I R Harvey was born in Cwmbran, Monmouthshire, but his family left Wales when he was a child, following his father's redeployment to Teesside. Growing up in rural North Yorkshire, he attended school in Northallerton. After working as a Residential Social Worker for 16 years, he re-trained as a primary school teacher. He taught for 12 years before becoming a deputy head teacher and safeguarding officer. I R Harvey took early retirement in 2017 to pursue his passion for writing. The Mabinogion, a book of Welsh history, myths and folklore was the inspiration for this story.

To my late brother Nigel, the artist, who should have illustrated this book.

To my dad, who never finished his book.

To the memory of David Gemmell, whose books still enthral me.

I R Harvey

EAGLE HEART

AUSTIN MACAULEY PUBLISHERS™

LONDON • CAMBRIDGE • NEW YORK • SHARJAH

A CIP catalogue record for this title is available from the British Library.

ISBN 9781398458536 (Paperback)
ISBN 9781398458543 (ePub e-book)

www.austinmacauley.com

First Published 2023
Austin Macauley Publishers Ltd®
1 Canada Square
Canary Wharf
London
E14 5AA

Thanks to:

My wife, Carolyn, for her unfaltering belief that I could finish the book.

My children: Jenna, William and Beth for all the scorn that kept me grounded.

My mum, a former English teacher, who was my proof reader.

Martin for technical support.

Lisa for the advice;

Matt for his insistence on a swamp.

And finally, thanks to Ian (Mr Turner) for making me want to try writing a book.

Chapter 1
Prologue

Narfi ran. Narfi ran for his life. His pursuers had spread out behind him, all older boys who would easily outpace him on the flat. His only hope was the woods; icily calm, he surveyed the land before him: the woods off to his right, across Forge Bridge, Mason's hill straight ahead. He headed on towards the hill, legs burning as he struggled up the slope, the heavy panting of his pursuers close behind, almost within reach. As soon as he drew parallel with the bridge, he darted sharp right on to the scree slope and headed back down. Digging his heels in as his da had taught him, he stepped at pace downwards.

Kobus bore down on him. Narfi sidestepped left as Kobus shot downhill, out of control to crash amid a pile of dust at the base of the slope and lie still. Narfi continued down, hurdling the prone, groaning figure and made for the bridge. Shouts and curses followed him but now he was safely across into the cool of the trees he knew they wouldn't catch him. Stopping behind a large oak he leant his back against the rough tree and pressed his palms against the reassuring bark. Slowing his breathing, he concentrated; feeling his skin energise as it prickled with elemental magic. Bark-like patterns flowed over his exposed hands and face—his clear, green eyes darkening to a deep emerald, even the whites, as his hair appeared to thicken like a tangle of shoots. The dark green of his shirt shimmered for all the world looking like leaves appearing to dance in the breeze, whilst his leather trousers blended with the bark of the tree.

With little effort now—his body infused with the magic of the woods, he scampered up the tall trunk soundlessly, then squatted down on a high branch to watch as his pursuers shuffled carefully into view. Kobus stormed into the middle of the group, face scraped and bleeding.

"Narfi! You foreign shit… You're dead, you filthy little midget!" The seven chasers stood and listened, glancing around the wood.

"How the hell can he hide so quickly?" This was Hennie, Kobus's hulking, sycophantic cousin.

"Maybe he climbed a tree," offered Blund.

"How? We'd have seen him. And anyway, there aren't any branches he could reach," Hennie muttered.

"Look for him," ordered Kobus. The other six began spreading out. Hennie grabbed a fallen branch and began scything down nettles and ferns.

Narfi pressed himself against the tree, invisible, heart pounding and waited for them to leave. These seven had tormented him continually through his life, tormented him for every way he was different to them: he was much smaller than these other boys even though he was the same age (midget); his skin was brown not white (filthy, foreign, shit-coloured); his eyes were a dazzling green (freak); he didn't attend the Chancel-run school (heathen); his mother was a hedge witch and the Chancel preached such people were evil (pagan; son of a witch-bitch); even though nearly everyone in Glanyravon came to her for medicines, healing and midwifery.

He watched the seven thugs with tears in his eyes; Kobus, the leader of the gang who was the son of the Glanyravon's wealthiest man, the Burgermeister Kerneels; Hennie, his huge cousin—already the size of a full grown man; Blund, who loved hurting anyone smaller than him—especially the young girls; Kees, who was so pale and blond he was almost an albino; Luuk, who terrified him the most as he was so quiet, but always seemed to be watching him; and the two brothers Wolter and Jacobine; both slow witted but willing to do anything Kobus told them. It was these who called him Narfi, which he suspected was some kind of insult, but it had stuck and now everyone called him that; even he thought of himself as Narfi. Only his mam and da called him his real name—Mab.

The seven moved on, still chuntering and occasionally calling insults out. Narfi watched them go, despair clawing at his stomach: he resolved then that as soon as he was old enough, he would leave. There was no life for him here. The summer croft where they went to pasture their sheep up in the hills over the hottest summer months was empty the rest of the year. He would live there. Alone. He didn't care about friends—he'd never had any, the seven bullies made sure no one ever spoke to him.

There had been a girl called Sara, who'd played with him every day when they were small. Her family lived near to his own home. But when she was about five years old, she had 'got lost' one evening on the way back from the Chancel school. Everyone had looked for her but it was the seven bullies who had found her, or rather Blund had, in the woods. The girl refused to talk ever since. He knew they had led her away and done something terrible to her that had hurt her so badly she screamed if he went to see her. Even worse, he knew it was because of him they had hurt her. The adults all called the boys heroes for finding her, but he knew them; he knew what they were like. So, he knew in his heart of hearts that he would leave and never come back to Glanyravon, the village that had been the only home he had ever known.

Fourteen Years Previously

Ceinwen sat on a small sandy bank of the Little Ban River, her feet swishing through the cool water, enjoying the shade of the great willow. Her morning collecting herbs and roots for her cures and remedies had gone well. Her reed trug beside her was packed with essentials, including lovage, new nettles, wood sorrel, wild garlic and even a rare and precious tryffyl that would fetch a whole silver at the market. She ruffled the fur around Rhosyn's neck. The young boarhound grumbled in pleasure as he rubbed under his ear, pressing his cheek into her hand.

It had been a good day under a hot sun. She could just see Hywel further downstream, paddling his coracle into the shaded side of the bank. She wanted to shout out and ask if he'd caught anything, but knew he'd glower at the noise she was making, then claim she'd scared the fish away. She watched him cast a line into the water then sit, solid and still, as patient as time. Her husband. It still sounded strange. No other man had even looked at her, the Wicca woman, as a possible wife. But Hywel. Yet even now, past the age when most women stopped bearing children, she still had not given up hope of having his child, refusing to believe she would probably never conceive now. Ironic, when she had brought so many children into the world that her own child had died in the birthing.

Rhosyn's low growl and sudden alertness tore her from her musings. The great hound stood and stared into the distant trees, still rumbling, before letting out a short bark. Ceinwen stood and looked to where Rhosyn stared,

"Stay," she murmured softly. "Stay." Picking up a water-rounded pebble from the sand, she turned and launched it towards Hywel in his coracle. In her mind's eye, she saw him start and turn angrily towards to face her. Eyes fixed on the woods, she held her palm up to warn him something was wrong and beckoned him over.

Rhosyn took a short step forward just as a running figure broke cover from the woods. A woman judging by the skirts flapping around her legs. Judging by the type of cloth, all tartan patterns, but with only shades of greens and brown, the woman was from forest stock. As she drew nearer Ceinwen saw she was carrying something. She was making towards the left, away from Ceinwen when Rhosyn barked again, catching the woman's attention. Her running slowed to an indecisive jog as she looked around, seeing Ceinwen and the dog, she suddenly changed direction towards them.

As the woman neared her, Ceinwen could see that she was on the verge of collapse: her head was tilted back and swaying from side to side; she seemed to be struggling to hold on to her burden which was clutching tightly to her chest. Finally, plaid skirt flapping against her legs, she lurched to a halt a few feet from Ceinwen. The woman's hair was plastered to her forehead with sweat and she took huge gulps of air as she sank slowly to her knees, her burden a large bundle of blankets cradled on her lap.

"Please," she gasped, "my child." She offered the bundle to Ceinwen, who just stood, her eyes fixed on the woman's delicate face. Brilliant emerald eyes, impossibly green, a small sharp nose, high cheek bones and her obviously olive skin was flushed red with her exertions. Ceinwen stepped towards the woman, ignoring the proffered bundle and brushed the woman's rich brown hair from her face behind her ear.

"Celtyth," she gasped, shocked at the sudden realisation that one of the ancient people stood before her.

"My child, save my *mab*," the woman pleaded. This time Ceinwen noticed the singsong lilt of her accent, and looked back into those emerald eyes. Looking down at the bundle she saw Rhosyn snuffling at the blankets just as a tiny hand came from the folds and grabbed at the dog's ear. The dog jerked back but then her head edged forward towards the reaching hand and sniffed it carefully before licking at the tiny, chubby fingers. Ceinwen just stared, but was suddenly startled by a distant rumbling, punctuated by a shout. The Celtyth woman jerked her head to look back, let out a sudden, heart-wrenching sob before bending to kiss the child within the blankets. Eyes brim-full of tears, she lurched to her feet, handed her child to Ceinwen and headed from the river and away from her baby.

Still too stunned to move, Ceinwen watched the Celtyth-woman run. The baying of hounds suddenly flew across the meadow. The Celtyth woman turned slightly to see what followed and stumbled before heading off—fear lending her another burst of energy.

Ceinwen looked down at the swaddled child in her arms, Rhosyn lay with her head protectively by her side, ears alert and staring towards the distant sounds of thunder, baying hounds and inaudible shouts. Not thunder, horses galloping, Ceinwen realised just as Rhosyn growled deeply before jumping to her paws and whining softly at Ceinwen, who finally sprang into life. Decision made, she snapped up the bundle and ran for the river, turning left at the bank and heading down towards where Hywel's coracle bobbed in the current, her husband fishing line abandoned, paddled to hold the coracle mid-stream, concern etched on his face but oblivious to the unfolding drama.

"Hywel," she hissed urgently, waving him over, "come into the bank now." Seeing his wife's need and sensing her urgency, he eased into towards the riverbank where she stood, anxiously looking over her shoulder.

"Quickly Hywel," she ordered, "quickly." Hywel identified the near panic of his wife but could not thing what was causing it. Ceinwen was up to her thighs in the water now, the bundle of blankets and baby held out before her. As soon as the coracle was in reach, she deposited the bundled child onto Hywel's lap. "Go downstream to the wood before the bridge at Glanyravon and I'll see you there."

"What…" Hywel uttered looking between his wife's urgency and the bundle of blankets on his lap.

"Don't ask, just do," she ordered her husband. "Go." She waded back to the bank and turned to watch Hywel until the current had eased him around the bend in the river to safety, before heading back to the sandy bank where her shoes and basket of herbs and leaves stood. Away from the rushing of the water, the sound of the Celtyth-woman's pursuers was reaching a crescendo.

Thinking quickly Ceinwen whistled Rhosyn over to the sand, retrieved her lead and tied it on to a great log washed onto the shore. The dog stood and faced the growing noise, ears alert and tail aloft. Leaving her basket, Ceinwen stepped back into the water and made her way to the steep bank to her left and began pulling at the wood sorrel just as three great hunting dogs, tied to the pommel of a large horse's saddle burst into view. Rhosyn, larger than the hunting dogs, growled.

"Stay," Ceinwen ordered, standing stock still. Following the houndsman came several guardsmen, all mounted, and another man who was clearly the leader. This man was riding a huge, grey horse and was dressed entirely in grey but wore a black, banded leather shoulder guard that had a golden crooked cross adorning it. The man was a Knight Confessor; the punishers and torturers of the Gilded God; the most feared men in the realm.

As the hounds sniffed at the ground where the Celtyth-woman had knelt before pulling to go after her, the rider's eyes fixed on Ceinwen.

"You! Peasant!" he bellowed. "Come here." He pointed at the ground in front of his horse. Ceinwen quickly made her way out of the water, wood sorrel in hand and hurried across to stand near the confessor's horse, her eyes fixed firmly on the floor. He stared at her for a few seconds then said, "We are looking for a *narfi* bitch who ran this way. Tell me what you saw." His high-pitched voice carried an unspoken threat.

Ceinwen raised her arm without looking up and pointed in the direction the woman had run, feeling honesty was her best plan, or at least, some honesty. The Celtyth woman was clearly intent on sacrificing herself for her child. No-one could escape these huge hunting dogs. "She ran that way," her arm pointing off to her left. She then added, "She came over here to the river Lord, but saw she couldn't cross, then turned and ran. She was carrying something but I couldn't see what it was because I was in the river, up the bank aways." She risked a glance up at his face.

The Confessor stared at her without blinking. The skin of his thin face was unnaturally pale, accentuating the darkness of his eyes which seemed to be sunken into his skull like face as though they were hiding from the light. *He looks cruel*, Ceinwen thought.

"Bring the hounds," he suddenly ordered the man with the dogs leads fixed to his pommel. The dog man brought them over. Ceinwen was too frightened to move as the great slavering hounds strained to reach her. Closing her eyes against the certainty she would be attacked, she could hear Rhosyn growling. She was sure the smaller hunting dogs wouldn't get close to the boar-hound but she hoped with all her heart the men would ignore her low rumbling growl and leave her alone. The three hounds snuffled around the ground where the Celtyth-woman had knelt, just in front of where Ceinwen was now standing, then one jumped up at her, paws pushing into her midriff and knocking her down.

With a small yelp, Ceinwen turned and fell to her hands and knees. All three dogs were now on and around her, sniffing and pawing at her. Rhosyn's growling suddenly increased in volume and she saw her dog was up on its paws again, straining against the lead. But before she could say anything to calm her hound, the three hunting dogs pulled away having picked up the trail of the Celtyth woman, and within seconds the hunting party had moved on with a thundering of hooves and a cacophony of shouting. She opened her eyes, startled to see the Confessor still sitting on his huge horse, staring at her.

"You are from Glanyravon," he said. Ceinwen sensed a threat in that simple statement, not even a question.

"Yes Lord," she answered quietly, eyes down. The Confessor stared on before tutting once, then he spurred his horse asway. Ceinwen let out a shuddering breath as he left. Rushing over to her beautiful dog who licked at her face, nuzzling into her with her cold, wet nose. "We did it, Rhosyn, we did it." Then snatching up her basket of herbs, she headed down the river bank, away from the terror of moments before, towards the woods near the bridge at Glanyravon.

A mile to the southeast, the pursuing group finally caught sight of their quarry. The Celtyth woman was staggering now, on the brink of exhaustion. At a command from the Confessor, the hounds' man released the three, slavering hunting dogs. The great beasts flew from their handler at an astonishing speed, eerily silent now, to drag the woman down. Hearing the shouts of her pursuers the Celtyth-woman turned and saw the great hounds tearing towards her. Her shoulders slumped, then she dropped to her knees and pushed her hands flat against the grass of the pasture. "*Ddaear cymer fi*," she uttered softly, 'earth take me.' Then grinding her fingertips into the turf, she pressed her forehead to the ground, pausing to let the magic flow, just as the rushing hounds saw her.

With a deep breath and a final thought of her beautiful baby boy, she said, "*I ildio!*" A brief flare of light lit her face and her body sank down. Within seconds the dogs had pounced on the woman and savaged her. Canines ripping at her throat and neck, tearing at her face, then dragging her body apart. By the time the pursuing party reached her body, there was little left. The Confessor, eager to see the blood and gore, leapt from his horse and strode quickly to kick at the corpse. Plaid garments of various shades of green and brown flew aside to reveal a few bones and a lot of dust, as though an old sarcophagus had just been emptied out. He pulled a baby's soft woollen shawl from the mess and held it for a few seconds before dropping it back on the pile.

"*Narfi* bitch was a magicker," he told the group surrounding him, before hawking a gobbet of phlegm and spitting at the pile of rags.

"Makes no sense," said the houndsman making the sign of the crooked cross on his chest. "If she could magic like that, why not use it on us?"

"Bloody tree huggers, that's why. Soft as shit," one of the guards said. "They won't take life. That's why they're such easy prey—great sport for us, eh lads?" he added, to nods and grins of agreement.

Staying silent, irritated that he had been deprived of his sport, the Confessor mounted his great grey horse and turned to leave, cantering away as his party rushed to follow, the houndsman last to follow having tied the dogs in. As the party moved from sight a deep, green glow blossomed from the holes the woman's fingers had made and four green shoots grew impossibly quickly from the ground, then flowered into beautiful, blood red poppies that danced in the gentle breeze. The houndsman swallowed hard and quickly mounted, urging the horse to make haste and catch up with the others.

Ceinwen's heart was still pounding when she reached the woods near Glanyravon, where she at last slowed to a walk in the shallow water and checked the bank more carefully, looking for sign where Hywel would have dragged the coracle out of the water. She had long since stopped looking over her shoulder, knowing that if the Confessor's group had followed her, either the hunting dogs baying would have alerted her, or Rhosyn would have. She had waded into the river farther down passed the bridge, then doubled back in the shallows, her skirt sodden and heavy. Hywel had taught her that: how Rhosyn would lose a scent in the water, but pick it up if the quarry just crossed in a straight line to the opposite bank. Still, she wouldn't feel safe until she got home. Rhosyn gambolled along beside her, bounding in and out of the river, biting and snapping at the water as he did.

However, as she kept moving along, there was no sign of her husband or the coracle. The thought that they had been taken began to gnaw at her confidence. Where was he? Why had she taken the Celtyth-woman's child like that? Moving further on, fear rising, she had just decided to turn back and retrace her steps in case she had missed something when Rhosyn suddenly stopped, ears and tail alert, before rushing off into the woods. Ceinwen paused and listened carefully and heard the great hound barking, then it crashing through the undergrowth as it bounded joyfully back, followed more sedately by Hywel.

"Ceinwen," his deep voice asked quietly, "whose is this child?" She stopped and looked at her husband, and felt her worries and fears subside. He was so calm and reassuring, nothing perturbed him. A tall man, not handsome but well-made none the less. His nose was crooked from being broken; his dark greying beard covered pocked skin, but his dark eyes, always warm, smiled from the face she loved. He was holding the child so carefully in his strong arms. He had discarded the blankets and she noticed how the child was awake and staring at his face; one tiny hand wrapped tightly around Hywel's right index finger as though the child had claimed him.

Looking at Hywel's face as he mothered the baby, she thought to herself, *Perhaps it has.* She quickly and quietly told him of her encounter with the woman, not mentioning she had been a Celtyth, and the Confessor's party. Hywel simply nodded, never taking his eyes from the baby as the bay kept its eyes on him. Ceinwen held out her arms to Hywel who reluctantly passed the child over. She straight away checked the child over. Hywel saw this and stepped closer, looking at his wife's fingers gently trace the upper curve of the child's jaw, noting how the babe's skin was as dark as his wife's tanned hand. He looked into his wife's eyes and read the concern.

"Tell me," he said softly.

"Oh Hywel, there was a woman… young she was, running from the Grey men and a Confessor. I'm sure she was Celtyth. She gave me the child and told me to keep him safe and she ran. The Chancel men were minutes behind her. I didn't know what to do. It was heart-breaking to see her give up her baby and sacrifice herself to save him—you know what those damn Chancel men are like… what was I to do?" Hywel waited. "They Confessor questioned me but the dogs took off after the woman's scent. We're safe. I'm sure we're safe," she said again to convince herself as much as her man.

Hywel stood for a few seconds before nodding again. "Best get the child home then," he said. "We can move up to the croft in the Banna Hills a few weeks early, stay out of folks' way. Child looks small. Maybe if we're gone for the rest of autumn and the winter, we can pass it off as our own. I'll take you up the day after tomorrow after I get the sheep gathered today. We'll drive them up together." With that he turned and headed back into the woods, returning in moments with his coracle slung over his shoulder. He stooped and took Ceinwen's herb basket, smiling at her briefly and set off for home. Ceinwen followed, heart fit to burst. It was going to be alright.

****

17

Narfi stayed in the great oak tree until well after the other lads had given up. They had wandered away, back to the village shouting more names, obscenities and threats at him, promises of violence that he had no doubt they would keep. He thought again about telling his da, but knew it was probably best not to. After his mam had been accused of witchery, his parents didn't need anything else to worry about. He decided he would ask to go up to the summer croft for a couple of nights and let things settle while he thought through what to do. His mam and da had told him using his magic on others would be the death of them all, but there must be a way he could fight back. With heavy heart he climbed down, realising again how comforted he felt by touching the living wood of the tree. Slowly, sticking to the shadows and shade, he edged his way back home, wishing Rhosyn was with him, knowing the huge boarhound would keep the bullies at bay.

Easing his way through the huge reeds that bordered the stream near Forge Bridge, Narfi could smell the smoke of Kort's forge. He decided to watch the bridge, just to check that Kobus and his pack of brutes weren't lying in wait. Whilst he was waiting, no sign of his tormentors, Kort ambled out of his river side forge. The short, squat man threaded his fingers together and reached his arms high, palms up, to stretch out his back. After he'd done this he spoke to someone by the side of his forge, out of sight. Narfi knew then they were waiting for him, so he eased away from the bridge and back into the woods. There was no obvious way to get across the Little Ban near the village as it was too wide to jump and too fast flowing and deep to cross.

But he had a plan. Jogging through the trees he reached a large oak close to Dinnon's workshop. Dinnon harvested the reeds near the river to weave baskets; his open workshop faced the river. He sat there now, using a plane to smooth out a large plank of wood. Narfi knew he shouldn't risk getting caught using his magic, but he had already decided he had no other option. Laying his hands on the bark he summoned the magic to his skin. Perfectly camouflaged now he climbed the tree with ease, virtually flying up it, the magic on his hands and feet giving perfect grip on the rough bark. Once up high enough, he eased along a huge branch that jutted out over the river towards its centre.

Approximately two yards away from this branch, the tree that shaded Dinnon's workshop on the opposite bank, reached across the rushing water. Near to the end of the branch he felt the limb begin to dip towards the water. He shuffled a couple of steps back and then, without thought of failure, leapt across the divide to land, perfectly balanced on the adjacent branch. The sudden rustling of leaves and movement of the branch jerked Dinnon from his task. He looked up at the swaying branches and gazed around for whatever creature was leaping about, but saw nothing and went back to his task. Slowly releasing his tightly held breath, Narfi eased along to the trunk, where he clambered around the trunk so the great tree was between him and Dinnon before clambering down. From here he should be able to see his home in the distance. But all he could see was clouds of thick smoke. He stared hard, straining to see through it and suddenly caught the sound of barking again, and then a flash of flame where the thatch of his home was burning.

With panic welling in his chest, Narfi jumped the twelve feet from where he was standing in the tree and sprinted for home. Some small part of his brain processed the knowledge that he had jumped so far with ease and had no injury whatsoever. As always, he marvelled at how, when he was cloaked in magic, he seemed to be able to sprint and dodge so effortlessly quickly through the trees, skirting the open spaces up to his croft. As he grew closer to his burning home, he could make out figures and horses through the smoke. He also recognised Rhosyn's ferocious barking.

She's protecting the cubs, he thought as he ran. That meant there were still strangers there. His mind instantly thought of Kobus and his threats, perhaps it was one of his gang at the bridge. As his concern deepened to dread, he slowed to a jog and eased a little deeper into the wood to hide his approach.

He knew there were people outside his home, but there was no sound of urgent shouting, of people trying to put the fire out. He remembered when Dinnon's forge had caught fire two winters ago. How everyone had helped and shouted and called. This was just quiet, but why? Surely the neighbouring crofters and farmers would be rushing over at the first sign of smoke. Even Rhosyn had stopped barking. He told himself that must be good, the danger had passed. He told himself, but knew he didn't believe it. Slowing to a walk now he drew level with his croft, and stood in the clouds of thick smoke, which was about twenty-five yards beyond the trees where he was standing. Still cloaked in his magic and hidden by the smoke. He couldn't make out anything through the smoke that was drifting straight towards him, the magic protecting his eyes from stinging.

Knowing he would be unseen, he quickly scaled the tall oak that shaded the hens and eased along the thick branch that his childhood rope swing still hung from. He stopped abruptly when he saw Rhosyn. The great boar hound lay peppered with arrows, blood pooling around her head. Her body was lying against the southern wall of the wood shed, her back legs and rear end underneath the timber wall. Narfi knew that she had been defending the pups that were in the den she had dug under the shed. Not even his da could get close to them. His breath caught in his throat when he saw the small bodies just beyond where their mam lay. 'They must have attacked to protect her,' he reasoned. But only three. It was then, as his eyes misted that he knew his mam and da were likely dead. Neither would suffer to see Rhosyn hurt, let alone the pups.

Narfi steeled himself, rage and grief fighting for control as his hands gripped the branch tightly as he tried to master his emotions. His hands squeezing into the wood as though it was soft clay—and it was then like a fog had lifted. His mind calmed and cleared. His enhanced vision seemed to take in every detail, looking through the thick smoke as though it was nothing but a light mist. He heard the unmistakable sound of horses galloping away, but could still see two hitched to the post where his da hung the ravens and magpies he killed. Looking now towards the front of the croft he saw what he had been dreading. His Da, arms tied around the trunk of the lightning blasted oak, so they were behind him. His eyes were gone. He was sitting, arms tied backwards with his legs outstretched, his feet still smouldering in a fire.

Unable to comprehend the scene before him, he jumped down and approached his da, solemn, huge sobs stifled like thunder waiting to burst. It was as he neared, that he saw his mother; naked, tied spread-eagled on the ground, hands and feet pegged out where her Da could see his wife; her face battered beyond recognition, the fire on her stomach, still smouldering. Calon coughed as the smoke filled his lungs. His stinging eyes told him the magic had left him. He felt as if he was someone watching himself. "This can't be real," he muttered.

"Where the fuck did you come from?" a coarse, loud voice barked behind him. Narfi paused, breathing out a long breath, then slowly turn and faced his questioner. Three metres away, a tall man faced him. He was dressed all in grey with a homemade crooked cross stitched badly onto the right upper arm. His pasty, long face was unshaven and greasy hair was combed forward over an obviously balding pate. His mouth was virtually toothless, his lips bruised and scarred. Not a Confessor but obviously a Servant of The Crooked Cross—the local militia men known as Grey Men. Behind him he could see another Grey Man sitting on the tailgate of his da's cart, grinning. This man was fat; his uniform strained across his large belly so the white flesh glowed from beneath the grey cloth. Toothless strode towards him, stopping abruptly when he caught sight of Narfi's eyes.

"Well, looky here," he shouted back to his fat friend. "We got us a greeny-eyed Celtyth boy." Still grinning his gummy, fat-lipped grin, he took the sword from his belt and walked straight up to Narfi. "You're the little freak we've been looking for. Toad, get over here. We're gonna tie him up and wait for the Confessor to get back, then we're gonna be rich."

"Ten gold pieces," Toad offered. "Five each," Toad enthused as he jogged over. By now Toothless was within grabbing distance of Narfi, who still stood, staring at the man in front of him, towering over him. Slowly he leant to his left, head tilted slightly, and watched the approaching Toad, who had stopped, returned to his da's cart and was rummaging around for some rope. As the men drew towards him, something extraordinary happened. Later Calon would reason that rage or desperation was his motivation as his magic flowed through him like never before.

"What the…? Where did he go?" Toad exclaimed. Calon, who hadn't moved, turned his magic-filled gaze back to Toothless, Narfi clenched his right hand into a tight fist, then, impossibly quickly, he hammered his fist straight into the middle of the Grey Man's chest. Narfi felt as much as heard the crunch of Toothless' sternum as it caved in. Toothless took three steps backwards then crumpled onto his back, his face already bright red, gasping for air. Narfi stepped forward and lifted the sword the Grey Man had dropped.

Toad shouted in alarm as his friend staggered backwards before collapsing on the ground. His mouth opened and closed in confusion and disbelief. But before anything else could be said, Narfi ran straight at the fat Toad, swinging the sword in an overhead arc as he leapt into the air to cover the last few feet, the sword a blur as it scythed down through Toad's skull and straight through his body. The two separated halves staying balanced for a few seconds before falling apart in a wash of blood and offal. Hearing a harsh gurgling noise Narfi turned round. The Grey Man was desperately gasping for air like a fish out of water, hands gently laid on his demolished chest.

Narfi approached him and bending down grabbed one ankle. Lifting his leg he changed hands, his back to the gasping Toothless, then strode towards the burning croft, effortlessly dragging the large man. The flames had died down, but the bright embers glowed hellishly in the night. Narfi dropped the man's leg, grabbed the front of his grey, homespun tunic with his right hand and hauled the man up so their eyes were level. Reaching for his little belt knife with his left hand Narfi regarded the man dispassionately, head again tilted slightly to one side, before stabbing both of the Grey Man's eyes out.

Then, with virtually no effort, he heaved the man onto his shoulder and launched him into the centre of the croft, sparks, glowing cinders and smoke leaping up high as he landed. Stunned by all that had just happened, Narfi just stood stared into the embers, his mind numb and wearied. A gurgling cough roused him from his stupor. Whipping round, he saw his da's head move. Rushing across he fell to his knees by his da's side, cutting through his bonds with his knife then lifting him easily from the fire his feet were in before laying him down gently on the soft ground by the herb garden. He ran and grabbed his mam's dress and dunked it in the water barrel they used for the garden. Going back to his da he lifted him, then sat down, cradling the dying man like a new-born child; his mam's wet dress draped across his da's feet to try and cool them.

For what seemed like hours, his da did nothing. Narfi squeezed water from the dress into his da's mouth, and did what he could to sponge his face clean and soothe his ruined eyes. But other than shallow, laboured breathing his da, all strength and energy, seemed incapable of anything except dying. Narfi gently rocked him, spoke soothing words and said repeatedly how much he loved him. Not knowing what else to do Narfi started talking about times they had gone hunting together, Narfi had talked and talked without looking at his father's ruined face, but felt a slight shifting, so steeled himself to look down. Two hollow, bloody sockets seemed to be focused on him. His Da's mouth moved, but there was barely a whisper, so he bent his head putting his ear close to his father's mouth.

"Summer croft, quern stone. Summer croft, quern stone. Summer croft, quern stone." Over and over his da muttered it, until a cough racked him into silence. His head lolling to one side against his son's chest. Narfi watched his breathing slow to barely nothing, before his da went so very still and his skin suddenly paled as his heart stopped beating. Narfi hugged his father's body tightly, soundlessly weeping, stopping only when his tears had dried up and his arms ached. Laying him gently down Narfi stood. Lifting the wet dress from his father's body he took it and laid it across his mother's mutilated corpse. Almost trancelike he walked over to his da's cart, stopping at Toad's carcass, which he lifted with one hand and dragged towards the burning croft where he flung it into the embers to sizzle and crackle.

Going back to the cart, he lifted the long-handled shovel from the hooks that held it on the side, and walked over to the herb garden. On the ground his mam had cleared for planting winter crops, he dug a shallow grave wide enough for both of his parents. He then returned to his mother, freeing her from the savage restraints and laid her down in the grave on her side, facing into the centre. Lifting his da, comfortable now with how strong he was when this magic was on him, and laid him down on his side, so his parents were facing each other. He'd never really thought how much smaller his mam was than his da, so he moved her down so her head was rested against her husband's chest; their arms wrapped protectively around each other.

Before filling the grave, he sat and used his knife to cut lavender—mam's favourite—from the garden and laid the purple flowers across their faces, before placing his mam's dress over their heads to keep the soil off them. Then with one final goodbye, he gently pushed the earth back into the grave by hand. Finally done and with the fire light fading as the night descended, Narfi lay down on the grave hoping with all of his heart he would wake in his own bed. Tears flowed again. Turning over so his face was against the earth he screamed his anguish into the soil. When finally, his sorrow was spent he pushed his hands down to lever himself up, then found he couldn't move. He looked down, alarmed, and saw that his fingers had delved down into the earth. He felt the familiar rush of magic, a faint green glow seemed to illuminate the length and breadth of the grave.

Narfi began to feel light-headed and seemed to be looking at his hands from a great distance. Frightened now, not sure what was happening, he strained to free his hands, yanking them free with a spray of dirt. The glow increased in intensity for a few seconds before fading, as a cool breeze seemed to blow across his face. Narfi knew the magic had left him. His hands were just his own skin again and his vision had gone back to normal. He also felt unbelievably tired, heavy of heart and limb. He realised this must be because the magic had been boosting his strength. As the glow finally faded completely away, he noticed the whole surface of the grave seemed to be moving. Easing back, he watched, fascinated, as lavender grew impossibly quickly from the grave soil—a whole year's growth in a minute—that then flowered and gave off the rich scent his mother had loved so much. It was a sign, he decided, that he had done the right thing. It was little comfort, but comfort none the less, that his parents were together in death.

"Summer croft, quern stone. Summer croft, quern stone," he said to himself. Realising how much it had meant to his da to stay alive long enough to tell him that, so it must be important. Narfi pictured the croft in his mind and could visualise his mam's quern stone, set next to the hearth stones, where she always complained it was too hot for grinding the grain when the fire was lit and asking his da to move it. He remembered his da always telling her to move it herself if she wasn't happy with it where it was, then they would look at each other, mam would shake her head and keep grinding and sweating. A distant whimpering reached his ears.

Turning around, he tried to make out in the dark where it was coming from. Instinctively, he headed for Rhosyn's den under the wood shed. He could make out the great boarhound's body as he approached and saw, movement as a small form moved around her, keening. One of the pups he realised. One had survived. He rushed over and knelt by the pup, no bigger than a cat, which growled at him and rushed to stand between him and his mother, protecting her. Narfi remembered his da saying that the pups were ready for weening, so knowing she would be hungry he decided to leave the puppy there for the moment and begin collecting what he could salvage to take with him to the summer croft. It also dawned on him that he had to be away before morning as whoever had left the two grey men here would be back.

He began by checking the cart. There was an old oil cloth Da used to cover the wagon, big enough to completely cover him if need be, that would keep the rain off. He took Toad's bow and the quiver of arrows he had dropped. He also claimed the sword Toothless had carried. This he stuck through his belt. He rummaged around in the cart and found the pan on the floor under the driver's seat where someone had left it. The pan had a wire handle like a bucket and was slightly tapered so the base would fir exactly into the stove when cooking in it; and as it was wider at the top the cleaned and cool stove could fit snugly into the pan making it easy to carry. Da usually hooked it on to a bent nail on the back of the cart.

Next, he rushed across to the smoking shed; the lean-to built against the stone chimney stack so it was outside the house. The heat emanating from the burnt house was fierce, but the chimney stack gave just enough shelter. He saw that the door itself was smoking as the croft fore had been so hot. In hope, rather than certainty, Narfi pulled his sleeve over his hand and yanked the hot door open: four sides of salmon hung on the drying rods that were lowest down. Higher up the bacon that was cold smoking was sizzling and dripping fat onto the salmon that looked baked rather than smoked. He piled all of the salmon on his left arm and topped it with some of the bacon and headed from the heat, aware that even those few seconds so close to the simmering shell of his home had brought him out in a heavy sweat.

He headed over to the pup to feed it some of the fish, but just before laying it down, he paused. He lay the salmon sides on the ground behind him, skin side down and flaked off a piece that had bacon grease on it. Rubbing his fingers on the greasy from the bacon he knelt down and offered his hand to the pup so it could lick his fingers. A sob that turned into a coughed laugh burst from his mouth as he remembered his da telling him that a pup will love the one who feeds him. The pup busily licked at his bacon greased fingers, its tongue sure and soft. Narfi then fed the young dog small piece after small piece. Pausing in between feeds to get the pup's attention by whistling, just as he had remembered his da doing with other young from Rhosyn's earlier litters.

When he judged the pup had eaten enough, he picked it up, letting it nuzzle under his chin to get used to his scent and took it over to the water barrel near the herb garden. He put the pup down and cupped his hands to dip into the water. He then offered the pup the water, warm as it was. It lapped thirstily and Narfi had to repeat the process twice more before the pup was satisfied. He sat down and moved the pup into his lap where it settled in a curled-up ball, obviously exhausted from its ordeal. Narfi watched the glowing ember and occasional flames as his home and childhood burned to nothing. He sat there trancelike for some time, till he was snapped back to reality by a loud bang as a stone from the chimney stack must have succumbed to the heat and fallen hard, sending a shower of sparks into the hot air.

A clopping noise sounded from the dark behind him. Narfi's chest lurched. The Grey Men were back! He whirled around but saw nothing—staring into the embers meant his eyes would need to adjust. Remaining still, he waited for his pupils to dilate, seeing as they did a horse-like shadow standing some distance from the burning croft. One of the horses of the men he'd killed, he realised. He began to relax, but then sprang into life again when he recalled the other grey men who could return at any minute. He picked the pup up and took it over to the cart. He found a burlap sack and set the pup on it on the back of the cart so it wouldn't off, but the pup decided to settle down to sleep.

Narfi picked up Toad's bow and slung it and the quiver of arrows over his left shoulder. He rolled the oil cloth long ways into a tube which he slung over his right shoulder, binding the two ends together with some twine to stop the flapping about as he moved. He found some rope which he looped a few times around his waist thinking it may come in useful at some point. He then retrieved the salmon sides and took them over to the cart. He folded them before moving the pup and sticking them in the burlap sack, skin sides out. The sack already had string wound around its opening—he pulled this tight and threw that over his shoulder as well. He decided against taking the sword, opting instead for his da's wood axe, and discarded the pan as well, the less he had to carry the better. Hefting this in his right hand, lifted the pup from the cart and held it in his left arm like he'd seen village women carrying their babies.

With one last glance at the lavender that hid the place his parents' bodies were buried, he turned and headed into the sanctuary of the trees, somewhere he always felt safe. As he walked it suddenly occurred to him that no one had come to see what had happened. All the village must have seen the fire, but not a single person had come to help. They were either frightened of the Chancel men, or more likely, Kobus and his family had called them in. Without even breaking stride Narfi resolved to leave and never come back. "I hope the Confessor kills the lot of you," he muttered to himself. By now he had just about reached the tree line.

As he entered the woods, he stopped and looked back, alerted by the sound of horses galloping. He heard shouting, but indistinct, and figured the Grey Men had returned, so he headed quickly into the deepest part of the woods, woods he knew like the back of his hand, and headed west. By his own reckoning, he was nearly fifteen years old and, apart from the pup, he was alone in the world. His only goal was the last thing his da had said before he died, *summer croft, quern stone*, so he would head there then decide what to do.

Chapter 2
Escape

After fleeing throughout most of the night, sticking to the heavily wooded valley that ran west of the Little Ban River, splitting the Banna Hills, Narfi finally slumped to the ground exhausted. He'd removed his over shirt and created a sling of sorts to carry the pup, who was proving surprisingly heavy. Setting the young hound down, he leaned his back against the trunk of a great oak, bowed his head and wept again. As the pup wandered off, tentatively exploring this strange new environment, great sobs racked his chest as he covered his mouth in a desperate attempt to hold the grief in; afraid it would escape and overwhelm him. Everything was beyond him. He was fourteen years old, nearly fifteen, with no family. He couldn't care for himself or protect himself from those who would now surely do him harm. The pup clambered on to his face and licked at his cheek.

"Well, not completely alone hey pup." He scratched behind the dog's ears and realised he would need to name her. He'd need something suitable.

Lifting the pup off his lap he dragged his pack on to his lap and rummaged around inside for some scraps of bacon. He glanced towards where the pup was watching him carefully, ears pricked alert and eyes attentive. He tossed a couple of scraps towards her and watched her rear up, tail wagging to snuffle around on the forest floor as she sniffed out the tasty morsels. He observed her closely: her fur was completely black apart from an odd shaped white patch, the size of his hand on her chest. The patch was more or less round but tapered to a point on one side, a bit like a bird's beak he thought. The pup by now had snaffled the bacon scraps and Narfi realised she was watching him, ears up and head tilted slightly to one side.

He rummaged in his pack for a couple more bacon scraps, saying as he did so, "Black and white, with a bird beak marking, how do you fancy Magpie as a name hey?" He then tossed the scraps a little further away from the pup, much to her delight. As she sniffed them out, he called gently, "Magpie, Magpie." But got no response from the hound, but he still liked the idea of a bird's name. "Not a Magpie then. How about… raven, hawk, eagle, crow." The dog ignored him completely. Narfi then had a sudden memory of crows. His Da would throw stones at the pests as they pecked around at the dogs gnawing-bones. The crows would squawk and flap about but always come back. His Da would look at Roisin and point at the crows and shout, "Bite the Bran, Rosie, see 'em off!" and Roisin would bark and scare them away for a minute.

He had asked his da what a bran was and his da had told him it was the name of crows in the old tongue. "Bran," he softly called at the pup, who immediately stopped and looked at him. "Bran," he said again and this time the pup looked at him then suddenly barked. Narfi supposed the pup remembered his da shouting the word and his own mum barking, but somehow it fit. He held a piece of bacon in his fingers and called the pup over, his voice gentle and pleased like his da would call the dogs. "Come Bran; here Bran," and to his delight she lurched excitedly towards him and snatched the bacon from his fingers. "Good girl Bran," he said ruffling the fur behind her ears.

He resolved to train her as he'd seen his da do with countless pups. He knew as well how loyal this breed were, so he knew he'd never be truly alone. He realised as well that Bran gave him purpose; something to care for, something other than fear, dread and grief to think about.

After a good hour of coaxing Bran to come to him at his call or whistle, which was moderately successful, and a completely fruitless five minutes trying to get her to sit at command, he let Bran wander and sniff, whilst he thought about his next move. He could never go back to Glanyravon. His home was destroyed; his parents were dead. Thinking of his parents brought more tears. He tried to remember them as they'd been before, but all he could picture was their bodies in death; tortured and defiled. In turn this brought to mind his father's last words to him, *Summer croft, quern stone*. In turn he remembered his plan to go there. This he realised was something he needed—a goal to get him through the next few days.

Feeling intensely weary now he knew he needed to sleep. He knew he needed to eat as well but that could wait. He and Bran had drunk their fill of water on this journey, from the cold-water streams that flowed down from the hills and mountains to swell the Great Ban and Little Ban on their gallop to the sea.

Looking up he surveyed the branches above him and saw a nice fork, perhaps twelve feet up, where two huge branches erupted from the enormous trunk. He whistled at Bran who surprisingly came instantly to heel and he scooped her up and nestled her inside the makeshift sling again. Placing his hands on the trunk he leant his forehead gently against the rough bark and closed his eyes.

He seemed to slip in his 'otherness' so easily this time; but then he realised that for the first time ever, instead of questioning why he could do it, he had just accepted that he could. Then he realised he would never have to hide it if he lived by himself in the great forest, and no one would ever find him. For once he was able to enjoy the slight prickling sensation as his skin bristled like a cooling breeze across face. His eyes now saw more clearly in the dark and he could make out the patterns on the back of his hands. As he had always done as a child, he laid his hands on the trunk and enjoyed barely being able to see where it was, though he could feel it against the bark. Hands pressed tightly against the rough skin of the oak he climbed swiftly and easily up, marvelling at how he was able to do this; how his hands just adhered to the trunk; how he was able to feel the bark of the tree with his feet even though he wore moccasins; how his clothes seemed to camouflage as well as his skin.

Lowering himself down onto the wider of the two branches, he contemplated this for a short while, but soon felt his exhaustion taking him. Lying flat on his back, Bran curled quietly in the crook of his right arm, he looked up through the oak and felt a great calm wash over him. Safe. He felt safe.

Narfi jolted suddenly awake, instantly aware that Bran was squirming beside him inside this overshirt. He felt completely refreshed and ready to get up and get moving but lay still for a while longer, looking up at the canopy of leaves above him. He held up his hand to brush through the leaves and noticed he still had the magic on his skin. Bran, who had squirmed free, was now perched on his chest, tail between her legs, looking thoroughly uncomfortable with her arboreal elevation. She began to whimper and fret, her paws restlessly stepping up and down, but suddenly she stood stock still, ears alert and head turned to the left towards the great river.

Narfi held his breath, watching the pup, breath frozen. The unmistakable baying of hounds chased the last of the night away, as though they crested the waves of morning in pursuit. Putting Bran down on the wide branch he swiftly climbed high up to the very top of the huge oak. From here, higher than most of the other trees, he could just make out the silver sheen of the Great Ban through the forest canopy about a quarter of a mile to the east. He judged by the baying that the hounds were still getting closer to him. He waited, hoping to see who followed. A sudden shouted command, the first human voice he had heard, cut the hound's frantic noise dead. Then he saw movement. Smudges of darkness on the far bank that seemed to flit between the trees. Narfi realised they were searching the other side of the river. At last the group moved out of the forest and stood on the river bank.

Narfi saw there was a multitude of big hunting dogs and one smaller hound, marshalled by several chancel men, obvious in their grey uniforms. The smaller hound, a sniffer dog he thought, milled about on the bank then headed a few yards closer towards his position, before it stopped, rigidly poised looking across the river at its narrowest, but fastest running point. Narfi wished he'd thought of this, being pursued by dogs, and kept to the trees but it was too late now. At least, he hoped to himself, they won't figure how he crossed. Wading was impossible as the flow was too fast, probably even for a horse, but he'd adapted a trick his da had taught him to cross streams to keep his feet dry.

Having identified the closest target on the opposite bank—the overhanging branches of a huge river birch on the opposite bank that had half collapsed across the water, as though bowing for a drink, he'd cut a long yew branch to make a pole. He scooped up Bran and tucked her tightly into his shirt then moved her around so she was wriggling against his back. Bran seemed to like the feel of his skin when he magicked it, so seemed fairly content to just rest against him. He then walked as far back as he could and holding the pole in front of him like a lance, teeth gritted, he sprinted for the river, planted the far end of his pole into the fast-flowing water and used his momentum to bend the pole, whilst he held on tightly, and was vaulted into the air, his 'otherness' wrapped him and seemed to help him slice through the air and travel twice as far as he'd ever thought was humanly possible.

As the bent pole snapped straight, Narfi timed his jump, a prodigious leap which meant he landed higher up the tree than he'd expected. Grabbing on to a fairly sturdy branch which again he found easy, as though the tree helped him hold tight, he swung his legs up so he now hung upside down by his arms and legs. A large splash made him whip his head back, fearful the pup had fallen, but he realised as he did that it was the pole, falling into the river and feeling the scene on the fast current. Once he had hauled himself up to a sitting position on the branch, he reached into his shirt and manoeuvred a squirming Bran around to the front. He then eased himself along the branch to where it joined the trunk and climbed down a few feet before jumping down to land softly on the forest floor.

After sagging to the ground and resting for a while the adrenalin rush long gone, Narfi realised that he'd need to eat and sleep soon or he'd become exhausted. He trudged deeper into the wood that seemed much denser on this side of the river. He laid his open palm on many tree trunks as he went by and seemed to know them when he did—how healthy they were, how high, how strong—another mystery he needed to unravel when he was safe and settled at the croft.

Bringing his attention back to the men on the other bank, he saw they were now gathered into a group and had begun debating. The Confessor, who stayed mounted on his horse, just listened as the dog handlers seemed to be doing most of the talking. The man with the bloodhound was especially animated, turning and pointing over the river then holding his right arm out, gesticulating upstream. This action created a furore as the other handlers all started waving their arms downstream. Eventually the Confessor must have heard enough and raised a hand, stilling the men instantly. He spent a few moments speaking then gestured to the blood hound master who immediately began moving up stream.

The Confessor behind him and the rest of the group: dogs, handlers and grey men all stepping in behind the horse. There was also, he observed, a small man or child staying close to the Confessors horse at all times; a servant he supposed. Narfi knew they were looking for a place to cross upstream. He had no hope that they'd given up on crossing the Great Ban and were just heading back to whence they'd come. He resolved to keep moving towards their summer croft in the far west of the Banna Hills.

He remembered travelling with his da to the croft, they only went with the sheep which seemed to take days to herd them up there. He had no idea how long it would take without the sheep slowing him down. He could recall Da's insistent whistling at the dogs to keep the flock moving. He could remember his Mam and da telling him tales when they were at the croft, tales of how the Banna Hills slept at the foot of the great Eiran mountain range and other shepherds wouldn't herd this close to the Eirans—the barrier that kept the Celtyth separate from civilised people. His parents would laugh at the stories other folk told of the

Celtyth stealing babies and children for slaves; raiding people's farms for sheep and cattle; and killing innocent crofters.

Mam had said they were a peaceful people who never harmed any living thing—something Da scoffed at. They both agreed that the Celtyth were unholy and likely to suffer the anger of the Chancel. Especially as they used magic. The Chancel preached that magic was a great evil that the Celtyth used to bewitch those good folk who strayed too close to their lands. Da used to scoff at this and say the Celtyth had never been seen this side of the Eirans, so they were perfectly safe staying at the croft because only idiots believed such stories. And, as all bandits, rustlers and thieves were obviously idiots, they wouldn't come stealing and robbing this close to the Celtyth lands. Narfi remembered how he would ask question after question about the Celtyth, but his mam and da would never really answer them, often giving each other 'looks' that Narfi thought meant they didn't want to tell him so as not to frighten him. Now he'd never know what the 'looks' meant or find out more about the Celtyth.

Throughout the morning, Narfi kept trudging west, thankful that his da had taught him so much about tracking and finding his way through woods and forests. He knew he was further north at the moment than their usual route to the croft with the sheep. He remembered seeing the great forest on their right as they travelled along the drover's roads and trails that ran close to the farms and pastures along the river Great Ban as it doubled back before heading down south. He knew where the forest ended, the Banna foothills began, so he just had to keep moving generally west. Once the Eirans were insight he could easily find his way, heading straight towards the tallest peak, where the eagles soared and swooped. A huge mountain with its huge curved slope that da had told him was the back of a dragon, half buried in the rock and turned to stone by Celtyth magic.

As he'd travelled with his mam and da over the hills south of the trees, the dark, forbidding wall of forest always looked unwelcoming to his young eyes, yet now he'd never felt so much at home. Or as tired. He'd only been travelling a few hours but he was already done in. He sat down beneath a huge willow that stood recklessly close to a small, shallow stream—it's roots visible as they trailed from the bank down into the gently flowing water. The stream was only a jump across, but Narfi decided it was ideal for a quick wash. Stripping bare, of magic and clothes he lay down in the middle of the stream, the water just breaking over his chest was crystal clear and beautifully cool.

He noticed how filthy his hands and arms were, and could only imagine how dirty his face and hair were. After rubbing himself clean, he set to scrubbing himself with some lemon thyme he'd gathered on the walk. He rinsed out his clothes—pounding them against the willow's trunk like he'd seen his mam do. He was somewhat taken aback by the amount of dirt that fled downstream as he rinsed his clothes, so went through the process twice more till the water ran clean. Thoroughly cold now and shivering, Narfi sat under the willow, realising it curtained around him like one of the round circus tents he'd seen at the Glanyravon May fayre.

Deciding a small fire would be a great comfort and a good means of drying his things, Narfi had gathered twigs. He had stripped some bark from a mature silver birch on route and spent some time carefully stacking the smaller twigs over the larger pieces of bark, he roughed up some of the fibres from the biggest piece into a small wad, then struck his precious flint against the roughened steel bolt he always carried, showering the birch fibres with sparks. Once a large glowing ember had developed, and after some serious huffing and puffing, he placed the glowing bundle into his tinder stack and blew some more to get the flames going. He felt secure in the knowledge that the huge willow would dissipate any smoke—he was careful about only burning dry sticks and some bracket fungus he'd found. Besides, he reasoned to Bran, the Confessor and his troop were miles away.

As the midday sun reached its peak, he lay his clothes on the ground next to the small fire and, wrapped in his blanket, watched the cloth steam. He took the last side of the fire baked salmon from his pack, and fed Bran first, who scoffed it down before amusing herself by jumping about in the shallow stream. After finishing his share of the fish, he added some thicker dry sticks to the fire then lay down, enjoying the warmth of the small blaze. He began to wonder how they would feed themselves now, but was asleep before he'd finished the thought.

Something soft and wet roused him from his deep sleep. Narfi pushed Bran away and decided opening his eyes wasn't an option. Unable to form any conscious thoughts of rousing himself, he was soon asleep again, dreaming of Bran barking furiously. The dream went on and on until it was disrupted by the pup thudding its paws on top his chest and barking at his face. Narfi pushed the dog away again, muttering, "Bran, shush for heaven's sake." But the barking continued.

Finally, Narfi was able to peel his eyes open and look at Bran, who was now facing away from him, hackles up, tail and ears alert. He reached out to stroke her back, smoothing the fur and noticed she was standing in the ashes of his fire. He put his own hand onto the detritus, expecting some warmth, only to find they were stone cold. Looking about he realised it was getting dark. The fire would never have cooled completely in that time. "I've slept all night, a day and into the next night. A whole day!" he said to himself, incredulous. "Nobody can do that. No-one gets that tired," he was muttering as he tried to stand up, but only succeeding on stumbling two steps to his right before falling down.

He turned on to his back and smiled; remembering the may fayre game of *dancing the churn*, when the young men would spin around a milk churn with their forehead pressed to the handle of the lid on top—ten times round then run and sit on a girl's lap. The girls would be sitting on milking stools a good twenty yards away. The dizzied boys invariably just veered off to one side, usually ending up in the duck pond much to the delight and amusement of the girls and other boys. No boy had ever made it to a girl's lap to win a kiss and the first dance. He laughed as he lay there, but sadness was never too far from him when he thought of home.

Gingerly sitting up, he looked around for Bran, but the pup was nowhere in sight. He sat still and listened, Bran's furious barking sounded again, followed instantly by a long, not too distant howl and men shouting encouragement. They'd found him. He staggered to his feet, whistling for Bran. He was very aware that panic was reaching for him and tried to stay calm. 'Think,' he told himself. He reached for his magic to camouflage himself, but nothing happened. He held his hands in front of his face; this had become so easy, why was it failing now. Thinking quickly, he rushed to the trunk of the willow and placed his hands on it—concentrating hard, imagining himself at one with the tree. He felt it, stir. His hands flickered between human and bark skin, but still the magic eluded him. In a last desperate attempt as his pursuers approached crashing unseen through the undergrowth, he pressed his fore head against the rough bark, and almost felt he had pushed into the tree. His hands now were hardly visible against the bark, and he knew his eyes had changed as his vision had sharpened.

The first hunting hound, taller than his waist burst into the space under the willows branches and began moving quickly about sniffing the floor. Narfi realised that it couldn't see him. He quickly scaled the tree, silent as smoke, and moved to the top of the main trunk where most of the branches forked from. He rested there, concern for Bran flooding his thoughts. A few seconds later the rest of the hunting hounds burst into the space and began milling around in confusion. The blood hound, held by a rope was next, beetling around the space, unable to settle or fix on any one thing, his handler clinging on behind him, panting and sweating. The rest of the men arrived in a similar state, he counted sixteen in all, some in grey, some in soldiers' uniforms. They all did the same thing; stopped and looked at the bloodhound and his handler.

"What," the handler whined. "There's no scent here." He was about to say more when a soldier walked into the space, arm outstretched, hand gripping tightly to Bran's scruff as the pup snarled, growled and waved its paws at the huge man holding him. Another soldier limped in after him, holding tightly to his left calf.

Good for Bran, Narfi thought. There followed a big argument as the grey garbed soldiers shouted at the dog handlers, the bloodhounds man in particular, and the handlers shouted back. It was only the arrival of the Confessor on the horse that quietened things down. Narfi was amazed at how such rough, scary looking men were cowed without anything being said or done. They just fell silent. The Confessor stopped the horse and stared at the men and hounds before him. Jerking his hand, a small hooded figure stumbled forward from the other side of the horse where he'd been standing, the child Narfi had seen before.

Now he saw there was a fine chain held by the Confessor shackling the child; judging by the metallic clink as it moved, the chain was made of iron or steel. The chain he saw led under the child's hood and he suspected that it was attached to an iron collar around the figure's neck. Keeping hold of the chain the Confessor climbed carefully down from his horse and began bunching up the chain, forcing the hooded child close to him. Standing, surrounded by the other men Narfi suddenly realised how short the Confessor was, in fact only the child did not match the church man's height. This made the response of the soldiers and dog handlers even more surprising: they seemed to shrink away from the Confessor as though the man was radiating some kind of awful power over them.

"Hold this," the Confessor demanded quietly of the biggest soldier. A hulking brute, the man shuffled over with his arm outstretched as though wanting to avoid getting too close to his leader. When he was close enough, the Confessor simply threw the chain at the huge man's face, striking his mouth. The Confessor then reached for a riding crop looped over the pommel of his saddle. Narfi could see the unfortunate soldier wiping his sleeve against his lips as he backed away holding the chain. The child didn't move. "Tell me why we have not found the little heathen bastard! Tell me why there is not an iron collar around his scrawny neck!" The man's voice was high pitched; incongruous in a man of such obvious influence and command. The soldiers as one turned to look at the blood hound handler, who was keeping his eyes focused on the ground in front of him.

"Well…" the Confessor demanded.

"We found his dog, sir," the man manged to utter, bobbing his head subserviently as he did so.

"I don't want his dog," the Confessor replied so softly that Narfi hardly heard him. The church man then advanced on the handler saying, "I. Want. The. Filthy. Heathen. Brat." and every word was accompanied by a lashing of the crop across the man's chest. The handler had made no attempt to protect himself, he'd just taken the blows. Watching on, Narfi saw the Confessor punch the man straight on the side of the head with the butt end of the riding crop. This sent the dog handler reeling and swaying, before abruptly collapsing to the ground where he jerked a little before lying still.

The man's hound whined and licked at his master's face, until the Confessor's boot connected mightily with its ribs; its yelp almost dragging Narfi from his hiding place to protect the dog. Narfi breathed out very slowly, hands gripping the tree so hard they began to mould the trunk as though it were clay. Softened wood and bark oozed between his fingers. He eased his hands out from the now oddly sculpted trunk. Resolving himself to silence, even as a guardsman sliced a sharp knife across the injured hounds throat, Narfi became suddenly aware he was being watched.

The child below who had stood with its back towards him, had turned its head and seemed to be fixated on the great tree where Narfi was perched. A small brown hand reached up and tugged the hood down. Bizarrely cut, curly brown hair framed a girl's face. From where he was, with his magic on him, Narfi could see the girl had eyes as bright and green as his own and light brown skin like his. He'd never seen anyone else like himself before. He also noticed how ill she looked; face drawn and dark rings beneath her eyes. She also stood as if she was sick, barely moving and sort of droopy. Their eyes held for a few moments before the Confessor's hand grasped the collar and wrenched the girl around to face him. Narfi could see the pain that assault had caused her.

The Confessor lifted his still bloodied crop and pressed it against the girl's cheek, the tip threatening her open, unblinking eye. This was defiance, Narfi realised. The girl wasn't cowed, and stared back at the church man, the two almost equal in height.

"I've told you before," she said to the Confessor. "Dogs cannot track magic. All they were following was the boy's puppy, and now you've separated them, you'll never find him." She gestured to the forest and looked around and suddenly her eyes were staring into his again. "He'll head for the mountains now for sure." Was that advice? Or a trap? He wasn't sure. But one thing he did know, Narfi loved her voice: it was strong and had a strange, musical accent to it that he couldn't place.

"That's why you are with us," the Confessor replied, lashing the crop against her cheek, just hard enough for a cut to open. The girl didn't flinch, or even blink.

"Take off the iron and I will find him," was her flat response.

"I am nobody's fool," he told her, wiping his riding crop clean against her clothed chest. "Un-iron a filthy *gentes*, I don't think so." And with that he punched her full on the side of the head, sending her staggering back to fall in a heap, face down, arms cradled around her head.

Narfi's breathing quickened—his da would never tolerate hitting a woman or girl. Again, he calmed himself. He had still to figure why they so desperately wanted him, but knew if they caught him, judging by how the girl was being treated, it was not going to be a good experience. He resolved to listen and learn as much as he could. He also resolved to try and free the girl; there was more to her than he'd first thought. He was sure she'd started straight at him, but hadn't given him away.

He realised that the Confessor was addressing his men again. "...the night here. Stake that puppy out and make it squeal every now and again. You guardsmen, fan out around this tree and stay alert." With that he strode across to the stream and sat on a rock. The guards disappeared whilst the hounds men instantly began making a camp of sorts, whilst their dogs all tied, lounged near the stream, most sleeping off their exertions. Some of the men gathered kindling and wood; others were filling water bottles; two men had removed a pack from the Confessors horse and were emptying it—a large canvas sheet was laid out then one of the men ran off to the trees with a hatchet in hand.

Meanwhile, the big man holding the girl's chain had taken a huge wooden stake and pressed it into the ground through a large ring that was at the loose end of the chain. He then unslung a great axe from his back and, using the rear of the blade, hammered the stake deep into the ground through the iron ring, holding the chain firmly in place. He rummaged around in the pack the dead hound's master had carried and took a length of twisted leather. This he tied around Bran's neck, then secured the other end to the same stake the girl was anchored to. He aimed a swift kick at Bran, who dodged it easily enough, snarling as she did so. The oaf tried twice more with the same result. He then snatched up the leather lead and yanked it hard, causing Bran to yelp loudly.

"Again," shouted the Confessor. "Again." The oaf did as instructed and set to tormenting the pup for a few minutes more before the church man waved him away. Once the fire was going and their meat was roasting, the camp eventually settled down and quietened. The aroma of the meat had Narfi's stomach gurgling until he heard one of the guards say to a huntsman, "This dog tastes good. I'm glad you've brought a steady supply of fresh meat with you. Which one shall we eat tomorrow lads?" Whereupon a huge argument broke out that threatened to spill over in to a genuine fight as the two protagonists squared up to each other. It was only a shouted command of "Enough!" from the Confessor that stilled the action.

As night fell, Narfi, still wedged into the tree and beginning to feel uncomfortable, watched the girl carefully. She'd curled into a ball and seemed to be sleeping, but had done nothing else. He'd smiled to see Bran settling down into the space between her lap and chest about an hour ago and he noted now that the girls arm lay across the dog almost protectively. It was now as the group settled into sleep; the Confessor in his tent; that Narfi began to consider moving, freeing the girl and Bran, then getting away. He'd already thought his plan through. By walking along the branch that stretched over nearest where the two lay tethered, he could make it dip down. Fortunately, the wind was blowing hard enough to rustle the trees and rain had started falling to add to the noise. The guards he could see were all facing outwards, and he reckoned most of them would nod off soon enough.

Narfi remembered his da telling him once that the hour before dawn was the stillest time of the day. So it was at that time that he began to move. He checked he was cloaked in his magic, simply by looking at his hands. Then he moved slowly out from his waiting place. Any noise he made was lost in the constant rustling of the leaves as the heavy burst of rain deluged down. Another mystery he couldn't fathom was that although his clothes were soaked, his skin felt dry. His magic skin seemed to keep the moisture off him.

He shook himself from his deliberations and kept moving, picking out the long branch that stretched out over the centre of the camp below, closest to the tethered girl and his Bran. The pup had moved away from the girl now and was curled up beneath a thick shrub about four yards beyond her. This branch was thinner than he'd first thought but he believed it would bear his weight. Easing carefully forward in a crouched position, his right hand pressed against the branch behind him for balance, he made his way painfully slowly over the girl. As he'd hoped, the branch began to dip the further along it he travelled, but not nearly enough to set him to the floor. His earlier hours of planning now bore fruit.

Focusing on his right hand pressed against the branch he willed it to bend. He'd practiced this through the night and knew it was just a matter of concentration. He just had to picture in his mind what he wanted to achieve and it was as though the tree knew what he wanted. Suddenly and with little warning the branch just bowed down, its leafy tips touching the sodden ground beyond his target. He was close enough now to just ease himself off the branch and land soundlessly on the ground several yards from the girl and pup. He'd expected the branch to then shoot back up, but it just remained where it was. This was a bonus he hadn't expected as the leaves dipped down like this provided good cover and he also realised that he'd only planned getting down to the girl and Bran, but had given no thought to how to escape. This was perfect. They could just climb back up.

Moving stealthily across to the girl, he saw she was sleeping, so he moved past her to the stake. Here, rather than try and pull it out, he gripped it in both hands next to the wet ground and squeezed with all his focus. The wood simply acted like wet clay and squished between his fingers, toppling the stake. Narfi lifted the iron ring and eased back towards the girl and his dog, holding the chain low to the ground so it eased through the grass and mud without clinking. Once back at the girl, he reached out his hand to shake her shoulder, stopping suddenly when her eyes opened. She stared intensely at him.

Neither moved for what seemed an eternity, then the girl lifted the chain and held it out towards him with one hand, but grabbed his shirt with her other hand and wrapped it around the cold iron. She nodded at him. She wanted him to wrap the chain in his shirt to stop it clinking as they ran. He however had another idea. Leaving the china on the sodden ground he looked intently at the collar. He saw it was solid iron, something he'd worked before, so he just gently lifted her chin and grabbed the collar with both hands. A little concentration and the iron parted like wet bread. He put the broken collar carefully down on the wet ground, standing on them to push them into the sod. He suddenly realised that the girl had gone very still. He looked at her and found her staring at him open-mouthed. He stared back, assuming she must be amazed by his cloaking, but then thought, *She can see me. Why is she amazed at that?*

He shrugged back into his jerkin and then reached across her to wake Bran. The girl had other ideas though and snake-like her hand shot out and grabbed his wrist in a solid grip. He looked at her and she was shaking her head. She sat up using his arm as leverage. Letting his wrist drop she grabbed his face with both hands and moved her head towards him. *She's going to kiss me*, Narfi thought excitedly, his stomach flipping. She didn't.

Instead, she turned his head to one side and pressed her mouth to his ear—he could feel her warm breath against his lobe. "*No,*" barely audibly whispered. "*Their dogs are tracking you by following the dog's scent. Leave her or you'll never get away.*" She let his head go and he turned and looked at her. She stared back. Narfi looked across at Bran deciding that he'd rather take his chances with his dog than the girl. But she had other ideas. Grabbing hold of his head again she whispered into his ear. "She'll be fine. They will use her to follow you. The big man liked her and the Confessor said he could keep her. Let's go."

He was about to argue but didn't feel right grabbing her as she'd grabbed him, so he just sat moving his mouth open and closed, thinking back to Rhosyn, Bran's mam. He recalled his da telling him something when he'd asked why Rhosyn always followed his mam, not his da or him. "Loyal to death, Boarhounds," his da had said. "Biggest, fiercest dogs there are, but they bond with their first human contact. That's why we see she whelps outside, away from people, so the man who buys the pup is its first master. Be no good selling the puppies only to have them all coming back here 'coz they'd bonded with us. So, mind you stay clear of them."

Looking at the girl's bruised and bloodied face dripping with rain brought home how precarious their situation was. Knowing in his heart she was right he steeled himself and stood, gazing for a final time at the pup he'd come to think of as his only friend. The girl, who by now had quietly stood reached across and took his hand, gently squeezing it once. She smiled him a sad smile and led him towards the stream. As soon as they had reached the bank, she grabbed Narfi's arm and pulled him down behind a stand of reeds. The crescendo of rain on leaf increased as she pulled him around and motioned him to drop his ear to her mouth once again.

Holding his head gently, she told him, "*The iron has left me too weak to cloak myself, put your hands on either side of my head and you can hide me too.*" He did as she asked, blushing as his palm alighted on to her soft, wet cheek, feeling a little thrill as he did so. He also watched amazed as his magic spread like flooding water over her exposed skin. She tugged his hand again, leading him towards the stream. She eased straight in front of a previously hidden guard who was sitting the other side of Bran's bush; looking around. Narfi wanted to stop but she dragged him on, quietly sneaking a few yards in front of the man—the big oaf. He was looking right at them, rain pouring down his face, but doing nothing.

He can't see us, Narfi thought pausing, until the girl dragged him onwards—away from the camp and into the stream. She managed to get him to sit in the water with his feet pointing downstream as she did the same, then she lay back, dragging him back to so that they were floating but with their heads up looking at their feet as they began to drift free of her captors. Still holding hands, the two drifted to freedom. His thoughts with Bran, wondering if he'd see her again.

Chapter 3
Berys

Chilled to the bone, drifting quickly on his back, legs stretched out in front of him, Narfi thought he'd have loved this 'stream sailing' if only he wasn't frozen. Narfi shouted out to the girl that he had to get out of the bitter mountain water. The girl was drifting along a few yards behind him so he had no idea if she'd heard him or not. Still, he thought, she'll see me get out of this infernal stream and follow. Narfi manoeuvred himself in the fast flow to get closer to the right-side riverbank and lowered his legs, but didn't try and stand until his heels had touched the stream's bed.

As cold as he was, standing and walking proved almost impossible. He shivered ferociously once out of the water and struggled to put one front in front of the other. Three times he fell, and three times faced the agony of getting back to his feet before he made it completely clear of the water. Finally, on the bank he collapsed into a foetal position and hugged himself in a futile attempt to generate some body heat. His shaking was now so extreme he couldn't rub himself with enough force to generate adequate friction to create some warmth. In this position, teeth chattering alarmingly, he saw the girl get out of the water with no effort and walk calmly over to where he was lying.

Crouching down close to his head she looked at him, her mouth upturned into an amused smile, before she suddenly burst into even more amused laughter. She laid her hand on his forehead—it was very warm; beautifully hot against his frozen skin. Narfi couldn't even summon an angry response. He tried to ask her what was so funny, but the garbled unintelligible noises that burst from behind his chattering teeth and out of violently shivering body made no sense and only served to increase the girl's amusement.

"You have magic," she explained, still smiling broadly. "But no idea how to use it. Here." With that she placed her hands, painfully warm to him, on to either side of his head, her palms covering his temples. At once, he felt warmth rush through him, from his head where she held it, down through his torso then out into his limbs, arriving at his fingertips with an excruciating burst of pins and needles. His body relaxed and he rolled onto his back. The girl still held his head in both hands and he now began to feel hot.

He reached up to stop her as he began feeling uncomfortable, but she said. "Not yet. A moment longer, then I'll dry your clothes." With that she moved her hands, palms facing him about half an inch above his clothes, all over his front; along his arms and then along his legs. When bidden he rolled over and she did the same to his back. He could almost feel the moisture lifting from him like a wet towel being taken off. Exhausted by his escape; exhausted by his near freezing and now thoroughly warmed through, he just felt the need to sleep. The girl, however, had other plans. She sat him up then sat down cross legged before him. He looked into her green eyes, then quickly away, unable to match her critical gaze.

"Tell me why you dropped your *croen clogyn*?" she asked. He had no idea what she was talking about and was sure he hadn't dropped anything and told her so. "Your *croen clogyn*—your cloak skin I suppose you would say in your tongue. Why didn't you stay cloaked?" Narfi had no idea what to say.

"I… When I jumped in the water it was so cold, I couldn't think about it."

This brought more smiles. "You really have no idea, do you? The *croen clogyn* can keep you dry and protect you from the cold."

"Well, how did you stay warm then? You didn't have a *croen clogyn* when we escaped." He felt himself blushing and growing angry. The girl responded by slowly disappearing in front of his eyes. Her eyes became a deep green and the rest of her just blended into the background. He had a sense of her there and vaguely could see her if she moved. The girl then reappeared, much more rapidly than she had vanished.

"I used it just before I hit the water," she offered with a shrug. "There is so much you need to learn."

"But I can't just cloak myself like that," he protested.

"Well, I will have to teach you how," she said. With that she stood up and walked into the woods, her voice arrowing out after her, "Come on, we need to keep moving so we can rest when it's dark."

Narfi quickly stood and followed calling after her, "What about the dogs and the soldiers, they'll follow us." There was no reply but he saw her stop and turn to face him.

"I know. But remember, they can't track us if we're cloaked and dogs can't follow our scent through water. That's why we're going to run until nightfall. We'll cloak which will make the dogs next to useless and those humans couldn't follow a footpath, let alone two cloaked Celtyth in the woods." With that she disappeared again leaving Narfi pondering her last statement. 'Celtyth? Me?' he thought, 'I can't be. I grew up in Glanyravon with my parents.' He noticed he was alone. "Wait!" he called desperately. "How can I follow you if I can't see you?"

He saw the girl reappear some thirty yards away, so far so quickly he thought. She strode back. "Cloak yourself," she said. Narfi looked around him, turned and started to move towards the nearest tree, but she grabbed his arm and spun him around to face her.

"What are you doing? We need to move."

"I told you, I need to hold a tree to 'cloak' myself," he told her. "I'm not like you. I can't just do it. I have to be touching a tree and really concentrate to do it."

"Press your hand onto my hand," she ordered, holding her right hand up in front of him. Narfi did so. "Now, cloak yourself." Narfi focused and immediately changed.

"Whoa! How did that happen so suddenly?" he asked her. Turning his hand over in front of his eyes, as always amazed he could do this.

"I did it for you," the girl told him. "Cloaked with the *croen clogyn* we can move a lot faster than normal and remain invisible to human eyes," she added.

Narfi instantly thought of a problem with that. "What if I get lost, or I trip and you don't notice and keep moving? How will I find you?" The girl looked at him. He could see he had made a good point. She stood for a few seconds more, then began teasing out some of her hair. She took her wooden knife from her belt and sliced some long strands off. She knelt down then, beckoning Narfi to do the same and watch what she was making. She removed a bracelet from her own wrist that looked suspiciously like plaited hair to Calon, and unwound a few strands of this. He could see there were various colours of hair all wound together. She spent a little time extracting strand of different colour, before placing her own bracelet back on her wrist and fastening it somehow. Then, holding all of the loose hair she had gathered, she held them up by one end so the hair dangled down, swaying in the soft breeze. She began to chant quietly, lifting her other hand so the hair brushed against her palm. As she chanted, she moved her hand slowly down the long strands, almost cupping them. Narfi watched in stunned fascination as the hair seemed to intertwine of its own accord, plaiting itself. When the whole thing was one interwoven band, she asked him to hold out his hand flat and then laid the plaited hair on top of it.

"Don't drop it," she told him. "And keep still." Then she reached up with her knife and cut some of his hair off, as close to the scalp as she could. He saw she had taken only a few strands. These she divided into two roughly equal amounts. One she told him to hold with his other hand. She then removed her own bracelet again and added his hair to it, chanting again. The hair just sort of wove into the bracelet and then she fastened it on to her wrist again. She repeated this with the hair he was holding.

"This is what we call a *llinach*, simply put, it is a magical charm; now hold out your right wrist," she told him. Narfi did so and she gently draped the llinach over it and fiddled around with it before letting go. Narfi saw that the bracelet was firmly bound somehow. He could see no join. 'Magic' he thought to himself.

"I can explain all this later, but basically this is a bond between us. While we live this is unbreakable. It is a magic bond. When you are cloaked, think of me and hold your left hand tightly over the llinach." Narfi did as he was asked. "Now turn away, but don't let go of the llinach, and I will hide. Count to ten and turn around." Narfi heard nothing, but sensed she was gone. He counted to ten (quite quickly) and span round. Nothing but woods. He thought of the girl and a faint light extended about two yards from the llinach, pointing to his right. He saw her then, crouching behind some gorse, or more correctly, he had a sense of her. The girl stood and waved him over.

"How?" he began to ask, only to be told to shut up and start moving in order to put distance between them and their pursuers and set off. This time Narfi could somehow *feel* where she was, an awareness like when he knew he was being watched. Grinning with excitement, his tiredness forgotten, he set off after her, the trees and shrubs whizzing by as they sped through the woods stretched out endlessly before them.

Hours later and miles away from their captors, Narfi was sitting slumped, back against a dark pine. The girl was busily arranging their accommodation for the night. They'd climbed well above sea level into the Banna Hills that stretched west towards the Eiran Mountains majestic peaks. His legs felt incapable of supporting his weight now. They had run non-stop, cloaked by the croen clogyn; the magic sustaining their physical effort, but he was paying the price now. The minute he'd stopped, his *cloaking* had dropped; he'd collapsed and lay where he fell, shattered.

The girl, who seemed untroubled by running for hours, had found a stand of three tall saplings and somehow bent them together into a tent-like structure. She had then walked around the odd structure, manoeuvring branches, muttering to herself. Narfi lay, amazed, as the branches seemed somehow to knit themselves together into a living wall. She had then helped him to his feet and half dragged him inside, where she sat him down against the trunk of the tallest tree and made him remove his leather topcoat. He had gazed around stunned at the inside. The inner branches had all been manoeuvred sideways from the trunk to add to the 'walls' whilst creating a good space inside for the girl and he to move around in.

The smell was lovely too—it reminded him of the Martyrs' Solstice celebrations they'd had in the winter when everyone filled their homes with evergreens to honour the Five who'd died on their crooked crosses. Da had told him that was horse shit and that they'd celebrated the winter solstice for ever, welcoming the end of the old year and the passing of winter. The greenery was a reminder to spring that it was time to come back and warm winter away.

The girl came back through the entrance to their lodge. She'd taken his leather jerkin with her and bustled in backwards, backside leading the way, dragging his jerkin, on which she had placed several good-sized rocks he could have held in one hand and a large flat rock the length and width of his chest. He watched her curiously, only too aware of her womanly shape in her tight-fitting leathers. She placed four of the smaller stones in a square then, with some effort, heaved the large flat rock on top, creating he supposed, a table or stool.

"You need warmth and food to help you recover from that. I can just remember how taxing I found wearing the *croen clogyn* for a whole day the first time I did it. Your body will adapt the more you do it. I suspect you've not used it much, which is why you find it so hard. Magic comes from within, so it will tire you, but it's like your muscles—the stronger it gets the easier it is to use with less effort. Right. Food next," and with that she left the lodge again. Narfi stretched put his hand and felt the lodge 'wall'. It was as though many pine branches had been pressed together into an almost smooth sheet—in many ways like a living blanket. He could hear the wind blowing outside yet there was no draught inside. Whatever the girl had done, she had created a windproof, and he assumed rainproof material. He looked up and saw that the lodge surface provided a roof as well. In fact, it seemed to be just one piece of 'material' moulded around the tree trunks. He decided he would ask her about it when she returned.

He awoke when she bustled back into their lodge with a selection of things in her hands. She put these down next to the odd table she'd made and then produced more things from inside her tunic, including some long strips of bark.

"Look, I found… some…" she held up a familiar, yellowy looking mushroom but seemed to be struggling for the name.

"Chicken of the woods," he told her. She repeated what he had said, then stated, "So you know something then!" rather too pointedly for his liking.

"What's your name?" he blurted out, not even aware he'd thought to ask that question, his queries about the lodge walls forgotten, but it seemed to be the right thing to ask her. The girl looked at him, head tilted slightly, and smiled.

"One whole day we've spent together and now you ask what my name is."

"I…" he paused to think. "I guess I just thought of you as 'girl'."

"Girl," she repeated. "You think of me as a girl." She said this with no malice, which surprised him. Then she laughed and asked, "How old do you think I am?"

"About my age, I suppose," he told her.

"Which is…?"

"I'm fourteen. Nearly fifteen. That's what my mam and da told me."

The girl looked at him sternly then. She seemed to be considering this carefully. After a long pause, she said, "Berys."

A short, awkward silence followed that until he offered, "Narfi." Berys looked up in alarm and stared at him, appearing angry for the first time. He stumbled on, "My name that is. My name's Narfi." Berys just stared, then most unexpectedly guffawed somewhat loudly, then spent the next few minutes laughing, stopping but the minute she looked at him would burst out laughing all over again. At first Narfi was hurt by her response, but the more she laughed, the more he decided he liked the sound of her laughter. Eventually, when Berys had laughed herself hoarse she approached where he was sitting and knelt down in front of him and gently took his face in both her hands—her warm palms caressing his blushing cheeks.

"If there's one thing I do know about you, your name is not Narfi," she said softly. "In the language of the Celtyth, Narfi is a word used to describe someone who doesn't belong. Humans have heard it being used about them and for some reason it has become an insult about our darker skin colour. It has never been a name. It would be like giving a child the name 'strange'. Surely your parents didn't call you Narfi."

He thought about this then told her, "My mam and da always called me Mab," he said. "But they're the only ones who did. The other children and their parents all called me Narfi."

"Well, I can't call you that," Berys told him. "That's our people's word for son. I'll just call you my friend until such time as we can think of a name. Now let's eat."

With that she reached for the bark, keeping one piece for herself and throwing the other one to him. Narfi looked at it.

"I'm not eating birch bark," he declared. "I'm not that hungry."

"It's not to eat, you idiot," Berys said patiently. "It's to make a bowl with so we can put food in it. Copy what I do." Leaving him no time to protest, argue or ask questions, Berys took her knife and began explaining the process; squaring the piece of bark off with her knife first she made short diagonal cuts from the corners towards the centre, then folded and shaped the four sides together. Then she spent some time moulding the bark with her hands. As she worked, Narfi looked hard at her—her eyes were quite wide apart and large. They were almond shaped like his and seemed to match her high cheek bones perfectly. Her mouth was slightly upturned as though she was permanently smiling.

She's probably seen her hairstyle in a mirror, he thought to himself; her curly hair was tufty and stuck out here and there. Two obviously longer pieces by either ear she had twirled around and tied into small buns that looked like horns. He watched her eyes as she concentrated on the bowl they were, brilliant green so they almost shone out of brown skinned face, when she suddenly looked up at him and beamed. *Beautiful,* he thought.

"Now I'll use magic to seal the joins," she explained as her hands, and only her hands were cloaked. Narfi, who had just about kept up, decided his effort wasn't bad for a first attempt.

"Now watch," Berys told him. Taking her bowl in her left hand, she showed him her right hand. She wiggled her fingers to make him watch and he saw the magic cloak just her index finger and thumb. She then used these two digits to massage the joins of the bark. Narfi watched, transfixed by the fact that nothing seemed to be happening. Berys then gave her bowl to him and took his to perform the same action on the cruder bowl he had fashioned. He looked at the bowl and was amazed to see there was no join—it was a continuously smooth sided bowl now. He looked up at her to find her smiling at him while shaking her head.

"No questions now, we'll talk about this another time. One question always leads to twenty others and I'd rather just eat." She then spent the next few minutes slicing the mushroom, chopping up some wild garlic and peeling a strange purple looking root, which she the sliced very thinly. She then laid all of these very carefully and close together on the flat rock she'd set up earlier.

Berys obviously sensed he was about to launch into another question because she held her palm up to him and repeated, "No questions now. Just watch. This is how we cook food." Placing her open palms on either end of the stone slab, Narfi could see her concentrating. Again, he was underwhelmed by her display as nothing seemed to happen. It was only when the faint sizzle of cooking food and the lovely scent of cooking garlic reached his nose that he realised she was somehow heating the stone. "No questions," she said again. "I'll just leave it a while to cook through while I get some water." Taking both birch bowls with her she left the lodge.

Narfi shuffled over to the stone and held his hand over the flat rock, before dragging it back quickly. The rock was too hot to touch, let alone hold. Looking at it closely he could make out black lines and layers within the rock. Berys eased back into the lodge and set the water down and seeing his scrutiny told him it was called *hearth-stone*. Berys went on to explain that it was the only stone magic her people could do, and then only if there was enough of the black veins in the rock which many of her people suspected was a type of fossilised tree, which was why they could use their magic on it.

She used both bowls to refill a leather water skin she had produced from somewhere inside her clothing. She then shared out the food into the two bowls, before producing a bundled cloth tied with a lace. She untied and unrolled this to reveal a selection of small pockets inside in two rows, each one marked with some kind of symbol. Opening the two right hand pockets she took a pinch from one of what looked like salt and sprinkled his on both portions; then took a pinch of something else from the second pouch and placed this in her palm. "This is mint and a special moss called *druss* that only grows on trees our people have woven. It tastes wonderful and helps restore energy." She offered him a pinch.

Our people, he thought. *She thinks I'm like her, a Celtyth.* As he worked out how to question her about this, he took it and doubtfully placed it on his tongue. He could taste the mint instantly then a wonderful flavour filled his mouth, making it water—his question forgotten. "Lemons," he proclaimed. "I had them once at May fair; it tastes of lemons, but not so sharp it makes your eyes close."

"I don't know what lemons are," Berys replied. "Sprinkle it on your food," she said handing him a pinch more. They ate their meals in a companionable silence, both too hungry to do anything other than eat. Narfi found the food immensely satisfying. He had worried a few vegetables wouldn't fill him up, but he felt replete.

"You should sleep now," Berys told him. "The lodge will keep us dry and the hearth-stone will keep us warm. You should take your heavy shirt off or you'll be too hot." Berys pulled her jerkin open and from a pocket inside, one of many pockets he saw, she produced a small piece of material unfolding it to reveal a translucent, body length cloth. Laying that down she began to strip off. Narfi couldn't decide if he was alarmed, embarrassed or mesmerised or all three. He'd never seen any girl undress. She had removed all of her outer clothing, and now stood with her back to him waring only a very short loincloth. Turning her shirt inside out and rolling it before placing it on the ground for a pillow, then wrapped the long cloth around her. He could see her breasts pressed against the material and began to feel decidedly uncomfortable.

"Your *cynfas* is there," she freed an arm to point to a small square lying near his feet. "Wrap yourself up or at least lay it under you so the ground doesn't make you damp and cold." Narfi had no intention of stripping off just yet and revealing his ardour, so he laid the cloth down lengthways and stretched out on his side. The two companions lay curled around the perimeter with the warm stones in between them. He heard her snigger, then the rustle of her sheet as her warm hand pressed against his forehead. He was afraid to open his eyes knowing what he would see. She laughed again then said, "*Cysgu.*" He felt weariness pouring over him and he slept.

Narfi woke the following morning to the smell of food cooking. He could hear rain pounding the lodge whilst the wind howled, but the inside of their shelter was wonderfully warm and weather free.

Berys was sitting cross legged watching the food—two fillets of what looked like trout and some more of the sliced purple root they'd had yesterday. As he lay watching her, she reached across and grabbed his bark bowl, placed a trout fillet and some of the strange root in it and handed it him. "Eat," Was all she said. The trout was delicious, the root less so, although it was strangely satisfying once eaten.

"Why did you say 'our people' yesterday? You're Celtyth but I'm not—my parents were human, so I must be human too," he told her.

Berys regarded him for a few moments. "You are Celtyth. No human could do what you can do. Look at your skin colour for a start. Humans from this land are pale skinned; you are dark skinned like me. You have magic and no human ever had magic. I suspect that those you call your parents were no such thing."

"No way," he shouted. Narfi could feel himself getting flustered. "They were my parents, so don't you…"

"How old are you?" That question stopped him.

"Fourteen summers," he told her. She continued to stare at him.

"And compared to the humans you grew up with, you are small for your age?" Narfi was stumped. How could she know that? He floundered for something to say but Berys talked amiably on.

"Celtyth people are much longer lived than humans. We live about two hundred and fifty years. You being fourteen means you are still a child. You won't be fully grown until you've passed forty so the human children you knew would have got bigger more quickly." She said all of this matter-of-factly, then added, "They didn't like you, did they?"

"No," he replied. "They called me *Narfi* and *runt*, sometimes *squirrel* because I always hid in trees they couldn't climb. They didn't like me—saying I was a *darkling* or a *breed*. My mam and da said ignore it. We lived out of the village because my mam was a Wicca woman, so they didn't like her either. They said I was tainted because my mam was a filthy witch." Tears welled in his eyes, so he turned away from Berys.

"Stand up!" she ordered. He wiped his eyes on his sleeve, sniffed and reluctantly climbed to his feet when she tugged at his arm. She stood and faced him, her arms holding his elbows to his side. They were of a height, but she was perhaps an inch taller. Their eyes met and their gazes locked. "How old do you think I am?" she asked him.

Narfi thought. She still had a boyish figure (he'd noticed that), was slim and lithe. "About my age?" he responded uncertainly. That firm gaze of hers held him again.

"Thirty-nine."

Narfi laughed aloud. "I don't think so Berys. You'd be older than my man. She was thirty-eight. No way." She simply smiled at him and shrugged.

"We need to get moving. Gather your things. Roll your *cynfas* and give it to me." He gathered from that, that their conversation was over, which was fine by him. He rolled the *cynfas* and handed it over. Berys tucked it inside her tunic then, once everything was stowed, she simply changed. Her *croen clogyn* just appeared as easily as blinking. "Stand still," she told him, then reached out her hands and pressed her palms to his temples. He felt the magic flow over him like a shiver, what his da called 'someone had just walked over his grave'. The minute his eyes cloaked, he saw the world in such sharp contrast it took his breath away.

"Now stand where you are. I need to put this right," she said gesturing at the lodge. Berys then began muttering in her own language whilst she moved around the inside of the lodge, smoothing her hands over the walls she had created, which looked exactly the same. She shuffled around the whole lodge, repeating this with no visible effect Narfi could see. She told him to follow her outside. The wind and rain, he noticed, didn't affect him in the slightest as he was cloaked—one bonus of his magic. Berys then bowed to the lodge before spreading her arms and then clapping her hands together loudly.

The tree branches she had moulded into walls simply sprang back into their original state, whilst simultaneously the trees flicked back upright, their tops unbinding where Berys had woven them together. Then finally she placed her palm flat on the cooking stone for a few seconds to cool it, before lifting it and placing it flat on the ground, rolling the four support stones away. It was as though he and Berys had never been there.

"Right. Let's move," she said, turning to leave, but Narfi grabbed her arm and Berys turned to face him.

"Where?" he asked. "Where are we going?"

She turned and pointed over to her left. "West. To the lands of the Celtyth. Back to my people. Your people." Narfi said nothing, still seething from all she had said. West was fine because that was where he wanted to go—his da's last words still burned, *Summer croft, quern stone.*

"West," he nodded but with no intention of going anywhere near the lands of the Celtyth and the two set off, running through the trees.

They ran for the whole day before, once again, Berys stopped them and set up a lodge. She'd explained on the way that they were heading for where the Great Ban River left the mountains as this was the only way to get into the

Celtyth lands. Narfi had nodded at that. He knew that river. Once they'd found that he could navigate his way to the summer lodge because his mam and da had seen to it that he could find his way. Stay south of the river; line up the peaks of the Dragon's Claws, keep heading west along the wooded valley of the Banna Hills and follow this valley to the highest hills. The lodge was built against a shallow cave in an old quarry. Overgrown now, the quarry was just part of the wooded ascent to the top, so the lodge was well hidden.

Exhausted again by using the magic all day, as well as running all day, Narfi dropped to the ground inside the newly created lodge while Berys gathered food and stones she could heat for cooking and warmth. She came back with two fat pigeons she'd already cleaned and plucked; a large beige *chicken of the woods* mushroom; more wild garlic and some birch bark for making bowls. Once the bowls had been fashioned, she went out again in the fading light and collected water. Narfi could hear a stream babbling its merry way down to wherever, wishing he could be so carefree.

Berys made a stew of sorts with the food, which she cooked on a large hearth-stone she had heated with magic; then surrounded the bowl with other heated rocks that she formed into a cairn over the food to make an oven. Her explanation of this process was their only dialogue; he had no desire to talk and she didn't seem to care. His resolve to travel the summer lodge had deepened during the day—the thought of entering the essentially alien world of the Celtyth had no appeal. Looking back at his life he'd always been an outsider and had no wish to repeat that way of life; he would be happier on his own. He had to stop himself thinking about Bran, wishing she was with him. He knew it was right to leave her, but he missed her. As he had no wish to share conversation with Berys, he ate, thanked her for providing everything for him and said he needed sleep, which was true.

The following morning followed the pattern of the previous one: breaking camp; putting everything right and then running. By now they were within a sight of the great Eiran Mountains that hid and protected the Celtyth from the human world. Throughout the late morning, Narfi caught occasional glimpses of the imposing peaks through the trees which were thinning out as they moved up into the Banna Hills. He knew the great forest would end in a few miles and from there he could follow his own path at last. When Berys finally stopped around midday at a rushing, mountain-water stream, Narfi could recognise the little cluster of small mountains, their peaks swathed in cloud. He told Berys, who was drinking the icy stream water, that he knew the mountains, pointing up to the seven granite peaks.

Berys looked up. "*Y Morwynion*," she told him.

"Dragon's Teeth," he insisted.

She regarded him for a moment, her head slightly tilted, before smiling and shrugging. "We know them as *The Maidens*," Berys explained. "Legend says that they are one of the guardians of our lands. They sit and wait at the entrance to our lands—Penrhyn and Torffan. They will awake when the Hounds of Annwn call them, if the land of the Celtyth is threatened. They are said to be stone skinned giants who will bring death to any not of Celtyth blood. Further on is the tallest mountain that we call Gwen Fawr—in your tongue that means 'big smile'. I was told that any Celtyth returning from away knows they are home when they see the peak of Gwen Fawr and they smile a big smile."

Berys stopped and looked at the distant peak. Narfi thought she didn't look too happy to see it, but didn't say anything. Berys continued, "And I am glad to be so close to home. When I was taken, I never thought I would be so close to these mountains again." With that she crouched down and put her hands into the water, splashing her face.

"You've never told me about you being taken," Narfi said as she filled her water skin.

Berys stood, eyes once again fixed on the distant Gwen Fawr.

"No," she replied softly. "No." With that she turned from him and headed up the hill.

"Berys," Narfi called after her. "I can't go there—to the mountains. I have to go somewhere. My dad said I should go…" He choked then and couldn't think how to continue. Mixed emotions swirled through his mind. Berys had stopped at his call and now turned to face him from higher up the hillside. "I have to… I'm so close to the summer croft."

Still staring, Berys nodded once then softly said, "Then go." Eyes clamped on his, she then disappeared behind her croen clogyn. Narfi saw her shimmering form as she leapt the steam. He gripped the llinach with his hand to his chest and the bright connection leapt from it tracking her as she moved away. Narfi let his hand drop and hoped she found her way home.

"Thank you!" he called, then louder "Thank you!" his voice echoing slightly. The silence was suddenly overwhelming as the bond thread slowly faded, but a sudden flash of light caught his eye. A sudden pulse of energy made his wrist twitch and Narfi was forced to take a deep, involuntary breath as though he had been winded. Then the most wonderful feeling he had ever experienced consumed his senses for a few seconds, before lapsing into a satisfied feeling that all was well with the world. Narfi had never felt happier. Or more ready to move. Stooping to the stream for a quick drink, he gathered himself and with one glance back to where he had last seen Berys, he set off towards the croft. He realised as he walked away that perhaps this was why the mountain was called the big smile if this was what the Celtyth felt when they saw it.

Chapter 4
Summer Croft

About an hour later, Narfi had reached the path that led down towards the quarry and the summer croft. He stopped on the slope and looked at the trees crowding into the narrow valley. He could hear the stream as it bustled along over a multitude of stones and rocks that his da said had been quarried then dumped in the water. He knew that this smaller steam joined into the Great Ban River that his da said rushed over a great waterfall in the Eiran Mountains before it reached the Banna Hills. He'd told Narfi that's why the water was so cold, it was ice melt. Narfi made his way to the start of the path that stretched diagonally along the hillside. The track that led to the quarry and the croft forked back on this path and led along to the wooded crown of a small hill that had been eaten away by whoever had quarried the stone, leaving a hill that looked like a giant had taken a bit out of it.

Eager to get there, Narfi pushed on without stopping to wonder at the beauty and majesty of his surroundings. As usual the track heading up was easy to follow as animals used it daily. The way into the quarry however was overgrown, as was usual for this time of year. Narfi pushed his way through, for the first time wondering how their sheep would fare. He supposed that one of the other villagers, fat Devyn no doubt, would claim them as his own. Once through the initial growth that filled the entrance to the small quarry, it opened out into a reasonable space, Da always said it was the same size as the Chancel of Sarum, and echoed the same way too. The lodge was built against a shallow cave at the back of the old quarry, facing south so the sun shone down on it most of the day during high summer.

The lodge had been built from smooth stone with a door and two windows. A long slate roof angled down from the quarry rock face. Whoever had built it had somehow inserted the top layer of slate straight into the rock of the quarry wall so no water could drip down inside. This high, pitched roof also housed a narrow platform in the loft space where he would sleep at one end. The other end he spent hours carefully stacking wood for their fire. Da had slid one of the slates out and rigged it up like a flap to act as chimney that would funnel out the smoke. He'd grumbled every year that whoever had built it hadn't finished it as there was no fire place or flue; that or it was never meant to be lived in.

Narfi eased open the solid wooden door that Da said had been there when he first came to the quarry and stepped inside. The place was full of dust and cobwebs as it always was on their arrival. He could picture his mam bustling about cleaning and sweeping to get the place clean whilst he and his da sorted the sheep and gathered wood. He marvelled at the craftsmanship of the builders—all of the walls were beautifully smooth with several sconces in each. Mam had wondered at this, presuming they were for candles, but da had pointed out there was no soot on the inner roof of any of them so nothing had burned there. They were also too small for anything but the smallest stub of a candle.

In the centre of the room was the great quern stone where mam had ground their grains for flour and pounded the wild garlic and herbs, she flavoured her stews with. The stone, which looked like a huge shallow bowl, sat on a very low solid rock table. He remembered his da trying to lift it but it was either stuck to the stone table somehow, or as mam had suggested was all one piece of rock carved to look as it did. Moving to it Narfi knelt down and reached underneath the low stone table. Scraping at the dust and sand that had accumulated underneath, he revealed a long slate.

He slid this over to one side to reveal a small, stone trough. They'd never figured out was this was for, other than making an excellent hiding place. Inside was the familiar leather satchel which he hauled out. Easing back on to his haunches, Narfi took a deep breath and undid the ties before opening the satchel. Inside he found a wooden tube, a whetstone, a skinning knife, a curious wooden disk and his da's spare flint and steel. Nothing else. He picked up the foot-long tube and looked through it, suddenly realising that there was something inside. Using his index fingers, he eased it out. It was a rolled parchment. He opened the scroll and looked at it. It was covered in some kind of writing—unintelligible. He could barely read normal words; mam had tried to teach him rather than send him to the Chancel school with the others.

Tears formed in his eyes. His Da had clung to life to tell him about this and it was useless. A sudden bark outside caused him to jump and drop the parchment. Grabbing the satchel, Narfi took the small knife from it, then flung it back into the trough, throwing the tube, disk and parchment on top, before placing the slate back on the trough and quickly sweeping sand and dust back over to conceal it. He heard voices now and more barking. They had found him.

When Berys had left Narfi and run off into the woods, she'd had no intention of letting him go his own way. She had sensed that whatever he wanted to find was important to him, so she gave him some space. She was easily able to follow him as she was cloaked and he wasn't. He never once looked behind him anyway. She stayed within the trees high above him so if he did test their bond, he wouldn't be able to discern how far away she was, just that she was further north. When he diverted into the quarry, she had been standing on the top of the cliff wall looking down at him. Still masked by the trees and gorse at the lip of the quarry she also had been taken by surprise at the sudden appearance of their pursuers. They could only have followed them this quickly if they knew where they were going—or knew where Narfi was going.

Cursing to herself, she moved quickly along the rim of the bowl created by the quarrying of the stone. The opening that Narfi had walked through was lower down to her right. The trees that grew at the ground level had grown almost as tall as the rock face so this would give her a good way down. She reached the edge and waited. A dog appeared first, dragging a small man dressed in grey. They headed straight into the quarry through the opening following Narfi's tracks through the overgrown area, which were obvious to all. The man and his bloodhound were followed by four Chancel men and a strange, pale, young man who looked about Narfi's age. Their voices echoed up the walls making eavesdropping easy.

"See," the pale youth was saying, his voice an almost petulant whine, "I said he would come here. I said I knew where he was going." The four Chancel men drew their swords and moved quickly after the dog handler. The blond youngster trailed behind. Berys quickly jumped across to the tree, climbed down most of it before jumping soundlessly onto the ground. She eased her way inside the quarry, cloaked in her *croen clogyn* but still keeping behind cover. She could hear laughter now and moved further in to get a good view of what was happening.

Narfi stood in front of the open door of a cabin, a small knife held out in front of him, faced by the four well-armed men who were taunting and jeering at him. Berys could see that his eyes were darting left and right looking for an escape route. Berys sensed he was on the verge of panic as she watched him shuffling his feet, edging back towards the croft. One of the soldiers lunged forward at him, smacking his wrist with the side of his sword blade and sending his small knife flying. This brought more howls of laughter from the men. Narfi clutched his wrist and Berys saw blood oozing through his fingers.

"Aart, Gerben, grab his arms," ordered the one who was in charge. "And Kees, go to my pack and get the collar and chain ready." Berys couldn't see their faces and from behind, in uniform, they all looked similar: more or less the same height and all fairly lean. Yet the man who spoke had a swagger about him, a confidence she didn't like. As the two sheathed their swords and advanced on Narfi, Berys pressed the palm of her right hand to the llinach on her wrist, cloaking herself and willing Narfi to cloak himself. Without waiting to see if it had any effect, she moved in.

Narfi was frozen to the spot, close to tears and sure he was going to die. Then the warmth of magic swelled in his chest, almost taking his breath away. He felt the *croen clogyn* cloak him. His fear evaporated. He now felt calm and in control; his sight had sharpened dramatically, he felt light on his feet and ready to move. By contrast, the two men who had been advancing towards him quite briskly and purposefully, now seemed to have been slowed dramatically; their movements were almost comical as though time itself had decelerated.

The two men halted; complete shock registered on their faces. He heard the man who had commanded them shout, "Magic. Filthy little savage. Little shit. All of you swing your swords, but don't kill him." At his command the other three began swinging their heavy blades in a vain attempt to strike something. Narfi became transfixed by their movements. They seemed to be dancing, deliberately and carefully like the mummers would do at the May Fayre. The polished iron blades catching the light. His fascination was abruptly broken when Berys' voice whispered urgently close to his ear, "Move, you idiot."

Narfi stepped back as one of the blades arced towards where he had been standing, avoiding it easily. He was aware of Berys standing to his left as the four men hefted their swords for a few minutes before the one in charge told them to stop.

"Fuck me," one said, gulping for breath. "I've got the sweats."

"Shut it Gerben," the one in charge ordered. "We need to listen. See if we can hear him moving about."

"You're always sweaty, Gerben. I can smell you from here." The man in charge stepped over to this man and cracked his open palm against the man's mouth, covering it.

"I said shut up. That includes you, Aarl. Now listen. If you hear movement, strike." All four of the soldiers stood, straining to hear something. The leader was deliberately and as quietly as possible moving, placing his feet carefully to avoid making noise. Calon stifled a giggle. It all seemed preposterously slow. Even the dog had quietened, and he remembered Berys telling the Confessor that dogs couldn't follow them if they were cloaked. He felt Berys' hands on his cheeks as she pulled him close to whisper straight into his ear. Her lips brushing his earlobes deliciously.

"Stay here and stay cloaked. Do not try and help me. You'll get hurt." With that she moved past him to stand in the midst of the four men, although they couldn't see her. Then Narfi witnessed the most astonishing and dramatic thing he'd ever seen in his life. Berys clapped her hands together softly, the sound drawing the attention of all four men to where she was standing, legs slightly apart, arms held ready like one of the bare-knuckle fighters he'd loved watching back home. Then Berys raised her arms above her head, clapping her palms together loudly this time, before elegantly moving her arms, still straight, stretched wide, down to her sides, releasing her *croen clogyn* gradually as she did so.

Narfi watched her reappear from the head down in one beautiful, graceful motion. He had never seen anything or anyone so stunning. The four men, stood aghast for a few heart beats, then all at once they screamed and launched themselves, swords swinging at Berys. What followed lasted only a matter of seconds but with his magic cloaking him the action was slowed so seemed to last minutes. As the men swung their swords in huge deliberate arcs, Berys, with balletic poise and grace, moved irresistibly between them, evading the dangerous blades with ease. As she did her hands snaked out, fingers stiff and rammed each man in the centre of his chest with frightening force. The men all crumpled in identical fashion; mouths gaping, gasping for air, hands clutching at their chest. As soon as all four were down, Berys turned to face him, smiled and bowed towards him.

Kneeling down by the man nearest to her, who had curled into a foetal position, she pressed her palm against his temple, pushing his head firmly against the ground. He noticed light pulse briefly from the man's eyes as she did something to him. He closed his eyes then and his body relaxed and stilled. She moved to the second man and repeated this. As he knelt by the third man and pressed her hand to his temple, Narfi registered the pale young man for the first time. Kees, the blond bully, one of the seven who had made his life hell. Kees, a large knife held in his hand, move quickly and quietly forward towards Berys who had her back squarely to the advancing assassin. Narfi, years of hurt and rage propelling him, exploded forward. Kees had only a few yards to go to reach Berys but Narfi, cloaked as he was, covered three times that distance in moments before cannoning into the blond youth.

The effect of this was not what Narfi expected. Kees was stopped in his tracks, whilst he bounced off, landing flat on his back at his target's feet. As he landed, his *croen clogyn* vanished abruptly. The young man stared down at him, at first bemused, before his mouth twisted into a broad, triumphal grin. It was only then that Narfi saw the knife was sticking out from his chest.

"Narfi, you filthy piece of shit," Kees hissed at him. "You're as good as dead you son of a bitch-witch. Just like your fucking freak parents." As Kees bent down to grab the hilt of the knife, Narfi scrabbled his hands around, connecting with a large chunk of quarried stone which he swung with every ounce of strength and hate he could muster straight into the side of his tormentor's grinning head. The would-be killer dropped to his knees with a scream clutching the left side of his head. Narfi raised himself up on one elbow, his chest bursting with agony, and saw one of the swords. Still enraged he grabbed at it and swung it around in a wide arc at Kees.

"Narfi, no!" Berys shouted but too late to stop his momentum. The sword clove straight through Kees' wrists and halfway through his skull. Blood pumped and brain matter oozed out of the dreadful wound as the bully toppled forward, face down into the dirt. His legs kicked at the ground a few before he twitched a final time and lay still. Narfi collapsed back onto the ground, sure he was dying. He heard feet pounding and realised that the dog man with his bloodhound were fleeing the scene. He stared up at the sky, his heart pounding, in so much pain he thought his chest had been split open. Expecting to die, he saw grey clouds drifting lazily against the blue sky.

Berys' face appearing in his vision brought him back to his reality. She lifted her hands, now cloaked in magical power that glowed blue, to his face and felt with her index fingers along the line of his eye brows, finding two small notches. She then pressed these notches hard causing excruciating pain to his eye sockets for a few seconds. When she lifted her fingers off his head all of his pain eased away completely and he felt as though he'd spun around quickly too many times.

"Lie still," she ordered him. "Try to breathe slowly. You will be fine but I want to stop your bleeding as quickly as I can." With that she began to press gently around the point where the knife blade was buried in his chest, ripping his shirt open to expose the wound. She tore some of his shirt away and wrapped this around her hand to avoid touching the iron knife, he thought to himself. "It seems you were lucky my friend. The knife is stuck in the bones; stuck between two ribs. If it had gone in any other way it would have pierced your heart. I will pull the knife out in a moment then I will press my hand to the wound. You will feel heat but lie still and endure. Do you understand me?" Narfi nodded. "Don't nod, speak. Repeat the words 'lie still and endure' before I begin," she told him.

"I will lie…" he began but got no further as she swiftly removed the knife. He felt it grinding his bones as she withdrew it. Her hand then pushed down firmly on his chest. Narfi was glad he felt no pain. As his head swam, a steady warmth began to flood his skin beneath her palm, getting steadily hotter. She pressed her other hand to his forehead to steady his head, which had begun rocking from side to side. He became aware that she was muttering barely audibly in her own language whilst she was doing this.

At the point where the heat became strangely uncomfortable, yet still pain free, Berys lifted her hands from him and sat back on her heels. "Stay where you are for a while. You need water to replace the blood you have lost."

Narfi saw her stand and walk off towards the quarry entrance. She returned with a water skin and held it to his mouth whilst supporting his head to let him drink. He realised he was parched.

"Don't take big gulps," Berys told him. "Take lots of small sips and swallow little amounts or you'll end up being sick." After what Narfi decided was nowhere near enough water, Berys took the skin from him. He watched her as she stoppered it and placed it on the ground. She reached inside her jacket, withdrawing her strange herb pouch. She unrolled it and took a pinch of something from one of the pockets. She saw him looking quizzically at her. "*Druss*," she told him. "To revive you." She then carefully crumbled the dried moss into the water skin before fastening the stopper back in and squishing the skin around to mix the moss into the water. She then un-stoppered the skin and helped him lift his head as she held it back to his lips so he could drink again. The lemony flavour was somewhat diluted but was still wonderful. Helping him to sit up, she left him with skin and moved over to the body of Kees, the young man he had killed. She stood and stared for a while and Narfi could see her lips moving as though she was saying something, but he couldn't hear what it was. Berys then knelt down beside Kees' body and straightened the legs and placed the arms by the side of the torso. She then began speaking again before leaning over the body and pressing her arms down onto his back. Narfi wasn't quite sure what he was seeing now, but the body seemed to just collapse. It was as though the flesh had disappeared all of a sudden and left the bones bagged up in the clothes Kees had worn.

"What have you just done to him?" Narfi managed to croak as Berys stood up after dealing with Kees. She turned to face him and he was surprised to see a tear rolling down one cheek.

"Death should always be avoided," she told him. "We Marwolleth are not the wanton killers the Hethwen would have you believe. We kill if we must but incapacitate where possible. If you are to live with us you will have to learn this; all life is precious."

"What are you talking about, Berys?" he asked. "He was going to kill us." He got no response. Instead, Berys walked over to him and held out her hand to help him up. He could tell she was in no mood to answer his questions. She gestured to the four men she had overcome so easily.

"We have about twenty-four hours before these men wake. Gather your things and we'll start moving. More of them may be following; he hound master knows where we are." With that she turned and headed back to the entrance to the quarry. "I'll get my things and come back," and she was gone. Narfi turned towards the croft. He needed to get the pack out, find his da's skinning knife and grab anything else that might be useful. Berys had decided he was going with her and as he had no idea what else he could do or where else he could go, he supposed he should do as he was told. He also thought he should thank her for saving his life again. He was thinking this as the ground suddenly smacked into his face. Berys found him there a few minutes later.

Narfi came to as the sun was setting. The light had dimmed but he was still able to see. He felt refreshed, as though he'd slept for hours but he knew that couldn't be so. He was in the croft, lying on his side near the door, his head cushioned on someone's cloak. He sat up and looked around. The four soldiers had also been dragged in and all lay comatose against the wall to the right of the door. He felt heat radiating from inside the croft and turned around expecting to see a fire, but there was nothing in the makeshift grate. He stood up, swaying a little, then stretched his arms out wide. He felt a slight pulling in his chest and opened his shirt expecting to see a bandage. Smooth skin was all he saw, with a feint, pale line the only evidence of his wound. He touched it, expecting to feel something, but it was as though he had never been stabbed at all, let alone a few hours ago.

"You've healed well, my friend," Berys said as she walked into the croft. She held a full skin of water and a small bark bowl. She set the bowl down on the low stone table in the middle of the room and poured water into it. She then took out her pouch and added a variety of dried leaves to the water. Within seconds the water began to steam. Narfi realised then that the heat was coming from the stone table. It was like the ones she'd made in the tent only much bigger. He walked over to it and reached out to touch it, feeling the heat increase as he got close.

"I wouldn't touch it uncloaked," Berys warned him. "I made it really hot so this would boil quickly."

Narfi looked up at her. "Is this meant to be, like, a heating stone?" he asked her. "Bit of a coincidence if you ask me."

Berys regarded him thoughtfully. "I forget how little you know." She gestured around the croft with her arms. "This was crafted by the Cawrrocs hundreds of years ago. Didn't you wonder how smooth the walls were? Look how tall the door is! All woven by powerful stone magic." She knelt at the stone table where the bowl of water was now boiling, cloaked her hand and lifted off. Blowing across it, before placing it on the ground beside her. "All of our heating and cooking is done on stones like these. We don't use fire. Fire is reckless and likely to cause our homes to burn. The smoke poisons the air. We never use fire."

"But how do Celtyth cook who can't warm the stones?" He asked.

Berys laughed. "This is a *carreg aelwyd*. Although most just say *carreg* usually; a 'hearth stone' humans would call it. All Celtyth can heat hearth-stones," she said, "even you. Someone just has to show you how." Narfi was about to protest about being Celtyth when he suddenly remembered the satchel under the stone. He quickly fell to his knees beside the hearth stone and reached under, but it was so hot he immediately withdrew it.

Berys laughter rang out again. "What *are* you doing?" she asked him. He quickly explained what was hidden under the stone. Berys listened and chuckled at his description. "You hid your belongings in a…" she struggled for a translation, "we call it *popty bara*, to cook bread." It dawned on Narfi then.

"An oven," he told her. "But…my stuff!" he said pointing at it.

"You never learn," Berys said shaking her head. She cloaked her hand and forearm then reached under the hearth stone, brushing away the sand and dust before sliding the slate away. She reached in and removed the satchel, which by now was beginning to blacken along the edge that had been closest to the slate. An acid smell wafted into the room. Berys reached back in and felt around the smooth stone vault. She took out a solid rod of stone about two hand widths long, then reached back in and pulled out a round disk of some kind. She put this next to the stone rod. She reached back in a final time and felt around the space but took nothing else out. She then picked up both objects and muttered a few words in her own language and blew a long breath over them. She repeated this strange ritual with the satchel and the hearth stone. This time Narfi felt a hot wind wash over him.

"They're cool enough to touch now," she told him, reaching out her now uncloaked hand to pat the hearth stone. Ignoring the two objects, which Berys seemed quite interested in, Narfi took the satchel and opened it. The parchment was tube was fine. He took the scroll out and unrolled it, turning it over to check for damage—it was fine. He was about to put it away when Berys spoke to him.

"Why have you got a Celtyth scroll?"

Narfi looked up at her. "I only found it this afternoon. My Da… When my Da was dying he told me to come here and look under the stone, so I did. The satchel was in there and this was on top," he handed it to her, so she could see it.

He watched Berys carefully. He thought she was reading it because her eyes were darting along the lines of runes. When she got to the end, she looked up at him. He was a little concerned that her eyes looked a bit teary. "What?" he asked her. Berys looked down at the scroll again. She took a deep breath and said,

"It's from your real mother. I'll read it to you."

My dear Calon, if you are reading this then I succeeded in getting you to safety somewhere. It is such a long story that led to me leaving you with somebody that I don't know where to begin. Easiest for you is to find your grand uncle Emrys, or your aunt, who is my cousin, Briallen—who are the last of our people left in Penrhyn. Know this Calon-Eryr, that if I gave you up it was only to stop the grey man killing you. Leaving Penrhyn was a mistake and tried so hard to make it back. Tell Emrys I tried. Tell I'm sorry I should have listened to him. Your father, Cadellin, sailed for the Western World before you were born and I wanted to take you to him. Seek your grand uncle—my canllaw, it will get you there. Avoid the Gwerin, they have doomed the Hethwen. Go to Penrhyn. I wish I had time to write more. All my love, your mother, Eirianwen.

Narfi was stunned. He asked Berys to read it again. "My name's Calon," he told her.

"Calon-Eryr in full. It means 'Eagle Heart'. A good name. A good warrior's name."

Calon detected a meaning in how she said that.

"Why did you say it like that? I'm Celtyth like you, aren't I?"

Berys looked at him. "Yes and no. You have so much to learn, Calon." He liked the sound of his name. "I am Marwolleth, and we are a warrior people," she went on, "Once we were all Hethwen; once, but there was a rift in our ancestors' time. The Hethwen are a peaceful, non-violent people but our lands were invaded and the people slaughtered. There were some who wanted to fight back and kill the humans who, aided by the Gwerin—the mountain folk—attacked our lands. In the end the Hethwen Council agreed to give these warriors, The Ryfelwyr, their own lands on the peninsula called Penrhyn. After that our peoples lived separately. The Hethwen called our people the Marwolleth, the death people. They would rather die than take a life.

"With the aid of the Cawrrocs, the Eiran mountains were fashioned into a great unpassable barrier. The humans settled on one side and the Celtyth lived in peace on the other. But Penrhyn is not good land—all mountains and evergreen forest, so most of our people, led by your father left for the land across the sea, guided by the *Rhedwr Mor,* the wave dancers—those Celtyth who can weave water. Your mother and my mother were both heavily pregnant and not fit to travel so stayed behind, and I wouldn't leave my mother. Emrys stayed, he was the oldest of our people, because he felt it was his duty.

"My mother died giving birth to my sister, so your mother looked after us. But my mother's death was hard on her. She left with you, impatient to leave Penrhyn, anxious to travel to Ynys Aderyn and ask the wave dancers to take us all over to the western world. We now know she never made it." Berys stopped and read the scroll again before rolling it up and placing it back in the tube.

Calon had questions but sensed there was more to the tale.

"They came back for us, but your mother had left by then, and Emrys wouldn't leave without knowing what had befallen her, and you. So Seren and I stayed. Emrys is the only family we have known. Until now that is." She stopped and looked at him then, smiling at his dumbfounded expression. "We are related. Our mothers were cousins, as close as sisters."

"You knew my real mother?" Calon asked.

"Yes," Berys replied softly. "She was lovely. A great healer, Emrys told me. Which is why she blamed herself for my mother's death. She loved you dearly; was so proud of you. She just wanted to be with your father, Cadellin." Calon was numbed by this, not knowing how to react. "She would never have given you up while there was hope," she told him. "Her love was too great." From where he was kneeling, Calon walked over to the side of the room where he had slept, lay down and faced the wall. His grief, his loss, his abandonment, a hard lump in his chest. Berys left him there, walking outside, her memories shadowing her all the way.

Over an hour later Berys' insistent shaking roused Calon. "We must move on Calon; cousin."

Calon opened weary eyes and looked at her. She smiled warmly at him and helped him up to his feet before drawing him into a long, hard hug. Unsure how to react at first, it was a few seconds before he hugged back, and it felt good. They stood for a minute or so like this, needing the companionship and love of another.

"Something has changed in you Calon," Berys stated as she held him at arm's length.

"I do feel different," he confirmed, rubbing the ache in his chest. "And it's not just the name Calon, although I like it. It feels right. I've decided to do as my mother wanted. I'll go with you to Penrhyn and meet Uncle and learn how to use magic…" He noted her expression harden. "What?"

"I'm not going *to* Penrhyn," she told him. "When the Chancel men captured me, I was heading to Torffan—the Hethwen lands. I had decided to settle with them. There is a skilled weaver who lives in the Karas hills—the mother of Emrys children—called Cariad, our great aunt I suppose. I have met her twice and have accepted her offer to live there and learn from her. Emrys and Seren… I don't want to fight or kill; or wage war with anyone."

"But Penryn? You'll still take me there won't you?" he asked her.

Berys shook her head. "I would if I could Calon. I will take you to the Eiran Mountains, but I have no wish to return just yet. That amulet your mother left is a *canllaw*, our word for guide, a magic token that will get you over the mountains and guide you home. The Cawrrocs and Marwolleth put such powerful enchantments on the mountains, any who try to cross end up coming back with no idea where they have been. They just say they will never go back to the mountains. Many are driven mad with fear, so on-one ever tries now." Calon pulled the *canllaw* from his pocket where he had stored it.

"But my mother made it across."

"She was Marwolleth." Berys said patiently. "The *canllaw*."

He still held it in his hand and looked at it, turning it over. Calon could see it was just a smooth looking wooden disk; perfectly round with a thin edge and fat middle. "I can't see that this is an amulet. It's just a smooth, wooden pebble," he told her. Berys smiled at this and told him to grip it hard in his fist. Calon let it rest in the palm of his hand, it felt warm and silky, then closed his fingers over it tightly. Bright, violet light suddenly burst from it. His instinct was to drop it but his hand refused to open and if anything gripped it tighter. His body was seized with a sudden warmth. He felt no fear at all.

He watched in awe as the light seemed to crawl under his skin and light up the veins in his arm, moving quickly through his blood stream and into his head where, for a couple of heartbeats, he was filled with intense pain as his eyes blazed, making everything look violet. As suddenly as it had blazed, the light flickered out. Only his hand tingled now, and looking at it he saw violet flames dancing over his clenched fist before they too died.

He opened his hand then to reveal a beautifully carved wooden amulet. It seemed to weigh twice as much as the plain wooden bauble he had held moments before. It was still the same shape, but he could see intricate knot work decorating the edges of one side with an eagle motif etched into the domed centre, wings spread. He turned it over and saw this side was entirely covered by tiny Celtyth runes running in a spiral around a silver sun motif in the middle. He showed this to Berys, who took it and read it out loud to him, turning it as she spoke. "*Let the dawn kiss the sun and guide you home.*" She then handed the *canllaw* back and told him, "Your mother did that. She attuned the magic to you. Hold it tightly and the light will guide you home. All Celtyth who leave Torffan carry one as it's the only way to get back through the mountains from this side. Mine is here," she said, patting her chest. "When you're not holding it, it's just like a piece of wood. You can shape it; disguise it in some way. Most warriors just wear it as bracelet or arm torc; sometimes a necklet. Some prefer to make some kind of hair band. Whatever you can weave it into I suppose."

"How can I disguise it?" he asked her. "I can't do what your people can do."

"*Our* people," she reminded him. She then reached across and put her hand over the top of his, sandwiching the disk between them. He looked at her eyes as she focused on the *canllaw*, feeling it warm up slightly. When she lifted her hand, he looked down and saw she had somehow transformed the disk into what looked like a carved circle. She lifted his right sleeve up high and had him hold it. She then opened the ring and looped the circle around his arm just above his elbow and below his bicep. She then pressed the two ends together and he observed, stunned, as the two ends joined together and wove into one piece. He felt it tighten just enough that he could feel it, knowing it would stay in place.

As Berys rolled his sleeve down, she told him, "This is how Emrys wears his." He was about to ask how he could take it off when her finger pushed gently against his lips.

"Later," she said, "we must go. There are things I can explain, things I can teach you, but not until we are safely on our way to the mountains." She held his gaze, her finger still pressed against his lips, which he was rather enjoying. She then leant forward and stretched up to kiss his forehead. "Let's get you home," and with that she cloaked both of them, turned and jogged towards the entrance to the quarry. Calon looked around, pressed his hand to his chest without thinking, so he could see where she was heading and ran after her.

Chapter 5
The Grym

The next two days of careful travel, attempting to avoid leaving tracks or a trail for dogs to follow, were as draining as running for a day. Berys had explained that staying cloaked continually was not an option, it would end up with them both burned out and sleeping for a day. Far better to cloak occasionally, especially having waded along and crossed streams, sometimes swimming or floating down the deeper sections in an attempt to fool their pursuers. After nearly two days, the stress of pursuit combined with the physical exertion of running combined with occasional intervals using magic, meant fatigue was getting the better of Calon.

Towards noon on the third day, they finally reached the end of the great forest to find themselves on a slight rise overlooking a narrow plain that stretched across to the foot of the Eirans. The river snaked along to heir right and Calon would have thought it spectacular if it wasn't for the mountains that loomed before them. Calon had never seen them from this close, so imposing and unwelcoming. For as far as he could see to either his left or right, huge, sheer cliffs stretched up, but it wasn't their size that was so arresting, it was their uniformity. The cliff face from ground level to, he estimated, a height of fifty yards was smooth, blemish free stone. It almost shone it looked so polished. Nothing, other than the patterns within the stone itself, marked the glassy surface. This continued without change as far as he could see in either direction.

He turned as Berys muttered something, and looked at her, but she just stood misty eyed, staring at the peaks in the distance. "I never thought I'd see this again," she said, hugging herself tightly.

"I wish you'd change your mind and come with me," Calon told her.

"No Calon. I am not the same person who left. My way lies south and my immediate future is to be with Cariad. And besides, I can't travel across those mountains, I have no amulet to shield me from the magic. I will see you on your way and then follow my own path."

"But, I'll never find two people in all of that," he protested pointing at the Eirans.

"I have thought of that, and I can aid you there," she told him. Sitting down, she removed her own llinach and carefully extracted a single strand of hair from it. She then repeated the process of threading this into Calon's llinach. "That is my sister Seren's hair. How you find me, you can now find her. Seek her when you cross the mountains." Then smiling she added, "She is less likely to kill you without asking who you are." Seeing his shocked expression, she quickly added, "Don't worry, that was a joke. They will see that you are Celtyth and will aid you."

After resting for a brief period, they moved on onto the plain. He saw that the trees seemed to stop at a uniform distance from the cliffs in both directions which he thought was odd, but not as odd as the feeling he was getting from the cliffs. Calon moved up close to the cliff face and placed his palms flat against the rock. "It's impossible and unnatural," he said to Berys, "no one could have smoothed this so perfectly. How is it kept so clean and shiny? And it makes me feel… comfortable I suppose." He paused for a moment lost in thoughts of stones and rocks.

"How do we get over the mountains if we can't climb this," Calon protested, running his hands slowly over the smooth stone. The polished rock felt cool and strangely comforting under his touch. "Why is it not even damaged? Anywhere?"

He turned to Berys again to see why she wasn't saying anything, noticing instantly that her demeanour had changed. He regarded her thoughtfully; her eyes were wide and she seemed almost agitated.

"What?" Calon protested. "What have I done now?"

At first, she just stared at him. "You don't feel anything, do you?" she asked him. "It's just stone to you."

Calon still continuously feeling his hands along the rock where he stood replied, "It's just smooth stone. Nice and cool though. It's just good to touch. Feel it."

Berys, instead of moving closer, actually took a step back. "I can't. It's wrong. I don't know why you can bear to do that if you're a wood weaver. Cawrroc stone weavers created this to protect our lands from human incursion.

These mountains stretch like this for the entire length of the Celtyth homeland, Torffan. But the Cawrrocs, they didn't just smooth the stone to make it impossible for anyone to climb, they wove a glamour into it and that's all I can feel. I can sense it from here. It's…" she paused to find the right word, "unpleasant. Ugly. Humans can't bear to stay here for longer than a few minutes. I'm told they develop a great fear that drives them away, then when they're far enough gone, they can't remember why they left—and steadfastly refuse to come back. If I wasn't Celtyth I would be running away now. Even with my *canllaw* I'm finding it hard to stay." With that she moved further back.

"What's a *cowrock*?" He asked tentatively, before he suddenly thought of something else. "If you can't bear it, how did you get out?" Calon asked. Berys began to unbutton her leather shirt and pulled out a woven band with a black object hanging from it. She moved further away and beckoned him to follow. They stopped some thirty yards away from the cliff, where she untied the band and handed the object to him. It was her *canllaw*. He first noticed how warm it was because it had been next to Berys' skin. It was a piece of shaped wood, but a dense black wood, that had been moulded with smooth ridges to fit her fingers perfectly when she held it in a fist.

As he closed his own hand around it, he felt a sudden urge to drop it in disgust as his stomach lurched, so he quickly handed it back, then began massaging his hand to try and remove the odd sensation, a bit like pins and needles from his palm. The feint queasiness he'd felt eased almost entirely the second he'd let go of the wood.

"You felt that, didn't you?" Berys said. "That's what the cliff stone does to me, only it's bigger so it feels…" she couldn't finish this sentence but held her arms wide and stretched them. "The *canllaw*, you'd say weaver-wood, that you held is attuned to me. As I told you all Celtyth who leave Torffan carry one to get them across the mountains. Holding this tightly we can ignore the glamours that the Cawrrocs covered the range with. Glamours more powerful than the one here." This reminded Calon of his earlier question.

"What is a *cowrock*?" he asked her. Berys smiled and shook her head slightly.

"I forget you know nothing of your own people or the land. Your heritage has been denied you. Once we get to the mountains if we're not followed by the humans, I'll have time to tell you many things." She seemed about to leave it there.

"And *cowrocks* are?" he asked her for a third time.

Berys who'd just turned to walk away, turned back towards him. "They were an ancient Celtyth race, not like us, who were very strong stone weavers, *gwehyddion cerrig* in our language. I don't even know if they still exist. None have been seen for hundreds of years." She'd decided that was enough. "Come on we must get to the *grym*." She turned away and headed north along the great cliff wall. "And no, I won't explain what the *grym* is—you'll see soon enough." They walked, uncloaked by magic, for the next few hours. The great cliffs stretched high on one side and the forest crowded on the other side. In between was the land they travelled; a wide expanse of grass and scrubland, punctuated by occasional trees and shrubs. The width of this open land seemed to be consistent for the entire length of the mountain range, as though the trees wouldn't come any closer but gathered at a safe distance to look.

He asked Berys about it and she said that she thought it was something to do with the glamour on the stone. She seemed reluctant to talk about anything, so he gave up trying. Calon could sense Berys' disquiet and assumed it that being so close to the cliff was stressing her. He had no such feelings and if anything felt uplifted being close to the smooth stone of the great mountains.

As the afternoon sun dozed sleepily into evening, Berys, who had forged ahead, suddenly stopped and pointed ahead of them. Calon followed her finger and saw a gap in the mountain range and could see that water was tumbling from it by the haze of water vapour that sat above it like a cloud. "The grym," was all she said. She waited for him to catch up, then for once walked beside him as they approached the gap. The noise of the rushing water growing to a crescendo the closer they got.

"The *grym* is the only way into Celtyth lands," Berys explained. "In ancient times, this great river flowed gently down a series of shallow rapids in a wide valley. Mighty Cawrroc weavers then tapered the valley to a gorge we call the *grym*, so that the wide river was forced through a constricted opening making it rush like fury. The Cawrrocs fashioned the cliffs so that the river that is hundreds of yards across is gradually funnelled through this narrow ravine that is only a third of the river's width and roughly one hundred yards long. The huge rush of water picks up speed dramatically on its journey through the passage as it narrows into the *grym* before it finally drops down a series of steep steps into the hills and then the plains beyond the mountains.

"This huge mass of water is so fast flowing it's impossible to swim against, wade through or take a boat up. Added to that, we'd have to go against all that power whilst moving uphill through a waterfall, standing on rock that's been woven and worn smooth so it's as slippery as ice, that holds a glamour convincing you the attempt is futile. It's the greatest defence the Celtyth lands has."

As they got closer Calon was awestruck at the majesty of the *grym*. The high walls stretching straight and impossibly high, caught the dipping sunlight in places the making the *grym* sparkle beautifully like a clear night sky. He observed that once into the valley the river widened again, gradually spreading out until it was a few hundred yards across, the white water diminishing as it slowed.

"What is this river called?" he asked Berys. "I thought the Great Ban was big until I saw this."

Berys gazed across the valley at the great undulating mass of water. "This is the Great Ban, you idiot. Our people call this the *Mam Afonydd*; the mother of rivers. It narrows and speeds up as it passes through the forest, then loops around the Banna Hills and down south into the sea." She looked back towards the *grym* and pointed out the smooth walls inside the opening.

Calon found himself focusing on the huge cliffs they had followed and saw something in the rock close to where the *grym* burst from the mountain wall.

He realised with a start that Berys was still talking. "The cliffs in the gorge are magically smoothed so there is nothing to hold onto to climb the high cliff faces, walls that slightly overhang to make scaling even harder. Emrys said that only a Cawrroc could have managed that," she explained before looking at Calon and adding, "Or perhaps a Celtyth who can weave stone can climb that way."

She went on but Calon was bewildered by the majesty of the grym the closer they got to it. The water cascaded down, roaring like thunder, but catching the light of the dipping sun. As they finally approached the river bank, his thoughts turned to how they were going to get passed the grym. He was just about to ask Berys when he noticed again the slight change to the smooth, cliff wall. As they neared, he saw it was a rectangular shape.

"What's that door there, Berys?" he asked her, pointing to a place just left of the waterfall where spray and mist clouded and hovered. Berys turned.

"What? There is no door," she told him.

"No, there is something…" he began before walking the twenty-odd yards to it. He ran his hands over the rectangular feature that was just a paler colour than the rest of the wall, but quite distinct. He felt no difference between it and the cliff face. Running his hands over the entire perimeter he felt no crack or blemish. "Here," he called to her. "It looks obviously different but feels the same."

Berys by now had moved beside him, clutching her weaver-wood pendant tightly. "What are you talking about? There is no difference at all. It all looks entirely the same to me." She watched his fascination as he smoothed his palms along the same bit of stone. "Describe what you see to me again," she asked him.

"It's… it's like there is a pale shadow of a door here. The rock looks lighter. It feels the same though. It starts here," he said crouching to his left at ground level, "and reaches up to here." Calon followed the discoloration line up and over his head, jumping once he'd reached as high as he could. "But it's another yard or so higher than I can reach and it is this wide," he told her walking about three yards to the other side of the shape.

"I wonder if that's a Cawrroc thing. They were said to be taller than us. Perhaps they sealed a door up?" she suggested. Whilst Calon began examining more of the cliff face for more shadow features, Berys thought an idea through before asking Calon if he could weave stone like he could wood and iron. He turned back to look at her.

"I've never tried," he said, "but you can do that stone thing, isn't that weaving?"

"No. I can heat stone, but that's it. Most Hethwen can and we're wood weavers, it's just simple magic. But I think if you can weave stone, that's why you can see something in the rock that I can't." Calon looked at his hands then the rock somewhat sceptically.

"I'll give it a try. What do I do?"

Berys walked over to him and told him to cloak himself. "Concentrate, like when you snapped the wood and iron, and just see what happens." Calon turned back to the discoloured door part of the rock wall and placed both palms flat on the smooth stone. He willed with all his being to be able to open the door, leaping back instantly when his fingers pressed into the rock leaving eight holes and two grooves where he had pushed. The two friends looked at each other, then back at the holes which were refilling as they watched, so that in a matter of seconds it was smooth again. "Well, that was interesting," Calon exclaimed at exactly the same time as Berys said,

"You can weave stone!"

"No Berys, I didn't change it. It was just that there was nothing solid there. It was like pushing my fingers into soft, silky sand. It was so easy." He stepped back to the wall and pushed his cloaked hand against it again, this time he just hit rock. He saw Berys' quizzical look. "I think I have to concentrate on it opening," he told her before trying again. This time his hand disappeared straight into the cliff face up to the wrist before he pulled it back. He moved to one side where the wall wasn't different and tried, but all that happened were a few small dents in the surface which instantly smoothed over. "It's definitely different," he told Berys. Moving back to the shadow door, he focused and tried both hands together, grinning as they slid into the wall up to his elbows.

Berys was desperately trying to remember if she'd ever heard Emrys talk of something like this, whilst also realising that Calon could probably climb up the wall of the grym and into Torffan if could harness what he'd just done.

"Berys!" She looked around at Calon's cry of alarm. He was trying to pull his arms back with no luck. "Someone's holding me," he shouted on the edge of panic, "I can feel their hands on…" and he disappeared into the rock completely. Berys ran to the wall, cloaking as he went, and thrust her hands against the rock that was just that; cold, smooth rock. She called his name and was about call it again when a strong hand burst from the wall and grabbed her throat roughly; squeezing hard and cutting off her air, hot pain stunned her. More than that, she was able to reason when her *croen clogyn* failed and her ability to fight back with it. 'Iron,' she thought in her panic, 'He's using iron'. Her breath seemed to be sucked out of her as the hand dragged her forwards, leaden legs stumbling, she began to black out, stunned at the last thing she saw—a pale, sharp featured face as it slowly eased through the rock, grinning.

Calon lay bound on his side, his right cheek against the cold, stone floor of a dimly lit, square room. His arms and shoulders ached as his hands had been bound at the wrist behind him. Smooth dark walls flecked with quartz exactly like the mountain cliff face he'd been admiring. A tall man dressed in dark clothes that looked woollen was standing at the 'door' that he'd just pulled Calon through. Only from this side it was like a window, with a clear panoramic view of the open ground between the mountains and the forest. It seemed to bow out in a large curve somehow. The man backed into the room and Calon saw that he had Berys by her throat and he could see her face darkening as he hauled her in, her legs dragging along the ground, eyes wide and bulging. The man suddenly jerked backwards and flung Berys into the wall behind where Calon lay, her legs lying over his waist and thighs. He went back to the window and stood there for a few minutes, looking. Calon tried to gently elbow Berys in the leg to try and rouse her. She groaned loudly, not the result he'd hoped for, causing the man to turn around. He was strangely pale, his skin seemed to be too translucent. Calon had the feeling that in better light he would be able to see inside him. Other than his sallowness and unusual eyes, his face was unremarkable. His nose was perhaps a little large and what Calon had thought was a grin seemed to be his permanent expression.

His eyes however, were remarkable. They were quite large, and almost entirely, very black—a stark contrast to his white skin. In fact, to think of them as eyes was wrong, they appeared to be two black chasms, revealing nothing about their bearer—if as his mam had always told him, that a person's eyes were the way to view their soul, this creature was as friendly as death. His hair and eyebrows were the same soft looking dark hair; the eyebrows growing right around each eye and halfway under, which also added to the oddness of the being in front of him. When he grinned with his mouth open, Calon noticed that his teeth seemed small, like toddlers' teeth, and well-spaced.

He met Calon's eyes then, grinning a big, wide simpleton grin, and still holding his gaze he strode over to his two captives, bent down and grabbed one of Berys' legs and yanked her off Calon to lie on the floor beside him, her head bouncing sickeningly with a dull thud on the hard floor. Berys groaned again. The pale-man, still grinning, kicked her hard in the chest, bringing another tortured sound from Berys. He held up his hand revealing fingers each adorned with two metal rings, his thumb with one. Calon could see that each ring was spiked on the palm side. Calon swung his gaze to Berys, seeing now the blood trickling from puncture marks where the metal, the iron, had pierced her skin. He had nullified her magic before she had a chance to fight, he thought to himself, anger beginning to stir within him.

Their captor had removed his heinous rings and put them down on a stone wrought able, from which he picked up a heavy looking circlet of stone. The pale-man moved back to Berys and did something to her that made her whimper. Calon couldn't see what until the pale-man stood, obviously happy with his efforts and he back to his vigil at the window. Calon turned his eyes back to Berys now, shocked to find her eyes open, tears brimming and then slowly traversing her battered cheek. The circlet had been clamped around her neck and

Calon had seen enough iron ore at Kort's forge to recognise it. He felt his rage building, but Berys, barely perceptibly, shook her head. She mouthed something at him, having to repeat what she wanted to convey a few times before he realised what she was conveying. "No magic?" he mouthed back, at which she nodded before closing her eyes.

Calon was at a complete loss. The journey with Berys had seemed exciting and wonderful. Her magical ability had constantly amazed him, especially as he knew he would be able to do some of the things she could. It had all seemed like a big childhood adventure with him as the hero. But now, faced with this harsh reality, he knew he was just like a child, lost in a dangerous world with no idea how to escape let alone survive. As for helping Berys, he had no earthly idea what to do.

Calon awoke sometime later to the sound of voices. He looked around and saw he was alone in the room, Berys and the pale-man had gone. It sounded like two men were talking outside, but their conversation was just a low, muffled noise. There was a pause and then a much higher pitched voice, Berys, followed by the two deeper voices conversing once again. Once it ended, he heard urgent footsteps as the pale-man and another moved across the room to the 'doorway', which was opened to allow the other man to leave. Calon had caught a glimpse of grey clothing and a grey robe to know a Chancel man. He knew they were in dire straits. A short while later he heard more noise; a dragging, scuffling sound getting closer, and then Berys was propelled back into the room, with the pale-man's hand around the back of her neck, guiding her at arm's length. She was barely able to support her own weight her left leg buckled every time she tried to walk on it.

He shoved her over towards Calon where she stumbled to her hands and knees, yelping in pain, before the pale-man turned her into a sitting with her back against the wall, hugging herself and with her legs straight out in front of her. He pressed her neck back against the wall and said something as he did, before standing back. Stone rings, obviously shaped iron-ore, were secured around both ankles and wrists; identical to the one around her throat. Calon could see that she had been badly beaten as her left eye was now swollen shut and her nose looked misshapen, probably broken. Blood was smeared all over her face and he saw the front of her tunic had been torn open.

Before he could even think what to say to her, the pale-man kicked his bound legs and barked something at him. Calon stared at him, terrified. The pale-man spoke again, slowly and deliberately, but Calon could only shake his head. The man came towards him then, knelt and grabbed his throat, but stopped short of squeezing his neck when Berys mumbled something to the torturer. The man had looked at Berys but now hauled Calon up to a sitting position and spat into his face.

"Human taint. Hethwen but not Hethwen." The pale-man searched Calon, looking disdainfully at the small knife he found. But he was more interested in his arm ring—his *canllaw*. He did something to widen the ring and pulled it free from Calon's arm. He stood, and let go of Calon's throat but grabbed his tunic at the back of his neck and hauled him back against the wall next to Berys. He then took a slender length of iron-ore from a pocket in his clothing and wrapped this around Calon's neck. Finally, as he had done this to Berys, he pressed his hand to Calon's neck ring, pushing him back against the wall. Calon felt the ring start to heat up, before suddenly cooling when the man took his hand away.

Standing back, the pale-man held up Calon's arm ring, still grinning like a dolt. The pale-man's hand cloaked as he began to mutter. The ring began to blacken and smoke before bursting into flame. They watched as green flames hissed from the weaver wood, but all too soon it was ash in the pale-man's hand. Their captor bowed theatrically, giggled and left the room. Calon, too terrified to move, listened as the pale-man's footsteps echoed away. He tried to move, to go to Berys, but found his neck ring was fastened to the wall so he couldn't move—he was helpless. His hands were bound behind his back so he couldn't even reach out to Berys, who was in a seriously bad condition.

He couldn't even turn his head as the neck ring allowed no room for manoeuvre at all, or reach out as his hands had been bound behind him. He simply had to sit and stare ahead, out of the weird window, into the dark beyond. He felt hopelessness wash over him again, and felt a pitiful, large sob building in his chest but was stopped by Berys touching her hand to his face, the backs of her fingers gently rubbing his cheek.

"Calon," she croaked, even her voice, which was barely a whisper, sounded broken. "I'm sorry. The *Gwerin* are waiting for Chancel men to come. They will be here soon. You have been sold to them… they said for slaughter… to Sarum with the Chancel men. Me… I…"

Calon answered in a whisper, "It's not your fault, Berys, you didn't know about this anymore than I did."

"No. I mean I'm sorry—I can't go with the humans again. What they did to me before…" her voice died to a gentle sob and she was silent for a time. "You have to free me, Calon; release yourself and free me." He was about to ask what she meant when he remembered freeing her from the Confessor's camp by melting the chains and shackles. Her hand moved to his chest, barely reaching the centre. "Free yourself and release me," she croak-whispered again as her hand fell away. Calon asked her how but she had obviously passed out again.

He tried everything he could to focus himself and bring the magic, but to no avail. His hands were bond in such a way he couldn't reach the llinach on his wrist, which enabled him to cloak so easily. It was only as despair began to settle on him that he remembered when he'd first seen Berys, how he'd moulded the living wood when he sitting in the tree watching her being hit, that he recalled he'd been incredibly angry at the time. "That's it," he said to himself, "I just need to be angry."

With that he looked again at Berys' slumped form, taking in the blood and bruises. He forced himself to think about what she had just told him about her previous capture by the Chancel men. He focused on this. In turn this got him thinking about the Confessor and he recalled vividly the damage inflicted on his mam and da. He relived every moment he could recall until it felt his blood was boiling. He then closed his eyes and imagined he was back home in the woods, hands pressed to a tree and willed himself to cloak. It was easy. His *croen clogyn* just slipped over him. He twisted his hands around underneath him and eased his legs through his bound wrists and arms. He put his fingers to the bindings on his legs and neck and they just melted away. He couldn't get his fingers to the iron-stone manacles on his wrists, but didn't care. Berys was his concern.

He shuffled over to her and gripped the manacles on her wrists and squeezed his fingers through them like they were made of butter. He repeated this for the manacles on her ankles, then finally and carefully, he removed the iron-stone collar from her neck. He gently touched her face and whispered her name. Her eyes fluttered open then closed again, leaving him unsure as to whether she had registered his presence. He thought back to when she had healed him. She had pressed her hand to the wound and it had grown hot and it had healed. He tried that now, hoping that focusing on healing might help her. He pressed his palm against the worst bruise on her left cheek and willed it to heal. He felt warmth, but nothing else happened. He then tried touching her forehead and asking her to wake up. That had no effect either. Ever conscious that their captor could come back at any moment he did the only thing he knew would wake her up—he grabbed her broken nose and quickly dropped his hands to cover her mouth.

Her eyes flew open and mouth gaped into a muffled scream. She took a few moments to focus while he pressed her lips and then nodded to him, telling him he could let go. "Tell me how to heal you," he whispered to her.

She responded by grabbing his wrists and holding them up in front of his eyes. She gently pulled them apart as far as they could go, her voice barely a whisper, "Just… keep focused… pull your arms apart." He did as she'd suggested and the manacles dropped almost instantly. They looked at each other for a few seconds than she bade him to help her to her feet. "Get us through the door thing," she ordered him. He had to support her weight as they crossed the room to the window. He pressed his hand against it, but before pushing it through, he turned to Berys.

"How will you get through?" he asked her. She responded by touching his chest and drawing up their bond, then cloaked herself.

"I'm not sure," she said weakly. "But we are linked. Just keep hold of me. The *Gwerin* pulled me through easily enough." With that he pushed his hand through.

"It's like putting your hand into a tub of skin warm water," he told her. Still supporting Berys they then walked straight through the wall together, stepping out into the dark night on the other side. He then tried to urge her into moving quickly back along the cliff wall, the way they had come, but she just fell to her knees and put her hands to the ground. "Berys, come on, we have to go," he begged her.

"No Calon, I can't," she said. "We cannot escape the Gwerin, I'm too broken to move quickly and the humans will be here soon. I can't."

"We can heal you…" he began. "You're already stronger."

"No, Calon. You have not the skill. The gwerin put iron in my blood. It will days before I could attempt that. Even cloaked I cannot run on a broken leg. The Chancel man knew what he was doing." She looked up at him then and beckoned him over. She reached up to grab his arm and insistently pulled him down towards her. He knelt as well so they were facing each other. "Closer, so our knees touch," she told him. When he'd shuffled in, she wrapped her arms around his chest and hugged him tightly, her head against his shoulder. Unsure what to do, anxious to flee, he at first held his arms awkwardly before tentatively following her lead and hugging her back. It felt good. She then moved up and took his face with her hands, kissing him on the mouth. "I'm sorry," she told him again. "I think I could have joined with you if things were different, cousins or not." She smiled then kissed him again, only this time for longer. He enjoyed their lips touching but when her mouth opened, he began to feel a little odd. The tip of her tongue then touched his and he knew what she intended. Just their tongues touching had shared something. He wanted to argue but she had done something to him. He couldn't move or speak.

She reached inside her tunic and brought out her *canllaw*, the black, weaver-wood amulet she carried. Holding it in her open palm she reached across and grabbed his right hand and place in on top of the amulet, pressing her hand on his so that the *canllaw* and his hand were sandwiched between hers. "I must attune this to you. The gwerin destroyed yours." He could feel the ridges pressing his fingers and palm. She then muttered in her own language and the amulet began to glow a deep green colour. Calon felt the weaver-wood writhing against his palm, the ridges moving until they fitted his fingers perfectly. She let go of his hands, leaving him holding the *canllaw*. "Keep this and when you go through the mountains and it will protect you," she told him. She leant in then and kissed his lips again before easing herself away from him. Helpless, he watched her through blurred vision as tears filled his eyes.

She cupped his face a final time. "Tell Emrys and Seren I wish I'd listened; I wished I'd stayed. We have to fight them, there is no mercy in them. What they did to me… I couldn't stop them… I can't go through that again…" Berys then smiled at him one more time before dipping forward so her forehead touched the earth, with her palms flat on either side of her face. "*Ddaear cymer fi*," she whispered softly, 'earth take me.' Then pressing her fingertips down into stony ground said, "*I ildio!*" Calon watched, chest heaving but still bound by her magic, as with a brief burst of light from her hands, she just crumpled.

Her body just seemed to collapse in on itself amid a wash of light. Her clothes just fell, covered in dust. It wasn't until the light blinked out that Calon could move again. He lifted his hand to his mouth and great sobs wracked his body. He crawled over to what was left and tentatively touched her clothing. As he reached out, he noticed something on his wrist. He brought it up to his eyes and saw it was braided hair—Berys' *canllaw*. That brought more anguish and he curled into a ball on the ground sobbing.

As he calmed, he became aware that he wasn't alone. The gwerin stood by the side of him. He looked up and recognised his captor. He could think of nothing to say, so just lay down again and curled into a tighter ball. He never saw the heavy iron-stone club that knocked him unconscious.

Chapter 6
Mordwyn and Anghenfyl

Bound and hooded, Calon had no idea how long he had been captured. All he knew was that he was inside the mountain and they had been moving interminably. Apart from a few rests where he had been given water, although nothing to eat, he felt he had been walking for hours. His head still hurt from the blow that had knocked him out, leaving him groggy. He'd panicked on first coming to, but a few sharp punches to his midriff had stopped that. The total darkness that was not his worst torment, it was the loss of Berys; the constant agony that he should have done more was a raw pain, he carried like a dead weight. He had to avoid thinking about her for fear of sobbing again.

He'd also discovered something about his magic: raw emotion, be it anger or grief, made it far easier to manifest. The incessant dripping of water; the scattering of pebbles he'd kicked; the scrape of his feet on rock; and the constant banging into walls or the occasional tripping and grazing of his knees he found he could live with, because the concentration it took him to keep his magic beneath his skin was his only focus, wearing as it was. He'd also noticed how soundless his captor or captors were. They made very little noise, so he had no idea if it was only the one gwerin or if there were more of them. Apart from the occasional rustle of clothing and because of the quietly mumbled words in their own language, he thought there were at least two. He also began to wonder if the strangely soft bag on his head had anything to do with muffling their sound, but the noise his own feet were making gave lie to that idea. They were just unnaturally quiet.

His endless trek into the mountain, sometimes uphill, sometimes downhill, came to an abrupt end when a hand gripped his upper arm very firmly and swung him to his left. He stumbled slightly as he shot forward, but one of his captors grabbed his bound wrists to halt his fall. This caused agony in his wrists, rubbed raw by the rope that restrained him. He couldn't help but let out a yelp of pain. He was then grabbed and dropped abruptly to the cold, stone floor, face down so that his wrists could be freed. As blood rushed back into his fingers, pins and needles added to his immense discomfort.

Clawing his hands together, he opted to lie still, hearing a whisper of noise as his captors left, followed by a dull thud that echoed eerily, as the scrape of bolts being slid into place confirmed his predicament. He lay unmoving, straining to hear, but jerked suddenly when something wet touched his hand. He grabbed at the soft bag on his head and discovered that there was a knot tied underneath his chin, but with his fingers suffering from the after effects of pins and needles, he couldn't seem to grip the laces. Eventually, with some difficulty, when his fingers regained enough feeling, he managed to tug the bag off.

There was no light in the cell. Even if he held his hand up to his face, he couldn't really see it; even cloaked, he could just make out a shadowy blur. He could hear nothing. Calon decided to explore, walking forward slowly with his arms extended in front of him until he reached a wall. By the feel of the wall, it had been worked magically smooth by the same folk who had fashioned the great cliffs. The surface was as smooth as the glass in Dinnon's cottage window. The only glass he had ever touched. Keeping his hands pressed to the wall he traced his way around until he came to what was obviously the door. This was rougher to the touch and made from some kind of wood by the feel of it.

Quickly passing over it, he reached the other side and continued round—no corners. It was a round or oval room. Getting back to the door he put his back to it and paced across till he hit the wall. It was only six paces over. Feeling his way back to the door he laid his hands on the wood, debating momentarily whether summoning his magic would help. He decided it couldn't make things worse so pressed his cloaked hands into the wood—or tried to. It felt like wood, but he couldn't weave it or mould it. He guessed it was some kind of iron wood—he remembered Berys mentioning it—a material that was invulnerable to magic. He could feel the grain, but there was no 'give' like he found in living wood. He moved to one side and pressed his hands to the wall.

"It is *helyg-haearn*, iron-willow in your tongue," said a quiet voice just behind him. Calon jumped back, slamming up against the wall. A dim glow began to fill the cell. A dark figure emerged slowly, holding some kind of light emitting rock. Calon became aware of how small the cell was and was stunned that this person in front of him had not only been so quiet but had also evaded being touched. The gwerin lifted the rock up to his own chin and the light suddenly flared brighter, illuminating the bearer's face—the pale-man.

Standing before for the first time, Calon realised they were of similar height. He looked quite old to Calon, but perhaps it was the light so close to his chin that gave the gwerin a demonic appearance. The gwerin spoke to him then in his own language. Calon had no idea what he was saying so just stood and watched the gwerin, who seemed to take Calon's indifference for incomprehension. "Not Hethwen we, but *Gwerin Carreg*, the stone folk, in your tongue, although the Hethwen prefer to call us *Rhai-Coll*, the lost ones. I used to think that was because we went our own way, but more and more I think it's because we lost our magic when we came down here." The gwerin's voice was quite high in pitch and there was a strange, lilting quality to his accent. "Typical of your people to use double meanings like that. Unwanted cousins we, it seems."

"They are not my people," Calon responded. "I've never even heard of you stone folk or whatever you are before today, if it still is today."

"Ah," the gwerin said. "Indeed." He then looked at Calon for a few moments before taking two strides to stand face to face. The gwerin reached a hand up and pushed his hair aside, touching his temples. Calon stood transfixed, both too frightened and too battered and tired to move out of the way. "So, you have no idea you are Hethwen? Do you think humans can use magic like you?" He smiled as he said it but more, Calon felt, because he knew something that he didn't.

"You feel it, the magic, don't you?" the gwerin said. "Someone, your mother I would think, hid you among the humans. Why would a good mother do that?" With this the gwerin moved to the door, touching it with his right palm flat to the wood, bolts slid back noisily then the door swung gently open. He turned and smiled at Calon and laughed aloud as the light suddenly vanished. "We gwerin have perfect sight in the dark. When the door closes, you'll never know if I stayed inside with you, or left you alone in the dark." The door slammed shut in the darkness, the odd echo muffling any immediate sounds, and Calon had already experienced how silent the gwerin could be. He quickly spun around with arms outstretched trying to see if the gwerin was still there; he tried kicking and punching but his blows found nothing other than rock, and all he managed to do was hurt both of his hands. He knew the gwerin had tried to unsettle him. Both he and the gwerin knew it had worked.

Calon woke when the door to his cell slammed shut and the bolts ground into place. He was stiff from lying on the cold stone floor, but eased himself into a sitting position. He listened intently, but could hear nothing. Thirsty and hungry he hoped they# gwerin had left him something to eat and drink. He moved forward, shuffling on his hands and knees, feeling his way, until he reached the wall. He then proceeded around the circular cell, still touching the wall, until he came to the door. He felt carefully around the floor, but his hand knocked against something that clattered over. Cool liquid immediately flooded over his supporting hand. He quickly dipped his head to the floor and tried to manoeuvre the spilt liquid, water he was relieved to discover, into a puddle he could lap at with his tongue, but the process was futile. He had barely wet his tongue, when the darkness suddenly receded in the cell, hurting his eyes. He squeezed his eyes closed against the bright light, waiting for his irises to contract.

"I had suspected you were a powerful weaver. Now I suspect not." The same high pitched, quiet voice. Calon looked up to where the words had come from. Squinting up, directly above him, shielding his eyes from the glare of one of the strange light stones that was sitting on the door lintel, he saw the gwerin stuck to the ceiling. His fingers and bare toes seemed to be dug into the stone. The gwerin moved, spider like to one side. Calon was fascinated to see the holes his fingers and toes left fill up and smoot over, as if they were never there. 'It's like liquid' he thought to himself. He switched his gaze back to the gwerin who lowered his feet until he was hanging by both hands, straight down. He then let go with one hand and twisted his other wrist. Slowly and gracefully, the gwerin lowered himself the seven or so yards to the floor; his hand still holding onto the stone of the ceiling, but stone that stretched like well risen dough, until his feet came to the floor. With a flourish, he let the stretchy stone rope go and it withdrew in a couple of seconds back to the ceiling, where it reformed a smooth surface without blemish. Calon was aware his mouth was open, and was also aware the gwerin was showing off. But what he had just seen was incredible.

The gwerin grabbed the back of Calon's neck and dragged him to his feet. He walked towards a wall with him then propelled him hard into it. Calon just managed to get his arms up to protect his face, then crumpled to the floor. Expecting and dreading more casual violence, he curled into a ball, but all that happened was one swift slap to his arms, which he still held protectively over his head. The same pincer like grip clawed on to his neck and hauled him to his feet. The gwerin then placed both of his palms on Calon's cheeks, his long fingers pressed into his temples. Calon felt magic then, like Berys would do to him, but infinitely more intrusive. With the pain becoming excruciating Calon began to moan, then with a loud tut the gwerin shoved him away. Calon fell to the floor again.

That voice again. "A wood weaver could never have walked through that stone. I know it was you, but how? I sense nothing. You can't even summon light from a light stone, something children can do." With that he reached up and took the stone down from the door lintel, throwing it at Calon, striking him on the fore head as he dipped to avoid it hitting his face. A small trickle of blood began to leak down Calon's face into his right eye. The pain was enough to bring tears to his eyes.

"It's called a *carreg-fwyn,* a light stone, if you can't use it you'll have to die in the dark," the gwerin hissed at him, before clicking his fingers. The cell descended instantly into pitch darkness. There was a slight shuffle, then the noise of the door opening and slamming shut; bolts slid into place, but Calon was not confident he was alone. Struggling to his feet, he began shouting,

"I know you're still here you fucker," followed by a scream of primeval rage. Still clutching the light-stone in his fist, his rage gave him purpose and energy. He began swinging his arms violently all around him, smashing the walls with his hands, grazing knuckles finger joints. He even jumped and swung to try and connect with his captor, but all too soon he was exhausted and he sank to the floor. He curled himself into a ball again and, still dreadfully uncertain if he was alone in the cell or not, he wept.

****

In the deepest cave of the mountains a great stone sarcophagus rested, as silent as death in the blackness. The tomb stood in darkness no human eye could penetrate. If there were light, ornate gwerin runes would be seen carved across the marble lid, etched in gold. Around the perimeter of the great lid a two-inch-wide band of gold had been fixed. From this solid band fine golden wires had been fixed and then crisscrossed over the whole sarcophagus; a fine wed of magic that had been destroyed when the lid had been slid sideways to rest horizontally askew the tomb and allow access to what lay inside.

Within, that cavity was fogged with suspended decay. The magic that had held the corpse in stasis had been severely weakened when the lid was removed by the thief. The corpse within was rotting—gradually. The body that lay within was over six feet long, broad shouldered and its skin was now pulled tight across the skeletal frame. The head, little more than a skin covered skull, was large with a pronounced ridge that ran the length of the forehead just above the eyes. A Cawrroc skull. Incongruously, a round, flat disc of solid gold had been implanted in the centre of the forehead; its only embellishment was a pure diamond, shaped into a square based pyramid that rose an inch from the surface of the golden disc. The surface otherwise was completely smooth, but it's lustre amidst the dust of centuries in the tomb, was evidence of its very recent placement therein. The creature's left arm still lay against its chest, fist closed around a now desiccated parchment. The right arm however had been moved and now lay flat on the bottom of the sarcophagus, palm open. Whatever it had held stolen by whoever had violated the sanctity of death.

****

Over a century later, the perpetrator of that crime waited silently in the dark of the Calon's cell, watching him flail around beneath. The gwerin, fingers and toes embedded in the rock of the ceiling above, hung and watched with amusement, observing Calon's bloodied hands, waiting for his moment to drop to the floor. When Calon finally stopped and slumped, to the cell floor into a tight sobbing mess, the gwerin smiled; let the boy rest just a little while; let him start to believe he was alone. He watched the boy, who was lying face down on the floor, weep himself out then slowly and deliberately raise himself to his hands and knees.

Gently easing his toes from the rock, the gwerin eased his legs down slowly until he was hanging by just his fingers that were still hooked into the ceiling rock. Then slowly and silently he began to lower himself gently down towards the human below, the rock he gripped gradually stretching. Suspended like this he was completely taken by surprise when Calon, still crouched low to the ground suddenly leaped and spun, arms stretched upwards as he did so. His open right hand, flailing blindly, fortuitously struck the gwerin's chest, grabbed a handful of tunic and dragged the gwerin downwards.

Standing now, his tormentor located, Calon's left hand slammed into the middle of the gwerin's chest, grabbing a hand full of tunic and an amulet that had been tucked inside the gwerin's clothing. Calon kept hold of the amulet and pulling hard, snapped the chain. With this as a weapon he held the amulet tight and swung the chain around hard, hoping to hit his captor. The gwerin though had recovered and simply eased back, avoiding the blow. Calon, still blind in the pitch-black cell, continued swinging the chain from side to side, hoping to connect with his assailant. His efforts were cut short however as a powerful kick hit the side of his head on the temple and he toppled soundlessly, head bouncing off the floor with a deep thud. The gwerin released his hands from the rock and landed lightly on his feet beside the prone human. The rock of the ceiling above rippling smooth, like milk settling in a glass. The gwerin was relieved he could see the steady rise and fall of the Calon's chest, knowing a hard head fall on rock could easily kill. He bent down and took Calon's left arm, lifting it so he could unpeel the boy's fingers from his prized amulet.

He noticed with some disgust that blood from Calon's battered hands had covered the precious artefact. Holding it gently by its edge, he watched with interest as the blood on the golden surface seemed to hiss and spit as though being boiled, forming into small ruby like balls that slowly sank into the polished gold surface of the amulet. Sudden heat flared from the precious object, causing the gwerin to move it from hand to hand for a few seconds until it had cooled enough to handle. Puzzled, the gwerin looked at it but could see no discernible difference to his prized artefact. Satisfied that all was well, he turned his attention to the snapped chain, grasping both ends of the broken chain and holding then together.

Concentrating hard, he felt his fingers warm pleasantly as the gold, welded by magic, reformed a complete circle. Then, looping the chain around his neck, he tucked the amulet back inside his clothes so it rested on his chest, the gwerin opened the door and left. Closing it behind him with an ominous thud, he slid the bolts into place before heading off down the corridor, down into the mountains heart.

****

Deeper down still, in the tomb at the deepest point, where the huge skeleton lay in the marble sarcophagus, at precisely the moment that Calon's blood was absorbed into the golden amulet, the air shimmered and sparkled as the runes on the tomb's lid flared to life briefly, the cave then plunging once again into impenetrable darkness. Within that tomb, where the Cawrroc skeleton had lain undisturbed for centuries, a huge hand lay, withered and grey with age, skin stretched tight over decayed flesh and taught sinews and tendons; a hand so old no living being could remember who it belonged to; a hand so ancient only half remembered legends could recall it's ever being. A long dead hand that, as Calon's blood entered the golden amulet, twitched before curling slowly into a tight fist; a hand that like the being it belonged to was now free of death's cold charity.

****

Mordwyn left Calon's cell and hastened down into the depths of the mountains. Several months had passed since he had discovered the ancient tomb in the deepest part of the caverns. Even before being outcast from the residential levels of Parth-Cerrig—the gwerin kingdom, Mordwyn had spent years travelling through the lowest, uninhabited levels of the mountains, and somewhere in what was left of his sanity Mordwyn recognised that the spells in the tomb, the enchantments in the floor and walls, had changed and unhinged him beyond what he could control. He knew he had always been mad, but it was a madness he knew he could control. Now, his insanity ruled him and his desires. He dreamed of gold and precious stones, he dreamed of silver and diamonds and, most of all, Mordwyn dreamed of his revenge.

The gwerin King himself, Brenin, had ridiculed and banished him in the Barnwyr, the great court of the gwerin when all the male folk would gather to bear witness and pass judgement on wrongdoers. He'd tried to protest his innocence—he'd tried to assure the King he would never harm a child, especially not one as pretty as Sioned. Yet midway through his efforts to appear sincere and guiltless, he'd remembered the child clawing at the ground as he lay on her back. She was trying to crawl away and in attempting to drag herself from underneath him, she clawed the stone floor and two of her finger nails had been torn from her fingers. He'd giggled then. He tried to hide it, but it was so fucking funny, because he still had the fingernails.

The King had raged then and called Mordwyn insane, which had made him stop giggling. He had looked at His Right Royal Majestic pain in the arse Brenin, smiled and told him, "Yes I am. But you have no idea how mad?"

He knew it was the magic in the old Cawrroc tunnels and caves that fed his madness. For years he had explored the hidden tunnels and shafts, before finding the tomb. He had spent days in there, lost in his dreams, running his hands over the great walls of runes that lit up when he ran his hands over them; lit up and whispered things he couldn't quite hear. But after, he found he just knew things. Things like he did as they advanced on him in the Barnwyr, intent on collaring him in iron to bind his magic.

He had bowed low to the King, sweeping his arm down grandly so his knuckles touched the floor, then flipping his hand over, he had pressed his palm to the flagstone he was standing on and just descended through the rock to freedom, smiling as he went. That was still the longest journey he'd made through solid rock. It was like the times he'd been swimming in the great underground tarn, swimming but harder and slower. He'd nearly died as his held breath threatened to burst his lungs open, but he'd got through the floor and hung from the ceiling of the corridor in the level below. As he calmed himself and drew deep, long beautiful breaths, he vowed then to kill the king. Kill the king and take his place.

And for a few months, that revenge had been made real by the discovery of the tomb. However, the more obvious it became that he could not raise the ancient weaver, the greater his fantasies ruled him, fired by rage and insanity at his treatment by his own people and honed by the years of solitude and loneliness. Now, his only recourse was a pact with the humans; humans with their ridiculous beliefs, their bloody iron weapons of war and their lust for Celtyth blood.

For the first years of his exile, he had moved around unseen, spying on the gwerin, stealing what he wanted, mainly silver and gold. He'd found the King's treasury and begun moving it, hiding it where no one but he could reach it. The strange thing was, the more gold he had the more he became obsessed about having more. This led him to spying on the trade hall near the great waterfall, the grym, where the humans came with their gold and silver to buy iron ore from the gwerin. He had thought to steal the human's gold at night, when he could see and they could not, but he had seen Brenin there with a dark skinned Hethwen girl, an iron-collar around her neck as well as irons on her wrists and ankles.

He'd seen Brenin hand the girl over for three ingots of silver; silver so pure he could smell it. He heard them talking, they would be back at the next new moon and so, he had a means to acquire wealth placed before him. He could steal

Hethwen women and children, drag them through the mountains, imprison them in cells he had found and sell them to the humans. He noted the human who took the girl—a tall man in long, grey robes. He knew then he had one moon before they came back. One moon to take a Hethwen to trade for his own silver ingots. Following the King had led him to the hidden halls from which a door could access the human side. He had to wait two 'trades' before he learned the King's secret way, only succeeding by hiding himself in the wall, his face cloaked, the great Brenin oblivious to the fact he was within touching distance of he who hated him most.

Mordwyn could have killed him then, wanted to kill him then, but he knew he had to find the way through the mountain to the human side. Even so, he barely held himself in check. The King, dragging a young child by a chain, even looked about to check he was alone before etching a rune in magic on the wall directly in front of Mordwyn's hiding place. A rune thus etched firmly into Mordwyn's memory. He had a way through.

Stealing Hethwen women and children proved relatively easy. He already had his own way out of Parth-Cerrig and once into Torffan it was so easy for him to travel unseen at night and steal the wood-folk from their beds. He had spent days trying to work iron, finding in the end that shaping the ore was the only way he could weave it. Once he had iron on them, they seemed to lose all fight. The first month he had taken one small child, she was worth the risk, and exchanged her for three silver ingots. The chancel man had told him that he needed as many Hethwen as he could take, even promising to pay gold if he could take powerful magic users.

Seven months later, he was rich in silver ingots, and now with his latest acquisition he would get gold. It was such a shame that the female had surrendered herself. Still the male alone would bring him gold, almost making up for the disappointment of again failing to raise the big Cawrroc from his stasis. Mordwyn had reasoned he must have been an important weaver to have been kept whole by magic. The disc he had melded to his skull should give him control over the Cawrroc and once he had the ancient in his thrall, he could use him to create his own realm beneath the mountain. It had failed though. Another grand dream come to naught.

Mordwyn often enjoyed the irony of his endeavours; the gwerin had declared him outcast, which would have to his being iron-collared and exiled on the human side from where there was no way back in to Parth-Cerrig. Yet after escaping that fate, he had spent his years of exile looking for a way through to the human side. His long search only revealed routes closed off, magically sealed and long forgotten that he could not re-open. The answer to the riddle had been provided by the mighty Brenin. Mordwyn had his way through the mountains. His alliance with the human Chancel men would bring him the riches he desired soon enough.

One obstacle remained: there was not a direct route through from one side of the mountain range to the other without travelling across the lower levels of Parth-Cerrig. The gwerin would never allow that. The King and his weaver council, the Cildraeth, would oppose him and although he was the strongest gwerin stone weaver by far, he was no match for their combined might. His hopes had risen when he discovered the tomb of the greatest known Cawrroc stone-weaver of all who lay in limbo, waiting to be raised from death. With a Cawrroc to aid him, he had hoped the tunnels under the Eirans would have been accessible at last. Hope; a futile waste of time.

As he neared his own caves, he climbed high up onto the ceiling and hung there, waiting to see if he was being followed. He spidered a few yards back along to the nearest corner to double check, but no one had tailed him. Lowering himself down, he approached a smooth wall, and wiped his hand in a complete circle before etching a rune on the stone. Pushing his hand through the middle, he stepped through the wall; the rock oozing back into place behind him. He swallowed his nausea and moved about his home, touching the stacked silver ingots he kept here, talking softly to himself. He picked up a half ingot from the top of the pile; the half he'd received for the last Hethwen he had traded—an infant barely walking.

He held his hand out flat with the half ingot covering his palm. Then using his magic, he watched it slowly sag, flowing between his outstretched fingers as it liquefied—not enough to pour, but enough to melt it to a jelly. He loved the feel of the precious metal when it was fluid like this, wrapping it around his fingers and hand. So enrapt was Mordwyn by his sliver plaything that the *Seren-rocs*, the rock-lights, blazing into life came as an unbelievable shock. He screamed and dropped to the floor, cloaking as he did so, his eyes burning as they adjusted to the sudden brightness, his arms wrapped protectively around his head. In this state he listened but heard nothing. Slowly he opened his eyes and sat up and saw his room was empty. He stood and looked all about; nothing was out of place. Until that is, the lights started moving.

All of the *Seren-rocs* moved at once, flowing around the walls to the side opposite his entrance point. There they formed an arch shape nearly seven foot tall. Mordwyn, feeling more uneasy by the second, took a few steps back, until he bumped into the opposite wall. He waited, breath coming faster now, eyes fixed on the arch of lights. He noticed the wall inside the arch changing slightly, losing all form until it was the purest black he had ever seen, as though it was absorbing light into it. Nothing reflected from it at all. Mordwyn shuffled sideways to the point at which he could pass through the wall, keeping his eyes on the strangeness in front of him, he reached behind him and smoothed his hand on the rock in a circle before easing it through. He then stepped slowly backwards through the wall, inches from escaping whatever was happening.

A sudden hiss, an escaping of air, put paid to that, as halfway through the wall it solidified around him; not crushing; but not allowing any movement either. On the verge of panic now, he tried with all of his magical might to free himself, but to no avail. His head was held firmly so his face only was showing, other than that only his left leg from the knee down and both of his forearms and hands were still in his room. He had just decided that things could get no worse, when they did.

The rock within the lighted arch way opposite bowed out towards him, as though it was made of silk and was being blown. Then a face appeared, pushing through the very fabric of the rock, moving through it with ease, followed by a thin torso and long spidery limbs. Momentarily dumbstruck by the horror in front of him, Mordwyn's mouth opened wide, impossibly wide, but silent. He stayed like this even as the rock-lights suddenly dropped to the bottom of the wall, lighting the beast from behind so its front was draped in deep shadow, whereupon the horror lurched towards him. He screamed then, a violent thunderclap of a scream that burst from the depths of his lungs. The hellish apparition approached, one foot lifting then lunging forward and slamming on to the floor, whilst the other leg dragged without leaving the flagstones, creating a thump and swish as it moved.

As it got closer, Mordwyn noted how disjointedly it moved, almost as if its skeleton wasn't connected. As it drew nearer, Mordwyn closed his eyes, squeezing them shut against the pain and death he felt sure were only seconds away. Yet noting happened, except the noises of the creature moving had stopped. He could hear the creature's breath rasping in and out, so he knew it was there. Tentatively, Mordwyn opened his eyes to be greeted with an empty room. He was just about to believe that he had imagined it when he glanced down to see the creature, bathed in shadow kneeling in front of him, its forehead pressed to the ground an inch from his foot.

As he watched, the creature's arms gradually extended sideways, its hands pressed against the floor and the creature, head still bowed, rose. Its huge left hand shot forward and settled on Mordwyn's head as the creature extended to its full height. Mordwyn felt the longer finger slip inside the stone and grip his skull. Heat flared around his whole body and he was aware that he was being dragged upward through the rock. Just as suddenly the hand fell away and Mordwyn found himself still trapped in the rock, face forward but much higher.

The beast moved its hands in front then slammed its palms together, the loud slap sending the rock-lights up skittering up the wall and along to congregate above Mordwyn's trapped face, lighting at last the horror before him.

Mordwyn stared straight into the round eyes of nightmare before him. The right eye had an almost black iris that filled nearly the whole lens; a thin band of bloodshot white ringed the black pupil. The left eye was milky and white—a dead eye. What was left of its nose only a couple of inches from his own. Mordwyn next took in the flat golden disc he himself had implanted in the centre of the beast's forehead, with its pyramid diamond standing proud.

"I know you," he said more to himself than the creature. He then giggled, despite his predicament; his magic had worked.

The reanimated Cawrroc moved closer, its ruined nose cavities open to the world, snuffed, as one long, bony finger pushed at Mordwyn's face, then moving lower down around where his chest was trapped in the cave wall. Strands of long, lank hair matted together by some substance Mordwyn didn't wish to think about adhered to its head. In bald places, Mordwyn could see the knobbly skull of the Cawrroc through its greyed, taut skin. The Cawrroc stood straight again and raised a hand in front of Mordwyn's face. It lowered the hand down until it was level with Mordwyn's chest again, hidden within wall. This was no impediment to the Cawrroc who pushed its hand through the wall and pressed the gwerin's chest, or more specifically the amulet on his chest. The hand withdrew and the Cawrroc raised a finger that simply looked like skin covered bone moved in front of Mordwyn's eyes; the fingernail he noticed, was nearly two inches long, curled and encrusted with grime and filth. The Cawrroc, finger pointed straight at Mordwyn's face, moved its mouth, trying to speak. Fetid, soundless breath sighed out; yellowed teeth, the few that remained, were heavily stained with something brown. Mordwyn gagged. The Cawrroc persevered until it managed a single, barely audible word.

"Master." The long-nailed finger dropped and the Cawrroc shuffled back, raising both hands, grimy palms forward. Mordwyn experienced a pleasant warmth as the magic enveloped him and then felt himself sliding slowly down and out of the rock until he was standing in front of the Cawrroc. For so long he had tried to reanimate the greatest stone-weaver that had ever lived; years spent breaking enchantments and avoiding traps. And now, when he had all but given up, the dread creature had arisen. He looked hard at the tall corpse-like figure, who bowed low to his new master.

****

Back in his cell, Calon jolted awake. Head pounding, he sat up slowly, the cell still pitch black. He rose unsteadily to his feet and moved blindly forward; arms outstretched until he reached the wall. He tried once again to push his fingers into the rock, like he'd done before, but to no avail. With the thumping pain in his skull clouding his thinking, Calon could see no hope of escape, no hope of rescue. He turned and leaned his back against the wall, enjoying the smooth coolness of the stone before, and not for the first time, he realised how much he missed Berys; how much he'd relied on her. With grief now crowding in on him as well, he slid down the wall slowly till he lay on the floor of his cell. Tears falling again, for Berys and himself, he curled into a ball and sobbed.

Mordwyn quickly mastered control of the Cawrroc. When holding the amulet, or when it was touching his skin, he could simply compel the creature to do his bidding. Initially, for the first few minutes it was simple tasks he ordered the beast to do: moving stone; illuminating the rock-lights and have the creature move them—Mordwyn preferred them above him, like stars; smoothing the rock walls of his dwelling; but the gwerin was soon bored of this. He ventured with the Cawrroc into the tunnels and made for the higher, populated levels. He asked the creature to cloak himself, which the creature did in a dark cloud, so black it was impenetrable to even a gwerin's cloaked eyes. Mordwyn was ecstatic now, barely suppressing his gleeful laughter at his prospects. So busy was he dreaming up tasks for the Cawrroc, he was taken by surprise when a gwerin *out-walker*, those who patrolled the fringes of the populated levels and went above ground on errands, almost walked into him.

"Why are you done here?" the out-walker demanded. "You know…" his voice tailed off as he suddenly noticed the darkness gathered behind Mordwyn. "What the hell is that?" he asked, pointing at the nothingness. Mordwyn had expected to stay hidden, but an opportunity had presented itself. He lifted his hand to his chest and gripped the amulet.

"Kill him," he said softly, pointing at the out-walker. The darkness exploded forward and the unfortunate gwerin was raised from the ground, a bony, long fingered hand briefly appearing, wrapped around the out-walkers neck. With apparently effortless ease, the Cawrroc lifted his victim high, then turned his wrist and rammed the out-walker head first into the rock floor—his head disintegrating to a bloody pulp. Mordwyn then told it to hide the body, expecting the creature to drag it into a dark corner, but the Cawrroc's magic cleared the mess completely by pushing the body into the rock floor before smoothing it over so not even a speck of blood showed where a life had been so callously taken.

Mordwyn clapped his hands in delight. This changed his plans. He had a force of nature at his beck and call. Why stop at stealing the King's treasure when he could steal his throne. What a thought he'd just had. He giggled insanely, then turned and, making his face solemn, told the Cawrroc to go to the throne room and kill the king. The blackness quivered slightly then began moving, one leg dragging and one legging rising high before slapping the ground. "Wait," he called to the Cawrroc, "I want them to hear you coming. Make a loud noise. Band the floor or something, just make it loud." The darkness hiding the beast had stopped moving; it seemed to shiver at this but then moved forward again. At first there was nothing but the creature's feet, scraping and slapping and Mordwyn wondered if he had made himself understood. The huge boom that sounded a moment later put lie to that, causing him to jump. Dust and detritus rained down from high up, pitter-pattering on the hard stone floor. Heart still pounding, Mordwyn was now in raptures. "Yes, yes, yes. Again and again. I want him to know you are coming." The boom echoed relentlessly along the corridor again.

In the great hall of the mountain King, Brenin and his advisors paused from their deliberations as the first boom sounded. The gwerin looked at each other with alarm.

"Rock fall!" exclaimed Brynn, the King's Chancellor, standing and looking up.

"No," said Brenin, "I think not." A second boom sounded, followed by a boom every ten seconds or so.

Brynn moved a few paces to the hall door. "It's getting louder," he observed between the ominous reverberations.

"No Brynn, it's getting closer." The King returned to his elaborate stone throne and sat. Calmly and clearly, he issued orders to close and bar the great double doors to the lower levels where the rhythmic thudding was approaching from. He sent one councillor off to gather the royal guard and Brynn to gather the *Cildraeth*, the weaver council. The boom continued, monotonous and ominous, getting closer. The Cildraeth arrived; nine gwerin stone weavers all wearing the black robes of their guild, a white diamond badge sewn to the centre of the chest. Anxiety buzzed around them as they stood before their King.

"Seal the access to the lower levels," the King ordered pointing at the great iron-willow doors. The nine weavers hurried to the double doors, already closed and barred across the middle by a huge beam. The stood in a line all with both hands touching the iron-willow frame or timbers that made the door. As one they began to chant. Liquid stone rose from the floor, filling every available space around the door, rushing over the weaver's hands until the door thickness had made it all the way to midway up their fore arms. As one, they all stepped away, the holes where their hands had been, refilling and levelling off almost instantly. Still the incessant boom sounded.

The great hall was filling now as more gwerin, startled by the deep, hollow sound sought answers or refuge with the King. Frightened conversation and speculation hummed around the room, punctuated still by the portentous pounding from below, a hubbub that died suddenly as the booming knell stopped. There was a dread-filled silence then for nearly a minute. The King, sank back on his throne, his guard around him. The Cildraeth knelt in a tight huddle, all hands pressed flat to the floor, as they raised a dome that covered them and the King's council on the raised area where the throne sat. Just as a quiet murmur started, a piercing screech shattered the hush of the hall, as though something hard was being dragged down the outside of the huge doors. As suddenly as it started, the screech ended. The sound of shuffling feet now filled the great chamber as everyone bar the Cildraeth, eased back from the doors. The stillness stretched into another minute of agonising uncertainty. One gwerin's muffled sobbing drew the attention of the crowd as folk turned to see who it was, and at that exact moment the terror struck.

The huge iron-willow doors flew open, slamming into the walls with a crash that echoed around the stunned throne room. The stone and rock that had moments before sealed the doors shut now exploded and ricocheted catastrophically around the hall; huge jagged stones smashing gwerin apart; smaller shards punching straight through bodies or lacerating skin. Blood and offal were scattered and showered all across the chamber, accompanied by the screams of the dying. Save for area protected by the weaver's dome, the throne room now was nothing more than a charnel house. The enchantments on the great doors, considered unbreakable, had not even lasted one shove. Anyone left alive amid the slaughter cowered, ashen with dread, and stared at the space beyond, gwerin eyes able to penetrate the deepest darkness struggled to see what was coming.

Discerning only a deep shadow that seemed to pulse and breathe. Then it emerged. A vague figure swathed in blackness. Its physique hardly discernible in the shade or dark that seemed to emanate from within it. The mass shuffled forward into the cavern, raising one cadaverous arm as it did so to disperse the shadows that surrounded it, shadows for all the world like a swarm of dark *tywyll*, the offal-bats that ate the dead. With each slow movement it made, the scrape of dried flesh on stone rustled around the cavernous space. The King bolted to his feet.

"Do something!" he yelled at the Cildraeth. "Kill it! Stop it!" The fact he was on the edge of panic evident in the pitch of his voice, not only to the remaining gwerin, but to the creature also, who stopped and looked up, his one good eye fixed on the King. Brenin visibly paled under the scrutiny. He moved back behind the few Royal Guard still standing. The keening and groaning of the many injured filling the silence. Then Elyan, the Weaver-Prime stood, staring at the stationary beast, open mouthed. Slowly he raised his arm, pointing at the Cawrroc,

"It's a Cawrroc," one of Elyan proclaimed. "One of the old people. We thought they had all died."

"This one looks as though he has as well," Brenin said quickly.

"There is a legend that says the greatest Cawrroc weaver of all was buried alive in a magic tomb to preserve him should he ever be needed." They all looked at the dread creature before them' they all knew the tale.

"Anghenfyl," Elyan said, turning to the King, "he has risen." At the sound of his name the Cawrroc released a primal growl, crouching as he did, his eye

100

focused on the ground immediately in front of him. He then raised his right hand, balled into a fist and slammed it hard on the flagstones, releasing a huge surge of power as he did so. The floor rippled and a wall of liquid rock rose over the weavers still crouched and holding their protective dome in place. Their magic was nothing to the power unleashed on them. The liquid rock as it touched the dome hardened until the whole thing was covered, sealing away those inside, including Brenin the King.

They gathered together in the centre, all looking up as the beast walked up the dome, his dragging and stamping steps clearly audible. Once at the top he stopped. Fear surged among the trapped gwerin then, their wailing and pleading however was cut dramatically short by boom so loud it burst eardrums and left them all disoriented. This was accompanied by a flash of light so bright they all threw themselves to the floor of their prison to hide their eyes. None saw Anghenfyl descend through the ceiling of the rock until he hung mere inches from the floor, one foot held in a loop of the rock he had softened to lower himself down. He singled out the King and reached down, gripping Brenin's head with his huge hand, his thumb dug into the base of his skull and his fingers gripping the King's forehead.

With the king held firmly, Anghenfyl use magic to raise himself up, the rock rope retracting until the Cawrroc and his prisoner were standing on the apex of the rock dome. Anghenfyl held the King up before him, lifting his other hand towards the helpless monarch's face. One finger extended, its filthy nail curved and crooked, poised; with astonishing speed that fingernail sliced through Brenin's left eye and out again; blood and vitreous fluid were cascading down his cheek before the pain even registered. His scream began but was almost immediately halted by the Cawrroc dropping him to the dome where he plummeted straight down the curved wall and crashed into the rock floor at high speed. The King then felt himself being dragged away from the dome. He was turned to face back towards Anghenfyl, who was waving his arms surprisingly gracefully to manipulate the liquid rock that was manoeuvring Brenin so adeptly. The King was levered upright, rock smothering his whole body from the feet up, covering his mouth but leaving his nose and one eye uncovered.

The final indignity was a small tongue of stone that moved up over his chin and into his mouth, pressing his tongue down. Trapped like this, the King was incapable of any movement. The agony from his ruined eye was all-consuming and he could only watch the monster through the tears of his good eye.

Anghenfyl stopped waving his arms and hands then and stood upright on the dome. Raising his arms slowly, stretched them wide before lowering them down to his sides, his wrists cocked so both palms were parallel with the domes surface. Then bending his knees slightly, the Cawrroc forced the dome slowly and inexorably down. It moved inch by inch, lower and lower.

Brenin could hear nothing but could imagine the horror for those inside. Down the dome came, tortuously slowly, maximising the suffering and terror for those dying inside. Down it came until eventually the floor of the great hall was level once again. The only evidence that the dome had been there was a wide circle of clean stone amidst the blood and offal spattered floor of the throne room. Even Brenin's throne and dais were gone, crushed by the awesome power of Anghenfyl's weaving.

The Cawrroc turned and looked at Brenin then, and for the first time the King saw him clearly. Around seven feet tall but hunched slightly it was an imposing presence. Long centuries in the tomb, even though the body had been magically preserved, had left its skin grey and clammy looking; his gnarled joints stood out, white bone almost shining through the thin membrane covering them. The skin of its chest was crumpled and folded like it was too large for the body beneath and over its belly lay crusty flaps of skin, crumpled and folded like old parchment. The Cawrrocs head hung slightly forward as though it was too heavy for its now slender neck. All four of its limbs were devoid of muscle, the very thinness making them appear long and spidery. Sinews could be seen straining against the taught grey skin that clung tightly to the beast skeletal frame. A filthy loin cloth his only clothing, stained by the detritus of the tomb and the cadaveric fluids released in death.

The beast moved across the floor to stand in front of the trapped King, up close the monster was even more hideous. The diamond, Brenin could see had been embedded in the creature's skull. One filmy, white eye, the other virtually black gave it an unnerving stare. The grey, papery looking skin of its face had no sheen or vitality; so thin that the corded muscles underneath stood proudly, threatening to burst through. Up close, the beast reeked of death and putrefaction, which, added to the stone pressing into his mouth, caused Brenin to gag.

Despite the groaning and wailing of the survivors littering the throne room, someone singing drew his attention away from the beast. He swivelled his good eye to try and see who it was, but the sound was coming from behind him. He looked back at Anghenfyl and watched the creature's eye track the singer.

Whoever it was seemed very happy and completely unafraid of the monstrous Cawrroc dominating the room. In fact, the creature seemed to shrink slightly as though it was cowed by whoever had entered.

Brenin started when a familiar gwerin jumped in front of him hailing, "Greetings great King Brenin," before sweeping into a low bow. He then stood and gestured expansively around the great hall of the throne room, now become a slaughter house and added, "Lord of all you survey." Before giggling and bowing again. The gwerin approached the trapped King then, smile fading as he did so, until he was very close, his eyes fixated on the King's ruined eye. "Great King," he said teeth gritted and his voice low and menacing, "I am Mordwyn. I am the death of your house. And this," he pointed to the Cawrroc, "is Anghenfyl, the weapon of that destruction. The greatest rock weaver of all time, who sealed Torffan from the humans to keep their hate and violence away from the peoples of the Celtyth, will wipe out the ruling class in Parth-Cerrig, and I will rule here."

At this Mordwyn began to hum and mimed placing a crown upon his own head. Then he danced around the chamber, bending to pick up a severed forearm which he held up before him, waving it at imagined crowds of his subjects. The blood that leaked from the severed limb onto his hand stopped his performance dead. He turned towards Brenin and in a fit of rage hurled the offending limb at the King's face, but missed. Mordwyn bent and wiped his hand clean on the robe of some unfortunate courtier's corpse.

He stood and approached Brenin again, "And my first decision as King will be to destroy the Hethwen so the Gwerin will rule all of the Celtyth lands; we will be free to live above ground again. I will let the humans through these mountains, to wipe them out, and after they have done that, my loyal monster here will destroy their armies and the gwerin will be free. With the Marwolleth gone we will be free to mine the Cerrigaur Mountains in Penrhyn, where gold flows like water.

He stopped then, staring at the man who had been his King. Never taking his eyes from Brenin's face he gestured to Anghenfyl, to move back in front of the trapped King. "Seal him in." Brenin had barely registered what Mordwyn said; he watched a single, grey, viscous tear struggle to slide down the creature's emaciated cheek, then liquid rock was moving over his face; he never even had time to scream.

Chapter 7
Cadfan

In his cell, Calon had lost all track of time. Permanent and total darkness was beginning to shred his sanity. His resolve had died on the cell floor. He knew if he stayed angry, he would stay sane, but he just didn't care anymore. He missed his mam and da. He missed Berys. Loss and failure consumed him. Hours of sobbing had left him dehydrated and his throat sore. He knew he needed water. His thirst was consuming him. His mouth felt dry and sticky at the same time. He had tried licking the walls and floor, but even though that had momentarily helped it seemed too much effort now. His skin itched unbearably, but scratching had exhausted him and rubbed his skin raw. Worst now was his headache, he couldn't move if he'd wanted to; any time he moved, he felt he was spinning out of control.

Feeling the need to sleep, he made a monumental effort to bring his hands up so he could rest his cheek on them. Head spinning, he had lain like that for a short time when he realised he could smell Berys. In his head he tried to order his thoughts—she must be in the room with him. He tried to say her name but a barely audible, parched croak was all he could muster. Fighting his confusion and lethargy, he decided to just wait for her to approach him. In the meantime, he would just breathe her scent in. Her scent he decided was very comforting. It was the smell of her hair he was remembering when she had held and kissed him. Her hair. And then he had it. Her *llinach* on his wrist was what he could smell. He moved his hands up a little higher until he could feel the hair tickling his nose, and breathed in hard.

The effect was instantaneous; like lightning striking him. His confusion disappeared and he felt his magic again. He felt the *croen clogyn* sliding over his skin, cloaking him. He felt a power ease through him. He stood shakily and, swaying slightly he moved carefully forwards until he reached a wall. Clawing his hands, he tried digging his fingers into the rock with a small measure of success, his nails disappearing into the stone. Pulling them out he made for the door. Once the iron-willow was beneath his palms he pressed forward with what strength he had and willed them open. Nothing happened. He tried again, frustration lending him focus and anger.

This time he felt something give a little, so poured all his rage and fear into one final effort. It was as though the door simply stopped being there. Calon fell through, hands breaking his fall. He struggled onto his back, pulling his legs clear of the cell through the door that appeared to be undamaged in the grey half-light of the tunnel, but the effort had completely exhausted him and, as his consciousness faded, he moved his wrist to his face and kissed the *llinach* of Berys' hair.

Something pecking at his brain woke Calon. The insistent tapping on the centre of his forehead forced wakefulness upon him. His eyes opened to nothingness—pitch darkness greeted his return to consciousness. Still lying on his back, he groaned and rolled onto his side before carefully levering himself up to a kneeling position. He tried cloaking himself, but he was so weak and so tired that even the *llinach* Berys had given him was no help now. Steadily, he crawled forward, raising his arm in front of him every yard to search for a wall.

After a short journey, he reached smooth stone and used it to help him stand. Keeping one hand flat to the wall he began to walk tentatively forward along the corridor, which curved gently until he reached a door; a large iron willow door by the feel of it. He felt around but there was no handle or latch. He decided to move on, still following the curve. After a good few yards, he came upon another door. This too had no discernible way of opening it that he could feel. Calon guessed that the doors were evenly spaced. "They must use magic to open them," he muttered to himself.

He had just taken one more step when a familiar cackle of laughter stopped him dead. Light began to flood the darkness, gradually revealing his familiar surroundings. That familiar voice behind him, very close to his left ear, startled him enough that he skittered forward into the cell wall. "You really are quite an imbecile," Mordwyn exclaimed between bouts of guffawing. "You should have seen yourself," he chortled and began to mime Calon's efforts to travel along the non-existent tunnel. Calon, sitting now with his back against the cell wall, could only watch.

Mordwyn's demeanour changed abruptly from hysteria to seething rage. "Did you really think you could use as much magic as that and not be heard? Of course you did! You're an idiot!" Mordwyn stopped then and approached Calon, looming over him menacingly. Calon could see foamy flecks appearing at the corners of his tormentor's mouth, which were launched instantly into the air as he continued ranting. "Pray tell me, master weaver, how is it possible that a…a… boy with no skill in magic, no training in the mystic arts can go *through* an iron willow door when not even a weaver as powerful as I am can do that? Tell me? I want to know how you did the impossible. Iron-willow is magic resistant." The gwerin was literally screaming now, bending down to vent his full fury directly into Calon's face.

Mordwyn half raised his hand as though he was about to strike his captive, but seemed to think better of it and began pacing about muttering to himself, all the time clenching and unclenching his fists. Calon reached up to scratch nervously at his neck, to find an iron-willow collar had been wrapped around it. Now he was aware of it, he wondered why he hadn't noticed it earlier as it seemed to weigh so much. Whilst Mordwyn continued his frantic pacing, Calon quickly felt around the whole collar but there was no discernible catch or lock. He moved his hands to the back of the collar and found the hinge. He tried invoking his magic but he felt almost nauseous at the thought of it.

Then he suddenly remembered Berys' llinach, resolving to try one more time, hoping his desperation would give enough magic. He touched his fingers to her hair and felt the familiar prickly heat building. He quickly reached back for the hinge of the iron-willow collar and simply pulled his fingers from the base of his neck, up through the collar, grabbing both ends as he bent them apart. Magically infused, he felt energy and vitality return to him in a hedonistic rush.

Climbing to his feet, he faced his captor, who had been alerted by the sudden movement of his prisoner. He stopped raving under breath and pointed a finger at Calon who calmly tossed the iron collar at the feet of Mordwyn with a loud clang. The gwerin's mouth dropped open. He looked down at the iron-willow collar then back up at Calon. Incredulous, he took a step away from Calon, his back now against the cell wall. *He's frightened*, Calon thought to himself.

"Anghenfyl!" he bellowed. "Get in here, NOW!" Calon heard movement behind the locked door and prepared himself to power past whoever it was that was about to come through the open door. Only the door didn't open. An apparition of death and decay simply lurched straight through it—the most hellish being Calon had ever seen. The creature towered over him, it's huge grey, skinned clammy hand reaching out towards his neck. Calon could discern no expression on the beast's face, other than ugliness and putrefaction. The hand stopped inches short of his throat and stayed there, time stretching as Calon and the Cawrroc stared eye to milky eye, as a strange sensation began to fill Calon's senses.

"Kill him!" screamed Mordwyn breaking the spell. "Kill the little fucker." But the monster did nothing, simply stood and kept staring. Calon felt the magic pull him, as though something had grabbed him inside and was drawing him gently forward. Mordwyn's ranting and raving was muted now and seemed to be coming from a distance away, as the two appraised one another. Calon became aware of a bright gem on, or in, the creatures forehead. He saw the giant's mouth moving and heard the grating of bone on bone as his disconnected jaw struggled to articulate the sounds the monster needed to make to speak.

After a long battle the Cawrroc managed to push two words out. "*Rhoddwr gwaed*," he grumbled, the sound barely a whisper of air. Calon stood nonplussed. The creature's mouth began another barrage of rattling and grinding before pronouncing, "Blood giver," in its dry drawl. Whereupon it sank slowly to its knees before bowing down and touching its bejewelled forehead to the floor.

Realisation dawned on Mordwyn; the pathetic boy's blood on his amulet. That was what had woken Anghenfyl. He was not the true master at all. Apoplectic with rage, Mordwyn ran forward and launched a kick into the midriff of the Cawrroc, the audible snapping of ribs testament to the damage he had inflicted. The creature appeared not to have felt a thing. Calon's ear fog cleared suddenly as Mordwyn continued to rant at the beast to kill him. Anghenfyl raised himself to his feet, turned to his apparent master and said, "No."

Mordwyn reached inside his tunic and grabbed the amulet that controlled the Cawrroc. Holding it tightly, his voice dropped to a sibilant threat, he waved his fist, the amulet clenched inside, and hissed, "Kill. Him." Anghenfyl simply turned away to look back at Calon who took his chance at the distraction. He launched himself at Mordwyn, punching up hard onto the elbow of his outstretched arm. The arm jerked violently as Mordwyn let out a piercing scream and clutched it to him. The amulet meanwhile dropped to the dungeon floor and skittered into Anghenfyl's foot. The huge Cawrroc bent surprisingly quickly and lifted the artefact; his bony, cadaverous hand gripping it tightly. His face twisted into was should have been a smile of triumph, but looked instead looked more like a grimace.

Mordwyn, panting, rushed for the door, pushed it open with ease and fled into the dark corridor. Calon wanted to follow, but the creature before him, despite its obvious limitations and disabilities, stopped him with ease, gently pressing his large hand onto Calon's chest. He watched the creature open its other clenched fist and regard the amulet. The brief second that his hand was open, a darkness descended and ripped the artefact clear before spinning away, through the open door, which instantly slammed shut. Stunned by Mordwyn's theft, Calon looked up at the Cawrroc. Whose one good eye lifted to observe Calon in return, and its mouth began its contortions again.

The creature spoke to Calon who couldn't understand a thing it was saying. The creature eventually seemed to sense this, and began slowly talking to Calon in his own language. "We must destroy the amulet," he said. Gesturing Calon to follow he added, "Marwolleth, come with me." But as the Cawrroc tried to exit the open door he slammed to a halt, his free hand swung up and clutched his forehead. Calon heard a groan of pain.

"What is it?" he tentatively asked. Anghenfyl, standing head bowed, gestured at the diamond embedded in his forehead.

"Too much pain," he uttered after the unusual struggle. "I cannot leave here. This…" he indicated the diamond on his forehead, "holds me here. The gwerin has trapped us both."

"But you are a great weaver. Surely you can take it out?" Calon asked him. Anghenfyl looked at Calon again for fully a minute before he could get his words out.

"Not myself. Can't do that to myself. You could," he said, pointing at Calon. He came over to him and knelt in front of him so his head was slightly below his. Taking Calon's right hand, cloaking it for him as he did so, he pressed it between his own clammy palms. "Now feel your hands warm," he tapped the amulet, then pointed up to the thing in his forehead, "Lift it from my head." He took Calon's left hand and lifted this to touch the gold base. "Hold it. Pull it free."

Calon's left hand felt light and tingly, it was so easy to bring his magic up with the Cawrroc's help and he felt as though it was spilling out of him. He focused his concentration on the gold base of the implanted object, feeling it warm. Anghenfyl obviously sensed it too as he grabbed Calon's left hand again and pushed it against the stud in his skull, encouraging Calon to rub his fingers and thumb over the diamond set in the middle, before letting go. Calon looked at his fingers, they felt strange. He saw a silvery glow emanating from the tips, the intricate swirls highlighted beautifully. Anghenfyl nudged him, "Pull it free," he told him again.

Calon reached up placed his fingers on the gold base and pulled gently. His fingers couldn't grip the gold. It was like trying to lift melted butter. It just dripped back into place.

"*Diemwnt*," the Cawrroc grumbled. Calon guessed he'd said diamond, so switched to trying to grab that. The diamond stuck to his fingers like the glue his da had made from bones. As it lifted clear, as easy as picking an apple, the gold base simply fell from Anghenfyl's skull and landed on the floor, leaving a neat hole in the skin of his forehead that revealed a creamy square of bone beneath, which immediately began to ooze with a thick clear pus. Calon marvelled that the Cawrroc seemed to feel no pain. He bent down and picked up the gold. Anghenfyl held out his hand and it took a moment for Calon to realise that he wanted the diamond and golden base back. He placed both into the large, slender hand and watched the spidery fingers close around them.

"We go now," Anghenfyl said, turning and heading for the door. The Cawrroc eased through it as though it were dense fog, Calon rushed to follow and slammed into the door nose first. Clutching his face, eyes watering, Calon called out. The Cawrrocs face appeared through the door, followed by a hand.

"Hold on to me, I will pull you through," he ordered. Once through, Anghenfyl regarded Calon carefully.

"You have need of rest. I fear you must travel in the dark as cloaking will tax you too much. Stay close," he warned as he headed off. Calon followed, but found in the corridor that he could not see well enough to follow the Cawrroc. The slap and shuffle of his peculiar gait echoed around the walls so Calon found it hard to pinpoint exactly which direction it had come from. The first fork in the passageway they came to, Calon realised he had lost the creature he was following. He wanted to call out but couldn't quite remember the Cawrroc's name.

"Ang!" he yelled. "Ang! Where are you?" He stood still, holding his breath then so he would here if the creature responded. Within a few seconds the tell-tale slap and swish began to sound. The darkness seemed absolute to Calon yet he was able to discern the ominous shape of the creature bearing down on him when it was about twelve yards away. Anghenfyl barely discernible form stopped in front of him.

"Follow," he told Calon, turning to walk away.

"Ang," Calon responded, "I can't see, you have to go slower." The Cawrroc stopped and turned. He approached Calon again, and took his head into his grey hands. Calon had half-expected the creature's skin to fell dry like parchment, but should have remembered the palms were cold and clammy and made him shudder. Ang, which Calon had decided was what he would call him from now on, held up the diamond and made glow softly, enough that Calon could see, even though he was not sure that observing the Cawrroc this close in good light was actually a good thing. Ang lowered his head so his eye was level with Calon's.

In the half-light, Calon saw the disjointed mouth open and its great tongue as it began to protrude towards him; dark purple on the outer edges but with a greyed yellow centre covered in some sort of death slime that seemed to reflect the light so the centre of the tongue glowed. It felt that the Cawrroc was looking straight through him and he was about to ask him what he was doing when the beast suddenly gripped the back of his head hard and pulled it towards his own. Ang's fingers fixed onto his eyes and yanked the lids up, causing Calon to yelp in pain. A hurt soon forgotten when the slimy, corpse tongue licked him, depositing something deathly cold and equally horrid on the lenses of his eyes.

The stinging was so intense his eyes immediately watered and his nose burned and began to run again. The pain was extreme for a few seconds then faded just as quickly. As his vision cleared, and as his mind was now able to process his anger and discomfort at the violation, he took a deep breath to remonstrate with the Cawrroc but instead held it before releasing it slowly in a loud hiss. The underground world he'd experienced so far, all impenetrable darkness and grey, unending rock and stone had vanished. In its place was a corridor of wonder. An unimaginable array of reflective surfaces glittered and sparkled on the walls and ceilings all around him. For all the world like a midnight sky warped into a tunnel. Only the floor was different, with great lines of alternating blacks, greys and sparkly granite flowing along the pathway's folk would walk.

He could see the Cawrroc limping along further down the sloping passageway and ran to catch up, marvelling as he did at the beauty before him, as well as the gross act of magic that had altered his vision. He was almost boiling with questions by the time he caught up with Ang, who completely ignored everything Calon asked him as he shuffled and lurched along endless, downward sloping corridors; through gloriously jewelled caves; past fast flowing, subterranean streams; even at one point just walking through a wall. Anghenfyl had gripped his upper arm and just dragged him through. Calon had barely registered what had happened when he was running again to catch up with the Cawrroc, whose unusual gait belied the speed with which he moved. On they went, deeper and deeper into the bowels of the mountain.

****

Calon estimated they had been walking for about two hours by the time they reached their destination. He knew without question that left to his own devices he would die down here. The endless caves, tunnels and corridors had no pattern and they twisted and turned so often, he marvelled at how the great Cawrroc knew where he was going. They arrived at a dead end at the bottom of a gentle down slope. Loose rock was piled against the wall and littered all across the floor as though some part of the tunnel roof above had collapsed. To the left-hand side, a long diagonal scar, edged in some kind of glittery quartz, travelled a few metres up the wall. Calon wondered if he could only see it because of Ang's spit on his eyes. The Cawrroc moved towards the diagonal scar and just walked through it. Calon hurried after.

He touched the wall with his hand as Ang had done, but the rock was solid. He felt along the line of quartz and found it was a ridge, protruding roughly two inches from the walls surface. Looking behind it he saw the narrowest of gaps, probably seven or eight inches wide. He could hear Anghenfyl shuffling about on the other side so decided he would try and squeeze through. He made it most of the way, but became stuck. His chest compressed between the sides of the narrow cleft. He'd already scraped his cheek and could feel blood trickling down the right-hand side of his face and neck.

"Ang!" he called out, but the words lacked any power with his chest squashed as it was. He was about to call again when Ang's milky eye appeared in the gap. Calon had thought that this eye was blind, but the fact that a large grey-skinned hand reached into the crevice, gripped his neck and just pulled him through the rock as though it was water, put lie to that. Once clear of the rock, Calon had expected Ang to let him go, but the opposite happened. Anghenfyl gripped the back of his head with his other hand and hauled Calon close to him; very close. The Cawrroc's face was barley an inch from his own.

Ang turned and lifted Calon so he was on tiptoe facing off to one side. He decided that Ang was looking at the scratch on his cheek and hoped he would heal it. Instead, Ang licked it. His large slimy slug of a tongue, accompanied by a miasma of decay and corruption, oozed up his cheek twice. Calon all but gagged and was abruptly let go. Ang turned and shuffled into the centre of the chamber they were in. Calon put his hand to his tingling cheek, expecting it to feel slimy and wet, but it was crusty and dry. It had scabbed over in seconds— Calon could feel the tightness in his healed skin.

He watched Ang head over to the far wall of the chamber, where he ran the palm of his hand repeatedly over the rough surface, smoothing it. As he continued the graceful sweeping of his hand, he began to chant quietly under his breath. Calon watched as the surface of the wall began to change—from rough to smooth initially, but the Cawrroc's magic polished the surface to a mirror like sheen in the shape of a prefect square, each side roughly a yard long. Ang stopped then and walked to the other side of the chamber. En route he bent to the floor and picked up something.

As he neared the entrance where he stood, Calon could see it was a small stone. He watched fascinated as Anghenfyl squeezed the stone in his fist—a faint blue light shone from between his clenched fingers for a few seconds, the large hand relaxing as the light died. Once on the other side of the chamber, Ang kept looking back at the mirrored section he had just created. When he was satisfied that he was directly opposite the square, mirrored patch he held the stone he had picked up against the wall. Calon could see now that what had been an ordinary piece of rock was a cube of blue crystal. Ang held this against the wall and a clear blue line of light appeared between the crystal and the mirrored square. The line reflected back at an angle.

Anghenfyl moved the crystal, reducing the angle until the beam of light was one straight line reflecting from the direct centre of the square that Ang had created. The Cawrroc's gentle humming changed pitch then, becoming higher. Calon watched in awe as the beam of blue light began to expand gradually at the far end until it matched the mirrored square precisely, creating a beautiful blue square that sparkled and flickered, bathing the chamber in a deep blue of a summer sky. All of a sudden, Ang's humming increased in volume before abruptly stopping. The square of light then sped across the chamber and impacted against the wall where Ang held the crystal. It blazed a brilliant, blinding blue for about a second then died away. In its place was a perfect mirrored square matching the first one Ang had created.

Anghenfyl walked right in front of the new mirrored square. Calon approached and could see his reflection repeated endlessly between the two squares. Anghenfyl reached out a hand and gently shoved Calon in the chest, easing him back. He then cupped his large, grey hands about his mouth, leant into the mirror so the edges of his hands touched the glossy surface, and bellowed one short loud 'oo'. The sound immediately echoed back from the mirror at the other side of the chamber and back, doing so repeatedly until it became a continuous sound; a long low 'oo'. Ang then touched his crystal cube back to the mirror.

After a few seconds, Calon heard the pitch of the 'oo' deepening and beginning to undulate. This he realised was happening in conjunction with the square, still centred on the same spot, turning gradually. The square turned and the 'oo' deepened and began to undulate until it was a throbbing almost too painful to hear. As the square continued to turn, the undulations began getting closer together and finally, as this square had completed a quarter turn so it now like looked like a diamond, the note became a pure, deep hum that seemed to reverberate through Calon. The sound then died away. Ang lowered his hand, still clutching the crystal, then awkwardly sat down on the rocky floor, before lying down on his side.

Calon approached the diamond mirror and touched it. The surface was warm and perfectly smooth. He angled his head to try and look into the square mirror opposite, again seeing himself reflected endlessly. After a few minutes of this he decided that sitting down was a good idea. He sat with his back to the wall. A sudden movement from Ang made him start. The Cawrroc, still prone on the stone floor, held up the crystal cube, faintly glowing again, and a small globe of light as big as the end of Calon's little finger, emerged from the cube and sped directly into the centre of Calon's forehead. He felt himself floating for a second, his left cheek touching the rocky floor, then drifted blissfully into sleep.

****

Calon came back to his senses, feeling completely refreshed and alert. He was aware of voices, a low murmuring coming from the far side of the chamber

113

he was in. He sat up and looked over to where two figures stood. One was obviously Anghenfyl; tall, cadaverously thin and stooped. The figure he was talking to was of a similar height, but there the similarities ended. The one talking to Anghenfyl was straight backed, stocky and powerful looking. He didn't quite match Anghenfyl's height, so Calon guessed he was just under six feet tall.

From where he observed, Calon could see that the new Cawrroc had a heavy brow and a square-looking forehead. Its hair was short, trimmed Calon guessed, and looked black. The creature's arms looked strangely long, like Anghenfyl's good arm, but were well muscled. In fact, the creature looked made of muscle, broad and powerfully built. The two Cawrrocs conversation stopped abruptly when Anghenfyl touched the other Cawrroc's arm and both turned to look at him. Both Cawrrocs approached, one lurching along, the other moving smoothly towards him. Calon was immediately surprised by the contrast of the two Cawrrocs; how open and friendly the stranger appeared. His dark eyes glittered and a wide, open face beamed happily at him. The stranger reached out a powerful hand towards him, offering help. Calon took it. The warm hand that gripped his was calloused and twice the size of his own. Calon was pulled up to his feet.

"Welcome," he said. His voice deep and resonant. "I am Cadfan. I have come at Anghenfyl's bidding to take you from the gwerin's mountain." His speech was slow and considered, Calon assumed that this was because he was speaking in a foreign tongue. "I hope you feel rested young one. Anghenfyl tells me that you were tired and needed… I think you would say, a good sleep. Anyway… he is anxious to move on," Cadfan gestured towards Anghenfyl, who was distractedly looking away to his right. "He also tells me you have many questions and he has bid me answer them for you once we have seen to his needs." With that, Cadfan turned and headed after Anghenfyl who was already moving away.

After walking for some time, the threesome stopped at the end of a long corridor where the ceiling had caved in. Large boulders had cascaded down leaving a gaping, dark hole high above them.

"This is our destination," Cadfan told him.

"What? Up there? It doesn't look safe," Calon responded.

"No not up. Underneath." Cadfan explained pointing at the rock fall.

"We have to move all that," Calon said exasperated. "That will take hours." Cadfan simply smiled and put an arm out to gently move Calon away from the rocks. Anghenfyl approached the base of the rock fall and raised his good arm so it was horizontally out in front of him, palm facing the rock fall. A deep, stomach-churning hum filled the corridor they were standing in, making Calon feel very uncomfortable, yet his eyes remained fixed on what was happening in front of him. Anghenfyl gradually began to raise his arm; as he did so the rocks seem to fall upward from where they lay, some pulling up left or right. As they rolled noisily up and away, they revealed an open shaft, as dark as death, beneath where they lay. Calon and Cadfan approached the hole and stood next to Anghenfyl at the lip staring down.

"Why can't I see down there?" he asked. "With what you did to my eyes, I can see perfectly in the dark. Why is that hole different?" Neither Cawrroc responded. Calon was about to repeat his question when Anghenfyl stepped into the black hole and walked down. The darkness swirled around him, staying on a level, so it appeared that the Cawrroc was disappearing by degrees. The level of blackness remained fixed. There was no visibility below the surface at all. After Anghenfyl's head had disappeared below the surface of the darkness, Calon looked questioningly at Cadfan who smiled at Calon's discomfort.

"It is what we call 'darkness like water'. It is an unnatural darkness, created by Anghenfyl. Without his blessing you would never see down there; you could never climb down; and you would live barely an hour without heat."

"Where is *there*?" Calon asked.

"*There* is the cavern where Anghenfyl was interred. The place he lay for hundreds of years before he was raised."

Calon thought about this. "But if no one can see in the 'darkness like water' how did that gwerin manage?"

"Ah," Cadfan replied. "Now that is a question." Calon wanted to ask more but had no chance as two small spheres of light rose through the dark layer and hovered in front of them. Cadfan stretched out his hand, palm flat, underneath one of the spheres that then lowered gently on to his hand. Calon copied this. The sphere of light settled on his palm and he could immediately feel that it was some kind of gem or stone that was heavier than he expected for something that had floated, and was warm to the touch. He watched carefully as Cadfan stepped into the dark, which to Calon's eyes was still just as impenetrable. He could see the Cawrroc moving down steps and disappearing much as Anghenfyl had done. As Cadfan's head vanished from sight, Calon stepped up to the black hole. He still could not see. He eased a foot through the 'surface' that proved to be just like water, although not wet and unbelievably cold. There was nothing for his foot to step onto. Withdrawing his now cold foot, Calon held the light sphere, still resting on his palm, over the hole hoping that it would provide the solution. Nothing changed. As he was contemplating his next action, Cadfan's head re-emerged from the darkness, seemingly floating on the surface. The Cawrroc chuckled warmly at Calon's confusion.

"There is much we have to teach you young Calon. I have been at fault in not explaining. You must grip the stone tightly and wish to see. You must focus. The darkness then will be but a thin layer."

"But it's so cold. How …" Calon started but the Cawrroc had submerged again. He gripped the stone tightly and looked downwards. Concentrating, he could now see, very much like looking through murky water, a few steps leading down. He moved onto the first step and felt his leg pass through a thin barrier of intense cold that seemed to move up as he moved down. As he continued, the intense cold moved over his chest and finally his face. Once his eyes were though the dark layer he could see clearly again. A perfectly cylindrical staircase wound down a few metres to a paved stone floor. It reminded Calon of the village well, only these walls were beautifully smooth. He noticed, with some trepidation, that about a metre down there seemed to be no more steps. He continued on descending but more cautiously and was surprised to see that as he moved further down, steps seemed to just appear. He stopped and looked back up.

The steps very near the surface had now vanished. Looking down again, he continued his descent until he reached the paved floor. The sphere he held tightly, flared very brightly, hazy blue light burst from between his fingers, and then faded to nothing. He opened his hand to see he held a sphere of some kind of crystalline rock, beautifully patterned and smooth. He felt it's warmth fading.

"It is quartz," Cadfan's voice startled him out of his reverie. Calon looked up and saw that they were now standing in a cave lit by one of Anghenfyl's spheres that bobbed relentlessly up and down in the centre of the space. Below this pale blue light, a large stone sarcophagus stood. Calon could now see that the tomb stood in the centre of a large, circular chamber that was otherwise empty. The domed ceiling, which was crafted from the same dark, crystalline rock as the small spheres, was polished to be almost mirror like and glittered like a clear, night sky.

This stone stretched around into the floor at the edges, barring a perfectly square, paved area roughly ten strides wide on each side. The slabs of perfectly square stone on the floor seemed to be either a very dull, grey granite, or startlingly black—so black were these several slabs, that they looked like holes; holes which the eerie light of the sphere seemed to disappear down. Calon moved close to one and tapped his toe on it, half expecting that there would be nothing there, and was rewarded with a dull, muted thud at every tap of his foot. The slab was just some kind of stone that looked polished but didn't reflect any of the light from the sphere at all. Strangely, he felt slightly nauseating tugging in his stomach as his foot come into contact with the black slab.

"Best not to touch that at all, young Calon," Cadfan advised softly. "Void-stone will steal things from you that will be sorely missed and can never be returned. Do not ever touch it with your bare skin for it will hold you tight and take that which makes you away. Void-stone is a fearful thing." Calon immediately jumped away from the slab. Looking around he noticed that there were a few other of these black void-stone slabs, which were interspersed with the grey slabs but in no discernible pattern. He found this confusing. He decided that he ought to go and see if the other stones felt the same way as the one he had just stepped on.

He was close to another one when a large hand clamped over his face and dragged him back, holding him tightly against a strong body. He immediately fought and struggled, desperate to get away and reach the black slab, but another large, powerful arm encircled his waist and held him tighter. He screamed in frustration and anger until the hand lowered down passed his eyes and covered his mouth to quieten him. His eyes immediately sought the black slab and stared intently at it, fascinated. He was aware that whoever held him was calling out, and recognised the word Anghenfyl but didn't know the language they spoke. He saw also, a strange disjointed figure limping towards him, and registered briefly that it held something towards him in its hand, but it all seemed so strange. He felt a tightness press all around his forehead and skull and then it felt like something 'popped' in his mind.

"Calon," a voice rasped. Calon shook his head slightly and focused his eyes on the face in front of his. Anghenfyl. His dark eye seemed to bore into him, whilst the rotten, milky eye repulsed him. He was aware that the tightness on his head was something the Cawrroc was doing and felt strong fingers pressing against his scalp. His mind began to drift again but the deep voice of the one who held him reverberated around him. "Calon," a sharp slap across his cheek brought him back to his senses. He could hear voices. "I had not guessed he was so sensitive to the magic as this Cadfan. You must teach him. I suspect only you can. I suspect also that he will be able to dream weave—I remember that you were thus affected near void-stone." The fingers at his brow then pressed again. Calon felt a sharp, intense pain for one agonising second, and his mind cleared. The huge hands relaxed but spun him around gently. Cadfan smiled warmly at him.

"You gave me a fright there, young Calon. Other than Anghenfyl, I have never known any Cawrroc be able to bring someone back from the pull of void-stone. I cannot, and I am considered the most powerful stone-weaver among our people. Now, tread carefully; touch the void-stone not at all. We must help Anghenfyl." With that Cadfan let go of him and walked across the room to the great sarcophagus, where Anghenfyl stood, fingers working at the stone.

The sarcophagus consisted of a huge tomb, made from the same glittery quartz as the walls, and a large lid that was just a huge rectangular slab of the same quartz. Around the perimeter of the great lid a two-inch-wide band of gold had been fixed. From this solid band fine golden wires had been fixed that crisscrossed over the whole sarcophagus like a fine web. The lid had been spun sideways so it was balanced horizontally across the middle of the tomb, allowing access to be gained easily from either end. Strange runes were carved across the marble lid, etched in gold. It was these runes that Anghenfyl was rubbing intently.

At first Calon assumed he was polishing them or reviving them somehow, but in fact he was erasing them. Cadfan joined him and the two Cawrrocs then set about cleaning the entire tomb; removing all the strange runes and the gold wire that had been placed in and around the sarcophagus. He'd asked why they were taking the gold away and Cadfan had mumbled something about the gwerin, but other than that the two seemed absorbed in what they were doing, speaking in their own language and generally ignoring any of Calon's questions. Calon got bored watching the two erasing the runes and began looking about the chamber. He started noticing how feint black lines formed a grid that covered the walls, as though a huge net had been stuck to them. He decided to examine these a little closer.

As he approached the wall however and reached out to touch the vein of black, he again felt pressure within his head as though something had tightened around his brow. He snatched his hand back—void-stone. He realised the room had gone silent and spun around to find the two Cawrrocs staring at him. He saw them turn and nod at each other.

"Be aware, young Calon, how easily the void-stone can take you if you let it," Cadfan told him. "Help us here, it will focus you. Take the gold wire and roll it tight," he added before turning back to his task. Calon moved over to the tomb and began winding the yards of gold thread into a tight ball, accompanied by the constant hum of the Cawrrocs' voices. Calon decided they weren't talking to each other but were reciting something over and over. He realised he was hearing the same phrases repeated over and over again. After a few more minutes they both stopped and stood back from the tomb. Calon finished winding the thread just after and held the ball of wound gold out to Anghenfyl.

Anghenfyl took it then looked hard at Calon. "If you can see the void-stone in the walls of this chamber," he told Calon, "you are equally blessed and cursed. I know. It will draw you towards it always. Cadfan will teach you how to resist it's pull. Few could pass on that knowledge save perhaps us two and maybe he who roused me. Him we must be wary of. It is known also as dread-ice or black-diamond. It is a mineral beyond our understanding; it is perhaps the hardest substance I know. It absorbs what it comes into contact with; anything that touches it. Light, sound, emotions and memories will all be lost to it.

"Only the strongest stone weavers can manipulate it if we 'skin' our hands with stone. The gwerin call it 'mind stealer stone' as it drives those mad who touch it. Is extremely dangerous to magic users—to humans it is just a mineral…" As Anghenfyl talked on, Calon became lost in his gaze, trapped by the darkness in Anghenfyl's milky eye.

Calon slammed back to his senses when Anghenfyl's finger touched his brow. The Cawrroc's face unreadable, but Cadfan's expression showed real concern.

"Calon, what has taken your concentration?" Cadfan asked him.

"Anghenfyl's eye. It …" Calon's voice trailed away as he struggled to express what had just happened. A long pause followed as Calon fought to retrieve what had happened. He looked all around him, in fact everywhere but Anghenfyl's eye. "His eye. It looks white and…dead, but it's like the void-stone," he declared at last. The two Cawrrocs turned to face each other. They had a rapid discussion in their own language then Cadfan stepped up to his fellow Cawrroc and took his head in both of his hands and stared directly into his good eye. Calon could see Cadfan's eyes flickering back and forth.

"I cannot look into his eye," Cadfan said. "I am compelled to look away, and when I look back, the same happens."

Anghenfyl turned to look at Calon again. "This cannot be. What I suspect. You must look again, young Calon. I will ward your mind as best I can." Reluctantly Calon stepped in front of the Cawrroc who stooped a little so their eyes were level. Anghenfyl's good hand reached forward and cupped Calon's head; his thumb pressed behind his ear and his little finger pressed onto the centre of Calon's eye brow. He felt a sensation within his skull, as though he were hearing a bee buzzing far off. "Now look again boy. Tell me what you see." Calon gazed back into the milky eye again, and unlike Cadfan, became absorbed by it instantly. He felt the pressure from the Cawrrocs hand increase and hear Anghenfyl ordering him to focus.

"Your eye is like the void-stone, it pulls me in, but I see nothing there," he told him.

"Cadfan," Anghenfyl ordered, "use some diamond dust to skin his fingers." Cadfan reached into his jerkin and withdrew a pouch. He opened the pouch and took a pinch of diamond dust, then taking Calon's hand he held it out horizontally, palm up, before dropping the dust onto the centre of his palm. He added another pinch then gripped Calon's hand from underneath and muttered something before blowing gently onto the dust on Calon's palm. Calon immediately felt warmth in the centre of his hand where the diamond dust had settled and was amazed how the warmth spread to his fingers.

Looking down, after a struggle to tear his gaze from Anghenfyl's eye, he saw a liquid silvery substance spreading over his hand, travelling down the length of his fingers and thumb before settling on his fingertips, as though he's dipped his hands in silver paint. Cadfan then said something else and Calon felt an immediate cooling on his fingers and watched as the silvery gloss turned transparent. As Cadfan let go of his hand, he brought his fingertips together, rubbing them against each other. He felt an uncomfortable sensation, as though he had something on his hand he needed to wipe off, but where he had expected the diamond dust to feel hard, it was in fact soft.

"You will feel very acutely with diamond dust on your fingers. Everything you touch will feel alive. Void stone will not penetrate it however," Anghenfyl explained. "Now touch my eye."

Looking back at Anghenfyl's dead, white eye, Calon felt himself drawn into distraction and confusion again, but with the pressure of the Cawrroc's finger on his forehead, he was able to maintain enough self-awareness and focus to concentrate on his immediate task. With extreme care he reached up his hand, index finger extended and gently touched the pale, spongy surface of Anghenfyl's eye. The eye went immediately black, in fact Calon's first thought was the eyeball had disappeared leaving a gaping chasm in the Cawrroc's skull. Simultaneous with his eye going black, Anghenfyl jerked his head back violently enough that he stumbled away from Calon who remained where he was, transfixed on the end of his finger. Without the Cawrroc's steadying touch on his forehead, he had become fixated on the void-stone again, only this time it was a sliver of the black-diamond, impossibly thin and as small as his little finger nail that was currently stuck to his index fingertip.

"*Anghenfyl*," he heard Cadfan call. "*Ay wych afechyon yr dych chiwedi datys*?" Anghenfyl simply groaned in response. Calon looked around to see the Cawrroc climbing back to his feet. He immediately took a step back, as did Cadfan; something was very different about the ancient weaver now. Power seemed to radiate out of him. His dark eye, now impossibly bright. Calon looked from the sliver of void-stone on his finger then to Anghenfyl's milky eye. He saw that it oozed now. A dark yellow, viscous fluid snaked slowly down one of his cheeks, for all the world like a tear. His grey skin was suddenly more alive. He seemed to be glaring at Cadfan.

"What did you say to him?" Calon whispered urgently.

"I just asked him if what had ailed him had been resolved. Nothing else." Anghenfyl approached Calon, his eye focused on the void-stone on his finger. He lifted his hand to take it, a hand that Calon saw turn silver as he raised it. He pinched the sliver between his silvered finger and thumb and knelt down. Now with his ruined arm he reached awkwardly inside his tunic and withdrew the amulet that had been embedded in his skull. Laying it flat on the floor, he placed the section of void-stone on top of the amulet.

Anghenfyl then held his palm over the two items, the silvery skin withdrawing, and began to hum. Fascinated, Calon took a step closer to see but Cadfan's large hand dragged him back and held him tight. Anghenfyl's humming increased in volume and lowered in pitch, causing the two items to vibrate. The void-stone then rose about nine inches above the amulet and red light began to spread from it, light that was then caught in some kind of vortex created by the void-stone so that it eddied and swirled from the base of the golden artefact into a cone of red light whose apex rose steadily and inexorably towards the void-stone. When it finally touched it, there was an eerily silent explosion of multi coloured light.

"It's like someone's caught a rainbow and trapped it in here?" Calon said in awe. The colours churned chaotically around the chamber before abruptly becoming intensely white and so bright that Calon was forced to cover his eyes. There followed a loud sighing noise and the light disappeared into the void-stone, like water down a hole, whereupon the fragment burst apart into dust that glittered as it fell to the floor. By the time his sight had recovered enough for him to see properly again, Anghenfyl had stalked over to the tomb. Calon watched the Cawrroc lift the gold thread that he'd twined into a ball about the size of a large cabbage. The weaver held it between his hands and proceeded to squash it smaller and smaller. Calon could see vapour or steam rising from the gold. By the time Anghenfyl had finished with it, the gold was perfect sphere which he tossed to Calon who promptly dropped it with a cry of alarm.

"That's bloody red-hot!" he shouted, wringing his hands before blowing on them. He glared at the weaver who smiled back, or at least half of his mouth did. It was the first time that Calon had seen his facial expression anything but deadpan and emotionless. The Cawrroc weaver approached Calon and picked up the hot gold. Calon could see his silvered fingers protecting his skin from the intense heat. Anghenfyl held the gold in his hand and let it fall from his hand, only Calon saw there was a long thread of gold still attached, running from the sphere of gold to the Cawrroc's palm. The sphere had almost reached the ground when Anghenfyl flicked his wrist up and the sphere rose back up to his hand again.

"Tricks," Anghenfyl said. "But you must learn this control. Come," he said to Calon, and lurched off towards the sarcophagus where he sat down on the edge. He bade Calon come and stand in front of him. Cadfan followed and stood behind Calon so he could hear what was being said. "You were not raised among your own people so you have little understanding of your heritage. It is well for you that we have found you for it was the Cawrrocs who first controlled the magic and taught the other Celtyth. Cadfan will teach you how to control and use the magic that you carry."

He reached out then and took Calon's wrist, lifting it and pulling at the *llinach* fastened there. "You do not know what this is," he stated, Calon shook his head. "This marks you. It is record of your lineage; your family's and your ancestor's hair woven into a magic charm peculiar to your people. Only a powerful weaver could have bound this to you. By this, all magic users will know you are marked as Marwolleth, a strong protection. It will protect you from many lesser magical attacks. Further, it will be imbued with a potency for some kind of magic the Marwolleth use; what that is I cannot tell. Its value will become apparent eventually.

"Although it is just hair, the fact that someone chose to give it to you, or died to seal it to you makes it unbreakable. Nothing can cut it, damage it or break it." He paused then as all three looked at the woven hair on Calon's wrist. "You however, can just take it off." Calon quickly looked up at Anghenfyl.

"If it protects me, why would I take it off?" he asked.

Anghenfyl thought for a while before speaking. "Because if you do, I can make it stronger. I can use it to help you against the void-stone. This I think is important as the gwerin who poisoned me with that dread mineral and bound me to his will, still lives. No Cawrroc or Hethwen will kill him or even oppose him, only the Marwolleth follow that path." He paused again and stared intently at Calon. "To our knowledge only three Marwolleth remain in Penrhyn. After Cadfan has taught you what he can, you must go there for you must learn their ways. You, I think, will prove a match for our gwerin friend."

He again lifted Calon's wrist and touched the *llinach*. "If he can manipulate void-stone, you are vulnerable, as you well know. I can use this to guard you against the pull of the black-diamond." Remembering how easily he had succumbed to the void-stone, Calon nodded his ascent.

"Simply pinch the *llinach* between your index finger and thumb and wish it undone," Anghenfyl told him. As Calon did this, vivid memories of Berys filled his mind. He held the hair up for Anghenfyl to take, feeling strange without the comforting feel of it around his wrist. The Cawrrocs both watched as, under the direction of Anghenfyl, Calon delicately removed one long strand, then handed the hair over to him, before refastening the llinach to his wrist. Calon wrapped the hair around and watched with fascination as the ends simply worked themselves together.

Meanwhile, Anghenfyl had extracted an incredibly thin strand of gold from the sphere he held, so thin it was almost invisible. He began to hum and mutter then, almost singing the magic as he began to wind the two stands together until it was big enough to form a thread. When he was finished, he looked up at Calon and smiled his crooked smile. Calon held his arm out towards him, wrist bared, but the Cawrroc weaver smiled and shook his head.

"This we will…" he paused struggling for the words he wanted, "hide in your skin. It is what we call a *craith*, I think you would say a scar. Once done this is a spell that only the weaver can break." Anghenfyl handed the strand to Calon as he began to root around on the floor. Calon was amazed how warm the strand felt. The two Cawrrocs began discussing something then, something Calon couldn't follow, but he was aware that Cadfan seemed to be against whatever Anghenfyl was suggesting. Calon noticed that the weaver had cloaked his hand and held it out flat, for all the world like a slab of granite carved to look like a hand. Although he could see nothing on it, his eyes were drawn to the open palm, so he knew what the Cawrroc held—void-stone.

"Calon!" Anghenfyl said sharply, breaking the spell of the void stone on him. "It is as I told Cadfan, we must protect you from the void stone. This was how I was shielded from it, and unless you touch it directly, it will never draw you. When I tell you, place the strand between my finger and thumb." With that he cupped his other hand over the void-stone and began to chant. The sudden surge of magic gave Calon goose bumps. Within seconds he began to feel the heat emanating from Anghenfyl's hands; within a minute the Cawrroc's cloaked hands began to glow red at the edges.

Calon looked at the weaver and saw the strain on his face. Another thirty seconds and his cloaked hands were bright red now, like the metal Kort would heat in his forge. "Now Calon," Anghenfyl barked, extending the hand that had been cupped over the void-stone; a hand as grey as stone, where a second ago it had glowed like the sun. Calon dangled the strand into the weaver's finger tips. With total concentration and infinite care Anghenfyl held the strand over this still outstretched palm.

Calon could see a small pool of black liquid boiling and churning on the flat of the hand, then watched, transfixed by the way the liquid surged and retreated as Anghenfyl slowly lowered the strand into the liquid, until the fingers that held it almost brushed the black, seething fluid. He then, equally carefully, lifted the strand from the liquid void-stone and held it aloft, before spitting on it. The strand blazed blue instantly, before fading back to what looked like a black strand of cotton.

After cutting the untreated end of the strand away, Anghenfyl spent some time examining his creation, an unremarkable looking piece of thread about four inches long, before stating he was satisfied that it was good. He then produced a wickedly sharp needle, curved at the pointed end to almost a right angle. He bade Calon to remove his tunic and lower his shirt, then come and stand beside him. He spoke to Cadfan, who joined them, and without warning grabbed Calon's shirt and tied it by the empty sleeves to pin Calon's arms tightly to his sides. He then gripped Calon's head very firmly with both of his hands over Calon's ears, lifting him so his toes were barely touching the floor before tilting his head to one side, exposing his neck.

"Quietly now, young Calon. This was necessary. Nothing we said would have made it easier. Scream if you must but it won't help you and may hinder me. I am going to place this strand within your skin—beneath the surface of it. It will hurt and it will take some time." He then lifted the curved needle to Calon's neck. "I'm going to make a hole here," he said tapping the side of his neck directly under his ear. "Then I will push the strand in. Following that I will need to shape it into a rune. You must endure."

Calon felt a small sting as the needle pierced his skin, followed by an altogether more unpleasant sensation as the strand was inserted. The pain was so intense that a soundless scream gripped him for the duration of the time it took Anghenfyl to force the whole thing in. Cadfan released him then, letting him stumble to the ground, arms still bound, panting and sobbing. Even had his hands been free, he would never have touched his neck; it hurt so much that even the thought of it being touched brought fresh agony. He was aware that Anghenfyl had knelt beside him and began looping great ribbons of stone he was teasing from the floor over Calon to hold him on his side and keep him still.

Three huge bands pulled tight around his legs, waist and shoulders, with a smaller one pinning his head down so that his neck was exposed again. The weaver lowered his hand over the thread hidden in Calon's neck and began to chant. Even through his pain Calon could feel the strand rippling within his skin; twisting and turning, ripping more agony from his neck, an intense torture that was over in seconds but had felt like an infinite to Calon. Cadfan knelt beside him then, pressing a cool hand to his fevered skin.

"Sleep, young Calon, I think you have earned it." He felt a surge of magic then and weariness overwhelmed him.

When Calon woke a few hours later, he felt rested and pain-free. He moved his hand to his neck, unsure at first whether he had dreamt or imagined Anghenfyl's ministrations. He felt a raised pattern of swirls on his neck. Standing, he looked around the chamber and saw that both Cawrrocs were now standing on the other side of the tomb, deep in conversation. He strode over, surprised at how refreshed he felt.

"You look much happier and healthier, Calon," Cadfan smiled as he spoke.

"I feel more alert and awake than I have in days. Probably just needed a good sleep," he told them.

Anghenfyl shook his head. "We have protected you from the magic in the roots of these mountains. Your mind is now free of the pressure of fighting against the void-stone. Also, any magic-wrought stone retains some of the magic that shaped it; this is how we find our way around." Calon nodded at that, finding it easy to accept. Raising his hand to his patterned neck he asked what they had done to him. Anghenfyl knelt to the floor and began to etch a symbol into the stone. "This a *triskelion*. This *craith* represents the three components of the spell—hair, gold and void-stone. To our people the *triskelion* is a symbol of strength; it represents the overcoming of adversity. It will protect you from the void-stone and possibly other magics as well."

"It didn't protect you though did it," Calon responded, his hand smoothing at his neck.

Anghenfyl laughed at that. "It would have if I had been marked as you are. My skin was marked with a different symbol, a *cylch,* we call it the knotted circle. Imagine a circle twisted this way, but still one whole unbroken line." He dragged the collar of his jerkin down and exposed a symbol. "This provides protection against the lure of magical wards and charms. It will ensure the bearer's mind is not confused or consumed, but it was not designed specifically to ward against void-stone, I could already do that. Or so I thought." With that explanation, he turned to Cadfan then, the two Cawrrocs pressed their palms together. Something seemed to pass between the two, before Anghenfyl turned away and approached the tomb.

Once there, he grasped its rim, magic humming around him, and simply walked through it, as though it were fog, and stood inside it, the stone behind him remained solid and untouched as though nothing had happened. He turned to Calon again. "One other gift I gave you while you slept." He indicated the other side of Calon's neck. Calon raised his hand and felt more ridges—another *craith*. "You will feel one large circle. Inside are three smaller circles each with a flame leaving them. This has two purposes.

Cadfan added his healing gift to the gold and also added a strand of his hair. This is the *awen*; it will aid healing as Cadfan can teach you, but it is also a call. If you are in dire need, press your palm to this symbol and when it warms say his name. He will come." Cadfan smiled and nodded at this.

Calon spent a while running his fingertips over the symbols embed in his skin, trying to visualise what his fingers were feeling.

"You know must search for your own people Calon. You never really fitted with the humans, did you?" Calon shook his head in answer to Anghenfyl's question. The great Cawrroc continued, "And I doubt the sedentary peaceful life of my people will suit you. The fire that burns within you will grow Calon, you must learn to control it. The only ones who can teach you that are the Marwolleth weavers in Penrhyn. Promise me you will go there and learn what you need. Seek Emrys. He is as old as Cadfan here. He can teach you I think, as he was once what you are now—all coiled and heated with conflict."

Calon nodded solemnly, holding Anghenfyl's intense gaze. "Go to Penrhyn and the Marwolleth; Cadfan will guide you," Anghenfyl repeated. Calon nodded once more, and with that the weaver lifted himself up, easing his legs out of the stone and sat on the tombs surface. "Why?" Calon asked suddenly, gesturing at the tomb. Anghenfyl turned and gazed at him, his one eye unblinking, but discerning Calon's meaning.

"I find this hard to explain," Anghenfyl began, before sighing and crouching down so their eyes were on a level. "I have lived my life Calon, I have died my death. I feel nothing now. The urge to simply lie down and die again is almost overwhelming now, and grows stronger every hour." He gestured then to the tomb. "I am passed my time. Cadfan has convinced me to do this, to stay in stasis. He believes the Celtyth are all but doomed by their peaceful nature, but he sees hope in you that at least some of our ways, some of our people will live on; as do I. So, we plan for a future none of us want. If our peoples need me, I will be here," he said gravely, placing his hand on Calon's shoulder before standing and turning for his tomb. Climbing into the stone sarcophagus, the great Anghenfyl nodded once at Cadfan then lay down. Cadfan bent and lifted the stone lid which they had been propped along the side of the tomb. He slid it onto one end and pushed it up so that only Anghenfyl's head was visible.

"Thank you my friends," he said, then clasping both of his hands onto his chest above his heart he said, "*Carreg dal fi.*" The tomb blazed with blue light for an instant. As it faded Calon saw that a feint blue haze remained, like morning mist on the wetlands. Cadfan told him to touch it, so Calon tried to place his fingers inside the tomb, only to find the 'mist' was solid. He looked questioningly at Cadfan.

"The question we need to ask is not, 'How is that done?' The question is, 'How was that undone?' Nothing I could have done would have broken that spell, yet our gwerin acquaintance managed it. But that, young Calon is a question for another time." He slid the lid over the final open section. Looking at the pattern on it, Calon saw that Anghenfyl had placed four bands of void-stone across the width of the great stone, and one long band down the centre, the ends of the bands curled outwards from the tomb lid. Cadfan cloaked his hands and grabbed one of the ends, dragging it down until it passed the join between the top and bottom sections of the tomb before pressing it flat against the stone. He had sealed the lid to the base. He repeated that process with the other nine ends then stood back, satisfied with his work.

"We talked long about this. Anghenfyl assured me that only two living beings can open this. The two beings whose hair and magic is woven into the void-stone. You and I. We are certain the gwerin could not repeat this feat and keep his mind. Working void-stone is one thing, working void-stone held by another's magic… not even Anghenfyl can do that."

Calon nodded his understanding at that, but another question had already consumed his thinking. "But he said if we needed him, we could rouse him. How?"

"Now that is a question," Cadfan smiled and turned away. "Let us leave here Calon, we have far to travel and much to discuss. We will go back to my people and I will teach you what I know." The Cawrroc turned and made his way back to the impossible stairs that they had come down on. Calon glanced once more at the great tomb then hurried after, chasing Cadfan with his questions.

Chapter 8
Journey Under the Mountain

After the first hour of the journey, Calon was completely lost. "This place is alike a maze," he told Cadfan. "How do you know where you're going? Everything looks the same. Also, you said it was a long journey, but you didn't take long to get to Anghenfyl's chamber, so why is it taking longer to go back?"

Cadfan answered as he walked. "I did not travel this way Calon, I used the *afon garreg*, the stone river. Other than a master weaver, none could travel this way. If you are attuned to another weaver there is a way to pass through rock that takes many tens of years to learn. If there is a bond that stretches between—"

"I have that," Calon interrupted excitedly, "with Berys. *Had* that. It's how I followed her in the woods."

"Even so," Cadfan agreed. "It is the same thing. When you know how, a powerful stone-weaver can travel along such a bond, depending on their mastery of the magic. I can travel though stone, but not water or wood, other than a few feet. Most Cawrrocs cannot travel through wood at all. Yet you, it sems, have the potential to master both, if you have the inclination to spend years under the mountains."

Calon thought about that. "Anghenfyl took me through a wall; and I fell through a door once by myself and didn't like it."

"Ah. That is possible. But had you gone into a *wall*, you would have died in the stone. It is best not to attempt unless you are trained how to do it. Without a bond to guide your way, it is certain to be fatal. Which is why you cannot travel as I did. You have no bond with a Cawrroc other than me and I am here." Cadfan paused but could predict Calon's next question. "And even if we make our bond here and I travelled home, you could not follow. It is not a thing I can tell you. It must be shown. If were a mile apart, I could not shout instructions to you, you would have to pull yourself along the bond. Given time I could teach you how, yet I feel that is not a thing you wish to spend time doing." Calon nodded to that, acknowledging that he preferred the open sky to the oppressive underworld

Throughout their journey Cadfan spoke about the Celtyth peoples and encouraged Calon to ask questions as he thought of them. It helped pass the time as they moved through the endless tunnels and caverns that led down to the heart of the mountain. When they stopped for a brief rest to drink and eat some of Cadfan's grey looking food, which Calon was happy to believe was mushroom of some kind, he asked the Cawrroc about Anghenfyl.

Cadfan looked hard at Calon. "I will tell you what I know of the history of Anghenfyl. He was a Cawrroc elder for many centuries and perhaps the greatest weaver of stone that has ever been known. He was also the first Cawrroc dream-weaver, a magic most rare among my people. Although I think the Hethwen and perhaps the Marwolleth are blessed with many more. Much of dream weaver lore was discovered by Anghenfyl. He it was who conceived and oversaw the great mountain wall that sealed off the western side of this island for the Celtyth peoples. Then, after centuries of service to all the Celtyth peoples, Anghenfyl just disappeared. The gwerin folk had taken him somehow.

"The gwerin are not like us. They had mostly lost their magic by then; living shorter lives. All they retained were small weaves that created light or heated stone. Where once we all lived in harmony, the gwerin warred on the other Celtyth peoples. They had harnessed something we could not combat; you would call it envy, lust and hate, and they had bound Anghenfyl to their dark purpose through some foul magic. But not as he was. His body and mind were all tortured and twisted by the gwerin. They had bored a jewel into his skull that carried a spell woven so powerfully that they gained control of the greatest weaver that had ever lived. The gwerin would appear out of solid walls.

"They stole Cawrroc young, they stole and enslaved any Hethwen they could, binding them in iron and using their fell ways to steal the magic from their captives which they used to prolong their own lives. A magic so old it was all but forgotten; a magic so foul it is anathema to the Celtyth peoples today—*hud gwaed*: blood magic."

"Is that blood magic how Mordwyn was able to get into Anghenfyl's tomb?" Calon asked.

"We suspect it was so," Cadfan told him. "It would explain much. Especially as your blood was instrumental in raising our friend. But as we know so little about it, it is hard to say with certainty how it was used to bind Anghenfyl to their bidding."

After a brief silence, Cadfan continued with his tale. "So it was that the gwerin lust for blood and power brought war to Torffan. We Cawrroc would not fight, so we just left the upper inhabited levels of the mountain kingdom and went deeper underground. The Hethwen too simply wanted peace and harmony; they refused to fight and withdrew from the land around the Eiran Mountains to live further west in the great forests, where the gwerin are not so comfortable. So many were killed, enslaved or simply just disappeared. Many gave themselves back to the earth rather than be taken.

"Thus it was that the Marwolleth were fashioned; the young Hethwen folk eager to fight back. And among the Marwolleth, one emerged who could weave more than just one element alone; Emrys. A dream-weaver. He it was who led the Marwolleth to fight against the gwerin, and he it was who mortally wounded Anghenfyl, bringing an end to the conflict. This bloodshed caused the great rift that led to the Marwolleth exile on the Penrhyn peninsula."

Calon interrupted, causing Cadfan to stop and face him. "Berys told me he is my uncle. Or was it grandfather," he added. "Family anyway."

Cadfan nodded. "That seems likely given you can both weave stone and wood." They continued walking as Cadfan resumed his story.

"Without Anghenfyl's power, the gwerin retreated back into the mountain and stayed there. Still stealing the Hethwen young, but selling them to the humans now. Of Anghenfyl we knew nothing until recently. They used dark practices to control him and I suspect he was aware of all he did under their power. Now one has emerged with the power to bin him and control him again. This is why he did not want to stay with us. His guilt, I think, was a burden he could not bear." Cadfan stopped then and lowered himself down to stare into Calon's eyes. "But you have freed him. I sense that Anghenfyl was correct that there is great magic in you young Calon."

"Someone called me Marwolleth," Calon protested. "What does that mean? How can you tell? I'm just me. I grew up with humans none of this makes any sense."

Dark eyes fixed Calon's for a time before the Cawrroc spoke. "The Celtyth peoples are peaceful folk, we live with what nature provides for us. We have no hatred and so have no violence. Our people do not steal, there is no need. We all share what we have. True, the gwerin took a different path, but not so different as the Marwolleth. Killing changes you Calon; sometimes for the good as you may find it abhorrent and never kill again, but rarely is this so. Most become intoxicated by the power of it. You Calon, have that look. This is why the Celtyth who chose that path were outcast. Marwolleth we named them, it simply means *death*." And that was the end of the conversation. The Cawrroc rose to stand, then gestured to Calon to follow him again.

After another seemingly endless downward trek, the Cawrroc stopped at an underground stream. Calon had heard the insistent gurgling from some distance away, echoing through the tunnels. Whilst he knelt to drink from the stream by scooping water up with his cupped hands, the Cawrroc spoke again.

"My people know Anghenfyl as The Icon. He was our hope of leaving the mountains and living peacefully with the Hethwen. His life is still told to this day." With that the great figure began to sing. His voice, though deep and gravelly, was surprisingly good.

Here he is—his might can see Beyond the halls of the mountain. Anghenfyl in pale robes has come And shown us our prison.
The icon has tamed the stone And shown us the blue beyond.
With heart we hope to walk the path To bide beneath a diamond sky.
But he fell to the dwellers and was lost Forgetting everything, loving nothing. And we forgot about everything
So faded away like a winter sun.

Immediately he had finished singing, the Cawrroc moved on. Calon hustled along behind him. Sensing a great sadness in Cadfan he kept his questions to himself for a while.

"Why are we going so far down?" Calon asked eventually. "How deep underground do you live?"

Cadfan responded to this with a question of his own, "How far down do you think we are?" To which Calon had no answer. "We are still above sea level at the moment." Calon's face betrayed his doubt and confusion. "Let me ask you this; when you were held captive by Mordwyn, where were you in the mountain?"

Calon thought about this. "I assumed we were underground somewhere I suppose." Cadfan chuckled at this. "Tell me how much of a mountain is underground?"

Calon thought about this and smiled before answering. "Well, none of it. To be a mountain it has to be above the ground, I guess. But being trapped in caves and tunnels with no windows made it feel like we were underground. How do all those people live in constant dark without the sun, without fresh air?"

"They don't Calon. The gwerin live high up inside the mountain. They have windows that are Cawrroc made; created from rock that can be looked out of, but not looked in to. They have ways in and out. They have valleys hidden from the human side where they grow food and spend time. The dungeons where you were kept were on a lower level, but still a day's walk up the mountain to reach." They kept walking as Calon thought about this, then Cadfan added, "We Cawrrocs live down at ground level. We made the decision not to fight or kill to keep our mountain home. The gwerin have no such scruples. They would have killed us had we stayed. So we left. We travelled to a place where they cannot go and will not find us. I am the first to leave in over three hundred years. In a short while, we will come to the end of this passage. Then you will see."

Another hour of trekking followed. As Calon stumbled after Cadfan, he began to feel a pressure in his ears and hear a constant hiss. He rubbed and poked at them to tray and clear the sound from his head. It was only as they moved ever onward that he realised it was getting louder; and it wasn't in his head; it was rushing water. Eventually he trailed Cadfan into a vast underground chamber, dominated by steep rapids where the river careered in a frenzy of white-water into a deep, churning basin before rushing headlong through a perfectly straight tunnel nearly twenty yards wide. Farther down the tunnel Calon could see that the river widened to a good thirty yards across and gave off an eerie green light as far as was visible. The river filled the tunnel. This one beach aside, there was nowhere else that Calon could see to get out of the water; once in the fast flow there would be no going back. Calon strolled over to his right where Cadfan stood beside a large stone on the bank. The Cawrroc offered Calon some more of the weird mushroom food, encouraged him to drink some water, then handed him something that looked suspiciously like moss. He told Cadfan as much.

Cadfan laughed. "That's because it is moss. Yet it is not the moss that is vital. The moss has been dried then soaked in *chouchen*, a drink like mead, made from honey. But there is something in this moss that feeds the heart, making it beat faster. You will be energised by this. Energy is vital here as I fear you would not make the journey without it's aid. Put the moss in your mouth and suck out the chouchen. Keep it in your mouth and keep sucking until you taste nothing. Spit

133

it out then." Calon did as he was bid and was pleasantly surprised by the taste and the warmth it created as he swallowed the liquid. It wasn't as sweet as the mead his da had let him sip; this left his mouth dry. After a few minutes Calon began to feel rejuvenated and heady. He felt his heart begin to race, his breathing quickened and he felt ready for anything.

"Are we going down there?" Calon asked Cadfan, pointing down the eerily illuminated tunnel. "That current looks very strong."

"No Calon, we are not going down there, we are going up there," Cadfan replied pointing up the waterfall. Calon thought about this then asked,

"Is this like the *grimm*; the way into the Eiran Mountains? Berys explained it to me. Without magic it is impossible."

Cadfan nodded at this. "Yes, it is the same, only for this you will need to be a strong weaver to make the stone obey you. Very few stone-weavers are powerful enough. This is how we keep ourselves hidden." With that Cadfan led Calon to the river and knelt on the rocky shore. Pulling up his sleeves, he cloaked his hands and gripping Calon's forearms to similarly cloak his. Cadfan put both of his hands into the water at the very edge of the rushing torrent, urging Calon to do the same. Even cloaked with magic as they were Calon could feel the cold as the power of the water threatened to drag his arms away. He remembered Berys could warm her hands when cloaked but he had no idea how. "Feel this ridge here," Cadfan told him.

Calon placed his hands adjacent to Cadfan's and found a raised ledge of rock he could grip with both hands. "Holding this, I will invoke the magic in the stone and create our way into *Lellacher,* our homeland. Hold tight so you can feel what I do. Aid if you can—I seek to lift this ledge closer to the surface of the water." With that, Cadfan's focus narrowed to his task. Calon immediately felt the stone begin to vibrate gently and raise slightly. He tried to pinpoint his concentration onto raising the ridge and found it rose easily so that it was just below the surface. He could see it now, almost as black as void-stone but speckled with quartz, so it sparkled faintly. Looking up the rapids Calon could see that the ridge extended all the way up and out of sight, staying about two yards parallel to the wall the entire way.

"I hadn't thought you would do that so easily, lift all of that rock, it's beautiful stone.

I like the way it feels… What?" he asked Cadfan who was staring at him.

"I didn't lift it easily, you did," he said bluntly. "I have never lifted that so quickly or so high." Calon didn't know how to respond so just shrugged.

"I just did what you told me," he said.

Cadfan continued to look appraisingly at Calon, before getting to his feet. "Night-stone. We call this," he indicated the ridge, "night-stone. Very easy to use magic on. The gwerin and Hethwen call it midnight lodestone. It is valuable to our peoples as it holds heat very well." Cadfan turned away then and sat to take the moccasins from his feet. Tying the laces together, he looped them around his neck so that they dangled on to his chest. Calon did the same thing, then stood beside the Cawrroc at the river's edge.

"Before we walk up the ridge, just lean on the wall here," Cadfan told him. Calon looked at the wall he had indicated, it was as smooth as the walls of the tunnel they were about to enter. He moved over to it, but when he was roughly a couple of yards away, Cadfan made him stop and stand with his feet together. "Now keep your feet still, as though you are standing on the ridge, lean from here and put both of you palms flat to the wall." Calon did as he was asked. The second that his hands hit the wall, they slipped straight down. Calon sat up from where he had landed.

"What the... Something pulled me down!" he exclaimed looking pointedly at his hands, then at the wall. Cadfan laughed.

"Not quite. This too is night-stone—enchanted to make that happen. If anyone touches it, down they go. Into that," he pointed at the rushing river, "and there is no chance of surviving a fall."

Calon looked up at the Cawrroc. "So, we have to balance on that ridge of super slippery rock, while water moving that quickly batters our legs and we have nothing to hold on to, and walk for... How far is it?" he asked, his exasperation clear.

"Over a hundred yards, mostly up hill," said Cadfan laughing again. "A hundred yards! I won't last an inch."

Cadfan then lifted his hands and touched his hands lightly to the wall as he muttered something. Calon watched with awe as the Night-stone seemed to move and flow over the Cawrrocs hands. Cadfan lifted them away, showing Calon that his hands now looked as though they had been carved from the stone itself. Bidding Calon lift his hands out towards him, the Cawrroc pressed his palms on to Calon's so their palms and fingers barely touched. As he did this, he muttered the same incantation and Calon's hands too became covered in the Night-stone.

"Now stand here, lean over and press both of your hands to the wall," Cadfan told him. Calon did and found his hands drawn to the rock. He tried to lift his hand off, but it wouldn't move. The Cawrroc showed him how to lift the heel of his hand off first and peel his hand away. Following that demonstration Cadfan told Calon to stand close to the wall before he lifted him up and telling him to reach up as high as he could before pressing his hands to the wall. Calon hung from the wall, his legs a good three feet off the floor. Cadfan gripped his waist and pulled him hard but to Calon's amazement he didn't move at all.

"You see," Cadfan told him, "you will not fall as long as you always have one hand fastened to the rock. It will be slow moving, as your arms must do all the work; your feet are just there to help take your weight. Sadly, only the walls are enchanted so. Now, if you do fall grab for the wall if you can and pull yourself up. But know this, that plunge pool where the rapids land will be your death. There is no enchantment there. I say this not to frighten you but to focus your mind. I will be behind you." The Cawrroc cloaked his and Calon's bare feet, then took a piece of grey material from a pouch on his belt. It had looked nothing more than a small square when he first revealed it, but when unravelled, Calon saw it was very thin material in a long roll, that was roughly three inches wide and several feet long. Cadfan began murmuring and ran the material through his Night-stone cloaked fingers, which seemed to darken the greyish looking strip of cloth, but still leave it malleable.

"This is material woven from the murk-wyrms that live deep in the mountains; we call it silk-sash. Used as a bandage, it covers wounds and binds well; but we also use it to make straps, ropes and belts. It is very strong. We use it to bind young ones to us when we travel. Had you been smaller I would have carried you through… as it is, I will bind you to me with this—the Night-stone I have infused it with will make it stronger." He then bent to bind the silk-sash tightly around Calon's waist, adding another binding around his chest. The two bindings were then roughly plaited together before Cadfan wrapped the free end around his own waist with a length of some nine yards between the two companions.

"Erm, shouldn't this be shorter?" Calon asked flipping the silk-sash up and down.

"No Calon," Cadfan answered patiently. "If you do fall, I will need a moment to brace myself to take your weight. This length I hope will give me that moment. Now let us be moving." The two moved to the water's edge. Calon looked nervously at the torrent raging through the tunnel. Even here on the bank it was hard to be heard, but Cadfan shouted to him and he could still hear.

"Now, the noise of the water is very loud inside the tunnel. It is virtually impossible to communicate. Let us agree if we need each other's attention that we will gently tug on the silk-sash." Calon agreed to this. Cadfan then asked, "Do you have any questions about this Calon? It will not be easy." Still buzzing from the *chouchen*, Calon told the Cawrroc he just wanted to get moving. Their shouting done, Cadfan eased into the water and Calon followed.

He immediately found that with his feet cloaked in magic he had surprisingly good grip on the ridge he was standing on; good enough that he had confidence he wouldn't slip, but the force of the water was incredible. He could already feel the coldness of the river sucking the heat from his legs. He remembered then how Berys had used the magic to warm herself. He hollered at Cadfan, who had taken a few paces into the tunnel, to make himself heard. The Cawrroc turned back towards him and after a few attempts grasped what Calon was saying. He then reached out a hand that he placed squarely on Calon's chest. He felt the warmth spread rapidly throughout his body, which was just as well because after only a minute in the river he could barely feel legs or feet, numbed as they were by the ice-melt water.

The following journey was interminable. Even cloaked in magic that made slipping or falling highly improbable, it was the most physically demanding thing he had ever done. He recognised as well that Cadfan was taking the full force of the water and shielding him from the worst of it. Before the pair had even reached halfway up the slope, Calon had reached the limits of his endurance. He tugged on the rope, causing Cadfan to turn and look at him. The Cawrroc could see that Calon was on the point of collapse. He eased back to Calon and mimed putting his hands flat to the wall. Then with great effort lifted him bodily out of the water before pushing him up the smoothed wall. With the magic of the night-stone on his hands Calon pressed his palms to the wall and was able to half hang, half rest on Cadfan to get his body out of the insistent battering of the water. He noticed that Cadfan was barely troubled by it.

Cadfan began shouting to him, but his hearing was fogged by the cacophony of the water slamming through the tunnel. The Cawrroc then wiped the soles of Calon's feet, grabbing his ankles quite firmly and sticking them to the wall. The Cawrroc then peeled his right foot off, lifting the heel first, before moving it right by about a foot, before easing his foot back down, toes first. Next, he tapped

Calon's left leg and indicated he move it the same way. Grasping what the Cawrroc wanted, Calon did. Realising Cadfan's intent, he moved his hands along in the same fashion. It took him a few minutes to co-ordinate his movements effectively, but once he had established a pattern of right-hand, left-hand, right-foot, left-foot, he began to move more quickly than he had been doing in the storm of water. It took concentration though, as a couple of times he didn't peel his hands or feet off correctly so that the appendage he was trying to lift remained fixed as he tried to shift his body weight, the missed step breaking his rhythm.

With Cadfan forging through the water at his side, the pair made better progress and eventually crested the top of the slope. Cadfan urged Calon to ease himself back into the water at the peak of the slope where the water looked as clear as glass as it surged over the edge and downhill. Calon immediately noticed the pull of the river was not as powerful here. When he finally rounded the end of the tunnel he could see why. The river was much wider before the falls; whose narrow opening narrowed the river dramatically, so the stone walls were almost squeezing the water through.

Having worked their way around the sheer walls that formed the opening of the waterfall, they found themselves on a ledge that jutted from the stone. The smoothness of the walkway telling Calon this was Cawrroc made. Cadfan bade Calon sit and rest whilst he removed the night-stone coating both of their hands and feet. He also used a warming spell of some kind to dry their clothes out and ease the ache in Calon's muscles. They had no food left, but following a drink of water, Cadfan assured him that they would be 'home' in a couple of hours. He stood then and walked over to the wall. Other than the smoothed walkway on which he lay, Calon could see that the rock was natural. Cadfan by now had placed both of his hands on the wall.

After a few seconds, a pulse of white light flew from beneath his hands along the wall, parallel to the walkway at about six feet up. Calon watched the sphere of light, for all the world like a shooting star, speed down what he could now see was a long tunnel, impossibly quickly. It disappeared from view, but the shimmer of its existence could still be seen faintly.

"Wow," Calon said, but was prevented from saying more by Cadfan raising his hand to hush him, before pointing to where the light had vanished. Calon could see that the far end of the tunnel was getting brighter, and suddenly the sphere of light was heading back towards them. It raced in silence, adding to the wonder, reaching the point where Cadfan had started it off, then bounced back down the tunnel, even quicker this time. Cadfan gestured for Calon to come over to the wall.

"Night-stone," he said, pointing at a thin vein of black, speckled stone set into the rock face, that stretched unerringly right down the long tunnel. "The light will travel faster and faster until it looks like one continuous line. You will have light then." With this he cupped his hands together, creating another sphere of light. Then he gently moved his hands forward and apart, sending the sphere gliding across the river at walking pace. It drifted into the wall on the other side of the water and then rolled down a few inches before stopping, roughly parallel with the pulsating band of light that was forming on their side of the river. The original sphere was now too quick to see and the illuminated line was nearly steady. With a wave of his hand, Cadfan set the other sphere into motion. Slowly it eased along the vein of night-stone opposite them, gradually picking up speed. Calon was mesmerised. And stood for a couple of minutes watching the light race back and forth, before it too became a steady brightness that flooded the cave with light. It was only when he tore his eyes from the light that Calon saw where they were.

The light, that still trembled slightly, gave the whole length of the cavern a warmth and colour, also revealing a sight he would only have seen in stages as he walked the length of the wondrous place. Huge, smooth rock formations, creamy white against the russet rocks of the wall, stretched down from the ceiling, for all the world like they were reaching for the water. The walls themselves were a rainbow of brown and yellow shades. Further up where the water was barely moving the reflections of the walls gave the appearance of a deep, covered canyon. So clear was the water, he could see perfectly how deep the river bed lay, at least twenty yards down from where he stood and looked, but much deeper towards the middle of the river. He knelt and reached his hands down to scoop a drink, rippling the surface, after one drink he reached in again only for Cadfan to snatch him back and away.

The Cawrroc then dragged him back against the cave wall, also pressing himself against it. Calon was about to ask what the hell was going on, but Cadfan's large, calloused hand clamped over his mouth. With his other hand, he gestured at the water. Calon saw nothing, save a few ripples, but sensing Cadfan's wariness, he eased himself as far back as the wall would allow, keeping his eyes fixed on the river. He caught movement in the corner of his eye a couple of times, a sense of something, and peeled the Cawrroc's hand from his mouth, nodding to him that he knew to be quiet. A knowledge nearly undone when something emerged from the surface of the water: a long sinuous back, eerily pale and translucent, veins and dark organs visible in the torso. It was snakelike but must have been a yard in circumference, and long. How long Calon had no idea. It eased back into the water so smoothly it barely left a ripple.

"*Sywenoer*," Cadfan explained a few minutes later. "I think you would say a cold eel. Just about the most deadly hunter that exists. They are lightning fast. Its teeth are fearsome and impossibly sharp. They are very few but live in the river, never sleeping, always moving. We don't know how many there are. Some say there is one only, but I think there are more. There are no *sywenoer* on the other side of the waterfall, something we often wonder at, but there are other creatures lower down that could kill you. Do not touch the water with any part of your body."

"But you took water from the river when we reached the top," Calon protested.

"No Calon, I took water from the fall. It seems the *sywenoer* avoid the faster flowing water." Cadfan stopped then and scanned the river. When he was satisfied that the creature had moved away, he told Calon to follow and set off down the ledge. "We do not know how they hunt, but it is not movement. Some say they sense warmth, some that is a 'blood sense' they track, or perhaps both. Just stay on the ledge; it has never taken anyone from the ledge."

"How do you know?" Calon asked, still eyeing the water warily. "If they'd been taken, how would you find out?" The Cawrroc stopped and looked at him carefully, nodding once, before moving on. Calon noticed he was walking closer to the wall now and did the same. After they had travelled out of sight and sound of the waterfall, they came to the end of the ledge. In fact, the ledge where it ended sloped down into the river. There was no way out or onwards that Calon could see; nothing bar a large stone trough, presumably drinking water he thought to himself. At least he thought that until Cadfan picked up one end of the trough and began shoving it into the water, its bottom scraping loud enough along the ledge that Calon backed into the wall again and looked fearfully at the surface of the river for signs of the scary eel. When he looked back at Cadfan he was stepping very carefully into the trough. Not a trough then, he thought to himself, but a boat; a stone boat. Something guaranteed to sink, and they were going to try and float in it.

Cadfan called him over and after stressing several times the need to avoid putting anything in the water, allowed Calon into the boat. Calon had expected the boat to rock unsteadily, like his da's coracle, when he climbed in, but it was very stable. He attributed this to the fact it was still grounded. He was also somewhat concerned about how they were going to float the trough, he couldn't think of it as a boat, off the bank. He asked Cadfan this. Cadfan rummaged around the boat and held up a rod. The rod was probably two feet in length, the width and thickness of the Cawrrocs thumb and looked to be made of night-stone.

"We use this to push ourselves off from the bank," Cadfan smiled at him. Seeing Calon's doubt, he added, "Watch." He then began to hum whilst at the same time he put his hands next to each other gripping the centre of the rod. He then simply eased them apart, stretching the night-stone until his arms had spread to their limit. He repeated this once more and was now holding a pole roughly nine feet in length. He then placed one against the bank and simply pushed them easily into the river. Pulling the pole back in, he manoeuvred it so that one end was between his palms. He began to hum again and rotate his palms across the pole. Calon saw that the night-stone rod was flattening out into a rough oar blade. He repeated this with the wet end and held up the paddle he had crested for Calon to see, before giving it to him.

"Before you ask, the *Sywenoer*, the cold-eels, have never attacked a boat or grabbed a paddle. Stone is cold," he added with a shrug. "Best to start paddling Calon, or we're headed for a trip down the waterfall," Cadfan said indicating the direction they were drifting in. Calon immediately set to his task. With the first pull of the paddle, Calon was surprised how little effort he needed, but even more surprised how far it had propelled them. He looked at Cadfan with raised eyebrows.

Cadfan smiled and simply said, "Night-stone." The two paddled through the fabulous cave in a few minutes, Calon engrossed by the rock formations and dazzling colours of the cave walls. As they turned around a long bend, the river was wider and slower flowing than previously, and Calon saw as the light that Cadfan had created began to fade that the great walls of rock here looked grey and unworked. There was no walkway on the bank either. As they continued Calon realised that there was enough light, just, to see where they were going— a strange green glow from huge swathes of what looked like moss. He remembered seeing something similar in the gwerin tunnels. The pair paddled steadily for upward of an hour before Cadfan announced that their destination was near and indicated to Calon that they should slow their pace until they were just drifting gently towards the end of their journey.

"There are things I would tell you, Calon, to help you through the next few weeks. We Cawrrocs are a race of powerful stone weavers as you have seen and will observe when we reach *Lellachar*, our home. The Cawrrocs created the great mountain defences of the Celtyth kingdoms before we came here. We are a gentle people like the Hethwen, but we were competing with the more aggressive Gwerin people for room underground, so we left. For centuries now we have dwelled in Lellachar, away from the world. Many thought us gone from Torffan to *Gorwynoll*—the Western World—or just 'gone' altogether. No Cawrroc has been seen for many lifetimes and it seems we have passed into legend. It was only the insistent echoes of Anghenfyl's magic that brought me out.

"We have watched the gwerin always, we have listened. Any magic could be a threat to us, so when a weaver used magic so powerful that the rocks hummed, we were worried. Then Anghenfyl called; Anghenfyl who we thought dead. The rest of my story you know." He paused then, considering what to say next, Calon thought. "My people will not be hostile, but neither will they be friendly or helpful. We have no intention of re-joining the Celtyth. We are happy here. Many were not happy that I answered the call of Anghenfyl. I fear we will be ignored you and I. But I will honour my pledge and train you—teach you what you can learn of weaving stone. Then I will take you to Torffan and the Hethwen. Would that I could return you to Penrhyn and your own people, but I cannot pass into that land and I would fear to send you alone."

"How long will I stay? It will take me years to learn magic," Calon asked despairingly.

Cadfan smiled at that. "First you must learn our language. Then knowledge I have accumulated over centuries and skills it has taken me years to develop, I can teach you in a week; but I think two weeks would be better."

"Two weeks! You must be joking," Calon cried. Cadfan chuckled at this. "You are joking. You had me going then."

"I said one week, Calon. I meant one week. I am a dream weaver—for all I know the only one unless Emrys and Cariad live. You will learn very quickly. Rather than explain it, let us wait a day then I will show you." They continued to paddle slowly in the dim, green light; Calon thinking about what lay ahead. "Now when we reach Lellachar, behave as we do. Offer no violence; stay calm and think before speaking. It is well that you will not understand us on the first day so no one can talk to you. Use this time to observe our ways and customs, how we interact, and learn. It will ease your stay." Calon was about to launch into a myriad of questions but Cadfan held up his hand, dropping his paddle onto his lap. "No questions. Learn to listen and think. Absorb what you can in this short stay." He picked his paddle up then and indicated that they should pick up speed. "We are nearly home," Cadfan said, twisting to point with his paddle. "One more bend and we will be at the *glanfa*… the wharf." He smiled then and returned to the task of paddling. To Calon the next few minutes drenched him in dread.

As they paddled, the river curved around to the right. The dull green light that had shown the way was replaced now by a brighter, yellowy light. Moving on, they found themselves in a narrow chamber with a long smooth, stone wharf on their left, but just a smoothed, rock wall on their right. The chamber was only as wide as the river and the wharf, but its height was immense. The walls rose up, meeting at an apex many hundreds of yards up. The wall beyond the wharf was also of worked, smoothed stone, and was completely solid bar a narrow fissure that reached high up into the vaulted ceiling of the cave. It was through this fissure that light flooded, bathing the wharf and river here in a pale light, for all the world like sunshine Calon thought. He helped Cadfan remove the boat from the river, dragging it up a slipway. As Cadfan gathered some items from the bow of the boat, Calon looked up again at the smoothed wall, noticing that higher up, a good thirty yards, the wall ended and huge beams stretched into space, with ropes hanging from them.

"Cranes," Cadfan said from behind him. "Much easier to lift things up than carry them manually up the stairs."

Calon nodded at this, then, "What stairs?"

Cadfan pointed over at the shaft of light that pierced the gloom and sparkled the water. Walking towards it, Calon saw that the fissure was just wide enough to allow only a single file procession, presumably to deter attackers he thought. Added to which, there were no stairs within it, the way up was a steep incline, very steep, leading up the thirty or so yards to the level of the cranes. He put his foot onto it to move up and immediately slipped. "It's that stone!" he exclaimed. "Night-stone." He remembered the effort it took to walk up the waterfall. "We'll never get up there."

"One step at a time Calon, one step at a time," Cadfan told him. "Look carefully at the stone of the slope." Calon did and saw feint lines running across the slope at regular intervals.

"Step-sized intervals," Calon said to himself.

"Indeed," Cadfan answered. "Now watch." He moved to the beginning of the slope and indicated the wall on either side. Calon saw that there were two patches, opposite each other where the rock wall had more sparkly bits. He said as much. "More quartz," Cadfan corrected him, then reached up and placed a hand on each of the quartz patches. He hummed in his own language then. Calon felt the magic as vibrations in his chest and watched with keen interest as steps pivoted up silently and smoothly along the entire length of the slope.

"You will also find that the… slipperiness of the stone is nullified. Once at the top I will return it to its original state." With that he started his way up with Calon shadowing behind.

By the time they reached the top Calon's leg muscles were burning. He paused after the final step, rubbing his aching thigh muscles, moving aside to allow Cadfan room to stand at the top of the flight of stairs and stretch his arms wide again, pressing his hands onto the two 'zones'. Calon watched as the steps eased back into one singular, smooth slope. From this vantage point he could also see that the night stone of the 'stairs' extended to the very edge of the wharf Smiling he pointed at t. "I see what you have done here. Any attackers would slide down that slope, across the wharf and into the water. I'd love to try that." Cadfan turned back towards him.

"I suspect you would have a wonderful time, right up to the point when the *cold-eel* attacks you."

"Oh yeah," Calon said, "I forgot about that. Maybe not then."

"Quite so," said Cadfan and indicated they should move on.

The light now was unbearably intense after so long underground with only glowing moss and magic to illuminate their way. Cadfan saw his discomfort and told him to stand and wait for a few minutes.

"We have been a long time in the dark. This was built in such a way that any who come up can give their eyes time to adjust to the light. You can see that we have another few steps to climb before we are in the full glare. This area is shaded, though I must admit it still seems too bright to bear." Calon, with squinted, teary eyes, gazed around as he became accustomed to the brightness. He could see that there was another level, roughly three yards above this one. A wide, stone stair led up to it, overlooked by a high wall. The stone had all been worked and was wonderfully smooth; the floor was a polished to a glassy sheen.

"Let us move on," Cadfan said heading for the stair. "Best to keep your eyes down at first, so the full glare is less of a shock." Calon followed in his wake, soon cresting the steps. With his eyes fixed down, burning slightly, he hadn't seen Cadfan stop and bumped into his back. The Cawrroc paid him no mind, but sighed contentedly, "I never tire of this sight." Calon glanced to his right and saw a large hall, very large, stretching into the distance, sunlight flooding in from his left. He stepped around the Cawrroc and froze; unable to believe the sight before him. The huge hall was wide, and the walls tapered up to an apex above them. The wall behind had been worked for the first two metres up, after that it was rough stone. The opposite wall however was something else altogether—it was transparent, the whole wall simply a giant window through which the sun burst. Beyond was a panoramic view of a cultivated valley—all green and alive. Calon was stunned.

"This is why we call our home *Lellacher*; in your tongue it means 'bright place'." Calon walked closer to the window wall and stared out across a small valley. To enter this mountain cavern was to become engulfed in warming light. Calon stood awe struck, remembering a time with his mam, holding her hand tightly, as she spoke to one of the river traders—a big, lively woman with ruddy cheeks. She had told his mam of the giant window in the Sarum cathedral—filled with coloured glass that shone magnificently in bright sunshine. The reverence and wonder in her voice as she described it made sense to him now. He moved forward to stand right up against the window-wall. He placed his right and flat onto the surface and found it warm.

Looking out over the vista of the valley, he could make out Cawrroc folk hard at work; tilling the ground, weeding rows of crops, whilst some stood and chatted. Three children were playing in a small waterfall that tumbled over a rock ledge from a stream that wound down the mountain side. He could see how the Cawrrocs had channelled the water at various points to irrigate the crops and thought how such ingenuity would benefit the people of his own village. It all looked so peaceful and so… normal. He breathed out a long sigh. The familiarity of the scene before him made him believe he would feel at home here. He closed his eyes and tilted his face to the sun. After so long underground, the caress of sunlight meant so much; the warming touch as welcome as the sight of daylight.

He heard Cadfan's footsteps moving up behind him to stand at his shoulder. He looked around to find his friend beaming at him.

"We will come back soon," Cadfan promised. "Even wander outside in time. But we still have a way to go, so let us move on." With that the two companions strode across the great cavern. Calon glanced wistfully back for one last glimpse of the outside world, then they were back into a tunnel.

They travelled for some way, the worked stone of the great cavern giving way to altogether rougher terrain, their passing marked by the scattering of loose stones and other debris that Calon's clumsy feet disturbed. Ahead he could now detect the sound of water dripping into water. He was grateful that he could still see in the dark, silently thanking Anghenfyl for licking his eyes, however repulsive he found the thought of that act. He resolved to remember to ask Cadfan about that; would it wear off or would he always be able to see in the dark?

The further they walked, and they'd been going for over half an hour now, Calon found it stranger and stranger that they hadn't met another Cawrroc yet. He was intrigued to see if they were like Cadfan or Anghenfyl. Truth be told he wasn't sure what to expect. He said as much to Cadfan who strode on without stopping for a few seconds before gradually slowing and then finally coming to a halt. 'Thinking time' Calon thought to himself. Cadfan faced him and stretched out a large hand to gently squeeze Calon's shoulder.

"I understand," he said, "we are a mythical people to everyone except you. But think about that Calon. For hundreds of years, we have lived away from other peoples; away from conflict; away from aggression and violence; and away from others trying to use us. Answering Anghenfyl's call was not a popular choice among my people. Having you here will be even less popular, so they will avoid you, us. Do not be alarmed. You are in no danger but accept that you will not be welcomed either. Anghenfyl has bid me train you, teach you our language and return you to your own people and I will honour that."

He paused then, considering his next words carefully. "You are my friend, I think, and I would trust you. I know that those who would harm us and seek to control us, have already done you wrong. If they come here, it is not because of you. Remember that the gwerin Mordwyn had already found a way to rouse Anghenfyl. How long till he comes here? If he could undo the magics that protected Anghenfyl, he could do so here as well. This we must prepare for. I must warn all of my people and we must prepare our defences. This is why I hurry. I must train you and return you to the Marwolleth as quickly as possible so I can add my strength to my people's protection."

"You said that before," Calon responded. "But I won't be able to learn a language in two weeks." Cadfan laughed at that.

"Not two weeks to learn our language Calon. Two weeks to train you in everything and to teach you the history of our peoples. One night to learn our language." He laughed again at Calon's incredulous expression and was about to say more, but Calon spoke first.

"I know, I know," he said grumpily, as he brushed passed the Cawrroc and walked on down the tunnel. "I'll see! I can't wait to see." Cadfan, still chuckling, followed on.

Calon learned many things during the rest of the day. The Cawrrocs ate no meat at all – living off vegetables, fungi and occasional fish they caught, not only outside but also in the underground river. The Cawrroc farmed a huge variety of fungi, mainly in the dark of specially designed caves within the mountain but including one that only grew on south facing walls in the valley called *fysaru*. Cadfan explained this was especially vital to their food supply as it was very high in protein and vitamins. He remembered that Berys had been keen on feeding him mushrooms and surmised it must be a food stuff that all of the Celtyth valued. Like Berys they used no fire—instead they heated stone as she had done to cook or warm food.

Calon also discovered that the Cawrrocs all lived higher up in the mountains than he'd imagined. The 'rooms' he saw all had the transparent rock windows that he'd first seen in the great cavern, with views out across the valley. Cadfan had told him there were even a few such windows on the human side so they could keep watch on the lands the humans occupied. Calon had even walked out onto a ledge outside a window and tried to look in, but any transparency of the rock was undetectable; the whole side of the mountain from outside looked like sheer rock slopes and cliffs, but he knew how light flooded in. All the rooms the Cawrroc used to live in had a view. Deeper into the mountain were the storage and functional rooms. It was in one of these rooms that Calon found himself with Cadfan, ready to begin his training.

Chapter 9
Calon's Training

The room, really a cave that Calon and Cadfan were in, was cool but bearable. Although it had no natural light and was warmed through magic somehow, it felt comfortable and dry. The paved floor and walls were all worked smooth by the Cawrroc stone-weavers and patches of quartz were set into the wall that provided magic light that was as bright as the sunlight in the windowed chambers. The room itself had one large, raised area of stone in it that looked like a large table, although without space beneath to get your feet under. This was the only feature.

"This is where you will sleep, Calon," Cadfan told him.

"But I thought we were going to be training now. There's so much I need to learn. So much…" Calon trailed off, disappointment evident in his demeanour. Infuriatingly, Cadfan grinned the biggest grin Calon had ever seen him grin.

"You will train. You will also learn our language—the language of magic— and you will learn it tonight; in one night." Cadfan paused then, enjoying Calon's open mouthed confusion. "I am a dream-weaver. Not as powerful as Anghenfyl unfortunately, but good enough. You will sleep here tonight, and I will join you in your dreams and train you while you slumber. In just one night I can teach you what it would take weeks to learn if you were to train while you were awake. Time in dreams is a generous friend. Another benefit is that without the many distractions that would steal your concentration during the day; hunger, tiredness, thirst and so on; you will focus sharply on the task to be learned and absorb it so much more quickly."

"So when I wake—" Calon began, but was interrupted.

"You will be proficient in our language and basic stone-weaving skills," Cadfan explained.

"But how? I find dreams so hard to remember, like catching smoke. How will I learn if I can't recall anything?"

"You will learn, Calon, you will remember, and you will wake rested. It will take a few nights of training to really hone your skills." Cadfan paused then before adding, "Few are strong enough to be trained this way, very few. Anghenfyl tested you and insisted that I do this, for he said you are potentially stronger than any Celtyth for many years. Strong enough to dream-weave yourself even. Now help me here," he bade Calon, moving over to the wall opposite the entrance. He pressed his hand against a patch of quartz on the wall and a whole section of it slid down into the floor, a long black line now visible in the flagstones. Behind the wall were a series of large shelves, loaded with various items. Stooping to the bottom shelf, Cadfan hauled out a rolled-up mattress that he handed to Calon, telling him to unroll it on the raised stone base. He then stood and reached up to another shelf to retrieve a couple of blankets.

Having spread the mattress over the stone base, Calon was a little disappointed at how thin it seemed. Cadfan handed him the blankets and Calon was taken aback at how soft they felt. He then watched in fascination as Cadfan moved next to the bed and bent down to place his hand flat on the floor, Calon could see it was inside a black circle. Cadfan dragged his hand a little closer to the bed, pulling the circle that was part of the stone floor with it.

Calon looked on, incredulous. The Cawrroc then simply pulled his hand up from the floor, dragging a column of stone with it that reached to just above his knee. He then turned and sat down on it. Still concentrating, Cadfan then slid both of his hands under the mattress and held them there for a few seconds, before withdrawing them and turning to look at Calon.

"Sit on the bed now," he told him. Calon shuffled over and sat down, gasping aloud, when he sank down into the stone. "Relax," Cadfan told him, "I have softened the stone so that you can lie comfortably. It will mould itself around your body. You may also notice that I have warmed it slightly to help you sleep. Now lie back."

Calon did so, revelling in the warm comfort of the bed. It was the most comfortable he had been in weeks. Cadfan reached over and pulled at Calon's hair, causing Calon to yelp. Cadfan held up a long hair to show him before curling it around one of his fingers, he then rummaged around inside his jerkin finally withdrawing a sharp needle like instrument, very thin but with a wooden handle. He turned his left hand over and lay it down on the bed so that the palm was facing up. Next, he pulled at his sleeve revealing his forearm—this too rested on the bed. Calon saw a few dark swirls he recognised as runes from having seen them on Anghenfyl's tomb. Cadfan used his needle to prick at his skin just below the elbow joint, pressing down lightly and then trying to slide it in. When he succeeded at this Calon could see the needle under the Cawrroc's skin for a second before Cadfan pulled it out. Calon saw that there was no blood leaking from the hole.

"The trick is to just pierce the top layer of skin. Blood would hinder the magic. Now I will thread your hair into my skin and create a rune like these others." Unravelling the hair from his finger, Cadfan lay his bare forearm down again, and held the hair up so that the end trailed on his arm. Humming and muttering in his own language, he moved his right hand around until the end of the hair made contact with the hole and just disappeared inside. Cadfan then clamped his right hand over area where he had inserted the hair and chanted quietly for a few seconds. He stopped and lifted his hand away to show Calon his new rune; it looked like two spears intertwined with the blades at opposite ends. Calon reached out and touched it, running his finger over the skin he could feel it slightly raised.

"Now you must bear the same mark," Cadfan said whilst plucking a hair from his own head. He bade Calon raise his sleeve and lay his arm flat then repeated the whole process on Calon's arm, who was amazed that apart from some pressure when Cadfan made the hole the whole experience was completely pain free. His arm tingled a little when Cadfan clamped his hand over it but other than that he felt nothing. When it was finished Calon looked at his arm and saw an identical rune to Cadfan's. "With one more bit of magic we will be linked as brothers. It is this bond, if it works, that will allow me to train you while you sleep."

"*If* it works," Calon repeated. "That sounds a bit doubtful."

"Because there is uncertainty Calon. Only strong weavers can bond this way. You are still an unknown quantity, but Anghenfyl urged me to try this and he was certain it would prove successful. Now, place your right hand over my rune and I will pace mine over your rune. Grip it tight and do not move it until I have finished the incantation. It will feel odd but endure." When they were both set, Cadfan began to chant. At first Calon felt little, but then a sensation much like the itch of fading nettle stings began on his arm. The sensation grew harder to bear but he swallowed and gritted his teeth. Light began to glow underneath his hand, shining red through the skin where his fingers pressed together.

The sensation increased in intensity now causing Calon to writhe as Cadfan continued to chant until a sudden sharp pain, like the prick of a pin, brought an end to Cadfan's incantation and changed the itching to a pleasant warmth. Cadfan lifted his hand, indicating that Calon should release him. Calon immediately looked at his arm. It looked no different than before. He raised his eyes to look at Cadfan.

"Did it work?" he asked.

"Let us see," Cadfan replied, reaching over to press his finger to Calon's forehead. Calon felt the touch and immediately drifted into a blissful oblivion. "Yes, it worked," Cadfan said aloud to the sleeping Calon. "So let us begin."

Calon was aware that he was standing within his parents' home. A thin veil of acrid smoke filled the room and his senses, ebbing and flowing as though washing towards him. Mam's cook fire was burning in the hearth, but when he held his hands out to it there was no warmth; the beds were made; food was laid out—a loaf and a pot of mam's stew—the floor had been swept, but the whole room had an air of neglect and dereliction. Everything seemed to be in order, yet he didn't feel comfortable here. Or happy to be home.

He sensed movement behind him and turned to see a large man behind him. 'Cadfan,' he thought to himself. He gestured with his arms, indicating the whole room. "This is home, Cadfan, but I don't like it here. Why is it like this?"

"This is the home that you carry with you, Calon. Look," the Cawrroc said pointing to the side. Calon turned and saw a large, full-length mirror. He was puzzled for a second as there shouldn't be a mirror, but soon forgot that when he saw his reflection. Next to the other man in the mirror he was small and thin. His eyes were dark ringed and he looked afraid and tired. He touched his face and the boy in the mirror did the same. Cadfan walked into the reflection standing behind him. Calon looked to his left, but no one stood there. He turned back to the mirror and the other man was there still; older than he, tall, broad and lithe with a confident and challenging stare.

"They are both you, Calon," the Cawrroc told him softly. "One is how you perceive yourself, the other is how I see you." Calon took some time to think about this. "The experiences of your life have shaped how you think of yourself— by all accounts a small, frightened boy. Yet I see a different man. The challenge for me now is to have you see yourself as you truly are."

151

Calon was silent for a while. "Why here?" he asked. "My parents… the people who raised me… they died here. This is the last place I want to be. Why did you bring me here?"

"I did not. Here is where you chose to be, not I. Already I see that you know you must move on from this." Cadfan gripped his shoulders and spun him around so they were facing. He then pressed one finger onto Calon's forehead and began speaking in his own tongue. An endless stream of words the Cawrroc uttered, for what seemed hours. Calon found himself unable to move, just stare at Cadfan's mouth as he spoke, and in time he realised that his own mouth was moving, saying the same things. Intermittently at first but speaking more in time with the Cawrroc as time passed until they reached a point when they not only spoke in perfect harmony, but he understood every word that was said. He felt his excitement growing at his new talent, the room seemed to grow lighter, sunnier until Cadfan withdrew the finger from his forehead and everything stopped.

"Why did you stop?" he demanded. "I was just getting the hang of it."

"Which is why I stopped," Cadfan explained. "You 'had the hang of it' as you said. Why bother to learn something you can already do? If you can speak in the Celtyth tongue, why keep learning it?"

"But that's impossible," an exasperated Calon told him. "You haven't told me a single word. You just started mumbling and I followed along. I haven't learned anything." He stopped as a smiling Cadfan held a hand up. "What's so funny?"

"You speak to me in Celtyth Calon and rage that you cannot speak to me in Celtyth. That is funny. I am a dream weaver. Here I can teach you everything I know: how to speak in Celtyth; how to weave stone; I can heal you and show you how to strengthen your body so that you wake fitter and stronger. And I can teach you all this while you sleep. Here there is no time, we have as long as we need. That probably seemed like hours to you, but it was only a few seconds of your night. Also, a curious circumstance of dream-weave lessons is that anything you learn here you will never forget." Cadfan then touched his index finger to Calon's brow and gave the stunned him a gentle nudge. He toppled slowly backwards, expecting to slam into a hard floor, but simply woke to find himself sitting cross-legged in a cave, with two large rocks in front of him and Cadfan seated opposite.

"Now simply do as I do Calon," the Cawrroc told him and picked up one of the stones; Calon did so as well. "Now hold it and feel it, Calon." Copying

Cadfan, Calon rolled the rock around in his hands. It was night-stone and looked like a giant, dark egg, but he found he could hold it in both hands so that his thumbs and fingers just about touched around the circumference of the widest part. "Now as you hold it, think it warmer. Not so hot that you cannot hold it, just almost too hot to hold." Calon did this, surprised at how easy he was finding it, until he was forced to drop it as it was too hot.

Cadfan cooled the rock for him, simply with one touch, then bade him try again. After a few attempts and restarts, Calon finally mastered the control he needed, and held the hot rock proudly, shuffling it from hand to hand every few seconds. Cadfan expressed his pleasure at Calon's success that told him to watch as he then began shaping his own stone, much as Calon had seen his mam and da shape river clay. Without any urging from Cadfan he stroked and pulled the fabric of the stone, smoothing it and working it. When he had finished his creation, he looked up to see Cadfan had put his worked stone down in front of him; a beautiful smoothed black bowl, as though an egg had been severed in two and the two cupped ends fused together points first so that it stood on the smaller shell and the larger shell formed a deep, narrow bowl.

Calon put his own creation down in front of him: a rounded handle that he could hold in a fist; from the handle a large crescent-moon blade curved out so a fist could sit behind it. Two small straight blades pointed from the ends of the handle. Cadfan picked the weapon up, his face unreadable.

"It is well made, Calon. Hard and very sharp. If you were to weave runes into the blade, its edge would never dull. It is very well made," he said before putting it down.

"Can you show me the runes, Cadfan? I can add them now," Calon asked.

Shaking his head, Cadfan replied, "That is not a thing I would countenance, Calon. Were it a tool for cutting corn or wood, I might. But something designed to kill... I will not." Cadfan looked at him then. "I do not judge you or your path, Calon, but it is not mine. As I have told you, we Cawrrocs are a peaceful people. I think the rest of tonight we should focus on you learning more about our ways."

Picking up his weapon, Calon heated the stone and worked it again, this time into a bowl similar to Cadfan's, though not as elegant or pleasing to the eye. Cadfan nodded at his work, when he put it down next to the Cawrroc's bowl, and Calon sensed an approval at his decision to rework the weapon into something useful. An approval, he decided, that he cherished.

With Cadfan's guidance Calon learned how to choose stones to warm enough to cook food on; how to smooth rock; how to climb sheer walls by gripping the rock as though it were soft clay. He also spent time showing Calon foods he could eat in the wild; fungi, roots, berries and wild herbs and vegetables. By the time Cadfan finally told him to lie down, it seemed to Calon that they had been working on his talent for days.

Calon woke and stretched lazily, feeling relaxed and warm. He swung his feet out of the stone bed and sat up rubbing his eyes. He stood and reached his arms high, enjoying the cracks from his spine. He felt fantastic. Rested and ready for action. He looked around and saw that he was alone in the cave room. Thinking of Cadfan stirred memories of his dreams. He remembered Cadfan teaching him things, but only in odd snippets. He then recalled the Cawrroc saying that what he learned in a dream weave, he would never forget. 'Well,' he thought, 'I doubt that; I can't remember anything useful'. Hi musings on the night's activities were interrupted when Cadfan bustled into his room carrying a large flat stone and a hessian bag filled with something.

"Let us sort the room, Calon," he ordered. "Roll up the bedding and the mattress." He put the stone he was carrying on the bed base and gently lay the hessian sack next to it. He helped Calon roll the mattress and bedding together and return it to its storage. "Now young Calon, let's see what you can do." He pointed at the stone. "Heat that so we can cook on it. Place your hand flat on the surface and just… heat it."

Calon did as he was bid; placing his right palm flat on the stone he muttered, "*Cynhesu.*" The second that he uttered the word, he felt the surface warming. It had taken so little effort. His head whipped around to look at Cadfan, who smiled down on him.

"Magic is all a question of belief and certainty Calon. You knew you could do it, so it worked. Now raise your hand off the surface so you are not in contact with it but you can feel the warmth." Calon followed the instruction eagerly, lifting his hand about an inch of the stone. "Now, when it becomes too hot to keep your hand there, I think we will be ready." This took only a few more seconds and Calon jerked his hand up away from the heat. He immediately put it down flat on the cool bed-base and muttered, "*Oeri,* " to instantly cool his hand. "How did I know to do that?" he asked. Looking at the grinning Cawrroc. "I didn't remember that. I didn't think about doing it. I just did it. I knew what to do."

"Dream-weaving is a wonderful way to learn. Few have strong enough magic to develop their skills this way. You do. It seems Anghenfyl was right about you." Calon smiled at this, feeling his chest puff up with pride. "You probably recall very little of your night, but it is as I said to you—things you learn in the dream-weave you will not forget. You will find you just know how to do things." With that he emptied the hessian sack on to the bed base. A variety of vegetables and herbs tumbled out. Calon recognised mushrooms, leeks and onions as well as a sprig of thyme. There were a couple of things that he wasn't familiar with, but before he could ask, Cadfan was pushing him out of the room, along the corridor, towards an open doorway, through which Calon could hear the tumbling splash of water. Cadfan turned and walked through the doorway into a small chamber. Calon followed and was surprised at what greeted him.

"An indoor waterfall!" he exclaimed. The cave-room was relatively small and had a stone bench along the wall to his left, on which four, large wicker baskets stood. Directly in front of him was a smoothed wall with a round hole in it. This hole was lined with black night stone and was the source of a relatively strong draft blowing into the room. To his right, the fall itself fell over the lip of a large piece of night-stone that protruded from the wall probably eight feet up so that the water fell into the middle a depression in the stone floor. This seemed to prevent the water from flooding the room as it obviously sloped back towards the wall where it sluiced away down a hole in the corner of the room. To the side of the waterfall, about four feet up, a square of night-stone nearly a foot square was inset into the wall. From this a seam of the same stone ran up and connected with the great lintel, which was easily twelve inches wide, and over which the water flowed in a steady cascade. Cadfan told Calon to hold his hand in the flow of water. It was icy cold. He jerked his hand back.

Laughing he said, "Indeed. Some like it cold. Find it refreshing. But if you want it warmed, simply use your newfound skills and warm it." He pointed at the square of night-stone. Calon walked over and placed his hand on the black, speckled stone and heated it. He saw steam rising from the water and the basin where it landed. Cadfan continued, "It will cool gradually but you can easily add more warmth. Also," he added crouching down to place his hand on the floor, "for those who are modest…" He touched his fingers to another seam of night-stone that Calon hadn't noticed and raised a great sheet of stone up as high as he could reach, sealing off half of the room. He lowered it again so he could see Calon's face. "And throw your clothes over here. They need washing more than you do." Cadfan then walked over to the back wall, Calon could see his head retreating, where he stopped before coming back to Calon. He handed one of the wicker baskets over the modesty wall and explained that the contents could be used to scrub his skin with. Calon looked inside and saw the basket held many clips of what looked like moss but smelled of rosemary and something citrusy. He thanked Cadfan and began removing his clothes.

"Where are my knives and pouches," he suddenly blurted out, realising for the first time that he didn't have them. Everything had happened so quickly.

"We don't have weapons here Calon. I will return everything to you when we leave. Place your clothes on the stone bench at the back and I will see that they are washed and cleaned. I will leave you something else to wear in the meantime. Enjoy cleaning yourself." With that he turned and left. Calon placed his hands on the modesty-wall and found he could easily raise and lower it. He lifted it to his full reach and stripped off. He was immediately shocked by how dirty his hands were in comparison to the rest of his skin. Wrapping his clothes into a tight bundle, he hurled them over the modesty-wall and stepped into the water. It was only just warm, but it was blissful. He reached his hand across to the night-stone square and heated it. He found it much better to do this whilst under the water as he could get the temperature exactly right. He scrubbed himself with the fragrant moss, finding it slightly and pleasantly abrasive. It also left his skin tingling and wonderfully clean. He wasn't quite sure how to wash his hair thoroughly. The moss was not much help as his hair was shoulder length now, so his resorted to simply standing with his head in the rush of water and massaging his hands through it. It dawned on him then that as Cadfan had short hair, more like fur, that the other Cawrrocs must be the same so the moss was probably enough to wash their hair.

Stepping out from under the warmed water, the cold draft through the hole in the wall immediately bit into him. He looked at the hole to see if there was some way to cover it, but he couldn't see anything. Neither did he have a towel, so he had no way of drying himself other than waiting, until something occurred to him. He walked over to the hole, shivering in the chill blast of air and inspected it more closely. The hole was lined with night-stone for as far as he could see down, which was a few yards, so he simply placed a hand on either side of the hole and heated it. The air immediately warmed pleasurably.

Calon kept heating the stone until the air was warm enough to dry him almost immediately. He bent his head towards the hole and dried his hair. He thought to himself what a wonderful system this was and how his ma would have loved it. That last thought also, he realised, was about the first time he had thought of his mam without a lump appearing in his throat. He actually smiled at the thought of his mam washing here, remembering how she loved being clean. With that on his mind, he reached up and lowered the modesty wall so he could see over it. He just caught a glimpse of a swish of a plaid skirt and a moccasined foot shooting out of the door.

A hand then returned into the room and pulled at the door frame, drawing a sheet of rock across and sealing him in. Somewhat shocked, he looked around the room and saw that a neatly pile of folded clothes had been left on the stone bench and his clothes had disappeared. New moccasins had also been left.

Calon dressed in the clothes he had been left: soft buckskin trousers and a dark plum shirt of soft cotton and sat down to tie the moccasins to his feet. He lowered the sheet of stone that blocked the doorway to the wet room and retraced his steps back to the room where he had slept the previous night. There he found more food laid out next to the night-stone that he had used to cook with the night before. Unsure whether to eat or not, he sat down without eating to wait for Cadfan. He used this time to try and assess all that was happening and found he was still resolved to returning the place of his birth, Penrhyn, and meeting with his people the Marwolleth.

"You look and smell much better." Cadfan's voice startled Calon awake. "You look like a Celtyth now. Our clothes are suited to you."

"Yes, I like them," Calon responded. "This leather," he indicated his new trousers and moccasins, "is so soft. But I thought your people only ate vegetables. So how can you make leather?"

Cadfan pondered his answer before speaking. "We Cawrrocs for the most part do not kill warm blooded animals for food. The leather we collect is gathered from the creatures who die natural deaths, though many Cawrroc prefer not to use it at all. The Celtyth traditionally live in harmony with the land. We don't farm animals for milk or meat as we don't believe in holding creatures captive. Yet we do milk the goats that roam our lands. Some also fish and hunt for meat to supplement our diet. But these actions are part of a natural order and all of the animal that is slaughtered is used. It is viewed as a sacrifice. As far as I know the Hethwen still hold to these ways. The Gwerin do not and slaughter many creatures wantonly. The Marwolleth… as no one can enter their lands and they have not been seen for many, many years, I cannot tell you whether they hold with these traditions, but I hope so."

"If no one has seen them for so long, how did my mother get away and carry me to the human lands?"

"Now that is a question," Cadfan replied smiling. "And I think this is part of the answer." He held out his hand and revealed the *canllaw* his mam had left for him. "This tells us how she left—there magic held within would counteract the powerful charms in the Eiran Mountains. Though it does not tell us why she left her home. I hope you can find the answer when you get to Penrhyn."

Whilst that sat and ate their evening meal, Cadfan, in response to Calon's questions, told him more about the Celtyth peoples.

"When we made the decision to move here, we sealed ourselves off from the Gwerin completely. We work diligently to maintain an awareness of where they are delving and mining so that we can deflect any attempt to break through into *Lellacher*. We do this subtly. I and a few others worked hard to shield our mountain with void-stone and strong enchantments, turning back any who ventured too close so that they were too gripped with fear to ever retrace their steps or be able to tell others why they felt that way. This Mordwyn is different. Him we will have trouble with I suspect. We Cawrrocs are strong in stone-weaving, whereas the Gwerin have mostly lost their magic bar warming night-stone and creating light. We know they have not forgotten the *cildraeth*, a way of pooling magic to increase power, but they are still limited with its use.

"Yet Mordwyn it seems is unique in that he had more magic than was usual for a gwerin, and then this was greatly enhanced when he discovered that amulet which he used to enslave Anghenfyl; an artefact that enriched his power considerably. Now that we have taken it back, his power is not what it was, but remember, he made his way into Anghenfyl's tomb chamber, freed him from near death and bent him to his will. I fear we have not heard the last of that one." Cadfan paused then to eat a little more. Calon took his opportunity to reveal something that had been troubling him.

"Cadfan, why have I not met any other Cawrrocs?" he asked suddenly.

Cadfan offered his usual response, "Ah. Now that is a question."

"Well why?" Calon asked. "This place is all but deserted. I have seen some of your people outside at a great distance; one person took my clothes but all I saw of them was a skirt and a foot. Why?" Cadfan did his usual thing and smiled and thought for a while before answering.

"As I told you, they would be wary and uncomfortable around any strangers, but with you this is more. They know you are Marwolleth and mistrust you for that reason, but more than that, they can sense your violence, Calon; it burns from within you; the magic you have they see as tainted because you have killed in anger. It is this anger they fear."

"But you don't fear me," Calon stated.

Cadfan paused again before speaking. "I accept you, Calon, as the sum total of your experiences. I do not judge you, but that is not the same as not fearing you. My promise to Anghenfyl binds me. You should know that it was not a promise freely given, but the task I first resented I have now grown to treasure. I hope that what I teach you will help you see that confrontation, aggression and conflict are not the only ways to deal with those who would do you wrong. Above all else Calon, I like you."

Calon was a little taken aback by all of this and was, for once, stuck for words. He knew Cadfan would be staring at him, so he decided the best tack was to change the subject. "What are we doing today then?" he asked.

Cadfan smiled at him. "Now, that is a question," he said before laughing deeply at his own jest. "In these waking hours I thought I would teach you more control of your 'cloaking'. We could do this easily in one night, but sometimes failing is as valuable a lesson as succeeding. So, we will try and fail us two, that we may both become better. You more able to cloak and me more able to teach another. Also, as I have said, I enjoy your company."

There followed for Calon an almost continuous series of lessons and training in everything Cadfan knew. Most of his waking hours were filled with preparing him for his journey into Hethwen lands and then alone into Penrhyn. This day's training was focused on his ability to effectively cloak himself, which was instructive for them both. Cadfan showed him how to use shadow and disguise to hide himself among stone and rocks. He instructed him how to cloak himself using a 'rock skin' to protect himself so that weapons could not pierce or penetrate him. Cadfan was little help however, with wood-weaving. Calon was, as always, desperate to know more, desperate to improve, but as Cadfan told him, he would have to wait to spend time with the Hethwen or Marwolleth to truly understand this magic. He was instructed how to maintain a full body cloaking to increase stamina and speed, and likewise how to isolate parts of his body like his eyes so he could see in the dark. Most of this Calon could manage only sporadically at first until Cadfan embedded a strand of hair from the *llinach* that Berys had given him into both of his palms. This meant he could press his fingers against the hair and achieve cloaking instantly.

"This is quite a gift," Cadfan told him of the llinach. "This Berys was a strong weaver and I imagine not the only one among whatever of the Marwolleth remain. I suspect that this is their usual custom and she hoped once you'd made your way there that they would instruct you as I am." Calon still found it hard to think of Berys but for once felt a warm glow as well. This was followed by a surge of anger at those who had harmed her, something Cadfan noticed.

"That rage," he told Calon gently wrapping his hand over Calon's forearm, "is an emotion we are not used to here. It is a fierceness I know not how to help you with." Calon swallowed his anger as Cadfan looked on, concerned, before they resumed their training on merging and moulding rock; a weaving skill Calon usually found hard to maintain the focus for. Today was different. His hands simply entered the rock face as though it was water. Cadfan watched on, amazed.

"Step into the rock, Calon, but go in backwards and keep your face free lest you suffocate." Calon followed the instruction and eased his body into the wall as though he was stepping through a waterfall and then back out again. Cadfan then explained that there was great danger in this as if he lost focus, his body would be crushed instantly.

"Anger, it seems, is a good fuel for your magic," Cadfan told him. "Stepping through walls is its only real benefit, Calon. Would that Anghenfyl were here to instruct you. His mastery of this was beyond my understanding." Following a few days of this, Cadfan spent an entire dream-weave going over the skills to really instil them into Calon.

By day Cadfan prepared Calon for his journey; lessons on survival and feeding himself in the wild, which included skills such as cooking on heated stones; knowledge about foods such as edible roots and herbs; how to find water and the ingredients to create a broth that would sustain him on his travels when other foods would be hard to source. The broth, Cadfan called it *cawl,* was made from water and the dried orange mushrooms the Cawrrocs cultivated.

"*Chicken-of-the-woods*," Calon stated on seeing the vast rows of mushrooms growing vertically along a damp wall. "They look the same colour, only these are growing vertically."

"Ah yes," Cadfan replied. "I have heard of these *chicken-of-the-woods*. They are very similar I think; we call these, *ear-of-the-mountain,* for obvious reasons." Calon had to agree that they did indeed look like ears, big orangey ears. "We usually eat these cooked, but they can be dried to provide sustenance for those who need to carry their own food. They can be eaten when dried but are best added to water to make a broth with whatever else you can find, I like wild garlic, it provides energy and has restorative properties for the weary." He looked at Calon then and said, "I will provide you with a good supply, fear not."

After two more days of learning and practicing, followed by two more nights of relentless but refreshing dream training, Cadfan announced that they would be leaving Lellacher the following morning. "We will spend this afternoon provisioning you for your journey; tonight I will show you the healing arts and if you wish it, the weaving of a *craith*. But this morning, I have a test for you. I would see if you can do something that I, or indeed any Hethwen, Cawrroc or Gwerin cannot do. Follow," he said and set off down the tunnel that led back to the great chamber with the see-through wall.

They journeyed back to the underground river, walking along the bank side wharf, almost to its end, where a small flight of steps led down to the water. There Cadfan stopped and pointed across the river to the far side. Calon saw an opening in the opposite wall that was obviously a worked tunnel. "We must cross," Cadfan told him, "and we can cross as I showed you." With that Cadfan cloaked his hand and eased it into the rock wall before dragging his hand down, slicing off a section of stone nearly three feet long and two feet wide. Calon did the same. The two companions spoke the words of power and Calon immediately felt the stone section become almost weightless. Without any direction or instruction from Cadfan, he walked down the steps to the river, placed his stone shard on the water and simply willed himself across, the stone floating easily and sliding quickly across the water to the open tunnel on the other side. The water only flowed into the beginning of the tunnel as the floor had been worked at a gradient. Calon's shard hit firm ground and he jumped off, keeping his feet dry, before bending and lifting his shard and propping it against the tunnel wall. He watched as Cadfan swept over the river, grinning as the Cawrroc got his feet wet dismounting.

"You should have jumped, Cadfan," he teased him.

The grumpy Cawrroc retorted, "When you are over seven hundred years old, see how well you can jump." But there was no anger in it. He rather enjoyed Calon's boyish delight with his newfound abilities.

The pair, eyes cloaked to see into the darkness, moved down the tunnel which proved to be only to be twenty or so yards long. The walls were a combination of smoothed stone and rough natural rock. The rough, unworked patches were all similar; large patches of dark, grey stone, all angular and crystalline that glistened and shimmered. At the end of the tunnel, this strange rock was more evident. Lumps had been left strewn on the cave floor amongst the other debris. Cadfan bent and picked up one of these lumps; a piece of quartz rich stone. Holding it firmly in his now cloaked hand he bade Calon watch as he squeezed the rock and worked it into a perfectly round sphere, holding it up for Calon to see.

Cadfan nodded, again enjoying Calon's pleasure in his control of the magic. "Now Calon, fetch me some of the magnetite there," he pointed at a piece of the dark, shimmering stone. Calon fetched a fist sized lump of the stone and held it out for Cadfan who stood, eyebrows raised.

"What?" Calon responded to Cadfan's quizzical expression. "It's just a lump of rock.

What's so amazing about me picking it up?"

"Place it in my hand Calon." Calon did so and watched Cadfan's expression change immediately to one of intense concentration, almost distress, as he squeezed the stone.

"Why have you uncloaked your hand Cadfan? You can't think to work the stone with your bare hand surely?" he asked.

Cadfan dropped the stone to the floor and immediately seemed to recover himself. "I did not willingly drop my cloaking Calon, the stone removed it. This stone, magnetite, is what humans use to make iron. Iron is resistant to nearly all magic. It is why the humans bind their Celtyth captives in iron chains. Did you feel nothing when you picked it up?"

Calon looked at the rock that Cadfan had just dropped and bent to pick it up again. Looking Cadfan in the eyes he cloaked his hand in stone as easily as he had to handle and weave ordinary rock or wood. He heard the Cawrroc's sharp intake of breath. He then proceeded to heat the stone, using both hands to work it into a perfect sphere. He held the finished object up and showed Cadfan the magnetite transformed. The sphere, on its outside at least, was a smooth orb of iron. Cadfan was astounded.

"To my knowledge there is only one Celtyth who has ever been able to work iron-ore, the Marwolleth who I hope to send you to in Penrhyn. I suspect now that he is blood kin to you." the Cawrroc told him solemnly.

"Blood kin? You mean family? Berys told me I have family. Who is it?" The questions rattled out of a stunned Calon.

"Family I suspect. His name is Gerallt. He too is a powerful dream-weaver if he still lives. He was one of those who led the Marwolleth when they broke from the Hethwen. I know little else other than rumours that he could work iron. But as none but Marwolleth can enter their lands, we do not know for certain who is there, if indeed anybody at all. Now save your questions. I have much to think on." With that he turned to leave but shouted over his shoulder, "And leave that iron here." Calon looked at the sphere in his hand before dropping it to the floor and hurrying to catch up with his mentor.

Chapter 10
Torffan

Other than a few minutes on a mountain ledge overlooking the valley of the Cawrrocs, with Lellacher looming over him, Calon had been underground for at least a month by his own reckoning. Emerging into the spreading dawn, his first genuine foray outside in weeks, Calon was immediately cowed by the open expanse of sky. After so long with a mountain over his head he felt crushed by the weight of emptiness. The two stood on the side of a mountain with the Hethwen lands stretched before them; a living landscape of green trees broken by mountains and hills and the long, blue rope of a river lazily snaking across the land. The two made their way slowly down the mountain and into a steep sided valley, Cadfan leading the way. The Cawrroc seemed nervous and Calon asked what was troubling him. Cadfan had chuckled at the question.

"I have lived for centuries underground. This is only the seventh time in my life that I have been outside. I like it not." He waved his arms up at the sky. "There is too much… it is hard not to feel so small when there is nothing above you. I like stone. I love stone. Here I am… lost. But I will see you through the mountains and set you on your way. I'd hoped to arrive in the dark. I like the dark. I can't see how big nothing is." With that he continued down the narrow path, heading for the valley floor.

Once at the foot of the mountain, Calon followed the Cawrroc, who stuck to the shadows, along a narrow ledge that clung to the side of a large rock face. They walked along this for a good half an hour before Calon realised they were going up and away from their destination.

"We're heading away Cadfan," he told the Cawrroc. "We're going up not down."

Without pausing Cadfan called back over his shoulder,

"It will be quicker for you and easier for me if we go *through* the mountain. The valley floor is hard walking. Inside, we can move freely." They kept on for a few minutes more before Cadfan stopped abruptly at a rock face. Pulling Calon close he told him to cloak his eyes; Calon did so and the scene in front of changed immediately. What before had been an ordinary looking cliff face, now had a clear black, rectangular line displayed in it, tall enough and wide enough to fit a Cawrroc through it easily. Very similar he realised to the 'door' that he had found when he was with Berys.

"A door," Calon exclaimed. "How do we open it?"

This brought a deep chuckle from Cadfan. "You can't open a mountain Calon," he replied, stepping up to the 'doorway' and simply passing through it. Calon immediately followed, confident in his ability to do so. Once through the wall Calon found himself in a tunnel that bored through the mountain, exactly the same dimensions as the 'doorway'.

"There are many such secret entrances as these," Cadfan explained. "The wall is left perhaps a yard or so thick to form a way through that most stone weavers could find and use. The tunnels that link them cut straight through and make travel so much easier and quicker. It would take the best part of a day to walk around this mountain to the River Rhew, in here it will take us a couple of hours at most."

The going, Calon had to admit, was certainly much easier. After an initial uphill walk, they moved predominantly downhill. The walls and path had been worked smooth so there was nothing to think about other than walking. Cloaking his eyes to see in the lightless environment was also second nature now. He tried a few times to engage Cadfan in conversation, but he could sense the Cawrroc's discomfort at being so far from Lellacher so gave up. His own mood had darkened on this leg of the journey and with time to think, he had figured that suddenly being outside again had made him realise how much he had missed the forests and hills of his home.

Still in what actually seemed a short time, Cadfan stopped at another door, the outline on the inside of the mountain showing silver, so they had booth been aware of it for some time. Passing through the two companions emerged into the Hethwen lands of Torffan. They stood on a shelf of rock approximately ten yards long and only a couple of yards wide. To Calon it seemed they stood on the edge of a great precipice as there was no obvious way down and peering over the edge, he could see it was at least a fifteen yard drop onto rough, rocky terrain.

"I expect you have a clever piece of magic to get us down," Calon said to Cadfan who smiled knowingly and headed to the left most edge of the shelf on which they stood. Here Calon could see a channel running down through the rock.

"There are two options here." Cadfan told him. "Firstly, you could climb down using this channel for grip and purchase, or you could simply jump," he said jamming his right foot and his cloaked right hand into the channel as he began climbing down. As he moved steadily down, he called up to Calon, "It is night-stone. There are spurs to grip in to." And with that he was at the bottom. Calon followed his example and found the climb easy. Cloaking his hands meant he could force his fingers into the night-stone, so he felt very safe. He jumped the last couple of feet and turned to look at the path that led finally into Torffan.

Seeing the trail ahead, Calon set off, keen to get amongst the trees and have something overhead. He'd moved over fifty yards ahead before he realised that he was on his own. He turned back to see where Cadfan was. The Cawrroc still stood where they had climbed down from the mountain, his face tilted to the sky.

"Cadfan," Calon called, the echo adding an urgency to the call he hadn't meant. The Cawrroc looked down at him. The Cawrroc raised his hand, indicating stop, then put his finger to his lips, before beckoning him back. Calon loped back up the path, muttering impatiently to himself.

"I think we should wait Calon," the Cawrroc told him softly, his voice almost a whisper. Calon looked back at his friend and mentor and detected an air of tension coming from him—the Cawrroc was gathering his magic. Calon quickly made his way next to Cadfan, the Cawrroc's edginess had made him slightly nervous as well. Once he was at Cadfan's side, he tried to discern what the problem was. He saw nothing untoward; he could hear the babbling of a nearby brook hurrying down the mountain side but apart from that it was silent. As far as Calon could see the Cawrroc was being overly cautious and put it down to his unfamiliarity of the outside world.

"Look," he explained to Cadfan. "It's exactly as I'd expect. It's quiet because no one lives near here. This is how it is outside." He gestured expansively towards the valley and the world beyond with his arms.

Cadfan looked at him. "I understand that. It is, as you say, what we expected… bar one thing. What can you smell Calon?"

Calon sniffed the air. "Wood smoke," he stated. "But that's what I'd expect to smell. There must be people living nearby."

166

The Cawrroc, still worryingly serious, shook his head. "Think, young Calon. We are in Torffan, the land of the Hethwen people. Think. Tell me why I am worried?"

Calon was bemused at first before suddenly realising. "Fire. They don't use fire. So there shouldn't be any smoke." He was pleased with this deduction, but Cadfan urged him to follow that train of thought. It took another minute for Calon to suddenly realise. "Humans!" he blurted. "There are humans on this side of the mountain. But you said that wasn't possible."

"Now you understand my caution." Cadfan said seriously. "I think we should stick to our plan; I would know what happens here. But let us proceed with care." Cadfan had explained to Calon that they would find the Rhew, a tributary that fed into the River Tawe and follow this river south to Crowmere—the great lake that sat more or less in the middle of Hethwen lands where most of the people spent their time. Calon had agreed this was the best plan; meet with the Hethwen first to learn more of wood weaving and discover what they knew of the Marwolleth before setting off for Penrhyn.

The two companions continued down the steep mountain valley until they came to another cutting across it. This too was quite steep and had a stream cascading down it. At its widest point it was probably a good twenty yards across, and the water rushed quickly downwards, gurgling and splashing. Calon found the sound oddly reassuring. Stopping only once to drink, the pair made good speed, meeting the confluence of the Rhew and the Tawe in less than an hour, the smaller stream throwing itself over a twenty-foot drop to join the Tawe on its journey south. Calon stopped to admire the majesty of the water fall too long for Cadfan's liking; the Cawrroc eventually resorted to pulling him away.

Cadfan insisted they reach the river valley before night fall as there would be little shelter in the valleys and reminded Calon he was anxious to see him build a shelter for them. Through a dream-weave Calon had shown a fascinated Cadfan how Berys had woven the wood of trees into an airtight, rainproof shelter; a skill he had practised repetitively at the Cawrroc's insistence until he had mastered it, arguing such a skill could be vital to Calon's or their survival.

The Tawe was wider, deeper and slower flowing than the Rhew, though it still rushed through the forest with trees packed densely on either side making the travelling difficult. Near the waterfall a space had been cleared on the bank they were on, a boat with a hole smashed into the hull lay half in and half out of the water. Calon pointed out they could easily repair the hole with their combined crafts and broached the possibility of floating down the river to the lake. Cadfan had dismissed this immediately by pointing out that if there were human attackers in the Hethwen lands, they would be easily seen and targeted if they were in a boat, especially further down where the river widened and slowed, with no means of escape. "Far better we stay concealed until we know what, if any, danger there is," he had reasoned. Calon accepted this as sensible but still grumbled along through the densely packed trees.

By midday the trees had begun to thin and the gentle right meander of the river ahead showed a clearing lay ahead where another tributary joined the river. The two travellers stopped abruptly at the same time. Now their way ahead was clearer, both could see a pall of smoke rising from somewhere near to the clearing. Cadfan urged more caution and the two companions eased deeper into the tress away from the riverbank. Slowly now, painfully slowly, the two eased towards the site of the smoke. A shift in the wind carried the bitter tang of wood smoke along with an underlying scent, sweeter but sickening.

Calon could tell by the change in light that they were nearly at the end of the trees and could hear the water of the small tributary chuckling down to the Tawe. He stayed behind Cadfan now, apprehensive at what lay before them, but taking comfort from the Cawrrocs presence. Cadfan eased down behind the sweeping branches of a white willow, its leaves brushing the ground providing a dark shelter. Across the stream, which was fast flowing but only a few yards wide, Calon could see smouldering fires, the sight taking him cruelly back to his parents' home burning as he'd buried them. Cadfan's huge hand gently squeezed his shoulder, the Cawrroc sensing his discomfort. Easing further forward, but still under cover of the tree, the two saw more that caused them greater concern.

A Hethwen child, a young girl by the look of the colourful dress, lay dead on the opposite bank but a few yards from where they crouched, her head sagging down into the river so that her dark hair swayed in the water. A large arrow with black fletching had pierced the back of her skull and as her head bobbed in the flowing stream, the arrow danced in the air. The horror of what he was seeing abruptly faded to be replaced by a deep burning anger. He had to get her out of the water. Only Cadfan's iron grip stopped him.

Calon tore his gaze from the Hethwen girl and looked up noticing Cadfan's other hand pointing across the stream. Two Chancel men had appeared carrying a corpse between them, an older woman this time, naked. The two humans were struggling and cursing as they laboured along. The man travelling backwards carrying the woman's arms, stumbled and fell onto his backside. The other laughed and said something Calon couldn't hear. The fallen man cursed and regained his feet, giving the dead Hethwen a kick. He hauled her arms up and they carried her over to the fire, swinging her back and forward three or four times to build up some momentum before letting her go, the body landing more or less in the centre of the blaze sending a shower of sparks into the air amid a cloud of smoke. The two men congratulated each other then turned towards the Hethwen girl with her head in the stream.

As they walked over, the shorter of the two men grabbed his crotch and made a comment that made the taller man guffaw. Calon watched them. Both men were dressed in grey leggings and a black tunic. Both wore calf length black boots and a black belt with a scabbard and sword on their right hip, a sheathed knife at their left. They reached the dead girl and the short one grabbed her legs and hauled her out of the water. The taller man bent and pressed one foot to the girl's head then took hold of the arrow with his hands and yanked it out of her skull with a squelch and scrape of bone. Cadfan's gasp carried across to the two Chancel men who immediately drew their swords and surged into stream, the water swirling around their thighs.

"Hide yourself!" Cadfan whispered urgently, then, "Cloak yourself!" as Calon had stood unresponsive as the men lurched out of the water. Calon focused and felt the tingle of his body cloaking to merge with the willow branches.

The two men burst through the branches immediately next to where Calon waited and stood under the canopy of the great tree, swords pointed at the Cawrroc who simply stood and stared.

"What the fuck are you?" exclaimed the shorter man.

"Giant or troll," the taller man said, nervously licking his lips. Calon was so used to the Cawrroc he never really thought of him as tall, but he was a good foot taller than the men and considerably broader. The shorter man lunged suddenly with his sword before dancing back. Cadfan never moved.

"Whatever he is, he ain't got no fight," shorty said. "Same as the rest. We could take this one," he added lunging his sword forward again.

Fearful for his friend, Calon gathered his magic as the two men moved either side of Cadfan and started prodding him with their swords, moving to the stream. As the Cawrroc stepped into the water and the two men reached the tailing branches of the willow, Calon acted. Within seconds the branches, whipcord quick, had snaked around both Chancel men and pulled tight. Almost completely wrapped in branches now, the two men fell; Shorty pitched backwards but the taller man plunged forward before both were halted by the branches that bound them.

Using his magic, Calon had both men hefted upright, their feet a good yard off the floor. Cadfan moved back into the shelter of the willow with the Hethwen girl cradled in his arms. Both captive men began shouting and cursing at him, something Calon stopped by quickly feeding a branch into their mouths to gag them. They watched the Cawrroc lay the girl gently onto the ground and place his hands on her, before saying the words that would return her essence to the earth. The men watched in horror as the girl's corpse shrank and flowed back into ground leaving nothing but dust and brittle bones behind in a ruined dress. The two men immediately intensified their struggle and squirmed to release their bindings, but a tightening of a branch around each man's throat soon stilled them.

The two still had eyes fixed solely on Cadfan, who met their gaze unblinkingly before motioning with his left hand to Calon and telling him in the Celtyth tongue to slowly reveal himself. Calon stepped out of the branches, causing them to ruffle. Both captives' eyebrows raised and their eyes widened in alarm as Calon solely uncloaked himself and both began mewling in fear as he bent to pick up one of the discarded swords, running his fingers slowly up and down the iron blade.

"Calon," Cadfan warned, "no killing." Calon looked at the Cawrroc as did the two men, unaware of what had been said, but aware it was about them. Calon picked up the second sword and held both by the tips of the blades in one hand. Then cloaking his hands, he began to heat the metal, the iron glowing in seconds, before he suddenly twisted both blades together into one knotted, bent mass. He threw this knotted iron into the water where it disappeared with a hiss. He then took both men's knives and stretched their blades long and thin before wrapping each one around it's owner's neck with a sizzle of scorched skin before cooling the metal leaving them with a metal collar and the handle of a knife wedged under their chins. He then released them from the branches, both men falling to the ground and cowering. Cadfan looked at Calon, astonished.

"I suppose that is as good a solution as any," he told Calon before adding, "We must leave. There will be more. We head north now, I think there is too much danger this way." Calon nodded his acceptance of Cadfan's reasoning and turned after the departing Cawrroc.

The sound of the two terrified Chancel men ploughing through the water of the stream in the opposite direction accompanied him as he followed, raising a smile to his lips.

As they retreated from the death and burning, Cadfan told Calon that he had abandoned the idea of contacting the Hethwen, deciding instead to send Calon into Penrhyn to contact the Marwolleth.

"It is simply too dangerous here now. Even if you are able to evade capture, I see little that can be gained here. If the humans have invaded, I fear they will not leave and we Celtyth would never force them out. The Hethwen I think will do as we Cawrrocs have done and hide themselves away in the most unreachable or inhospitable places. Penrhyn is inaccessible to all except the Marwolleth. Perhaps peace could be made…," his voice trailed away and the Cawrroc stopped to look squarely at Calon. "You must tell them what is happening here. Urge them to let the Hethwen through into Penrhyn."

Calon nodded at this counsel but saw a problem. "Didn't you say you aren't sure if there are any of the Marwolleth left?"

Cadfan thought on this. "Yes, I did. But you are here, so they were in Penrhyn a few years ago. We must hope. You have the *canllaw*. Why keep it for you if there was no one to go back to? If they're not there, then you must do what you can to get the Hethwen through the wards that protect Penrhyn. There may be something there you could use. We must hope." He turned then at the sudden baying of hounds on the trail behind them. "Hope Calon, is a heavy burden but carry it we must." With that he turned and strode on.

By the time they had travelled far enough back upriver to where the Rhew crashed together with the Tawe at the waterfall, the baying of hounds was closer.

"Here we must part ways Calon," Cadfan told him. "I can be of no help to you from here and the Marwolleth ways are not something I condone. Remember that peace is a hard road Calon but the outcome is worth the journey." He reached out both of his huge hands and grasped Calon's shoulders. "You are a fine young Celtyth and I am glad you have helped me see the world again. Now, follow the Tawe up into the mountains. Look to the north, you will see a large mountain, Kirrid Fawr, taller than the rest. Head through the valley that leads northwest, and head back north through the forest. You will come to the shore of a great inland sea we call Llyn-dwr-Halen, for this is the boundary of Torffan. Follow this coast to the east as far as you can until you leave the forest. From there you have only two choices; turn back or go up into the mountains that border

171

Penrhyn. There is no path or easy climb, only a stone-weaver can scale the cliffs there. Your *canllaw* will see you through the wards. Good luck Calon. Stay hidden. Use your magic wisely. I hope you find family and peace." With that the Cawrroc turned and strode off, heading back up the banks of the Rhew towards home.

"Will I see you again?" Calon shouted after him. Cadfan stopped and turned, a loud guffaw burst from his lips.

"Now that is a question," he called back, laughing. Shaking his head, he waved once more and then headed back up the valley to the safety of the mountains and home to Lellacher.

****

Having parted company with Cadfan at around noon, Calon was facing his first night outside by himself since the attack on his parents' home and the rescue of Berys. A whole afternoon of running had exhausted him, but he'd certainly put some distance between himself and his pursuers; the baying of the hounds was but a distant noise now. He stood at the riverbank and looked around. From where he was standing, he could see a good way back down the Tawe but as the river curved and narrowed here, he couldn't see ahead very far, although he could hear the water crashing down through a narrow valley.

It was growing colder as the sun dipped, shining almost straight into his face, and he enjoyed the little warmth he gained from it. He sat cross-legged on the bank, his pack beside him and ate a little of the food that Cadfan had insisted he take from his pack. The taste was neutral but the sustenance would be welcome. He began casting around in the shallow water for a suitably flat stone he could use to heat some water when a sudden flash caught his eye from further down south. He stopped scanning for stones and looked down the Tawe. The flash repeated several times and seemed to be directed almost straight at him. He remembered a summers evening as a child sitting with his mam, using her small mirror to direct the sun into his da's eyes when he was concentrating on mending some harness; they had laughed at his faked anger. This was similar except there was a pattern of sorts to the flashes.

As he couldn't see anyone, he was sure they couldn't see him. He watched for a while longer. There was a pause of a few minutes then the staccato flashing re-commenced. He decided to give up watching and turned to move deeper into what remained of the forest. Heading north for a little way towards a stand of towering trees where the river curved to his right, he had taken a few steps when he detected more flashing from the edge of the trees he was moving towards. He froze for a few seconds before throwing himself to the right away from the water. They were signalling. There were humans ahead of him; Chancel men. He immediately cloaked and bolted into the nearby trees, furious with himself.

He waited for a good five minutes before he heard voices. The crashing water had drowned the noise they were making. Men appeared through the copse of great trees. Soldiers, all dressed in chancel grey and black with weapons drawn. They were all scanning the tree line bar one man who was staying on the bank, looking hard at the ground—a tracker. He could hear them shouting over the river noise, the words indistinct, but by the urgency of the tone he knew they were looking for him. Four of the dozen or so soldiers began moving towards him, scanning the trees and ground as they moved.

His options seemed few. He remembered Cadfan telling to pause and think when he was able, as snap decisions were often wrong decisions. He knew going back was not an option, these men were obviously making their way through the woods towards their comrades lower down the Tawe. He was trapped between the two groups.

Cloaked as he was, Calon knew how to hide. He took confidence from that. A childhood of avoiding the village bullies had taught him well. He mulled over spying on the men but Cadfan's insistence that he get to Penrhyn and the Marwolleth was his only goal beyond avoiding capture. Standing slowly and quietly he eased his arms around the tree in front of him, his magic blending the skin of his magical cloaking with the bark of the tree so they looked as one. He waited. Within less than a minute, a man swinging a great-sword passed within a few feet of him, oblivious to his presence. A second followed but stopped.

"Hey, look at this tree. Its trunk looks odd," He called to the man in front. Calon froze, not even daring to breathe, quickly formulating which direction to flee.

A sudden shout of triumph erupted from the men closer to the Tawe. "His kit! His kit!

Someone bellowed. This was followed by the men in the woods rushing down to the river, the odd tree forgotten. Calon eased a long breath out, angry he had forgotten his pack and the food he had hoped would sustain him for his whole journey. He stayed motionless, apart from easing his head around the trunk to watch what was occurring on the riverbank. One man held Calon's pack in the air triumphantly as others crowded round, making room for the tracker who had also come running. Whilst one man emptied his pack, scattering food, a spare set of clothing and a woollen hat onto the ground, the tracker who had been studying the ground carefully move away from the group directly towards him.

He stopped and pointed at the ground and turned to say something to the soldiers, all twelve had now gathered to listen to him, before turning and pointing almost directly at him. Fear coursed through him. He would have to run, but he knew that even cloaked he would be tracked and followed. Worse, these men seemed fresh while he had run for hours already. The twelve Chancel men fanned out into in a skirmish line, all just about within touching distance of the next man, and weapons drawn they slowly advanced. The tracker led them and was just about within twenty yards of him, when a voice whispered in his ear.

"Wait!" it ordered, barely audible above his own hammering heart. "Wait!" it said again. He kept his eyes on the tracker, still determined to run, when the man's head was flung back sharply by an arrow that jutted from the centre of his forehead, sending the man toppling backwards without a sound. Calon had barely registered the swish and thrum of the bow.

"Now run," the voice said, "head upriver." As he turned to do just that, he caught sight of the Chancel men scrambling for cover or throwing themselves to the ground. He turned and ran, heavy legs struggling to keep up with the vague figure that skipped ahead of him. As he laboured after the figure, various things occurred to him: the Celtyth was cloaked (like he was); they must have been either tracking the Chancel men or was being tracked by them; and more importantly, whoever it was must be Celtyth and had killed. *Marwolleth*! he thought to himself.

Chapter 11
Seren and Penrhyn

After an hour of running, the vague figure flitting ahead in front of him, Calon was almost at the pass where the Tawe emerged from the mountains. Cloaked as he was, Calon found running up the steep, boulder strewn incline easy, as the tress thinned out. Within minutes he had reached the end of the valley. A sheer cliff rose up about thirty or so yards high. To his left the river was relentlessly shattered by a majestic waterfall, it's mist and spray filling the air close to the river like clouds that had fallen to earth. He saw no sign of his rescuer. He turned and looked back down the narrow river valley. The voice startled him again.

"They will not be long in coming up here. They know we are trapped." A woman's voice; a woman who suddenly appeared in front of him, causing him to take a step back. She was dressed in soft, buckskin leggings and shirt, with a hooded cloak of a thin material with some strangely illusive pattern that he found hard to focus on. The hood was up, shielding much of her face. "Who are you," she demanded, "I can sense a familiarity about you." Saying that, she grabbed his arm, her grip hard and unyielding, pulling it straight towards her whilst simultaneously raising his sleeve to reveal his *llinach*. She placed her hand over it; a warmth engulfed his wrist for a few seconds, then she let go and lowered her hood.

"Berys," he gasped before finding himself flat on his back, winded, the woman straddling him holding a wickedly sharp blade that was pressed flat against his cheek, the point almost touching his eye.

"You know Berys?" the woman hissed. "Where is she?"

Struggling for breath, Calon managed to pant out, "I… I… Thought you were Berys." There was a long silence during which the flat of the blade pressed harder on his cheek. The woman, seemed both calm and on the point of killing him. "I knew her. She saved me."

"Knew," she whispered. She lifted the knife and sat back on her haunches. "You said knew."

Calon eased himself up. "She… died. We were about to be taken by the Chancel men and she was hurt. She… she… knelt on the ground and just… died." He felt the pain growing in his chest. Forcing the sobs down, he held out his wrist. "She… at the end, she added her hair to this," he said, revealing the llinach of hair again. He then fumbled inside his shirt for the wizard-wood amulet she had attuned to him. "And she gave me this *canllaw,* so I could return to Marwolleth…" His voice trailed away then.

The woman looked at him; he saw that silent tears rolled down her cheeks. She grasped his wrist and pulled at the llinach but couldn't break it. She then eased her knife blade underneath and tried to cut it free, but the hair seemed indestructible. She then grabbed his head and forced it to one side, revealing the *craith* that Anghenfyl had woven into the skin of his neck.

"*Triskelion.*" He heard the woman mutter. She then let go of his neck and pointed again at his wrist. "Take it off," she ordered him, meaning the llinach. Calon was disinclined to agitate her any further so did as he was told, wishing the llinach undone. He handed it over. The woman held it one hand and began chanting whilst holding her other hand palm down a few inches above the strand of braided hair. Calon tried to follow what she was saying but found it hard— she was murmuring about ancestors and blood as far as he could tell.

Gradually, he saw various strand of the plaited hair begin to glow separately, appearing to swell until he could distinguish three components. The woman ceased then. Whilst still holding the llinach, she reached up towards the hair at her temple, pinching a few strands before yanking them free. These she held over the llinach, then began chanting under her breath again. He watched in fascination, reminded of Anghenfyl's craft, as the woman's hair seemed to weave itself into the llinach of its own accord, disappearing completely.

She then handed it back to Calon and bid him put it back onto his wrist. He did so and looked up to meet her eyes. He immediately felt drawn towards her, her face seemed to grow larger as though she was lunging towards him; his peripheral vision blurred and faded so all he saw was the woman; a faint buzzing filled his ears and his whole body hummed. Then just as suddenly as they had started, the strange sensations stopped. Calon gasped and sagged forward, slightly nauseous now but elated at the same time. He looked up into the woman's eyes that now appeared greener than ever and seemed to be looking inside him.

"Seren," he said quietly. "I know your name. Seren." He seemed amazed by his own knowledge. "What just happened?" he asked her, holding up his wrist in front of his face to examine the llinach.

"Your *llinach*," Seren reached out to gently hold his wrist. "Do you know what it does? What if signifies?" she asked him.

Calon thought back over what he knew. "I was told it was some kind of magical protection given by the hair of my family and ancestors and that it had a power but I have no idea what that is."

Seren raised her eyebrows at this. "There is some truth in that but whoever told you that was not Marwolleth, so they were guessing or repeating half-truths and rumours they had been told. This *llinach*, it is a history of your family: your mother, father and their kin. It is what binds us to our loved ones. It does have magic, and knowing Berys it will help you heal; others and yourself. She was always healing…"

"Family," Calon repeated gazing at the llinach. "But you added your hair…"

"Then I must be family," she replied matter-of-factly. "I suspect that your mother was my mother's cousin. We have the same great grandfather."

"And you can tell all of that by looking at some hair," Calon stated sceptically.

Seren laughed then, despite her sadness. Calon smiled too at her enjoyment. "Some I knew, some the magic told me, some I think I have deduced, the rest Berys betrayed by giving you this *llinach*." She paused then becoming serious again. She reached forward and gently pinched a lock of Calon's hair. A small burst of heat warmed his scalp and he saw that she had removed some of his hair. Seren then lifted her arm and shook her sleeve down, revealing a llinach very similar to her own. She lay his hair on top and repeated her incantation. Calon's hair entwined itself into Seren's llinach.

"We are linked now," she told him. "If you hold your hand over your *llinach*, you will know in which direction I am. You will also get a sense of whether I am close or far away. What magic is woven into it we will have to wait and see."

"What does yours do?" Calon asked her. "Magically I mean."

Seren reached over her shoulder and grabbed something that had been stored on her back, bringing it forward. Calon saw it was a rod of smooth wood. Roughly as wide as her wrist and about a yard long, with some kind of string spiralled around it. Seren held it out vertically with a straight arm and showed Calon a triskelion symbol woven onto the middle of the rod. He watched as she pressed the pad of her thumb onto this. The rod immediately grew from both ends; extending at least yard each way, the string that had spiralled around the rod now stretched taut between both ends; she held a huge bow, the longest Calon had seen. He asked her what wood it was made from.

"*Ywen wrach* in our tongue; but we usually call it wych-wood, for obvious reasons." Flipping her cloak over on shoulder she revealed a quiver and withdrew one arrow which she fitted into the bow. Then turning to look back down the valley she waited, her head cocked slightly to one side, listening. Some distance away Calon heard men's voices, and he caught occasional glimpses of figures moving cautiously between the trees further down the valley. In a whirr of motion, Seren suddenly moved sideways to the advancing troops, still over a hundred fifty yards down the steep slope, drew and loosed an arrow. She lifted her thumb and the bow returned to its short state.

"My magic," she explained as she did this, and was interrupted by an agonised scream that echoed through the valley, "is that I never miss." The baying of hounds curtailed any further conversation.

"The hounds have tracked me here. That means there are more Chancel men than the twelve that were hunting me," he explained.

Seren looked around the valley they were in. "Me," she told Calon. "I have tracked them for over two days, killed many. You, I think, just happened to be in the wrong place at the wrong time."

"Or maybe the right place," Calon added.

"We'll have to climb," she said looking up. "And quickly. If they have archers, we'll be sitting targets on the cliff if they see us." She made to begin but Calon grabbed at her arm.

"The waterfall," he said, pointing at the space between the water and the cliff. "We can go behind it." Seren spat on the floor.

"No chance. Damn stone weavers have magicked it so nothing can hold to the stone.

Only a bloody Cawrroc could make that," she told him, disgust obvious in her voice.

"I can," he told her. Seren's disbelief was evident. "I can, I've done it before. A Cawrroc weaver showed me." He cloaked his eyes and approached the water fall. He saw it had been moulded so that the stone above jutted out from the cliff creating a good walking space beneath; a walkway that sloped gently down so there was no chance anyone other than a stone-weaver could walk across. The cliff face was night-stone so he would be able to manage his way across, but he knew that Seren would never make it and he wasn't strong enough to carry her across. Thinking back to his night-time lessons with Cadfan, Calon told Seren to quickly grab any sturdy branches she could find. He helped her and they had soon assembled a pile of twenty or so short branches at the start of the waterfall walk. He took off his moccasins and tied them together before swinging them around his neck.

Cloaking his hands and feet, Calon dug his fingers into the stone and moved onto the ledge easily. He had Seren throw him a branch. Holding it tightly in his fist, he pushed his whole hand into the wall, then withdrew it carefully, leaving the branch fixed. It took him a couple of attempts to work out how to manipulate the stone effectively and Seren pointed out that angling the branches up slightly would help her. He then moved along and fixed a branch that Seren had thrown him to the lowest point of the cliff face. He moved across repeating this alternate high and low pattern until he was at the other side. Seren had cut a few more branches to complete the rows of pegs.

Once Calon was across, he called her over. They could both hear that the hounds were close now, time was flowing away as fast as the water. Seren took hold of the first branch, not really trusting it but found it to be firmly fixed. She even pulled it with both hands but was unable to move it at all. Finally, she took a deep breath and swung onto the first with her right hand, immediately stretching out her left leg to reach the lower branch. Calon watched with admiration as Seren flowed across the pegs as smoothly as if she did it every day. She was across in seconds.

"Thank you for trusting me," he said as she grabbed him and hauled him against the cliff face just in time to avoid an arrow that hissed through the space she had just vacated.

"At least we can pick them off one at a time as they cross," she told him as she reached for her bow. Calon smiled at that.

"No." He put his hand on her arm. "Let a few climb on first." They swapped places. Calon cloaked himself to match the stone of the cliff face, silently thanking Cadfan for another of his lessons. Two archers stood at the edge of the walkway; arrows poised. Beyond he could see several soldiers begin readying themselves to make the climb. He watched, unobserved as they started making their way across. Their clumsy uncertainty a complete contrast to Seren's grace. He slid his cloaked hand onto the night-stone wall and waited until the lead man was holding the last peg before weaving a spell into the stone to release the branches. He had miscalculated the time it would take though and the first man leapt out from under the waterfall onto firm ground, only to be met by Seren's foot in his chest, which propelled him forcibly off his feet and down the waterfall to his death.

Calon saw none of this as he was focused completely on his own task, watching with grim satisfaction as the second man in line suddenly yelped in surprise as the branch he was holding came away in his hand, quickly followed by the branch he was standing on sliding out from the cliff face. For an agonised moment, the certainty of his death washed across his face. He showed great agility in getting both feet beneath him but they immediately cannoned off the stone and up into the air causing him to flip so that that back of his head crunched against the walkway and he slid into the stream of the water fall, lost. The undoing of the magic that held the branches fixed, rippled along the wall in no time, the six men who were clinging to the spars had no way to save themselves and within seconds they had all fallen to their deaths. Seren saw only the men hurtle off the ledge and was impressed enough to clamp a hand onto Calon's shoulder. She eased him back, nodding her approval and smiling.

"Now it's my turn," she stated. What followed was almost beyond Calon's ability to comprehend. Seren stepped into full view with her longbow ready and released several arrows in a blur of motion. The Chancel men fled or died. Some of the long ash, shafts had hit with such force that they had passed through one man and pierced another. Calon looked across and saw numerous bodies littering the other side of the river.

"That was unbelievable," he told her, awestruck. He watched an injured man, an arrow lodged near his hip, struggle to move into the cover of the trees. He heard the reverberation of the bow cord and his eye caught the blur of the arrow that hit then man just below his left shoulder blade.

"Heart shot," Seren replied coldly. "Instant death. That man was hit by an arrow that had passed through someone else." Calon could think of nothing to say. By his count at least fifteen men had died in a matter of seconds. "Let's move," she told him, heading quickly for the cover of the trees.

Seren led him downhill away from the waterfall, through the forested slopes of the mountains and down to a valley. Calon found this more taxing on his legs than climbing but said nothing. He had no reason to trust Seren as he'd only known her for a few minutes, but thinking about it, he did. He could see a vast expanse of water ahead in the distance and knew he was on course. He was about to ask her about Penrhyn and the Marwolleth when she stopped abruptly in front of him and cloaked, almost vanishing. Not knowing what she had seen, he cloaked as well.

The sun had nearly set now and it was only when he cloaked and his vision enhanced that he realised how dark it was getting. He could see her now, moving carefully down the slope in a crouch, her bow lengthened and an arrow primed. He set off after and caught up with her when she stopped behind a holly bush. Further down the slope he could see a squad of seven Chancel men traipsing along the valley floor. The whole squad carried shields on their left arms, facing up towards them and had bows slung across their shoulders. There was no slope to their right, a sheer cliff stretched up above them. All bar the front man carried a spear, although most were using them as walking aids. He was glad that they'd be able to avoid them easily as they had no tracker and no dogs. They could just hide.

As he watched them moving to bottom of the slope that led up to where they hid, he heard the hiss and twang of Seren's bow releasing. The arrow took the lead man through his back, disappearing through so that only the fletching and nock were visible. The man fell face forward without a sound. It must have been a two-hundred-yard shot. The effect on the others was instantaneous; they bunched together and faced the forest, kneeling to reduce the size of target they were presenting, their shields held covering their body. Their heads lowered to protect chins and faces with just enough room between shield rim and iron helmet to peer through. They held their spears at an angle, butts into the ground as they scanned the trees with obviously no idea where the arrow had come from.

Shortening her bow and storing it in her quiver, Seren pulled out a wooden knife from beneath her cape. The blade was about a foot long and had distinctive black grains laced through it. It was the colour of well-seasoned oak. He watched with fascination as she ran her fingers up and down the blade. He could see she was infusing or coating the wood with magic, so that when she had finished it shimmered. It looked like metal. Seren then pulled a flat round disc of the same black-grained wood out of a pocket, and held it flat in her left hand whilst with her right she began smoothing her palm over its' surface in a circular motion.

Calon was amazed. She was stretching the wych-wood into a much wider disk and in seconds had made a shield a good two feet in diameter.

"Stay here," she told him and set off down the hill. To Calon, she was walking brazenly straight towards the kneeling troops, but he knew they probably couldn't see her at all. As she neared the Chancel men and the ground levelled out, she began to jog, speeding up as she neared the kneeling men. When she was within ten yards, she uncloaked, revealing herself to the troops just as she bunched and leapt, over them, twisting in mid-air so that she landed facing the men's backs. She instantly stabbed two of the men before any of them had moved. The remaining men tried to twirl around but were encumbered by their long spears. The two men at either end of the line and out of range of her sword jumped up and turned and span to face her.

The other two had half scrambled up and around but made it no further as Seren drove her sword through the eye of the man to her right, before whipping her shield around horizontally into the neck of the man on her left. The rim of the shield sliced straight into his windpipe and almost severed his head. Blood spouted out of his neck as his head flopped down onto his back, whilst for a few heartbeats, his body remained almost upright before she kicked it squarely in the chest, toppling the corpse to fall beside the man she'd stabbed through the eye, who had just collapsed lifelessly on to his back.

There followed a few seconds of stillness as the two Chancel men, one to her right and one to her left, stood, shields forward and spears levelled some ten yards either side of her. Seren was motionless. The two both edged a foot forward, their movements looking nervous and uncertain even to Calon. Seren responded by cloaking. To her opponents she had simply disappeared. Calon saw her swing her left arm out away from her body, releasing her shield at the soldier on her left. The man had little time to react as the shield simply appeared out of thin air and sliced straight through his forward leg, sending him screaming to the ground.

In the same movement, she launched herself soundlessly at the other man who was momentarily and fatally distracted by the appearance of the shield. Seren ran towards him and grabbed his shield with her left hand, ripping it behind him to spin him round. Disoriented and off balance, he was facing Calon who saw the look of agony and surprise on his face as Seren's knife sliced through the tendons at the backs of his knees, dropping him in to a kneeling position. Seren used his shoulder to lever herself into a jump and then slammed back down, driving her knife down between his shoulder and collarbone. Pulling her knife free in a spray of blood, she watched the man fall face first onto the stony bank of the river.

Calon uncloaked and started down to the site of the carnage he had just witnessed. Dumbfounded that Seren had killed six men in a matter of heartbeats. He saw her move over to the man who's left leg she had severed at the knee. He held his thigh up and watched as blood poured from the stump, still screaming and crying. Seren reached him and took hold of his collar and unceremoniously battered the base of her knife handle into his temple to stop his screaming. The man was instantly rendered unconscious. Kneeling, she put both of her hands to his stump, stopping the flow of blood almost instantly.

By the time Calon reached the scene of the slaughter, Seren was using two captured water flasks to wash the blood off hands, before wiping her wooden blade and shield clean on a cloak one of the unfortunate soldiers had been wearing. She stood and faced him and he saw that she had doused her hair in the water to rinse the men's blood off. She began to steam and Calon knew she was warming herself to dry her clothes. He looked around at the dead men, the nauseating tang of blood, offal and opened bowls made him gag. He had no idea what to say to her.

"This," he gestured around at the corpses. "I mean, was it necessary? We could have hidden and let them go."

Seren stared back at him coldly. "Let them go? Back into Torffan to torture and kill defenceless Hethwen. Would you rather your own kind died at their hands? If they had taken you would they have let you go?" Calon shook his head. Seren continued, "They came here to a land not their own to slaughter, rape and enslave our people. I am here to hunt them down and pay them in kind."

"That man," he asked her, pointing at the unconscious soldier with a severed leg. "Why do that? Why heal him rather than kill him quickly? I mean, what if he survives and the other Chancel men find him?"

"I want them to find him alive," Seren replied. "Then he can tell them what happened here and the story will spread and their fear of us will grow." She took one last look at her handiwork and then gestured back up into the trees. "It is nearly dark. We should make camp further down towards, eat and rest up there."

"But what if more men come along and find…" Calon indicated the corpses. "If the fear of us grows, won't they kill more of the Hethwen?"

Seren smiled at that. "You think those zealots will let any Celtyth live? You told me on our way here how they slaughtered children. You told me how they raped and killed and laughed about it. This," she indicated the corpses, "will not make them worse, they can't be any worse. But it may make them think; it may mean they kill with fear in their hearts rather than joy." They waited in silence, looking at one another until Calon nodded his ascent. Seren began moving on towards *Llyn-dwr-Halen*, the inland sea, leading Calon who trudged along behind her. She had sensed his discomfort and uncertainty with her extreme actions, reminding her again of Berys. She resolved to tell him this when they had made camp, hoping he would like to hear the comparison.

Behind her, she heard Calon stumble, and the clattering clang of iron, as he tripped on something metallic he had kicked; probably one of the weapons a soldier had dropped. Without turning, she moved on and didn't see him bend and pick up a dropped sword, examining the metal, before sliding it through his belt and following her. After a few steps, Seren's shout to hurry up forced him into a jog to catch up.

Deep within the shelter of the trees, so tightly packed it was a struggle to walk without brushing against the branches, Seren slowed her pace looking for a good place to set up camp. She chose a site where four young trees stood in pairs either side of an animal trail. Calon helped her bind the tops of the trees with magic, causing Seren to look appreciatively at him.

"Berys," he said by way of explanation. Seren nodded and indicated that he should work the back of the shelter and one side. They worked in companionable silence, both intent on their weaving, until the walls were completed. He noticed that Seren's side was a lot smoother and more tightly knit than his, but still, he was pleased with his effort.

"How many times have you done that?" she asked him.

"This was the second," he told her. "I practiced it in dream-weaving a lot, but I only had my memory of watching Berys do it to learn from."

Seren sat with eyebrows raised, taken aback. "Well, for someone who only watched another do this, that is very good." She smiled. "I will show you more when we have time." With that she fussed over the whole of the inside, plugging gaps and smoothing branches and leaves. Within a few minutes, she sat back and sighed.

"Smooth the centre of the floor," she told him. "I'll be back shortly." With that she stood and left the lodge. Calon did as he was asked, knowing it would be where the heat-stone would rest. He knew from his trek with Cadfan that it could get cold, and they were higher up here, the stone would keep them warm throughout the night.

Seren returned after ten minutes carrying a large pack on her back. She eased into the lodge and shrugged the pack of her back. Reaching inside she began withdrawing the things they would need, including unstrapping a densely woven rug that they had to manoeuvre themselves around to spread it on the floor. A hole in the centre showed where the hearth-stone would rest. She provided a wooden bowl, a bag made of woven grass that contained food and finally, from the bottom, she revealed the hearth-stone, laying it in the gap. She fussed with the ground a little trying to get the stone perfectly level, before heating it then lifting the wooden bowl onto one half of it to boil some water.

As Seren prepared the food she had, Calon watched her. He found himself seduced by her concentration. She had dark skin, darker even than his, and emerald green eyes so bright it was hard to meet her gaze. High cheekbones gave her face a heart shape, even though it was a little thin. Her body was not as rounded or voluptuous as Berys, but Seren was quicker to smile and friendlier. She had her hair bound into six tight buns that looked for all the world like little horns about to sprout from her skull. She suddenly looked up at him, aware of his scrutiny, and smiled softly and knowingly at him.

Embarrassed, Calon shrugged off his leather jerkin as the interior of the lodge felt rather warm all of a sudden. He mumbled something about how amazingly effective a shelter the lodge was, eliciting a throaty chuckle from Seren, who went back to preparing their food shaking her head. Calon shuffled his things around to create a sleeping space, lifting the sword he had taken from the dead soldier. A shout from Seren made him jump.

"That's iron! How the hell can you pick that up?" she almost yelled at him. Calon looked at her pained expression then back at the sword, which he held by the blade. He shrugged, remembering how Berys had reacted.

"I've always been able to handle iron. It's just like handling wood or stone."

"Can you weave iron as well?" she asked, quickly followed by. "I know you can weave stone."

"Well, yeah. Cadfan taught me how to weave stone, but he said that Cawrrocs can't weave iron or wood. In fact, he was sending me down to the Hethwen to learn wood weaving, and he hoped that one of the Marwolleth might be able to show me how to weave iron."

Seren sat open mouthed. Gobsmacked. "Cawrrocs! I assumed you were joking or making up stories to impress me! We thought they were all gone!"

"No," Calon told her, "they have a new city under the big mountain. They call it Lellacher. It's impossible to get to unless you can weave stone. I was there for two weeks." He sat and waited for her to speak but she suddenly shouted and began sweeping the various mushrooms and roots she was cooking off the stone. Some looked a little wrinkled and dried out. She dropped them into the simmering water in the bowl.

"Stone, I can almost accept you can weave stone. But iron! I have never heard of another Celtyth who can touch it without losing all their magic." Calon told her then of how he had freed Berys from the iron chains and how he had wanted to find out more about his abilities but with the Chancel men pursuing them so avidly it had been impossible to spend any time just finding out what he could do.

"Cadfan, the Cawrroc who taught me, said there was a Marwolleth called Gerallt who could weave iron. He hoped he was still in Penrhyn."

"Gerallt," Seren repeated. "He was the brother of Emrys, my great Uncle. He went with our people across the water to Gorwynoll, the western world. I don't remember Emrys saying anything about weaving iron though. We'll find out when we get back."

"We?" Calon asked.

"Yes Calon, 'we'. I was heading into Torffan to meet someone when I came cross soldiers. I had thought to stay and kill any Chancel men that seek to head into the mountains here, but now I think we should go back to Penrhyn. Emrys must know about this attack. I also feel he will be fascinated by you and your tale. If anyone can aid you it is Emrys. We will leave in the morning." Seren laid out her bedding then and lay down, her back to Calon. "And keep that thing as far from me as you can."

"Shouldn't one of us keep watch?" Calon asked. "What if they come in the night?"

Without turning Seren told him, "One of us is keeping watch. Sleep. We have a hard journey ahead."

"But," Calon began.

"Sleep, someone watches over us. We are safe." After that Seren was silent. Calon pondered the someone she mentioned but drifted off to sleep before coming to an answer.

The following morning, the pair broke camp. Seren supervised him packing his things. She used young yew branches to weave a basket he could wear on his back. She insisted that his sword be strapped inside that.

"You must cloak yourself, it will make the journey quicker, though you will suffer when we stop. Two days of running will see us into Penrhyn. Try to stay with me. We will stop for water and something to eat at midday."

"I can use my llinach to find you, Berys showed me how," Calon told her, which got a welcome nod of approval. He smiled at that before asking, "What about the 'someone' who was watching us? Aren't they travelling with us?" he asked as she turned to leave.

Seren stopped and faced him. "She will watch our trail and warn us if any Chancel men are near." She thought then before adding, "She is not as trusting as I am. Now run."

Chapter 12
Penrhyn and Strife

Two and a half days of running was all Calon could manage. By the time they had eaten some lunch on the third day he found himself too weary too cloak, too weary to move. He had slumped to the ground to rest while Seren quickly scouted the way ahead after ordering him to pack their things away. He hadn't had the energy for that. He expected a tirade of admonishment when she returned, imagining her angrily pulling him to his feet; Seren did the opposite. She knelt down and looked into his face, seeing his exhaustion. She rose and he heard her rummaging in one of the packs before she returned. She encouraged him to lie down, pushing a spare, rolled shirt under his head and produced a cloth he recognised as a *cynfas*—a sleeping shroud. She covered him with it then knelt down by his head to give him some water.

"I'm sorry Calon, I should have stopped sooner. I forget how hard it can be to run cloaked when you are not used to it. I will leave you to rest for a few hours, but then we must move into shelter when it gets dark. Without magic, it will be too cold to sleep out in the open air. I will leave you for a while and set up a lodge. It may be for the best to rest now as we will be higher tomorrow and above the tree line so we'll need to keep moving then. Myllane will watch over you." She pressed her hand to his forehead and told him to sleep. He felt the warmth of the magic command seeping through his body and drifted blissfully away.

He woke a few hours later as it was getting dark. The cold had woken him. He groaned as he sat up, his whole body sore and still fatigued. A wolf was sitting facing him. Its eyes were level with his. He shuffled back a little, unsure how to react. The wolf tilted its head slightly and its tail wagged once. It's tail. Calon looked again and decided it wasn't a wolf—it was a huge fox: a big bushy tail that ended with a white tip and white fur down it's chest and belly. He also reasoned that unlike a wolf, the creature in front of him had a friendly face—a pointed snout, upright, triangular ears and long whiskers.

The two sat and regarded each other for a few minutes, Calon becoming somewhat disconcerted by the fact the fox/wolf was happy to meet his gaze when he'd always been told looking into an animal's eyes made them uncomfortable. Not this beast, Calon thought to himself.

"You've met then?" Seren's voice made him jump, though he noticed the fox/wolf hadn't even twitched and maintained its staring. She came into view and crouched by the side of the animal, hugging it. Calon noticed the creature's tail thumping up and down. "This is Myllane," she told him, scratching behind the animal's ear causing it to tilt its head and grumble loudly in its throat.

"When you said someone, I thought it would be another Marwolleth, not a wolf or fox whatever it is," he said softly, still distrustful of the animal.

"She, not it," Seren corrected him. "Myllane is a shadow fox. Our people have befriended and used them for centuries."

"So, it *is* a fox then," Calon said. "It looks just like a fox but three times as big and not at all timid or shy of people."

Seren laughed. "Not timid, no. We take them as young adults when they leave the litter. One person can bond with it and train it and it will stay loyal to that person unless they take a mate and they then revert to their wild state. They do sometimes let their old handler take a pup—which is how I got Myllane. The ones taken as pups tend to stay loyal to their handler."

Do they run in packs?" Calon asked.

"No. They are foxes in everything but stature. They are not pack hunters; they bond for life; and they are the most intelligent animal you could meet. Far smarter than dogs or wolves. But don't be fooled, they are vicious if they attack. They live high up in the Eiran Mountains, and hunt across the mountain slopes as well as in the forest. They also have the ability to blend into their habitat. Their fur seems to change colour to aid their hunt and they are very successful hunters. They will even take a young *Margaf,* the fierce goats that roam the Eirans and the forests." Seren reached out her hand towards him, helping him stand. "Come on," she insisted. "Night draws in. I have a lodge prepared and food ready." Calon found his legs were a little unsteady still, but Seren kept to a steady pace. The shadow-fox was already gone. He hadn't seen or heard it leave.

Twenty minutes later they arrived at the lodge Seren had prepared. The walls so carefully woven they looked solid. Inside it was warm. Looking around he saw that she had gathered ferns to sleep on and there was a wooden bowl on the hearth stone with a delicious smelling broth in it. He sat down. Seren reached into the pack she had been carrying and withdrew a leaf wrapped bundle. She unfolded the long leaves to reveal what looked suspiciously like two large steaks.

"Is that meat?" he asked her.

"Snow deer." Seren stated. "I believe you know it as venison. I hunted while you slept."

"But I thought the Celtyth peoples didn't eat any meat," Calon told her.

Seren laughed at that. "Why do your people think that? We don't live on meat as the humans do. We don't capture animals and make them live in barns or fence them up in fields. We hunt when we need to but every part of the animal is used. I would normally have saved the skin for making clothes and moccasins, but time is short and Myllane needs to feed."

"The Cawrrocs don't eat meat and Berys never did," Calon went on.

"Well, I can't speak for the Cawrrocs never having met one. There is so much to eat if you know what to look for and where to find it. Our peoples can live anywhere in these realms and survive easily, even in the depths of winter, without having to kill anything. Could you?" she asked him. Calon had no time to answer. "A little care in the cooking, the right flavourings added and we always eat well." With that she touched the hearth-stone, heating it, before dropping the venison on to it with a sizzle. She left it a few minutes and Calon's mouth watered at the smell as the he watched the dark red meat cook. Seren flipped the steaks over then reached for a small pouch. She took a pinch of something from the pouch and sprinkled it over the meat, a new aroma filled the lodge.

"Dried wild garlic," she told him. She produced her knife when she judged the meat cooked and sliced each steak into thin strips, before placing them into separate wide bark bowls she had obviously made earlier. She added some of the broth to it. And produced a small dark object from another pouch which she grated with her knife blade, scattering shavings of the thing over the food.

"Truffle," she said, adding. "Go easy it's still hot," and passed him one of the bowls and a split green stick with two prongs to eat with. They ate in silence. Calon had never eaten anything that had tasted that good and told her so. "Thank you," Seren said. "Drink the broth from the bowl, it's very nutritious." After, at Seren's instruction Calon lay down to sleep and drifted off to the sound of Seren clearing away and packing up as she explained they would be up and early and would need to leave quickly after his rest.

Calon woke to a grey sky. The lodge returned to just trees standing near each other. The shadow-fox sat upright nearby, looking down the mountain pass with ears pricked. He sat up and saw that another bowl of meaty broth rested on the hearth stone. His stomach growled, causing the shadow-fox to turn and look his way before standing and padding away down the pass. He picked the bowl up finding the broth warm enough to gulp down. He gazed around as he ate and saw everything else was packed and ready to go. He finished the broth and headed behind the densely packed trees to perform his ablutions. He returned to find Seren busily packing his bedding into her pack. She smiled at him warmly.

"It is good to see you rested, Calon. It will be hard going for the next two days and the Chancel men are near. We should leave now."

"They are near?" Calon asked. "How? Even if they travelled through the night, they could not have caught us. It would take…"

"A whole day," Seren finished his thought. "You have slept for a night, a whole day and a night." She laughed at his dumbfounded expression. "Valerian root in the broth I gave you."

"But they might catch us," he said. "You should have woken me."

Still laughing, Seren told him, "They will never catch us. Where we are going, you need to be strong so it was better you slept and rested while you could. I know now not to push too hard until you are stronger in your magic." She picked up the still warm hearth-stone and handed it him. "This is for your pack. I have found another. We will need them on the mountain. The night will bring the *dragon's claw*, a bitter, killing wind." She then pointed down to a bundle of branches, about twelve in all, each about eight feet in length. We will need shelter on the mountain for as you will see there are no trees that high. We will need to carry these between us." With that she eased her pack onto her back and handed him his. Once they were both ready, she bent and picked up one end of the bundle of branches, Calon taking the other. Then, uncloaked they set off.

The journey over the mountain was an experience that Calon would never forget: the beautiful desolation of the Eirans was something he would never tire of. The high peaks where Seren guided them on a crystal-clear day were like nothing he could have imagined. The views across the land bewitched him as effortlessly as the void-stone had. Seren had to stop and order him to move so many times that even she began to anger. By cloaking themselves, often just their exposed skin, he and Seren could protect themselves from the worst of the cold.

At noon of their first day Seren had said they could stop on the mountainside and they sat facing the way they had come until, at a distance, their pursuers emerged from the forest. Calon suggested they get moving but Seren just told him to wait. Within minutes the platoon of twenty-eight men were either wandering aimlessly around, sitting down or had bolted back into the trees. Incongruously, Myllane emerged from the forest at the same point and strolled through the men, who ignored her completely.

"These mountains are protected from intruders by very powerful enchantments,"

Seren told him, reaching inside her clothing to produce a weaver-wood amulet.

"A *canllaw,*" he said. "Berys gave me hers just before she, erm, gave herself back to the earth." He reached inside his own tunic and showed her the amulet her sister had given to him.

Seren was looking at him intently. "I had feared I would need to hold you as we journeyed here, but when you weren't affected as we left the trees, I knew you had something. Berys must have cared for you. I assumed you had your mothers."

"She left one for me, but after the gwerin took me…" he paused, "I think they stole it. Do you think a gwerin could use it to cross these mountains?"

"It would need to be attuned to the wearer, so no I don't think so. Besides, what harm could one gwerin do?" They went back to watching the men below them. Most of whom were just walking aimlessly around in circles. "They will walk till they tire, then lie down where they stand and die."

"What about the few who ran?" Calon asked her.

"As far as I know, they will not be coherent. Emrys says if they think about the mountain or try and recall their experience, intense fear and confusion will prevent them telling their masters anything useful." She stopped to greet Myllane as the shadow-fox approached and nudged its head into her shoulder. Seren reached up and rubbed her behind her ears, causing her to emit a satisfied rumble.

Their first night on the mountain, Seren constructed a domed framework from the branches they had carried with them. Four were used to create the dome, the other eight were threaded through these horizontally. Attached to her pack was a roll of soft animal leather which she draped across the framework, using magic to weave the wood into the leather, to hold it firmly and stretch the hides so they fitted tightly to the branches, leaving a couple of inches gap around the base. She told Calon to either find rocks to lay around the base to keep the wind out, and to use his magic to bend around the ends of the branches and put the largest rocks on the ends.

"Why not just cut the ends off the branches so we don't need to?" he asked. "Then the leather will reach to the ground."

"Because," she explained patiently, "without the rocks to hold it, the wind will blow it away. Snow makes this much easier, but as you can see, we have none. As it is, one of us will have to be awake to hold it down."

Calon looked back at the branches then cast about for a rocky surface. Twenty or so yards to his left he saw a wide shelf of stone that would suit his purpose. He asked Seren to

help him carry the shelter over to the rock and hold it down for him. Then, on his knees, he held a branch with one hand and placed his other hand flat on the stone, using magic to make it like soft clay, before pushing the end of the branch firmly down into it. He then solidified it again. He gave the branch a wiggle and found it soundly embedded.

"Well, aren't you a bag of big surprises," Seren told him. "That is very impressive." Please with her words, Calon repeated the process on all eight branch ends so that the shelter was in no danger of ever blowing away.

"Winds still getting in though," he told Seren, pointing at the base of the shelter where the leather was flapping in the stiff breeze. "But I think I can solve that too." He knelt to the ground again and began to weave the stone, drawing it up with both hands into a ridge of rock, a couple of inches high; he then fixed the leather into the rock all the way around, barring the door, until the whole thing was wind proof. Seren came over and stood next to him, wrapping an arm around his waist before leaning in to kiss his cheek.

"You are a revelation Calon," she told him. "Now we'll both be able to sleep and rest." He was so pleased to be useful. They had a comfortable evening in the dark of their lodge, sheltered from the scything wind, their hearth stones heated by magic warmed the shelter. He asked Seren about the fox, wondering if Myllane would be alright in the storm. She closed her eyes, concentrating for a few seconds, then told him to reach out his hand and push the side of the shelter behind him. He did so, his hand bumping into the fox who had obviously curled up in the lea of the shelter, protected from the worst of the wind. Not for long.

Within a few heartbeats her nose was pushing at the entrance flap of their warm shelter. Seren moved over towards Calon and opened it, letting the shadow-fox in, hugging her tightly. She ushered Myllane over to her side and got her to lie down next to the leather skin wall. Cloaking her hands she moved the two hearth stones beneath the opening, one stacked on the other.

"That should give us all enough room," she told Calon, "and leaving the hearth-stones here will mean any draft coming in blows as warm air into the shelter." Calon asked her again about the shadow-fox, and how it would have survived in the extreme cold of a mountain winter.

"Their fur is very thick. They can sleep out in the open as their tails are thick and can wrap around their faces to keep them warm. They'll find a place out of the wind if they're out in the open, but they would usually have a sheltered den; somewhere underground, or a cave. We even weave shelters for them if we have the wood." They sat in companionable silence for a while before she spoke again.

"Could you make this from stone Calon? If you had time? I just think to have a few shelters like his across the mountain would make journeying much easier. We could leave hearth-stones inside and you could shape a couple of bowls for water."

Calon thought about it. "Yes I could, if we had enough stones. If we could stack stones against the leather here, I could weave them much as you do with branches." He thought about this for a while, his thinking interrupted when Seren declared it was probably time to sleep. He could hear her fumbling around in one of their packs.

"The only thing we lack really is light," she grumbled. "Using magic all the time would be exhausting."

"Light," he repeated. "Of course." He cloaked his hands and reached over to the two hearth-stones. Using his magic, he gripped the end of one of the stones and with some effort he pinched a piece of it off. He tried to make it emit light, remembering his time in the gwerin's cell, but to no avail. He thought hard about the stones that the gwerin had used for light, realising as he did so that the stones had been shiny before they were 'lit'.

"Quartz," he said softly. "I think I need quartz."

"What's quartz?" Seren asked him. He explained it was a crystal, often found in other rocks in small particles.

"A crystal," Seren said, reaching into her tunic and pulling out something attached to a leather thong. She held it out to him and he took it, feeling it with his fingers. The top half was as smooth as glass and the lower half was just rough rock, with a looped stalk at the base through which the leather thong was passed. It was warm and he tried not to imagine where it had rested before she took it out.

"It's shaped liked an acorn," he said.

"My father said most of our people wore a crystal like this. They are passed down through the generations. There is always speculation about their purpose but most think it was a traditional wedding gift. It would be a nice gift. Humans call them diamonds. They seem to crave them as they crave gold."

Taking all this in, Calon began infusing the crystal using his magic as Cadfan had shown him, he visualised light emitting from the crystal in his hand, but hadn't expected the lightning bright glow that burst from the crystal, blinding them both and making Myllane jump to her feet whining. He quickly withdrew his magic, plunging them back into darkness.

"What the hell," Seren complained. He could hear her rubbing at her eyes.

"I think we've discovered what this," he said smiling. "It's a light. I put very little magic in and that happened. But stone-weavers have little use for such a pure light, so I suspect these were made for wood-weavers to use—hence the acorn. I doubt much magic will be needed to use this, same as the hearth-stones." He handed it across to her, holding her arm to place int in her hand. "You try. Just hold it and use it like the hearth-stones' only visualise light rather than heat."

It took several minutes and few brief flashes, but Seren soon mastered it enough to create a steady, warm glow from the diamond. Once she was satisfied with the level of light it was giving, she reached up and passed the thong over the branches that crossed in the middle of the lodge's roof and let it dangle, lighting up the interior enough that he could see her grinning from ear to ear. She responded by throwing her arms around his neck and kissing him full on the mouth. "You *are* a revelation," she beamed, before reaching for her pack to extricate their bedding.

Calon woke up alone in the morning. He assumed that Seren had gone to check on the Chancel men who had been following them, but we when he left the lodge and looked back towards the trees, he could see no sign of her or the fox. *Probably hunting*, he thought to himself. The sun was bright over to the east and the sky was a cloudless pale blue, a winter blue Calon thought. After relieving himself and checking his pack for food, Seren's was missing he saw, and finding nothing, he strolled outside and set his mind to the task of collecting some water.

Their lodge was on a flat escarpment, with a steep upward slope beginning some twenty or so yards behind it. The slope was mainly rock and he could see small runnels all over the rock with trickles of water dribbling down them. Seeing what looked like another ledge a good hundred yards up, he scrambled to it and found a small ridge stretching roughly twelve feet. He had hoped it would be a small pool, but the ridge sloped gently down so there was no standing water. Looking at it he realised that as it was solid stone, he could create a depression in the stone to capture the water that meandered down the slope. He began by cloaking his hands then just pushed into the rock, moulding it like sand, shoving it from the centre and rear of the ridge to form a ten-inch lip.

When he had finished, he was greatly pleased with his efforts and water had already begun to puddle inside what looked like a long, shallow trough. Looking down towards the lodge, he realised it would be an onerous climb up and down to collect water, but he realised he could do something about that too. Moving to one end of the trough, so he was directly in line with the lodge, he worked the lip of the trough down slightly into a spout, slightly lower than the side of the basin he had created. Water would pour from here when the trough was full. He then worked his way down the slope, using both hands back-to-back to push into the stone and pull it apart, creating a clear channel roughly eight inches wide and four inches deep. It took him a good twenty minutes to reach the flat ground level with the lodge.

He stopped and surveyed his work, seeing that he had not gone as straight as he had thought, but it was straight enough. Next, he went and stood near the lodge opening and looked for the best place for a basin. Slightly over to the right, about fifteen yards away he saw that the rock was slightly higher than the area the lodge sat on, but then fell away sharply. Crossing to it and looking back up towards where the slope ended, he saw he could divert his new channel to this area as although it looked flat it was still inclined down. He created another basin in the rock though not as wide but much deeper than the first, then in the same fashion he worked a channel back to join up with the one he had already formed.

Pleased with himself, and desperate to impress Seren with his ingenuity, he looked around for her, scanning the treeline below but still saw no sign of her. Turning back to his new creation, he hoped it could gather some water by the time she returned. He raced back up to the higher trough enjoying the quad burn, but was disappointed with amount of water in it. Looking either side, he saw water leaking away, water he could stream to his new creation if he created some long diagonal channels to feed into it. He set about this fervently, digging his cloaked hands into the rock and working his way higher, stopping after he created a long forty-yard gutter that would feed the trough. Heading back down he was pleased to see his idea working, and was even more pleased to see a half inch of water in the trough. He repeated his gutter, making out to the other side of the trough.

By the time he had finished the channel, he turned around and looked back down towards the lodge and saw Seren making her way up from the trees. He headed down, getting back whilst she was still some hundred or so yards away. As she neared, Calon waved and turned to head back to the lodge, nearly bumping into the shadow-fox who had been sitting behind him. In fact, he nearly hadn't seen her at all so good was her camouflage, but she had stood just as he turned, the movement catching his eye. He began to wonder if she'd been here all along.

"I have food, but no fresh water," Seren called as she approached. "The only water I could find was in a still pond," she said holding up the water skin and shrugging off her pack. "Bring the hearth-stones out here, it's nice enough out." He did as she had instructed, balancing the flat stones on pebbles he had manipulated so the hearth-stones would sit level.

Seren meanwhile had produced a brace of rabbits that she had already skinned and cleaned. He imagined that the shadow-fox had eaten anything she discarded.

"We can have fresh water," he told her. "I've set up a system to channel and collect it in a basin over there," he said pointing to his new pride and joy. "I've only just finished it though so there's not much in it, but the one up higher should be deep enough now." Saying that, he took the water skin off her and emptied it out, before heading back up the slope. Arriving at the trough, he was surprised to see it was nearly full. He knelt, pushing the skin down into the ice-cold water.

"I could have a bath in that," Seren laughed behind, making him jump. "That's wonderful. I'll certainly wash my clothes in it, I think."

"Er, I'd rather you didn't. This is drinking water." He pointed down the slope at the channel he had created.

"Oh," Seren said, "fair point, I suppose. I certainly wouldn't wish to drink your bathing water."

Ignoring her taunting, Calon continued, "When this fills, the water will stream out over this lip and head down to another, deeper basin there, close to the lodge." Water skin full they headed back down the channel to the basin.

"What we need," Seren said as they stood at the basin, "is a second one underneath that this one empties into when it's full. Then we can get drinking water from here, but use the lower one for washing and laundry." He could see she was as enthused as he was about this little project. "You get sculpting, stone boy, and I'll get cooking."

By the time that Seren called him over to eat, he had made a round basin roughly six feet in diameter with a stone 'bench' furthest from the drinking water basin. When the basin was full, a spout would direct water down a short steep slope to the 'bath'. Another lip in the side of the bath would allow the water to trickle freely away down the mountain side.

After they had eaten, spots of rain had begun to fall so they gathered their belongings and moved into the shelter of the lodge. Seren joyfully used her crystal to provide light and set to emptying her pack. She discarded a few items and repacked the rest, keeping a wooden brush in her hand. Holding the leather flap open, she called Myllane in and began rigorously brushing the shadow fox's coat. Calon noted how the fox seemed to enjoy the experience, something he was rather hoping that Seren wouldn't repeat with him. The rain by now was torrential and the fox, after it's brushing, was refusing to head back outside. They arranged themselves for the night with the fox curled up in the middle. Seren began moving about restlessly.

"No matter what I do, there's always something pressing into me," she muttered as she tried a different position. Calon moved over and told her to stay to one side. Cloaking his hands he smoothed them over the rock surface, ridding the stone of its rough edges.

"You're a wonder Calon," Seren said.

"You are welcome Seren," he replied just as formally with a bow and a grin. He turned to move back to his side.

"Could you raise a slight pillow for my head as well?" she asked. So, he moved back and pushed a smooth hump into the stone. Seeing the sense of it, he did the same for himself. He saw also that Seren had laid a rolled fur on the 'pillow' for added comfort. He was about to rummage in his pack for something similar when a tightly bound fur bounced of the back of his head. Picking it up he turned to see Seren grinning at him, teeth star bright.

"You're a wonder Seren," he echoed. Her throaty laugh music to his ears. It proved hard to sleep with the rain hammering on the lodge. "I wouldn't want to be out in this," he said to Seren. "We'll have to dismantle it and take it with us when we move on in the morning."

Seren made no response so Calon assumed she had dropped off to sleep. "No. We'll leave it here as it is," she murmured sleepily after a while. "We won't need the shelter on other side of the mountains. There are caves high up and we'll be back in the shelter of the woods before night fall." A few minutes later he could hear her breathing had slowed and this gentle sighing as she slept lulled him into a deep and dreamless sleep.

He woke in the morning to the shadow-fox sniffing and sniffling at his face. He opened his eyes warily, not wanting to startle her away. She then licked him along his cheek, an event followed by a peal of sleepy laughter from Seren who clicked her fingers, dragging the fox's attention away from Calon. He sensed the invasion of light as she opened the flap of the lodge to release Myllane out into the day. It was then he realised the staccato drumming of the rain had ceased.

"Do you think your pools will be full after all of that rain?" she asked him. Suddenly remembering his efforts yesterday got Calon moving.

"I'll go and check," he told her, stretching and getting to his feet. He walked quickly over to the basin and bath, finding both full as a steady slow-moving stream of water filled one and cascaded into the other. He cupped his hands and drank some of the icy cold water before calling back to Seren, "They're both full."

"I'm on my way," she called out from the lodge. He heard her stumble out a few seconds later and turned to say something but was struck dumb by the sight of Seren completely naked walking towards him, her clothes held in a bundle in her arms. Torn between tearing his gaze away and staring at her, Calon did neither. To his dismay Seren walked right up to him completely unselfconsciously.

"I've had an idea my red-faced friend," she laughed. "Bring the hearth stones out; you could use them to heat the water for me."

"Good thinking," Calon mumbled to his feet, before being disconcerted further by Seren leaning in and kissing his cheek. He stumbled in his eagerness to get away and was chased all the way to the lodge by the peals of Seren's laughter. He returned to find her sitting waist deep in the lower pool with her back to the wall as the water cascaded gently over her from above, eyes closed.

He knew she was using magic to take the chill off the water, but heating the stones was a better idea. He moved to the basin where they would drink water from and held both of the hearth stones. He cloaked his hands and lowered them into the water so the stones were submerged and proceeded to heat both to red hot. Bubbles began to seethe from the stones as the heated the water. A shout from Seren told him it was hot enough and he moved both stones as near to the lip as he could so the water tumbled in to the bath as soon as it was heated. He also had a sneaky look over at Seren's naked body.

"I know you're looking," she shouted up to him. "And thanks for heating the water, it really is wonderful in here. Strip off and join me." Calon had no intention of doing any such thing, but did remove his leather jerking and his shirt. Keeping his eyes down he moved down and around to the edge of the basin and dunked his shirt in, before pounding it on the rock at the side of the pool as he'd seen his mam do countless times.

"Give it here," Seren told him. "You're not making a very good job of that. I'll do it for you then you can get ii while the water is still warm. You might want to reheat the stones because it's cooling rather rapidly." Calon looked up to see she had put her wet shirt on, covering her breasts and reaching to her upper thighs. Unfortunately, the wet material accentuated her form even more than her nakedness had, reddening his face all over again. He moved back up and heated the stones a second time. When he stood and looked over, Seren was laying his shirt flat on a rock. She stood and smiled at him then turned and headed back to the lodge, using her magic to heat her body and causing the wet shirt to steam slightly. He watched her buttocks moving as she walked away.

I know you're looking," she shouted back to him without turning round. "Have a bath. You need it." Calon was dismayed by the amount of filth in his hair and on his clothes. The constant running water bore the dirt away but not before he'd seen how dirty he'd been. He stripped naked and washed his leggings and under things as well, enjoying the warmth of the water while it lasted. As it cooled, he turned his thoughts to how he could keep it warm. Remembering the waterfall wash room in Lellacher, he reasoned that by using hearth-stone for the spout he would be able to reach up to it while sitting underneath it to keep it hot and keep it heating the water. He would also be heating less water as the it would be heated as it flowed over the spout. He resolved to find a piece to use on his return. Looking across at the lodge he could just make out Seren inside packing her things away. He quickly stood and donned his wet clothes, cloaking himself to avoid the worst of the chill, before heading back over, before having to return for the hearth stones when Seren shouted out that she was hungry and wanted some hot food.

The following morning the pair set off from the lodge, filling their waterskins first. Calon was pleased to see how well his stone-weaving had worked. Seren rubbed his arm and told him she was proud of him as well, filling him with confidence. Looking down towards the treeline before they left, he saw the bloated corpses of the chancel-men, stretched out, grotesquely bathing in the sun. He turned sadly and followed Seren up the mountain, pulling his clothes tightly about him and cloaking his skin for warmth. Their journey over the next day and a half was uneventful and relentlessly dull. The mountain air blew as they crossed the high pass, a bitter rush, so strong at times they couldn't hear each other. Even cloaked as they were, they both felt the bite of the coming winter.

Once over the top, they descended down towards Penrhyn. They walked in a shallow ravine, shielded a little from the wind, and Calon could see the dark trees they headed for. Despite the fact they were heading down now, they seemed to move no more quickly. Walking on such jagged and broken terrain meant they could get no real speed up. As Seren had told him, it took them until nearly sunset to reach the trees.

Having grown up in the woods and forests that surrounded the Banna Hills, Calon was surprised how alien this environment was. There were no oak trees, no beech, no elm; as far as he could see there were no deciduous trees at all. The dark, evergreen trees were alien to him; rather than damp and rotting leaves, the smell was of sap and resin. The evergreens here were huge compared to the few he had come across, so large and tightly packed they seemed to be crowding together to keep the sun from the forest floor. After walking on hard rock, it was a pleasant surprise to stroll along on the spongy needles of the forest floor. Not much seemed to grow under the canopy so the way was easy going. As the gloom deepened, they finally came across a small stream, snaking its way through the forest. Seren turned to follow the water, even though they could have jumped it easily. He questioned why.

"We need to follow this down to get to the valley floor. I'm looking for a place to stop. It still gets bitterly cold even under the canopy. And it stays cold as no sun gets through. Look out for a tree with low branches. We'll need to make a lodge to sleep in if we want to stay comfortable and rest." They kept on trudging along for another few minutes before Seren suddenly deviated away from the stream and approached a tree that she considered suitable. Working together by the light of Seren's crystal, they fashioned their shelter for the night. Halfway through the wall smoothing, Myllane appeared with something furry and dead between her jaws. She dropped it at Seren's feet and moved off, disappearing into the darkness. Whilst he finished the lodge, Seren prepared the meat. Finally, having eaten, the pair fell into exhausted sleep, the hearth-stones warming their shelter.

The following morning, they set off and continued walking, but the gloom of the forest seemed to eat into their mood. Myllane wandered in and out of their company through the day and seemed unaffected by the lack of sunlight. Eventually, after walking continuously for what seemed like hours and hours, the ground began to level off and Calon could see the valley floor below, the stream widening as it switched from its mad rush down the wooded slopes to sauntering along the flatter ground.

Their good-natured silence was broken when, without warning Seren, who had been walking in front, suddenly stopped, took a step back and grabbed him by the arm, dragging him down behind a trunk.

"Cloak," she hissed. Calon did, oblivious to why she was so concerned. "Stay here," she whispered into his ear, before she moved down the slope to crouch behind another, wider tree trunk. She had her bow, not extended yet, in her hand and her gaze was fixed on the valley floor below. With intricate care they made their way further down the slope, Seren staying a few yards ahead and waving him on when she wanted him to move. Calon still saw nothing that would explain her caution or alarm.

When they were within ten yards of the stream that ran along the valley floor, Seren turned to her left and they edged along, parallel with the stream but hidden still in the trees. The pair crept along the course of the valley, moving from tree to tree; whatever had alerted Seren, Calon was still none the wiser and he felt it prudent to stay as silent as possible. After a tense half hour of slowly inching along, Calon was surprised to see Myllane. In fact, he only saw the shadow-fox as Seren ruffled her fur, suddenly revealing her as it changed colour. She was resting on her belly, ears alert, intent on something beyond the trees.

Calon could see by the amount of light permeating into the forest that the valley was open below them, whatever was wrong, this is where it waited. A sudden bark of raucous laughter split the silence, followed by a low, rumbling growl from the shadow-fox. Seren immediately prepared her bow, the ends lengthening, before she fitted the waxed cord. She removed her cloak, pulling out arrows that were stored in long pockets sewn into the lining, carrying them all in one hand. She moved further down, Myllane trailing behind, until she was behind a tree trunk on the very edge of the forest with a clear view of what lay beyond. Carefully, she pushed the arrows, eleven in all into the ground in front of her, keeping one in hand that she fitted into the bow. Calon eased down to an adjacent tree and finally looked upon what was concerning Seren so much.

A camp had been set up within the bend of the stream. One large fire with a metal framework scaffolded above it was smouldering gently in the dead centre of a ring of twelve large, canvas tents erected in an oval around the edge of the camp, with two square tents pitched inside that ring at either elongated end. A few yards from the smouldering fire, an iron rod had been hammered into the ground, beneath a square framed canopy, chained to which a large, bare-chested man lay with his back facing them, chains tightly wound around his legs. His arms were pulled behind his back and iron cuffs were fixed around his wrists pinning them together. Calon could see a rag tied around the back of the man's head so he assumed that whoever was held captive was gagged.

Judging by the amount of blood on his back, Calon assumed that he had been tortured. Calon could see several men in pairs, wearing the grey uniforms of the Chancel, patrolling the circumference of the camp and four armed guards stood watch over the prisoner. There didn't seem to be enough men visible for the number of tents they had erected. That meant there were more—either inside the tents or out patrolling. He was just about to suggest to Seren that they wait and watch for a while when she raised her bow and pulled the string taut. Calon immediately reached over and grabbed hold of the string. Seren's head whipped around angrily.

"Wait," he whispered. "There must be more. It looks like a trap."

"Emrys is down there," she hissed back at him. "There are only a few, more reason to attack now before the rest get back." She shrugged him off and pushed him so that he rolled on to his back. By the time he had gotten to his feet, he had heard three arrows loosed in quick succession. He was unable to stop her from launching herself forward, bow still shooting, as she raced towards the prone figure. By the time he looked down upon the camp, he saw that all four men guarding the captive were dead, heart shot, as well as the two pairs of guards closest to the prisoner. Seren sprinted down to Emrys and kicked at the iron rod to which he was chained. It took little effort.

Calon saw the rod fall surprisingly easily for something a man was chained to, but then he saw why. It had been rigged. As soon as the rod fell, it released the roof of the canopy over the man, a large net falling down and virtually crushing Seren underneath it. Not a net of rope, Calon realised, but a net of iron chain.

Myllane barked and growled and launched forward, reaching Seren in seconds, but a shouted command from her sent the shadow-fox back into the woods. Men ran from the tents and surrounded their new prisoner. As one, they turned at a shouted command. Calon looked and saw a tall, uniformed Confessor stride from one of the inner tents, followed by a much smaller figure, but one that Calon recognised only too well. The gwerin Mordwyn!

Chapter 13
The Marwolleth

The Confessor and Mordwyn approached the struggling Seren, who was fighting desperately to free herself from the iron net. Orders were issued and three of the Chancel men approached, one bearing cuffs, one carrying a chain and the third man a large hammer. The man with the hammer picked up the rigged spike and hammered it hard into the ground, the spike all but disappearing beneath the earth. Whilst he did this, the other two had reached through the iron net and pinned Seren face down on the ground before twisting her arms back behind her and cuffing her wrists. They dragged the net clear and proceed to wrap the long chain tightly around her legs.

Finally, the Confessor walked over to the bound Seren and placed something around her head. Calon saw it was an iron band meant to disrupt any attempts at using magic. When they hauled Seren to her feet, he saw blood running down her face over her eyes. *The band must be spiked on the inside, the iron is pressing into her flesh*, he muttered to himself, his outrage building. The arrival of a column of marching men was a timely distraction. The urge to charge down and try and free Seren decreased when he saw how many men there now were crowding into the campsite.

Taking stock, Calon reasoned that his best chance of freeing the captives was to wait until the dark hours before dawn when most of the men would be asleep. The men below hadn't bothered resetting the traps yet and this gave Calon some hope that they thought the two Marwolleth captives were on their own; this may make them complacent. They were also confident it seemed to Calon, that the iron would prove a suitable barrier for any of the Celtyth people. 'Not so,' he said to himself.

A sudden cheer drew his attention back to the campsite. Seren's chains had been fixed to the framework that had held the iron net, her arms now stretched above her head so her feet barely reached the floor. The Confessor had used his belt knife to slit up the front of her tunic, baring her breasts for the watching troops. She was spun around so that she faced a large post. Various men were invited forward and allowed to punch or slap her. Most aiming for the kidneys. Some loosened belts and used these to lash her bare back, the red welts and split skin soon very apparent.

His rage building, Calon was suddenly knocked sideways; Myllane stood over him, her paws on his chest. She looked calmly and directly at his eyes, before getting off him and turning away from him. He lifted his head to see two more shadow-foxes standing behind her, one similar in size to Myllane, but the other was slightly taller, definitely broader and far more powerful looking. It was this beast who came forward and put one paw on his chest, keeping him prone, before sniffing and snuffling at him. It paid particular attention to the *llinach* that Berys had given him, very quietly whining as he nudged it with his nose. He then began to lick at Calon's neck beneath his ear where Anghenfyl had threaded a *craith* that included a strand of Berys' hair into his skin. Whatever this meant he wasn't sure, but he was hugely relieved when the great dog fox began licking at his face.

"I guess that means I'm one of the pack," Calon muttered as he sat up, pushing the large shadow-fox away. The fox simply wagged its tail and came back in for more fuss. He looked back down at the camp and saw that Seren had been released from the frame and now lay curled by one of the central tents, an iron peg rammed into the ground beside her. He hoped that they would give her a blanket against the cold, but doubted they wood. He could see she had retrieved her torn tunic and had covered herself with it as best she could.

Whilst the shadow-fox persisted in its mission to lick Calon to death, he noticed that the other two shadow-foxes had vanished back into the woods now, so Calon was left with an animal that had the body of a killing machine but the mentality of a puppy. The shadow-fox would simply not leave him alone. He decided to move a few yards back into the darkness of the woods to avoid any movements being noticed, the fox nipping at his heels as he went. Just as he was about to turn, the fox grabbed his whole foot in its jaws and twisted it causing Calon to fall. He rolled over and sat up, only to be forced down hard on his back, the dog fox's paws planted on his chest. It began licking at his neck and face again. Whilst Calon struggled to playfully fend the fox off, he opened his mouth to speak and the fox instantly darted its snout forward, its incisors gripping on to

Calon's lower lip. Blood trickled into the back of his throat and panic threatened to overwhelm him, but the fox suddenly released him and began licking at the blood, its drool and spittle coating Calon's mouth. Calon sat up gagging and spluttering, spitting blood and mixed saliva out onto the forest floor, muttering and cursing as he did so. He stopped spitting and looked at the dog who was sitting tall, waiting patiently, its head tilted slightly to one side with its ears pricked up. Calon stared at the beast, not knowing what to think. The fox sat motionless, waiting.

"Bloody hound," Calon smiled at it, and its tail began to thump the ground. Calon couldn't explain why but he now felt completely comfortable and confident with the shadow-fox. He walked over and crouched down in front of it, rubbing his fingers over the soft velvety ears. The fox responded by nuzzling his head into Calon's hand, before standing and loping off into the gloom. 'It's going hunting' Calon thought. He didn't how he knew that, but he knew it. "Hela," he said to himself. "I'll call you Hela."

Calon settled down then and watched the flickering glow of the Chancel men's campfire. As dark settled in, vague forms moved about, many settling by the fire, either to eat or for warmth. He gradually lost clear sight of Seren, but knew she was still chained. It was going to be a long cold night. He decided not to cloak to stay warm, deciding that he would need all his strength, energy and reserves for the rescuing of Seren and Emrys.

Calon woke suddenly. The night was still dark. The overcast sky giving very little light at all. This was good Calon realised. Cloaked he and the two Marwolleth would be hard to see in daylight—in this pitch blackness, once free of the campfire light, they would never be tracked by humans. Sitting up he could see the orange, flickering of the camp fire. Three pairs of pointed ears were silhouetted against that glow. He could see Hela clearly, but the other two shadow-foxes sitting next to Hela, other than their ears against the firelight, were virtually invisible. He knew Seren or Emrys would have an explanation for this. He could probably see Hela as he had adopted her, although in truth he supposed that she had adopted him.

Calon, still cloaked, eased forward next to Hela and looked out across the camp. The fire in the centre was burning brightly because fresh wood had just been added. One man tended it, and had added enough wood for the flickering flames to light the camp's centre. There were brands burning on each of the four posts of the framework that stood above Emrys. These torches spluttered and spat. Calon remembered evening revels when he was a boy, the torches were dipped in pitch and spat like this. Two more illuminated where Seren lay, curled up in a foetal position. He counted eight guards standing motionless on the fringes of the camp. In addition, there was the man who was tending the fire and two pairs of men who patrolled around inside the camp.

He saw one pair approach Seren. One man knelt by her side, rolled her onto her back and obviously fondled her. He saw Seren lurch forward to try and bite the man's hand; he stood and kicked her hard in the midriff. The two men both spat on her and walked on. Glad she was conscious and willing to fight back, Calon watched for some time, seeing no one else. He had formulated a plan. He needed to get most of the men to one side of the camp, the furthest from Seren; he reasoned the old Marwolleth would be in worse shape and therefore need more help; he would need Seren's help with the old man.

What I need is a distraction, he thought to himself. He figured if he timed it right, he could infiltrate the camp, find an unused torch and fire the tent furthest from Seren. This would bring more men but he knew he could break Seren's chains in seconds. It would have to be enough time. He was about to head down when Hela walked over and stared at him. The fox blinked once, then turned and sped off—the other two darting off behind her like ghosts. Calon put this from his mind and crept in towards the camp, stopping at the last tree. He had waited until one of the torches had died. He watched intently as the man tending the fire walked over and bent down to a dark shape near the framework. He opened a flap of some kind, withdrew a new torch, lighting it from one of the lit ones, then replacing the dead one. He knew where he was heading.

Calon knew he had to time this right, wait for the two strolling guards who would be along with a skin of some kind to give the watchmen a drink. He aimed for a point between the two sentries who stood closest to Emrys. As the two strolling guards approached, he could see they were the pair that had just attacked Seren, the pair without the drinks. He saw the men with the wineskins stopping at the sentry on the opposite side. He'd have to be patient. He watched them give the wineskin or whatever it was to the sentry, one of the strollers patted the sentry on the back and they moved on.

Calon cloaked and jogged silently towards Emrys. He had reached the mid-point between two sentries, and the darkest part of the perimeter of the camp when Hela, Myllane and the other shadow-fox attacked. Hela leapt up, snatching the man's throat between his jaws and bearing him to the ground; one of the other two took the second sentry by the hamstring whilst the other leapt and hit the man in the chest, sending him sprawling. Both shadow-foxes then went for his throat. The guard managed one short high-pitched squeal before they silenced him. That squeal was enough to alert the closest guards and the shout went up that they were attacked.

The four guards all nearest Calon turned and sprinted across towards their dying comrades, the two sentries hefting spears and the two strollers drawing their swords as they ran. Calon had his chance. Sprinting in to Emrys, his cloaked hands ready, he knelt by the old Marwolleth and ripped the chains free, peeling off a heavy iron collar, before pulling the cuffs away.

"Get up and make for the trees," he whispered into the Emrys's ear, offering his hand. Green eyes opened and bore into his own, the reflected flickering flames seemed like rage burning in that gaze. He ignored Calon's hand and rose easily to his feet.

"Free Seren," he ordered, a harsh rasp of a voice. The Marwolleth turned towards the snarling and shouting mass and stepped towards the ruckus, cloaking as he did so, disappearing completely from Calon's vision. Calon ran over to Seren, disconcerted to see two of the sentry guards standing over her, spears levelled. As he ran to Seren, he heard Emrys's voice issue a command and the snarling of the shadow-foxes abruptly ended.

With no real plan, Calon used his anger to heat his iron rending hands as he advanced at pace towards them. He lunged at both men simultaneously, grabbing both by the front of their necks with his burning hot hands, gouging his fingers straight into their flesh and squeezing their Adam's apples. Neither made a sound as they collapsed, hands grasping at torn throats as blood poured out and life poured away. Cooling his cloaked hands, he freed Seren's shackles as easily as he had Emrys and was about to release the iron band from her head when a hand grabbed his shoulder and spun him round.

"Go," the familiar raspy voice ordered. The old Marwolleth looped his arms under Seren's legs and hefted her onto his shoulder, her torn tunic falling to the ground. To Calon's astonishment, Emrys was running easily for the woods. Calon followed, amazed at the Marwolleth's strength and fortitude. He was aware as he ran of the three shadow-foxes running beside and around them. Once in the safety and darkness of the trees, the Marwolleth slowed to a steady trot as he turned to his shadow-fox and said something Calon didn't hear. The three foxes all turned back. Behind him, moments later, Calon heard a chilling, wolf like howl. Immediately, two more howls joined it, the undulating wail the most unnerving sound he had heard. *Who knows what those Chancel men make of that*, he thought as he loped along behind Seren and her guardian.

After running for a few minutes, they crested a rise and began moving downhill, eventually they crossed a small brook and then followed that a little further, stopping when they reached a small waterfall that fed a pool. Emrys climbed down the eight-foot drop with some care, with his Seren still over his shoulder. Calon followed, jumping down a series of large boulders. From pool level Calon could see that the waterfall tumbled over a huge stone shelf. The old Marwolleth eased under this shelf and eased into the darkness beneath. Calon followed, amazed to see that the rock had been fashioned into a cave. A large iron-elm door lay discarded to one side of the entrance.

In the cave, Emrys lay Seren on the ground, demanded that Calon take off his tunic, which he lay over her before gently cupping her face. Calon finally saw to the iron band that had been fixed tightly about her head, removing it easily, but somewhat alarmed at the red, bloodied marks it left on the skin of her forehead where the spikes on the inside had punctured her skin. Her eyes fluttered open briefly, a half-smile crossing her lips, but she soon closed them again, lost in her own torments. The Marwolleth then turned to him.

"Who are you?" he asked. "Who are you that you can weave iron?"

"My name's Calon," he replied. "Calon-Eryr," he quickly added, remembering his full name.

The big Marwolleth's eyes narrowed. "Eagle-Heart," he said before stepping forward and grabbing Calon's chin, turning his head to odd angles. "You have your mother's face," he said softly. He let go of Calon's chin and patted his shoulder. The Marwolleth's whole demeanour seemed to change then, smiling he added, "I am Emrys. My brother Gerallt was your grandfather. I thank you for rescuing us from the Chancel men. You must have a tale and I would hear it from you, one that will be long in the telling no doubt, but we have no time now." Emrys looked back towards Seren. "She will need healing more than I can manage. Are you able, Calon?" Calon nodded and moved over to Seren, kneeling down by her side.

"I was given a *craith*," he patted the place on his neck, "and some teaching that would allow me to heal my own wounds… so I think I can, but I don't really know how."

Emrys joined him. "You must place your hands over the *craith* and cloak them. Gold is the colour of healing." Calon did, touching the craith, but when he cloaked his hands they were not gold. Emrys laughed. "No, I meant cloak your hands while you are touching the craith." Calon did, putting his right hand on to the markings first. When he pulled it back his hand looked normal but there was a faint golden glow. He repeated the process with his left hand.

"Now place your hands on Seren's wounds. The magic will dramatically speed the process her body is already performing." Starting with her bruised face, Calon placed his glowing hands gently on the swollen cheeks and split lips. "Take them off once you have touched them," Emrys told him. Calon did and saw that the gold glow now rose from the wounds he had touched, looking for all the world like golden flames flickering in the darkness of the cave, illuminating Seren's face. He turned and looked at Emrys, who smiled and nodded.

"I have never seen a healing so pure. Notice how the big swelling on her cheek glows more brightly. This means it is a more serious wound. I suspect her cheekbone is broken." Looking at Calon again, he said, "I will leave you to this. My grandniece has wounds I do not wish to see. Check her whole body." With that he left the cave and made his way into the trees. Calon watched him leave, horrified at the injuries that Emrys' back bore, but at the same time impressed by his courage and energy.

Resolving to treat Emrys as well, he turned back to Seren, removing the tunic that Emrys had laid over her. Her torso was a catalogue of torture. Her breasts had been bitten, teeth marks clearly visible; small cuts had been made across her nipples; lash marks showed where a whip had been used on her and great, purple bruises showed where she had been kicked. He could hear how laboured her breathing was, so started by placing his hands on her ribs. Seren groaned but remained unconscious. Calon focused his energy into his hands and began a slow process of feeling her all over.

When he had finished, Seren's whole torso burned like an autumn fire—the gold light flickering with real intensity around the ribs on her left-hand side. Satisfied he had set the healing in process, he saw to her bruised and battered arms next, before turning her carefully on to her front. Less had been done to her back, a few lashes of the whip, red and angry were all he could see. She had been chained from the top of her thighs down, so rather than remove her leather trews, he felt his way up and down both legs; the gold light only showed in three places on her right thigh.

Turning back over, Calon saw that the gold healing glow had dimmed slightly. He covered her up and looked about the cave. He saw a large, flat stone discarded against a wall. Retrieving it, he saw it was a hearth-stone. Cloaking his hands, he heated it, and left it close to her sleeping form, creating some warmth for Seren. Walking outside, he surveyed the pool in the spreading dawn sunlight, wondering if there were a way he could heat some water to bathe her wounds and clean the grime and dried blood from her body. He saw that the water to his right and furthest from the waterfall was fairly shallow. He waded into it and began hauling a few rocks over to form a small pond.

"Fine for bathing in," the returning Emrys commented across the pond. "But don't drink it, it's tainted." He pointed at a large black stone in the centre of the large pond. "Drink from the waterfall where it's still fresh." Calon nodded his understanding, watching the old Marwolleth who was carrying three or four long staves and a large bundle of bracken towards the cave. Intrigued by the large stone, Calon waded out to the centre of the pond, nearly falling a few times on the rough rocky bottom of the pond. By the time he reached the large stone, the water was chest high. He took a deep breath and ducked under to examine the big stone. He ran his hands along its length, about the same as his height and found he could get his arms right around it.

It was a perfect cylinder, clearly worked by magic, that stood bolt upright in the pool, its top a good few inches the pond's surface. The cylinder was beautifully smooth like glass, and Calon sensed the tell-tale 'wrongness' that indicated void-stone was present. He could also sense that iron was part of the monolith. Surfacing for breath, Calon resolved to get it to the shore so he could get a better look at it. Cadfan had shown him how to use magic to move heavier boulders than this and he knew that the water would help him manage the weight of it. He dived down again to examine the base, finding it sat on a wide block of granite. The base of the monolith had a channel worked into it that ran the length of the base; a channel big enough for Calon to slide his arm into. Halfway in, he realised that a large disk of hearth stone had been set into the granite and it was on this that the monolith rested.

Cadfan had told him about this; how hearth stone could be easily heated and made molten; other stones could then be welded to it so that when it cooled it was an unbreakable join. Unbreakable, but easily separated by a stone-weaver.

Calon heated the hearth stone, the water hissing and fizzing around him as he did so. Then breaking to the surface, Calon planted his feet and lifted the monolith from the base, quite comfortable with his arms wrapped around it. He struggled over to the shore where he had begun making a bathing pool for Seren and manhandled it onto the bank.

"You are a helpful person to know, young Calon Eryr," Emrys said smiling at him. "That must have been placed there by the Cawrrocs centuries ago. For as long as we have lived here, the Marwolleth have known this water was poisoned." Calon smiled and nodded at his great-uncle but headed straight back to the centre of the pool. Diving down again, he placed both hands onto the hearth-stone circle that had been set into the granite. He warmed the stone then gently pushed the backs of both hands into the rock until they hit granite on the other side.

He then filled the disk with magic and lifted it free, Cadfan's words running through his mind—*don't focus on the weight and what you think you can't do; focus on the magic and what it can do*—as he carried it back to the shore. Putting it down and freeing his hands he saw that the disk was a perfect circle, roughly a yard in diameter and a good four inches thick. Whilst carrying it back he had already decided how he was going to shape it and set to the task immediately. He worked the stone from the centre to the edge, pushing and smoothing the hearth-stone gently into the shape he wanted.

A few minutes later, he stood back to admire his efforts and was pleased with what he saw. He had extended the length and pulled the sides up to create an oval basin that would fill the area he had begun shaping. Ideally, he would have liked it deeper, it was only a shallow basin, but he wanted water to move across it, not stagnate inside it, and he can could fashion deeper sides from ordinary stone. The fact it was hearth-stone meant he could heat it easily for Seren.

"I have put Seren into a sleep," Emrys' voice jerked Calon from his thoughts. "So if you were intending to bathe her, it will have to wait till the evening." The Marwolleth scooped up some water in a bark bowl, turned then and walked back to the cave. Calon followed, his eyes fixed on the scars on his great-uncle's back. When Emrys sat down, Calon walked up behind him, his hands already a golden glow, and whilst Emrys wove his wood, Calon healed the wounds on his back. Emrys muttered his thanks when Calon had finished, his attention on the bow he was making from the strong yew he had collected; a bow that was fully six feet in length, thick around the middle and tapered towards the end.

"It's a long bow," Emrys answered to his question. "It has great power. Not as much power as my wych-wood bow. But the Chancel men still have that. Tonight, I will retrieve it."

"Seren had one," Calon told him. "They must have that as well. We must get it back."

His great uncle stopped and looked at him. "I go to kill Calon. You who can weave stone must have learned what you know from the Cawrrocs, a peaceful people who abhor violence. I fear to use you this night without any training. Once we have regained our things

I will teach you if you wish to learn. But one step at a time."

"What can I do?" he asked. "There must be something."

Emrys smiled and grasped his shoulder. "You have healed us and made us ready to fight. We could not have done that. If you wish to train, you will need weapons. Copy my bow as best you can," he said passing it over to Calon along with a second yew stave. "I will make Seren a bow, then sleep a while." Calon accepted the task and moved away to work by himself. He went and sat on the smooth black monolith he had hauled from the water. He could sense the faint pull of the void-stone and put the bow and yew stave down to better examine it. Cloaking his hands, he traced them over the surface, seeking to understand it's composition. As Cadfan had taught him he waited for instinct to tell him when and where to work the stone. Feeling the place was right he pushed the fingers of both hands into the monolith and pulled at the stone. Unexpectedly a shard, the entire length of the monolith sheared off in his hands. The shard felt light and he waved it in the air; the swish of the shard as he cut and sliced it through the air was very satisfying.

His actions had attracted the attention of Emrys who put the yew he was working on down and strolled across.

"I never thought to see blade-wood again," Emrys told him. Calon looked up, the awe in his great-uncle's voice was clear. "Your grandfather created a sword fashioned from this." He looked at Calon, adding, "He was not affected by iron like the rest of us, though he couldn't manipulate it as easily as you do. He had it with him when he left for Gorwynoll. That was the last time I saw it." He paused to look at the ruptured monolith. "We thought the Cawrrocs had destroyed it all, or hidden it deep within the mountains." He still gazed at the monolith. Calon joined him.

"It was hidden. It has been coated in a mixture of rock and a small amount of void-stone, look," Calon said, pointing at the place the shard had broken from. "That is why you stand a stare at it—pure void stone steals your mind away. The small amount here would make you forget you'd seen it the minute you walked from the pool. Also, you thought the water poisoned, but I imagine the Cawrrocs placed a ward spell of some kind on it to deter you from examining it." Calon ushered Emrys away from the monolith, to get him away from the pull of the void stone.

Once he had him settled to working on his long-bow, he went back and patiently stripped the void-stone infused layer from the great stone, separating the two types of stone. There was very little void-stone at all; the sphere Calon made of the pure black diamond was the size of an apple. He coated this with a six-inch layer of the limestone it had been fused into, creating a large boulder, rounded and smooth. Rolling it down into the pond, he waded back into the centre of the pool, carrying the sphere to where he had taken the monolith from. Ducking into the water, he eased it back onto its plinth and left it there.

He returned to the monolith to find Emrys sitting close to it, waiting for him. The blade-wood beside him has almost black but had a reddish tint to it.

"See how it is red here," Emrys said pointing to a red seam in the rock. "The Cawrrocs somehow fused it with iron which made it virtually unbreakable; and fashioned blades so sharp they would cut anything and never dull. The wood on its own could be made into weapons but they were too brittle. With the Cawrrocs helping him work the fossilised wood, your grandfather, Gerallt, was able to work iron ore into the blade-wood to fashion his sword. The Cawrrocs were appalled at what they had done, refusing to make more. Without them the skills were lost. I have never known any Marwolleth who could tolerate or work the iron. Until you."

"But you said my grandfather—" Calon started to say.

"Your grandfather could tolerate the iron, but working it enfeebled him and left his magic weakened. The iron in that sword tainted him forever. Yet that seems to be the root of your prowess, perhaps?" Emrys stood lost in thought before adding, "Your father was able to use that damned weapon as well. Its handle was made of horn so he was able to wield it, but no other of our people could even bear to pick it up." He stopped and looked at Calon. "But if you can fashion weapons from his monolith, they would be finest of blades. Make yourself a sword, Calon."

215

"Do you have a sword, Uncle?" Calon asked.

"Uncle, is it?" Emrys smiled. "I suppose that's as good as anything." He went and retrieved one of the unworked boughs of yew. Sitting down next to Calon he broke the stave into two pieces, one twice as long as the other. Taking the longer section, he spent a few minutes shaping it, weaving it into the shape of a sword with a slim blade slightly curved towards the end. He gave this to Calon to hold. The 'blade' was nearly four feet long and felt good in his hand as he swished it to and for.

"Here," Emrys said, holding up another blade. "Most Marwolleth use a long sword like the one you're holding and a shorter blade like this one for stabbing and close work." The second blade was straight and Emrys had curved a handle that covered the knuckles, a handle with sharp ridges on it.

Calon looked the two blades over carefully. "You said the handle of my father's sword was horn. How was it attached to the blade-wood?"

"We don't know. We suspect that the blade wood was heated and the horn forced on to it. That knowledge is lost as no Marwolleth could ever work the blade-wood with iron. You will find a way." Emrys left him and went back to fashioning another long bow. Calon studied the wooden swords and the blade-wood. He could see and sense how the iron and blade-wood had been worked into very thin strips then layered together. He could see the pattern of the twisting as the metal and wood have been twisted tightly, like the narwhal tusk he had seen at a fayre. The whole thing would then have been smoothed flat, perhaps hammered out even. He examined the monolith more closely and by uncovering more of the blade-wood he could see that long staves had been loosely melded together. Someone long ago had been prepared to made something from these long sections, swords probably, then changed their mind and worked them together into this large monolith which was then covered in void-stone. "Powerful magic," he said to himself, wondering about the one who had been able to do all of that.

Picking up the stave, he began trying to weave it. He cloaked his hands and tentatively tried working the blade-wood. The tightly packed folds of wood and iron had a slightly oily feel and he saw the blade-wood range in colours from a dep olive green to almost black, the iron giving it an occasional red glaze. He found shaping it ridiculously easy. Using the wooden sword Emrys had created he developed an idea of how to proceed. He began by taking thin strips of the blade wood. He found with precision and care, he could create a 'thread' of wood

216

as fine as spun wool. Within an hour, he had perfected his techniques and had reduced the whole shard to a pile of 'threads'. Laying them all out together, he packed then tightly and bound them with the 'thread he had kept for that purpose.

His next step was to fuse all of the 'threads' together for roughly a foot at one end. He drove this end into the rock at his feet to fix it then began the process of heating and twisting the blade-wood as tightly as he could from the base to the tip. When he was done the long twist of wood looked very impressive. He looked up to see if Emrys had been keeping an eye on him but saw that the old Marwolleth had fallen asleep. Turning his face to the sky he could see that it was noon or there abouts. He could see the two yew long-bows that his great-uncle had created and had an idea. He immediately sheared off another of the staves and began 'threading' it. It took him half the time the first one had taken him.

He then repeated the twisting process before shearing both 'twists' off at the point they reached the rock, leaving the untwisted threads in stone. He now had two long, twisted lengths of blade-wood, the twists spanning about five feet. He worked one a bit further, stretching it as he did from the centre out towards the end, replicating the shape and length of the long-bows Uncle had made. He was pleased with his efforts but knew the bow would be next to useless for anyone other than him. The iron 'taint' would make it difficult to use. Putting the finished bow to one side, he started the threading process again. This time however, he used his magic to tease the iron from half of the threads. He was about to discard these, but then tried working the pure iron into the unprocessed threads, creating a long thin, circular stave. Then using the pure blade-wood threads he had unravelled from its iron taint, he coated the iron rich stave completely in the wood, shaping a beautiful wooden bow. He was unsure if the iron underneath would cause a problem but he would let Uncle be the judge of that.

With real care, he then thinned out the centre before taking some of the hearth-stone from the lip of the bathing basin he had made Seren, moulding it in place to make a hand hold for the bow. He looked carefully at the ends of the bow to see how the bow string would attach. He then duplicated theses hooks in hearth-stone before attaching them on the tips of blade-wood bow. Now all he needed was a bow string, and his uncle to test it. Laying it down by the two yew long-bows, he turned his thoughts back to making a sword.

Calon began by holding the wooden sword and swinging it around. Hefting the wooden sword, he felt the length was right, so he severed the twist to match it. The process of shaping the blade proved a lot more draining than shaping the bow. Calon had to compress the blade-wood to make the blade thin. The sharp outer edge took a lot of concentration to create and he was glad his hands were cloaked or he felt he would have lost a few fingers. After a couple of hours, he had finished the basic blade and tang, but felt exhausted. He recognised the feeling as the way constant use of magic would drain him.

He looked at the unfinished sword and resolved to finish it the following day. He needed to attach a hilt, pommel and guard to the tang. The hilt he could make from hearth-stone, as he had fashioned the handle of the bow, meaning Emrys wouldn't need to touch the blade-wood. The pommel and guard were a different matter. As a temporary measure, and simply because it was an easy substance to work with, he used hearth-stone to coat the blade-wood pommel and guard. He hoped Emrys would help him solve the problem at a later date. Inordinately pleased with himself, he slumped to the ground, the completed sword in front of him. The dark blade almost shimmered; it's confusion of greens, reds and silver seemed almost alive.

He woke with a start as an icy pain bored into his temples. He opened his eyes to see a large hand spread in front of his face, middle finger and thumb pressed into either temple.

"Uncle," he croaked, the intense pain flaring behind his eyes. He tried to push the hand away.

"Wait, Calon," Emrys said. "This won't take long and you will feel better. The magic use drains the inexperienced this way." Emrys was right. After a few seconds, the icy agony dimmed to a coolness, washing his mind clear of pain and tiredness. Emrys let go and hauled him upright. "Seren needs to bathe now. You said you would heat the water." Calon nodded and stretched. He felt wide awake and well rested, as though he had slept for hours.

"What have you done to me?" he asked touching his own temples.

"I have used magic to restore you. Seren needs to bathe," he indicated the pond. "And I need you to show me these weapons." As Calon set to heating the hearth-stones to warm the water, he heard Emrys calling to Seren to come and bathe. He then grabbed Calon, telling him to collect the blade-wood sword and bow and the pair moved off into the trees.

"Are these safe for me to touch?" was Uncle's first question.

"I think so," Calon replied. He explained his processing of the ironed blade-wood and his coating of the bow. "I used hearth-stone to cover the blade-wood to create the grip. I thought to heat it so you could mould the grip to fit your hand. The sword is the same and I have coated the pommel and guards with hearth-stone to protect you, but I think we need something harder and more durable for that. I was hoping you could suggest something. I would love to see my father's sword to see how these parts were made."

"That I can tell you, but we have none here. There is a place in the far west of Penrhyn on the coast where giant trees of stone lay buried in the sand. On low tides you can walk out to touch them. This material, neither wood or stone, can be used. We weave this into strong blades. It is perfect for the pommels and guards too, but as for the bow I like the idea of hearth-stone on the grip. It would make it comfortable to hold." Tentatively, he picked up the bow with both hands, holding only the stave. "I can almost feel the iron beneath," he told Calon. "Like trying to remember a dream. This will be fine. More than fine."

Calon then had him hold the hearth-stone grip as tightly as he could, whilst he also touched it, softening it slightly so his great-uncle's hand squeezed gently into it, forming a perfect mould of his fingers. From beneath his belt, he produced a bow string. Looping one end over the upper notch, he played the string between his fingers and looped the other end over the lower notch. Calon knew the string was too loose and watched inn fascination as Emrys pulled the string back then let it go. The string snapped back, taut enough to bend the bow slightly. Emrys picked it up then, arm held out straight, he easily pulled the string back to his cheek. Looking puzzled, he repeated this a few times.

"The full draw is too easy," he stated. "I can't imagine there is any power here." Calon was crestfallen, sure this would have worked. Emrys saw his anguish and handed the bow back to him. "If we had arrows, we could test it and decide how to resolve the problem. Your idea is good, don't despair." Calon felt his uncle was being kind and watched as the old Marwolleth rummaged around in the trees for an arrow. He returned with a bent branch, thin enough to use as an arrow. He used magic to straighten, smooth and sharpen it. He bemoaned the lack of feathers for flights but said it wasn't necessary at this stage as they just wanted to see if the bow would propel it.

He was about to string the arrow to the bow when Calon made him stop. The youngster took the arrow and, cloaking his hands, began working at the wood towards one end. Remembering how his da would fashion throwing arrows with spiralled flights that he could throw unerringly accurately, he raised small wooden flights between his fingers that wound around the shaft of the arrow. He then looked around for a small piece of stone which he fashioned into a coned arrowhead that he wove into the other end. He handed this to the waiting Emrys who, nodded appreciatively. Fitting it to the bow he drew the bow-string back as far as he could, aimed at a large tree trunk some thirty paces away, exhaled and loosed. Neither of them saw the arrow fly. They both heard the sharp crack of it striking home. They looked at each other, then both looked at the bow. Then whooping with delight and gabbling simultaneously, they ran to find the arrow. It had missed the tree trunk he had aimed for and hit the rock face behind it. Looking around on the forest floor, neither of them could see the arrow.

"The flights can't spiral like that, Calon, they struck the bow as it flew, causing it to veer off. We need to stagger the flights so the arrow is loosed unimpeded." They were still searching when Seren strolled over, hair damp and all fresh-faced from her bathing. Her wounds had vanished and she looked healthy. She had fashioned a top of sorts that left her stomach visible but covered her breasts.

"What are you looking for?" she asked them.

"An arrow," Calon replied.

Emrys then began enthusing about the power of the blade-wood bow when Seren said, "This arrow?" They both looked up. She was pointing towards the rock face. Calon's arrow had pierced the rock, the stone arrowhead half buried in the stone. Seren, followed by Emrys, both tried unsuccessfully to pull the arrow from the rock. Calon removed it easily. Emrys repeated the need to alter the flights but Calon asked for the bow instead. With Emrys and Seren's help, he adjusted the grip of the bow, curving it slightly to allow the flights to pass the stave unhindered. On repeat shots, Emrys was able to send the arrow into a tree right up to the wooden flights. Seren surpassed that, sending it clean through the trunk.

"The power is extraordinary," she said softly, reverentially moving the bow around. "But the grip is uncomfortable." At Emrys' suggestion, Calon remoulded the grip for Seren's hand.

"She is longer-limbed than I," Emrys explained. "But has not the power in her arms. This bow was meant for her. She can loose arrows more quickly than I, and she never misses. The iron inside gives it such power."

"I have another idea I would like to try," Calon told them both. He explained how Anghenfyl and Cadfan had shown him how to create a craith using three separate strands bound into one. He took a hair from his own head and one from Emrys, but two from Seren. The first he wound around the grip of Seren's new bow, asking her to hold it tightly. He then put both of his hands around hers and worked magic into her hand and grip. He then asked Emrys to pick up and shoot the bow. Uncle was fine until he tried to draw the bow back, and wasn't able to move it. He looked questioningly at Calon, who laughed and clapped at his discomfort. The then wove the three strands of hair from each of them into the grip and repeated the 'tuning' process. This time Emrys managed a full draw easily. He handed the bow back to Seren.

"That is a rare and wondrous gift grandniece," he told her. "Now get to collecting wood for arrows." Seren, pleased as punch, not taking her eyes from the bow, headed off into the woods. "I would have liked that bow," he told Calon when she had gone. "But Seren needed something to take her mind off her capture and maltreatment."

"It was my pleasure, Uncle," Calon replied.

"Thank you, *Nephew*," Emrys responded, chuckling. "Show me this sword. I want my hair in the grip, mind."

When Seren returned with an armful of ash and oak branches, most of which were reasonably straight, Emrys was swinging his sword with gleeful abandon. He danced and twirled the blade in intricate patterns, almost blurring such was his speed of movement. Seeing Seren, he stopped and bowed.

"Well, granddaughter, you are not the only fortunate recipient of a wondrous gift. This sword…" He stopped lost for words. "It's as light as a cane and so easy to swing; its balance is perfect, despite looking too long. And Nephew here assures me it will cut through anything." He bowed once more before dancing away leaping into another set of drills. Calon simply raised his eyebrows as Seren looked at him, shaking her head. The two set to straightening the boughs and branches Seren had gathered, weaving the wood into beautiful arrows. Calon showed her the knack of the spiral flights and set himself the task of adding the bodkin arrow heads, fashioned from the iron corrupted blade-wood. By the time they were done the sun was setting and a harsh chill was beginning to settle. Emrys came back, his sword in his hand.

"Come inside," he told them soberly. "We must eat and then hunt the Chancel."

The both followed. "How will we find them in the dark Uncle?" Calon asked as he entered the cave.

Emrys looked at him. "I forget. You are so clever, so able, but you know little of out ways. The shadow foxes Calon. Where do you think they are? They trail the Chancel men, and we can always find a bond animal. Think of your fox, for he clearly adopted you, and tell me which direction he is." Calon thought of Hela and concentrated on trying to link. He felt a soft acknowledgment, almost a warmth, and turned to look into the descending darkness towards where he knew Hela stalked. Emrys patted his shoulder. "Myllane and Gelert, my fox, are there also. Now eat," Uncle said. "Then we hunt."

Calon ate and prepared himself for the night's work ahead. Uncle gave him the leather bands that had held his old sword to strap his unfinished blade on his back; he saw that Uncle had no way of carrying his own weapon yet, so just held it in his hand. Calon packed a small piece of void stone in his pack; collected his new long bow and arrows and walked up the steep bank, edging across to stand where the river tumbled over the rock ledge. He looked down and saw that Uncle was lecturing Seren on something; the pair were ready to move, fully armed. Uncle then hugged Seren and kissed the top of her head before waving to Calon and loping off into the darkening woods. Seren jogged up towards him, almost bouncing up the rough rock face to join him.

Seeing the question in his face, Seren answered it before it could be asked. "Uncle has changed his plan. Since he no longer needs to retrieve his bow and sword, he goes to try and get in front of the Chancel men; he wants us to get behind them and start picking them off, make them wary, frighten them a little, well, a lot. So, we'll head back to their camp and follow their trail from there. We'll need to run cloaked to catch up with them, and see where we're going," she told him. "Myllane and…"

"Hela," Calon told her.

"Hela," she smiled at the name. "Myllane and Hela are tracking them. Fasten on to Hela and you'll know which way to go if we get lost." With that Seren turned and loped off into the darkness. With their eyes cloaked, Calon knew they would have little trouble seeing in the dark, hoisting his pack onto his back and slinging his bow over his shoulder, he set off after her, Hela a warm acknowledgment in his mind.

After running through the night Calon and Seren caught up with the Chancel invaders. Seren slowed as they neared and it wasn't until she crouched down to her knees that Calon saw Myllane, the shadow-fox, motionless ears alert and attention fixed on a point beyond Calon's vision. He paused and tried to focus on Hela, but a cold nose nudging his hand negated that. He knelt and fussed the fox behind its ears.

"They are tired. They need to feed and rest," Seren told him. "Head back to the young pine trees and we passed and set up a lodge. I will track the Chancel men until dark, then head back to you when the foxes find me. Make sure they rest." With that she was gone.

Calon returned to a stretch of young pines that were growing where some old trees had fallen. He surveyed his options before deciding on a group of five trees that were close. His ambition took greater effort than he had expected but the result was well worth it. The lodge he had created had the tallest tree, branches wound tightly to the trunk, in the centre, whilst he had pulled the outer four trees into the centre trunk, before weaving the branches together to create the walls. He was dismayed to see more than a few gaps, but a fallen pine proved a good solution, stripping the branches with dense foliage to add to his walls. The result was not as smooth or neat as Seren would have managed but it was his best effort so far and more importantly, it was proof against the cold night air.

By the time he had set the hearth stone up and placed a couple of stone-lights on the central trunk, the two shadow-foxes were curled asleep, close together near the opening of the lodge. He could see the lodge was fairly circular, which he was pleased about, and a good twelve feet in diameter. He heated the stone to almost red hot to warm the lodge enough to take the chill from the air, before he lay down on a bed of bracken and fell into a deep sleep almost straight away.

He awoke some time before noon, mid-morning was his best guess. The two shadow-foxes still lay curled tight. Hela lifted her head briefly as he left the lodge. Although it was daylight, the dense canopy of pines made everywhere look dark bar the small patch of new trees where he now stood. He moved around his lodge, smoothing and reworking the branches that formed the walls. The great pine that had fallen, lay a few yards in front of the lodge and Calon walked over to it, removing some more of the branches, stripping away some of the bark he used his magic to mould a comfortable place to sit. His next task was to collect some fresh water. They had more or less followed the stream that led to the waterfall, so he knew he was close. Looking around he could see an animal trail heading of in roughly the right direction and followed that. After only a minute of walking he could pick out the sound of the babbling stream and was back at the lodge with fresh water in no time.

After cooking and eating, Calon went to the lodge for his pack and the unfinished blade-wood sword. As he had time, he resolved to finish the blade and grip while he waited for Seren. He had been thinking about how to complete the sword as he had run last night, so had a clear plan. He removed the void-stone from his pack and through trial and error managed to make a thin veneer of the void-stone that he coated the sword blade with. After coating the tang with a layer of pine that he moulded for his grip, he used coarse leather to make the grip. He had just enough void-stone left that he could 'thread' and loop around the leather grip, making the sword useless for anyone not made immune to the effects of the void-stone. The finished blade was wonderful. Calon swished it around in front of him, the black blade hissing through the air.

He was hungry now, and could see that the sun had passed its zenith, so he set about making a stew so Seren could eat when she got back. On his return to the lodge, he was surprised to see that the Myllane, Seren's shadow-fox had gone whilst he had been absorbed with his sword. He set to rifling Seren's pack and found a supply of mushrooms and roots he could add to the pot. He also collected some wild garlic when he went for more water. With the stew simmering gently on the hearth-stone he'd laid by his tree seat, Calon sat outside to enjoy the afternoon sun.

Still waiting for Seren to return, he decided that making more arrows would be a productive use of his time. It was while he was finishing the first arrow that a piercing shriek sounded straight above him, causing him to jump and drop the arrow. The flapping of wings told him it had been a hunting bird of some description, perhaps a falcon. As his heart rate returned to normal, the shrieking bird gave him an idea. Uncle had said to scare the Chancel men. Well, he reasoned with himself, if I could shoot arrows that whistled, or screamed, as they flew; and if I could shoot them at night, that would put the fear of death into the invaders. Remembering how his da made 'hawk' arrows that he would shoot over flocks of migrating birds, mimicking the cries of flacons and hawks. The geese or ducks would then land on the water for safety from the hunting birds, where his da could shoot them more easily with a normal arrow.

He remembered watching his da shape a cone of wood before splitting it in half across the middle. He would then hollow out the two halves using burning coals, a process that Calon was fascinated by: he could never understand how the coal would burn down as his da blew on it, before tipping out to let it cool a little. He would then add a slightly smaller coal and continue blowing. Once both halves were done, he would scrape the insides clean with his skinning knife, make two whistle holes, then glue the halves together. The weight of the whistling cone at the tip meant the arrows didn't need flights. With his ability to *weave* wood, shaping a hollow cone was easy.

He experimented with a few designs, finding that a shorter, thinner cone with narrow holes made the most jarring sound. He kept all the 'whistlers' he made, twenty-two in all, and knew he would have a variety of sounds. Testing them was enjoyable for him and Hela, who retrieved the arrows with great skill. He tried shooting two and three at once, with great effect if the whistles were of a different pitch, and Hela would somehow manage to retrieve all three.

Towards evening, the other two shadow-foxes had returned. He was standing, practicing twirling his sword, when all three suddenly stood, ears pricked up before Myllane gave a yelp and rushed into the darkness of the trees, tail wagging. Seren. Calon rested his sword against his shoulder and waited. Seren jogged into the clearing, Myllane at her heels.

"Calon, you lovely man, I smell food," Seren said with a big smile. Calon indicated the stew, simmering gently. "You've even made bowls," Seren exclaimed, holding up a beautifully smooth bowl. She held it up to her nose and sniffed it. "Smells a bit piney," she teased. "But it will add to the flavour." Calon coloured a little. He hadn't thought of that.

"Sorry," he told Seren, before adding, "I can probably line it with stone, it would—"

"It's fine, Calon, honestly," she interrupted. "Much better than I usually eat out of."

She began stirring the pot with one of the spoons he had also made from pine. "Smells good. What's in here?" she asked.

Calon told her what he'd put in. Seren then swung her pack from around her shoulder and placed it on the floor in front of her. She hauled a leg of something out of the pack, wrapped in wide, green leaves. "Deer," she told him. She set to with a knife, removing the leaves and slicing off chunks of venison into the stew. The rest she carved into three piles for the foxes. "Give it a few minutes to warm through and we'll tuck in." She nodded at his sword. "You've been busy."

Pleased he had a chance to show off his handywork, he hefted the sword in front of him and started twirling it as he had seen Uncle doing. Almost as soon as he had started, Seren called out, "Whoa! Stop!" Calon did and looked at her. "What you were just doing, Calon, it feels… wrong."

"I know," Calon said crestfallen. "I've watched Uncle, but no one has ever taught me how to sword fight."

"No, that's not what I meant. The sword… when you were waving it around, I was…sort of mesmerised by it. It made me feel *wrong*."

"The void-stone," Calon mumbled, his disappointment suddenly forgotten. "It's the void-stone I coated the blade with." He immediately threw himself into a frenzy of swordplay until Seren threw a pinecone at him that bounced off his forehead.

"Not in front of me, Calon, it's … not natural. Put it down. Practice with something else." Knowing the effects the void-stone had had on him under the mountain, Calon complied, before excitedly picking up his bow and his 'whistlers'. Seren was much more impressed by these. She even improved the concept by suggesting that if they could light the inside of the whistle with a glow, the two holes would like red eyes flying through the night sky.

After much discussion and practice with various materials, the pinecone Seren had thrown at him gave Calon the perfect material—the scales of the cone. By heating a scale so it was smoking then firing the arrow, the air had the effect of making it glow red, in some cases they even caught fire, but it was a great addition. The foxes loved the game too. The gathered and flaked a few cones before sitting down to eat. The stew was quite bland until Seren added a few things from one of her little pouches—including some salt, which made it taste wonderful.

After sleeping for a few hours, the pair rose, gathered their weapons and small packs and set out. They had agreed to leave the lodge as it was. Travelling at night was little problem as with eyes cloaked, they could make their way easily, the shadow-foxes drifting like ghosts ahead of them. Calon still marvelled at the odd grey world he walked through with his eyes cloaked. In his mind he felt he was walking through a charcoal sketch of the world, the lack of colour made the walking seem dream like.

As dawn threatened, they finally came within bowshot of the Chancel camp. Smoke in the air was the giveaway. Seren slowed and crept forward until they could just make out a feint, orange flickering from a camp fire. There they stopped. Calon questioned this, wanting to get in closer, but Seren, whispering into his ear, warned him the humans would be wary after his attack had freed her and Uncle, and sentries were likely.

"They have caught me once in a trap. Shame on me if they do so again." She told him as she held his face in her hands. She smiled as Myllane and Hela began nuzzling into them both, before trotting off into the gloom, seeming to disappear after only moving a few feet away. Within two minutes Myllane reappeared. Seren indicated they should stay silent and crept after her fox. They had stolen perhaps fifty yards forward before Myllane shrank to the forest floor. Seren and Calon stopped. Seren pointed off towards their right. At first Calon saw nothing. But a sudden movement of shadow caught his eye. The flare of a match that was then thrust into the bowl of a clay pipe silhouetted a man's head. He stood facing the camp, behind a tree as though hiding from his own colleagues.

The guard was on a rise that looked over a clearing below that lay in a bend of the river. Calon realised he was watching from the shadows, hoping to surprise any would be attackers. Looking carefully, he began to interpret the shadows, seeing that the man's crossbow was leaning against the same tree its owner was propped against. Seren took his head into her hands again and whispered into his ear.

"The dawn breaks. The guards are relaxing, thinking they have made it through the night. This is a good time to catch them unawares." She released his head and prepared her new bow. Selecting an arrow, she quickly aimed and released, before grabbing Calon's arm and easing him back into the dark heart of the forest. He was a little stunned. Calon knew that Seren's magic meant she had killed the man before he knew what had hit him, but the ease with which she took a life confounded him.

It wasn't until daylight had cleared the darkness that the dead guard was found. From where they waited, Calon and Seren heard the shouts of his fellows looking for him, calling him in. A sudden silence followed by urgent calling indicated that they had found him. Crouched in the shadows, Calon could make out the forms of the Chancel men in the distance, could see them backing down into their camp. He and Seren inched forward, staying out of view, cloaked to avoid detection, until they were back in sight of the dead guard. Calon had expected his fellows to take him or bury him, but he had been left where he'd died, skewered totally upright to the tree that he had stood behind, the arrow's spiralled flight was all that could be seen, jutting from his forehead. He could have been standing guard.

"This bow…," Seren whispered behind him, a reverence in her voice. "I think I'll take another shot. They are already unnerved." She took another arrow and eased to the top of the slope, still sheltered from view by the trees. It was a long shot to the camp from here, further than Calon had expected. They had pitched their tents on the other side of the meandering river, over two hundred yards away from their current position. "Let's see how this bow fares over a distance." She nocked an arrow and looked over at the camp. Men were scuttling around, packing things away, some taking down the tents. Others, mainly those holding crossbows, stood in an outer ring, surrounding the camp but facing outward into the trees.

Seren sighted on one of these guards, easily drew back the bow, aimed and released in one fluid movement. Calon tried to follow the flight of the arrow, but it flew too fast. He saw one of the crossbow men jerk upright then collapse where he stood. The nearest man to him rushed over, looked down at the corpse of his comrade then walked a few paces behind him. He bent and pulled the arrow from where it had landed. He raised the alarm, shouting out to the other guards to take cover. The camp was flooded with chaos. An officer shouted over from his hiding place behind a two wheeled cart carrying a water barrel. Calon couldn't make out the question from this far away, but he heard the shouted response.

"It went straight fucking through him." Directing men to move forwards, the officer continued shouting orders until Seren's second arrow slammed through his chest, poleaxing him. This was the final straw. A few of the crossbowmen loosed their bolts into the trees, none anywhere near to Seren's position and retreated back into the camp, grabbing bags and equipment before surging across the river. Calon and Seren had discussed their plan of action already and let the Chancel men leave without any pursuit. The shadow-foxes followed the invaders and would alert Seren if there were any waiting to ambush. Calon and Seren had a few hours to rest and prepare for the night ahead—they would start to harass the invaders in the afternoon when they were already weary from a day of marching and watchfulness. When the Chancel men stopped to set up camp, they would begin their campaign of terror and harass them through the night.

Chapter 14
Confrontation

Two days later, Calon surveyed the camp below him. The Chancel men's slow march had snaked along the river valley, the level ground of the valley floor benefitted the crawling army as they were using two-wheeled carts to transport equipment, so staying by the river side was really their only option. Water would always be plentiful as well. Tracking them from the slopes above was therefore easy for he and Seren, and the slow-moving convoy made for effortless shooting. Calon and Seren targeted men in the middle of the column to slow the train and hopefully split the force. Any attempt the Chancel made to retaliate or attack them was doomed as they had a hard charge uphill by which time Seren and he would have melted away into the darkness of the pine forest.

In an effort to protect themselves, they had made large shields which men carried on their outside arms in an effort to protect themselves and their comrades, who now marched tightly packed. There was little protection for them however. The bows Calon had made were so powerful that the arrows they fired went straight through the wood, skewering the man holding it.

Seren and he were on opposite sides of the advancing troops now. They loosed occasional arrows simply to keep their enemy on high alert and wear their confidence down. They had planned for Calon to simply aim at the bulk of troops so he would hit something; Seren, who was a deadly genius with the bow, aimed for the officers and sergeants, and had killed seven so far. They had estimated the force had originally been two hundred and twenty men, and Seren's efforts meant the enemy were running short of leadership. Altogether Calon reckoned they had killed or injured over thirty of the invaders, and the two Marwolleth hoped that eventually these deaths would fan the flames of panic and cause a mass desertion which would see the Chancel fleeing back the way they had come.

Seren had said that she would send Myllane and Hela to him when it was time for them to stop and rest. When the foxes arrived, he was to shoot one more arrow then head back into the forest to wait for darkness.

As evening approached, the men below him had stopped and the few leaders they had left were huddled between two of the carts in an effort to shield themselves. They had taken to walking there through the afternoon. Calon knew Seren would be looking to take another of these commanders out of the reckoning. He caught occasional, brief glimpses of the gwerin who had guided them under the mountains. He'd even aimed at him a few times bit to no avail. He had urged Seren to target him, but she had refused saying there was much they needed to learn from that *rock-goblin*.

There were still over one hundred and fifty uninjured men on the march so it was easy for Mordwyn to stay hidden in the morass of humanity around him. He hoped that Emrys would create a *craith* for him like Seren's so that he could shoot without missing. With his breath starting to mist in the cold air, he was relieved when Hela's cold nose nudged him. Myllane appeared to his right. Hela was his fox now, she had claimed him, but she still preferred to follow Seren and Myllane.

Seren had explained that until they could share their 'being', Hela would never truly be his. Calon wasn't sure what this meant but was happy enough to wait. Drawing an arrow, Calon looked at the men below. He decided that the commanders huddling between the carts would be his target. With the daylight easing into dusk, he pulled the bow string back to his ear, released his breath slowly as Seren had told him, then released his shaft when he was at his most still. In the gathering gloom he had no hope of tracking his shot, so he switched his gaze to the Chancel men clustered around the carts just in time to see a short barrel on one of the carts explode, spilling a liquid of some sort. He also caught sight of a man, an officer he hoped, keeling over backwards clutching his chest.

As one, men crouched, most hiding behind a shield bearer and looked towards his bank. This gave Seren an opportunity. Her arrow passed straight through one poor unfortunate and speared two other men together. One died as the other screamed and writhed to free himself. No-one came to his aid. His screams though were suddenly cut short. Calon heard the snap of a crossbow and saw that one of his colleagues had silenced him. His job done, Calon moved back in to the dark of the forest to lay up for a few hours, eat and recuperate. Myllane had vanished, probably back to Seren, but he was pleased to see that Hela followed him into the safety of the trees; the shadow-fox was a great comfort.

There followed three more days and nights of stealth attacks on the Chancel armed force. The invaders moved ever more slowly. They had followed the stream down to where it merged with the Glendow River and skirted a small lake on their journey. Burdened not only by the constant threat of attack, but also by the number of injured and dying men they were managing, their progress was stilted. Seren said this was a great benefit to them as the slower they moved the easier it was to target them. They had agreed to leave the injured alive as caring for their injuries and moving them all added to the slowing of their advance. He and Seren had killed over thirty of the invaders in that time and succeeded in sowing panic and despondency among the troops.

The few leaders left now walked exclusively between the carts, which were always ridden by men holding double shields. Despite only killing a small portion of the force, their attacks wounded twice that number and both Calon and Seren felt that the invaders were at breaking point. The night attacks with the 'screamers' had worked so well that the Chancel men could never settle. He and Seren took turns to rest and sleep while the other continued random attacks; sometimes sending screamers over the camp, at other times picking off sentries. Yet despite this, the soldiers marched on. There was still no sign of Emrys, but Seren's trust was total and Calon felt this too.

"This Chancel force has advanced down the Glendow River and are almost within sight of the Haur Hills," Seren told Calon at one of their evening rendezvous. They liked to leave the invaders alone when they were setting up camp, giving their enemies time to bed in, whilst giving them time to eat and rest. "That must be their destination," she continued. "We have little use for the gold there other than as ornaments, but from what we know of these Chancel men, they worship it more than their vicious god."

Calon nodded at this, adding his own knowledge of how wealth obsessed many of the humans he knew were. "Their obsession seemed to be in having enough money to pay someone else to do their work."

Seren accepted this but then said, "But what do they hope to achieve? They have so few men; they left most of their equipment at their first camp on the Glendow; they must know we will continue to keep picking them off…"

"They have that mad gwerin Mordwyn with them still. He will be at the root of their plan. He is a powerful weaver and I think completely insane. I dread to think what he could be planning to do," Calon told her.

"He may be powerful but Uncle is powerful also, and if we keep them in the trees, what use would a gwerin rock-goblin be surrounded by wood he cannot weave?" They discussed their options well into the night and decided to leave the shadow-foxes to trail the depleted and demoralised force they had tracked and head through the night along the Glendow River to the start of the Haur Hills in the hope of meeting up with Uncle.

A long night saw them covering over twenty miles in Calon's estimation. Seren had laughed at that and said it was more liked twelve as they sat in the cold night, eating the last of their food. They had started walking consistently up gentle slopes just before Seren called a halt. "We are nearly at the end of the forest; one steep climb away," she said indicating up hill. "We'll rest here and wait for daylight before we move on, the dawn is probably an hour away, so grab some sleep." Seren lay down on her back then before adding, "This trail we have followed will bring us out on one of the highest points of the hills and we'll be able to see for some distance if the day is clear."

Seren woke Calon when dawn was still a promise and they made the uphill trek to the edge of the pine forest. They left the comfort of the trees as the sun blinked weakly into view and crested the brow of the hill. Seren put her arm out and halted Calon, telling him to wait. He stood with her and watched the sunrise. From the early morning mist, the landscape emerged like an old man shuffling into the light. The trees beyond on the far side of the valley stood, silhouetted black, facing the dawn. The valleys and dales yawned in every direction with nothing to break the view to the north and mountains beyond, with peaks so tall, that the tops merged with the grey sky, holding it high above the cold, damp ground. To the west, the Glendow River sauntered away to the sea through a wall of trees, densely packed and forbidding.

The way south, Seren had told him, over the Haur Hills would take them to *Llyn-dwr-Halen*, the inland sea beyond. All this she had prepared him for, it was the smell that was out of place. It didn't smell right at all. Where he expected the tang of pine and the cool salty breeze off the water, the lingering fumes of many camp fires drifted through the air, alien and ominous; the cloying odour of the latrines permeated even the acrid smell of the smoke. Calon became aware that Seren smelt it too; her breathing quickened and laboured. He fought the urge to cling to the shadows and darkness, assessing there was little point. Wary and watchful she moved out onto the hill that overlooked the valley, beckoning Calon to follow.

Lower down, closer to the valley floor, the forest that should have been so alive, waited bleak and forbidding. The trees that had nurtured and sheltered them a contrast to the many that stood sentinel now, witness to the grim truth beyond, almost bowed in mourning. As the mist shrank away from the climbing sun, the unhindered morning light illuminated a field of tents and canopies, filling the valley that now seemed like an alien land. So many men.

"They fooled us," Seren muttered, almost to herself. "We took their bait and trailed that small force." She was silent then, thinking. "They had another way into Penrhyn; they had help. The Hethwen...," she began before lurching forward, moving out into the open, where she stood mute before one final desecration.

"Uncle," she whispered. Calon tracked her gaze. On a small rise in the middle of the valley, less than a hundred yards away from where they stood, a crooked cross had been erected—two curved boat keels slotted together, one perpendicular to the other. Uncle's arms were bound and nailed to the cross beam, his feet bound and nailed to the upright beam that bent backwards, pushing his chest out. His head was unbound but rested on the beam.

Seren's fury burned bright. "This is Penrhyn, our own lands..." Calon nodded dumbly by her side, suddenly aware that there was no one who would stand in the way of the humans now. He heard the rasp of Seren drawing her sword, not knowing what else to do he grabbed her arm. He had been about to say that there was nothing they could do, any attempt to take his body down would be in vain and Uncle wouldn't have wanted that. But he didn't say any such thing because before he could speak, Uncles moved his head and his mouth fell open in a silent scream. Seren spun to him then and grabbed the front of his clothing.

"You stay here. You cannot help me down there; you will only hinder me. If I fail, head back into the forest." With that she thrust her bow into his hands, cloaked herself and left him. "Don't," he muttered weakly, as her blurred form, barely visible, hurtled towards the summit of the hill where Uncle was bound. "It's bound to be trap." He had to do something. Impulsively ignoring her orders, he tried to follow but his feet would not move and he ended up falling forwards, putting his hands out to stop his fall so he was now on all fours. He looked at his feet and saw she had used her power to bind the long grass in which they had both standing, to his feet, trapping him.

A sudden scream made him look up. A soldier who had just emerged shirtless from the tent closest to where he was standing toppled to the ground, hands clasping uselessly at the terrible sword wound that had sliced him from shoulder to navel. Calon could just pick out the figure of Seren, racing towards the mound on which Uncle was cruelly bound. He watched her reach the bottom of the slope then just disappear from view. Instantly, canvass was flung aside and scores of soldiers emerged at a run, many with crossbows, converging on the place where Seren had vanished. A pit. It had been a trap. He watched with dismay as a dozen men bent and grabbed hold of ropes and pulled Seren up. She was trapped in an iron net, arms entangled and unable to call upon her magic.

A Confessor strode through the crowded troops, chains and manacles in his hand. He ordered some of the troops to free Seren's head from the net—Calon could see her cursing and struggling—so that he could clamp an iron band around her head, also tightly knotting a strip of cloth over her eyes. They then proceeded to release her from the net, adding the manacles as they did and tearing her jerkin and undershirt away. When they were finished, they hauled Seren to her feet.

He could see that her wrists were manacled to her waist on opposite sides, her arms crossed across her chest. Her knees and ankles were also manacled. He saw that Seren's posture was odd, her back was arched and her head tilted up. When they turned her, he saw a chain had been tightly strung from the band around her head down to the binding on her ankles, forcing her to lean over. There followed an agonising few minutes as Seren was moved. Walking was virtually impossible for her. She fell forward three times and with no way to protect herself struck the ground hard on each occasion.

After the third time, the Confessor ordered her to be dragged the rest of the way up the hill. When they hauled her back to her feet to the left of where Uncle hung, Calon could see blood weeping down her chest and arms where she had been dragged over the rough stony ground. A soldier reached up the butt end of his spear and jabbed Uncle in the ribs a few times to bring him to. Calon couldn't see if Uncle's eyes were open, but saw from the way his body suddenly tensed that he had seen his grandniece's condition.

"Help them," a voice fluttered in his mind. *"Walk to Seren and Emrys."* Calon looked about and saw no one. The voice in his mind seemed to have created a desire to obey in him. He thought of Seren telling him to run and hide.

"*No, help them,*" the voice repeated. Without consciously moving, Calon realised he had obeyed, the binding grass no longer held him and he was walking down the hill towards the grim tableau before him. He dropped a couple of metres down a short rock face, coming to a crouch as he landed. The sword on his back banging on the ground. He drew it free over his shoulder, thinking to hide it somewhere rather than have a Chancel man take it from him. Looking at the rock face he decided to embed it there, out of sight. The presence in his mind offered a sense of approval at this and Calon pushed the point of the sword against the rock, before realising it would take too much magic to bury it this way.

Instead, he placed the weapon flat against the smoothest bit of rock and simply eased it in, using his magic as he did toward the rock around it so that chisels would not gain any purchase to chip it out. He decided to place Seren's bow stave there as well. This way he could leave the weapons visible, but unreachable. His task completed, he continued his walk down to the crowd of Chancel soldiers massing at the base of the hill on which Uncle and Seren suffered.

As he approached, the first guard he walked past shouted in alarm, causing a mass drawing of swords combined with a steady drawing away from Calon. The shouts continued, but as Calon was now unarmed and simply walking through them as though he was strolling across a busy market square, there was a confusion; the soldiers did not know what to do. At a shout of command from the Confessor, the crowd of soldiers immediately parted, rolling away from Calon's path like surf retreating on a beach. Calon strode up the hill to the crooked cross where Uncle hung and Seren lay keening in his shadow. Still with no plan, he halted in front of the Confessor, arms by his side. He had done as the voice had asked and now had no idea what to do next. So, he waited.

The Confessor smiled at him, much the way a fox might smile on entering a henhouse, Calon thought. His confusion was ended when Uncle made a guttural sound, Calon turned towards him and saw Uncle's head lift slightly, his bloodied features a mask of pain. His battered mouth opened and Calon could see that blood had covered his teeth.

As Calon looked at him, Uncle opened his right eye, the left bulbously swollen, and looked directly at Calon. His whole bruised and beaten face then seemed to relax and it took a moment for Calon to realise that his great-uncle was smiling. Uncle lowered his head back on to the beam then, just as a piercing howl rose from the tightly packed forest to the west.

Calon turned to face the direction from which the howling had come, as did the multitude of soldiers below and around him. The howling started again; this time joined by an altogether different, guttural growling that seemed to shatter the air around them.

"What in the name of all that is holy is causing that?" the Confessor said. Calon, unsure whether the man was asking him or talking to himself, chose to say nothing, but Seren's voice, all hurt and suffering, croaked from behind them.

"The hounds of Annwn," her voice grated quietly. "The *helwyr-cwn*." Calon looked at her, as bemused as the Confessor. He saw that Seren too smiled as she forced the words from her mouth as though no pain, however great, would stop her. "The hunters are coming for you." With that she went quiet, the sound of her tortured breathing testament to the effort that it had taken her to speak.

The howling and growling seemingly crept closer and closer. Calon could see a line of trees swaying dramatically as though buffeted by gale force winds as whatever the hounds were moved closer. The noise became more threatening as it neared and was dramatically accompanied by a raucous cawing and flapping of wings, as a huge murder of crows took flight from the dark forest, sending a whole blizzard of black feathers flurrying as the flock rose majestically into the air: a furious, black tide that washed over their heads as the hounds' cacophony suddenly stopped. Calon reached out a hand and caught a falling feather in his hand, where it simply disintegrated like cold ash. He rubbed his fingers together, feeling the darkness it left, but seeing nothing.

"Look," a voice called, the alarm palpable. Calon looked. Deep into the trees, two lines of the densely packed line of pines swayed apart, creating a 'v' that surged towards the edge of the forest as though a great leviathan swam through it. When it reached the edge, two trees swayed away from each other leaving a clear entrance into the forest that was still so dark it glittered. The ominous silence was then littered with the hiss of a thousand swords being drawn and the shuffling of nervous boots as the army edged away from whatever was coming. At a command from the Confessor hundreds of men ran around to stand at the base of the hill between the Confessor and whatever monstrosity was coming from the forest; others moved to stand on the slope. A single note then sounded, a hunter's horn, a pure, clear sound that lasted for enough time that some men began to cover their ears. Then out of the forest stepped one warrior. He held a long spear horizontally at his side. Calon could see the hilt of a sword over the warrior's shoulder. The warrior paused to survey all that was before him, then looked back into the forest, raised his hand and gestured; from the gloom of the trees another figure emerged.

"Cawrroc," Calon muttered to himself. A good foot taller than the warrior and considerably broader, the Cawrroc looked a lot like Cadfan; stockily built figure and powerful looking, though he seemed taller, more like Anghenfyl's height, Calon surmised. From what he could see, this Cawrroc had features more akin to the Marwolleth; no heavy brow or square looking forehead; long, flowing hair like his own, not short, wiry hair like Cadfan's; arms in proportion to the rest of its body. In its hand, the Cawrroc held a long, curved horn, almost the size of the Marwolleth warrior beside him. He was dressed in clothing much the same as the things Cadfan would wear, but grey and black. From what Calon could see of his face, the right eye and cheek were covered in something dark, but he was too far away to discern what that was exactly.

One gesture of the Marwolleth's hand sent the trees snapping back into their natural position, a huge rush of foliage swaying to stand alert once more. The lone warrior moved languidly down the hill from the edge of the forest towards them. In contrast, the Cawrroc stood unmoving, for all the world like he had been craved from stone.

The Marwolleth strode towards them, eventually stopping in the centre of the valley at the foot of the rise that led up to where the army nervously stood at the foot of the hill on which Calon waited. The warrior faced the Confessor, looking up at him, back straight and chin held high. Dark skinned like all Celtyth, Calon could see that the warrior was well muscled and looked dangerous: threat seemed to ooze from him like heat from hot coals. Calon was aware that the soldiers around him had started reacting to the man's appearance: shuffling nervously, grabbing the hilts of their various weapons, coughing nervously and muttering.

The Marwolleth warrior looped the strap of the horn he held over his shoulder. He was dressed entirely in black: soft, suede trousers, moccasins that were laced up to his mid shin and a sleeveless leather tunic that was hung with a few black feathers. Smiling now, he raised the long spear to the vertical and held it out in front of him. A pennant on the spear caught the breeze displaying a raven; wings spread and blood dripping from its' claws. The warrior, after planting the spear in the ground, stepped forward a few paces, stopped and then bowed ostentatiously to the multitude of soldiers lined up before him. *Magnificent*, Calon thought to himself, *he is magnificent*.

After standing up straight again, the warrior reached both of his hands high into the air before lowering them down slowly until his arms were level with his shoulders. Then, abruptly, swung his arms above his head to clap loudly once. He repeated this motion and clapped again. On the third clap, he cloaked. Even Calon thought he had simply vanished. The men around Calon were completely startled and alarmed, many drew their weapons, murmuring nervously to each other, but all sound stopped dead when another clap sounded. It was as though time had frozen. They all waited in trepidation—a second clap sounded and men were inching backwards now, uncertainty sapping aware their earlier bravado.

On the third clap, the warrior reappeared, holding his hunting horn and backed this time by over twenty other warriors. Many dressed in patterned, brightly coloured trews and sleeveless jackets, but all of them armed in some way and to a warrior they were the deadliest looking group of armed men Calon had ever seen.

The ominous silence that followed was broken suddenly when the Cawrroc, standing on the edge of the forest, sounded one loud note on his horn. As one, the Marwolleth warriors dropped to one knee with their heads lowered.

"The hounds come," Calon heard Seren whisper to him. "Kneel." Calon immediately did as she had commanded, his knee touching the ground at the precise moment that three beasts surged silently from the darkness of the forest; not bursting through leaf and branch, destroying trees as they charged, but simply passing through the trees as though they were imagined. They covered the ground unbelievably quickly and in utter silence launched into the witing Chancel army. The slaughter was instant, terrible and real.

Within moments the army was put to flight. The three hounds rent and ravaged the humans like wheat. Bodies were torn and cast aside; huge claws sliced men in two. A miasma of death, blood, offal and excrement choked the air, as those who could, fled; harried mercilessly by two of the three hounds. The third hound came to a halt at the kneeling Celtyth warriors, it's great head swaying. Calon could see that the beast was easily eight feet tall at the shoulder and covered in brilliant white fur. In contrast the hound's face was fur less and looked like bone. This hound had a vivid black patch on one side that covered its dark eye, seemingly all pupil, but as intimidating as it appeared, it was the jaws that truly frightened. A great bony snout flared from the it's skull: the top splitting to form a long snout with two huge curved incisors that curved down; the bottom jaw tapered to form one incisor that curved up to sit between the upper two.

Hearing a muttered curse, Calon looked around him; there were upward of fifty soldiers ringed around the Confessor, eyes wide with terror. Calon turned back to find the hound's snout brushing his cheek. He lurched back in horror.

"Kneel," Seren hissed at him. "Be still." The hound snuffled at him, before stretching its jaws wide in front of Calon's face—it's throat and gullet black fleshed—then snapping them shut. Icy, cold air washed over him and the scent of forest bathed him, calming his desire to flee, before the beast surged through him and away. The sensation was almost agony—like jumping into freezing water but on the inside. He became aware of a sudden heat on his face and put his hand to his cheek to find blood oozing down.

"It bit me," he whispered, in disbelief that he still lived.

Seren's agonised croak behind him told him why. "It marked you. Only true Marwolleth are marked this way," as he lapsed again into tortured silence. Sudden movement attracted Calon's attention as the Celtyth warriors all stood and drew their weapons. Calon could see their skin cloaking with dark colours, rippling as the magic covered them, bar the leader, who raised his drawn sword and pointed at the fifty men ringing the Confessor. He held for a few heartbeats, then swiped his sword downwards. The Celtyth sprang into motion without warning, sprinting absurdly quickly up the steep valley towards the soldiers, who although they outnumbered the Marwoll two to one, could barely see who they were fighting. Panic reigned. Half the men turned and fled the rest tried to form together but the Marwolleth covered the ground so quickly they had no time to do anything other than die.

The slaughter was incredible. The ease with which the Marwoll warriors outfought and killed their human opponents was astonishing. Within moments the terrible screaming and shouting ended. Deathly silent. Calon was aware that the Marwolleth had made no sound at all in their frenzied butchery. Just as now they gathered in a wide circle around Uncle, Seren, himself and the two remaining humans who held them very close. The Confessor he saw, had pressed a knife hard enough against Uncle's throat that blood welled around the wound created. Similarly, an impressively armoured soldier stood with a spear point at Seren's chest, ready to throw his weight behind the weapon and down through her heart. Calon could hear his own breath had become shallow and rapid as he sensed the impending demise of his two friends. The leader of the warriors, still smiling, approached them.

"Far enough," the Confessor told him. The leader stopped, tilting his head slightly to one side, taking in the condition of the two prisoners. The leader then smiled and turned his attention to the Confessor. He regarded the human patiently. The silence stretched unbearably until the Confessor felt forced to speak. "Me and Gottfried, we will leave this old man here, but take this bitch here up the valley with us. My nice sharp knife held to her throat all the way. You let us ride out and we let her go when we're safely away." Although Calon could hear a slight quaver in his voice he was almost impressed that the Confessor was trying to command the situation. The warrior's leader wasn't. He smiled again, then reached inside his tunic, pulling out a dark, wooden tube, almost identical to the stone tube Calon had retrieved from the croft. The leader placed it to his lips and blew a loud, shrill note.

The Marwolleth all turned and looked back at the mysterious figure with the hunting horn. On hearing the whistle, he began striding towards them. There was a strangeness to his movements; he seemed to walk smoothly but at the same time no part of him seemed still. Even from a distance he exuded a restless energy that made it hard for Calon to really look at him.

"His magic boils within him, that is what you see," Gethyn said quietly beside him. I a few moments the Cawrroc was heading up the slope, the Marwolleth, peeling back to allow him a clear approach to the Confessor.

"No further," the Confessor warned, stooping the Cawrroc, who stared straight into the Confessors eyes and took two more paces towards him. The Confessor was beyond nervous now. "I'm warning you… no funny business or this sorcerer and the girl die. Do you understand me?" The Cawrroc simply held his gaze. The Confessor began to back away now, saying, "You let us go to—"

"No!" The Cawrroc's voice was quiet, barely louder than a whisper, but the single word had more command than anything else Calon had ever heard. That one statement had seemed to stop time. Calon had a good view of the Cawrroc's face now, if he was a Cawrroc. His body and size, probably six and a half feet tall, were all Cawrroc, but his facial features were entirely Marwolleth or Hethwen. The darkness on his cheek Calon had seen was actually a pattern of *craiths* that curled around his eyes over his cheek-bone. He knew these would be a source of magic and dreaded to think what.

The cold look on his face never wavered. Calon saw that the Cawrroc, he still thought of him as that, still held his long horn in one hand, the other was tightly clenched and constantly squeezing. Where the Marwolleth, he had met and Cadfan had been approachable, friendly and had a love of life, this one seemed to have no sense of benevolence. He seemed to be made of cold stone, and he had a curious smell. Like blood mixed with pine. 'Danger,' Calon thought, 'he smells dangerous.'

The Confessor obviously thought so too as he eased his blade slightly deeper into Emrys neck, twisting it slightly to make Uncle gasp. The Cawrroc's right eye, twitched and Calon felt the tell-tale tingle of gathering magic. The *craiths* on the Cawrrocs face suddenly lit up. Similar to the way the golden flames had healed Seren, green fire seemed to work its way over his face, and his cloaked eyes burned bright. He still said nothing but took one step closer.

The Confessor ordered his guard to kill Seren. Calon meant to surge forward to stop him, but iron hard hands gripped him and held him fast, one arm around his chest, one hand over his mouth. Gottfried raised the spear and paused. No-one moved, no one tried to stop him. Calon struggled, wanting to scream. Then the spear plunged down, striking Seren's chest. A great groan resounded wetly from Gottfried's mouth, followed by a gout of bright red blood. He looked down at his own chest; a great ragged hole gaped and oozed more blood, splattering over Seren as the man crumpled to the ground, dead. Seren wiped the blood from her, unharmed. The hands released Calon, who stood dumbfounded. What he had just seen was not possible.

Sensing his impending demise, the Confessor offered one last defiance. "I may die here, but I will join the Martyrs and live on," his voice tremulous and strained. The Cawrroc simply stared. With a scream of anger, the Confessor rammed in knife into one side of the throat of Emrys, ripping it through Uncle's windpipe and out of the other side with a flourish, but the triumph on his face was short lived as the wound in Uncles' throat simply healed as quickly as it had been torn open. Calon's gaze switched to the Chancel man. Breathing heavenly, the knife falling from his fingers, his hands reached up to his own throat which erupted suddenly in a wash of blood, his neck gaping openly as he toppled forward, dead before he hit the ground.

Stunned silence filled the space around the Cawrroc, who simply turned and headed back to the edge of the forest. Nothing was said, no one moved until he was walking across the valley floor. Calon watched, still spellbound, as the warriors surrounded Uncle and Seren. His relief that they would both be saved turning into disbelief as the warriors simply stood and stared at the two prisoners. Uncle's one good eye, barely open; Seren unmoving on the ground. "Do something," he demanded, getting back to his feet. "Help them."

Warriors stepped aside as Calon approached, suddenly aware of the size and power of the men he stood amongst. The leader turned and looked at him, head canted slightly to one side, though no smile touched his lips. In fact, Calon could read the pain on his face.

"How? How can we help them?" Turning, he pointed at Uncle's bindings. "Like you, we are Celtyth," he said his voice soft and low. "They are bound with iron—we cannot release them. Arawn," he gestured with his hand at the departing Cawrroc, "could not unbind this metal, what would you have us do?" With that he reached for the knife at his belt.

"Wait, wait!" Calon called.

"Wait? When every moment is agony as the iron poisons them. I cannot see them suffer this way and die a long death. Better it is quick and painless." He moved his knife towards Uncle's wrist then, Uncle's one good eye opened and fixed firmly on Calon, who grabbed the warrior's arm.

"Wait…" he began, but suddenly found himself winded, on his back, on the ground with the leader's knife at his throat. As the keen blade was pressed more firmly to his flesh, he managed to blurt out, "I can free them, I can free them!" The knife was moved from his throat, his arms were grabbed and he was dragged back to his feet.

"You are Celtyth," the leader stated. "How can you free them?" Shaking their hold off him, Calon stepped over to Uncle. Reaching up over his head, he could just about place his hand over the iron manacle that had been used to bind his left arm to the spar, Calon focused on the iron and simply peeled it away. With a gasp of pain from Uncle, his arm flopped down, the shoulder joint dislocated. Calon quickly ducked behind the crooked cross to release his other arm.

"Stop," the leader barked at him. Calon ignored the command. "Stop!" he ordered again grabbing Calon this time. Calon swung a punch that was caught in the leader's other hand.

"Let me free him!" he screamed at the warrior, struggling to break the grip on his arm. "Let me…"

"Slowly, slowly, young fighter, his feet first, or he'll fall," the leader said, a smile twitching the corners of his mouth. "Let us be ready in place to lift him down, or he'll simply fall to the ground." The sense of the argument took a few moments to dawn on an embarrassed Calon, who moved to the front of the crooked cross and released the iron bonds on Uncle's ankles. Four warriors, two on either side then moved to Uncle's aid as Calon moved to release the final binding. Uncle sagged down as the iron was released, the warriors struggling to support him without holding his dislocated shoulders.

They lowered Uncle, now unconscious, gently to the ground and Calon knelt by his side placing his hands on the iron that had been bound around Uncle's head like a crown. There was a gasp of horror from behind Calon as the iron circlet fell away, revealing a livid and suppurating wound, red and raw, as the iron tore the skin away.

"What has caused this?" the leader demanded, kneeling by Calon's side. "Is this some new poison?" But Calon shook his head.

"No," he said softly. "They used hot iron. They forged it onto him." Leaving Uncle where he lay, Calon moved quickly to Seren's side. Her chains and iron bindings came away easily. He asked for water to try and revive her but the leader eased him aside and placed his two palms on Seren's bruised and bloodied cheeks. He whispered gently and Calon saw a surge of green light, of power, flare from his hands. Seren's eyelids flew open, her eyes instantly alert.

"Uncle," she managed to croak.

"Seren?" he replied.

"No," she interrupted. "Not you, Uncle. Emrys; we call him Uncle now." The leader smiled at this before reassuring her.

"Rest easily, Emrys is safe and tended to. Your young friend…" The leader stopped as Calon knelt by Seren. Putting his hands on her cheeks Calon focused his energy into healing her bruises and cuts. She began to protest as the golden light flared over her skin that he should save his power for Uncle.

"I don't know how to heal him," he told her. "I need your help. Together, we should be able to strengthen him enough to move him."

Seren nodded at that, then looked back at the leader. "This is Calon-Eryr," she said to her uncle. "The son of Cadellin and Eirianwen. He can offer healing that no one else here can. You should leave us Uncle Gethyn, Calon will heal me and we will see to Emrys." Gethyn was about to protest, looking suspiciously at the wounds and blood on Seren's breasts but a look from his niece seemed to convey to him that all was well.

"I'll be close by," he muttered.

243

As much for my benefit as Seren's, Calon thought.

"I don't think he trusts me," he told her as Gethyn moved away. Seren smiled at that.

"He will," she told him. "Just give him a bit of time to get to know you." Turning his attention back to Seren's injuries, Calon moved to put his hands on the deep grazes on her chest, but froze. Seren's soft chuckle didn't help. After a few moments of nothing happening, she grabbed his wrists and pulled his hands down onto her wounds.

"*I* trust you," she whispered. Calon spent some time healing all of the grazes and bruises, recalling his time spent with Cadfan. Once all of her wounds were healed, Calon prepared to re-energise Seren with his magic. He remembered Cadfan teaching him this would work for a short burst, but the risk was that both he and Seren would be exhausted within a couple of hours—Seren especially as her body needed sleep to heal fully. Obviously sensing his intent, Seren opened her eyes.

"Not too much, Calon, just get me up. I need to rest but you may be needed." Calon pressed his palms to her temples and began to infuse her. Seren in turn gripped his hands lightly, suddenly pulling them free when she felt strong enough to get up. She stood a little unsteadily, Calon helping her. He shrugged off his leather jerkin and helped her put it on, using the belt he had taken off to secure it around her waist. It looked to bit but would suffice as a short-term solution. She leaned into him, her arm tightly hugging his waist for a brief moment. Then broke free and walked over to Uncle.

Seren spent a little time assessing Uncle's injuries, before calling Gethyn over. With as much care as was possible she instructed Gethyn and Calon on how to pop his shoulders back in, then with Calon's help they sealed the wound around his head and tended to what Seren suspected were several broken ribs. Calon watched as the golden flames flickered brightly over Uncle's side and chest, but could hear how Uncle's breathing eased and deepened as they healed him.

"Enough now," Seren told him. Calon looked at the bruises and grazes still raw on Uncles arms and chest.

"But—" he began before she interrupted.

"No, if we heal too much, too quickly, it will weaken him. We have done enough to make him comfortable. Let him rest now and we will do more tomorrow when he will be stronger and we more able to give of ourselves. Now, let me lie down for a while." She lay down beside Uncle's prone form, her back against his side and instantly slept. Calon also felt unbearably weary and sat beside them as they slept. He watched the warriors moving about the scene of the slaughter. All suddenly dropping to one knee as the horn sounded again, an ululating note this time, lower in pitch.

He turned and saw the Cawrroc on the forests edge, turn and head back into the trees, the horn in his hand. Gethyn, still kneeling, looked away to the south where the Chancel army had run. The dark cloud of carrion birds surged towards them, the three great hounds bounding along beneath the thundercloud of birds. The fearsome three came to a halt in front of Gethyn, all bloodied and chests heaving. Then as one they sank to their bellies on the ground in front of him, before leaping away after the mysterious Cawrroc, back into the forest from whence they had burst. The warriors all rose and at a command from Gethyn set off south to hunt for survivors, if there were any. Their intent was plain, none of the humans would survive.

Calon watched as Gethyn walked over and crouched down in front of him. Gethyn reached out and cradled the back of Calon's head drawing it forward to his so that their foreheads touched. Releasing him, Gethyn remained silent for studying Calon. "You did well here Calon. I am proud to know you. Seren and Emrys trust you and that is a precious gift, and not one given lightly." He paused then and looked around. "We must move back into the forest and provide shelter for them both; Emrys, Uncle, will sleep long and need more healing. Would that your mother were here."

Calon startled at mention of his mother. "Is my father here?" he blurted out— a suspicion he had held since first seeing the warriors. Gethyn, face solemn regarded him closely for a moment then dissolved in laughter, a rich chuckle that brought a smile to Calon's face.

"No Calon. Would that he were. I am your father's brother—your uncle. Your da, Cadellin, is in Gorllewinol with our people. We few came back to Penrhyn to get Emrys, your mam and you and Briallen and her girls. Arawn told us of your mam's death and that of Berys." Gethyn regarded Calon solemnly before adding, "To find your way here with no real help… you have done well. Your da will be so proud."

"You came back? How? Why did you all leave here? You talked in my head earlier. Who is Arawn? The hounds…?" Calon had question after question that Gethyn rebuffed.

Gethyn seemed surprised by what Calon had told him. "Talked in your head? Not I. Arawn maybe. He is fickle that one, and can use magic in ways none here could imagine—as we have just seen," he pointed at the two unfortunate Chancel men. "May be Emrys could explain more, but if Arawn can speak to you like that, you must be linked somehow."

"How did he kill those two me? The wounds they gave Uncle and Seren just appeared on them instead. How—"

"Peace, Calon. We will talk when you are properly rested. Sleep now and we will bear you into the forest to our camp." He insisted Calon lie down next to the sleeping Emrys and Seren, then he drew his first and index finger down Calon's face, over his eyes, and Calon slept.

After nearly three days of bed rest, Calon finally left the lodge he had been recuperating in. He had no memory of travelling to the lodge, only odd feverish memories of waking and being fed a disgusting drink by someone, and the comforting presence of Hela. When he finally woke his main concern was his sword. He'd asked one of the warriors who seemed to be guarding the perimeter, how to make his way back to the rock face where he had left embedded in the stone.

On his way out of the camp, he saw that other lodges had been set within easy reach. A large stone circle had been laid centrally to the lodges and he could see that most of the warriors were seated around a huge stone slab that seemed to rise from the earth. He approached the group, Hela beside him, somewhat tentatively as he was still unsure of his place among these people. The hum of conversation stopped as he neared and all turned to look at him.

Feeling suddenly out of place, he stopped, resisting the urge to turn back and just leave, but Gethyn rose and beckoned him over. He headed towards his newly discovered kin and was stunned to see that Seren and Uncle were part of the group. Seren looking back to herself and Uncle surprisingly well although he did appear fatigued.

"Come and sit, Calon," Gethyn said gesturing to a log beside him. "Before you ask… I felt it necessary to keep you sleeping while we decided our future." Seeing Calon's hurt expression, he added, "We had no reason to trust you, but Seren and Uncle have vouched for you, and your actions more so. Arawn also told me we should welcome you home."

"Arawn? The Cawrroc you arrived with?" Calon asked him.

"Well, I arrived with him, but he is not one of the stone weavers. He is the protector of Penrhyn." Calon simply nodded at the explanation. Having seen the way in which Arawn and his hounds decimated the human army, it was obvious that Arawn was a powerful ally. But Calon knew a Cawrroc when he saw one. The trouble was, no on other than him, it seemed, had seen one. He tuned back into the debate as Gethyn mentioned the gwerin again. "We found human soldiers here, with no understanding of how it was possible they could have crossed the mountains—and a gwerin with them." An awkward silence followed, finally broken by Seren.

"It was… *that rock-goblin*, who led them through the wards. How else could they have got through?" she hissed pointing behind where Gethyn stood. "Calon and I both saw him with the humans—not a prisoner as he claims; if anything, he was leading them."

"Yet we found him bound." Then for Calon's benefit added, "He claims he was held captive, hooded and chained, so had no knowledge of how he came into Penrhyn. He claims he was being taken to the reservation in Torffan, whatever a reservation is, to be imprisoned there." Gethyn shrugged as if he had nothing further to add. Calon walked across to confirm his suspicions. The gwerin lay bound with vines, lying on his side with his back to Calon. "We still believe no Celtyth, be they gwerin, Marwolleth or Hethwen would ever work in league with humans to attack their own kind." There was a murmuring of agreement from the gathered warriors.

"But I know him as you do not. His name is Mordwyn." Calon looked around the group and then in to his uncle Gethyn's eyes, holding his gaze. "He has no loyalty to the Celtyth, I watched him slaughter his own people with powerful magic. There is no kindness in him, only greed and lust for power. His mind is …" He could find no words to express what he felt or meant. Instead, he changed tack. "I have seen that humans cannot cross the mountains, and have no idea how a gwerin would know his way through the forests. But he is sly and clever; and he is a cave dweller." Then it came to him: remembering his journey under Lellacher to Torffan through the worked caves and tunnels. He looked up at Gethyn. "They didn't cross the mountains; they came under them." The momentary, stunned silence was followed almost immediately by everyone voicing an opinion. The noise only ceasing when Uncle bellowed for silence.

"I still doubt he could do that, but I'll accept it is possible. Even underground there are wards; protective magic created by the Cawrrocs. Even we would need help to travel that way. Only if, he had a *canllaw* would he be able to navigate the route, and that would only protect him alone *and* it would have to be attuned to him alone. How could a stone weaver, use his power on wood and attune it to the magic to negate the wards?"

"But he does have one," Calon interrupted. "When I was captured, he took the one my mother left for me. He must have…" The sudden quiet was almost tangible. Calon saw the anger simmering in most of the warriors, directed at him. Seren rose and stood in front of him, sensing it too.

"No blame on Calon," she ordered. "He is a boy. A Celtyth yes, but one brought up by humans since he was a babe, with no knowledge of his race, culture or heritage. Without one of us to guide him, we cannot fault his actions or choices," she offered, staring every one of them down.

"Seren is right," Uncle stood somewhat gingerly still. "If there is fault here it is mine. I should have kept better watch on Eirianwen and I regret not looking harder for her or her son."

Calon interrupted. The answer now he had thought of it was obvious. "Anghenfyl," he said with slightly more force than he had intended. The Marwolleth looked at him, doubt evident on their faces. Calon turned to his great-uncle. "You remember him? You remember his name?"

Uncle nodded. "Ay, he was mighty indeed, but long dead Calon. His life is nothing but a myth; a collection of bedtime stories to most of our people now. Surely he could not have…"

"No myth Uncle. I knew him. That gwerin," Calon pointed at Mordwyn, "raised him from death with blood magic and used it to control him." There was a collective hiss at mention of the use of blood. "I told you, he murdered scores of his own people. He could have easily induced Anghenfyl to craft something for him, a *canllaw*, to help him and his humans through the magic wards." Uncle looked up at Gethyn and nodded his agreement.

Gethyn paced for a few moments. "This foul creature would not have the lore to change that, Arawn has told me as much. But if a powerful stone weaver was involved, your theory seems plausible. What we need are answers." This seemed to placate the warriors, who turned as a yelp sounded. Gethyn had hauled the gwerin up and dragged him over to the stone, shoving him to lie flat on his back, his arms still bound behind him. Calon watched as the gwerin landed on his bound hands. Something gnawed at him, something he ought to remember. He shifted his gaze to the stone; almost black and sparkling with quartz; night-stone. The rock most easily manipulated by stone-weavers.

Calon knew what had troubled him at the same moment that, in full view of them all, the hateful Mordwyn raised his head and looked at them, the dark, sullen expression on his face transformed into a wide, beaming grin as he raised his now unbound hands in front of him to show he was free.

"No!" shouted Calon, lurching forward. "Grab him, he'll…" His worst fears instantly realised as the gwerin simply sank into the stone, smiling directly at Gethyn as he dipped below the surface, just as Gethyn's sword clattered the stone. Calon though kept moving, acting without thought, cloaking as he ran and dived onto the stone, pushing his arm down into the rock. His grasping hand felt cloth and he gripped tight, pulling for all his worth to haul the gwerin back. Seren joined him in his struggle and others moved to help, but all in vain, as the two friends simply vanished into the rock.

Chapter 15
Mordwyn's Quest

Calon came back to consciousness lying face down on cold rock. He turned his head painfully to the side where a feint light glowed. As his eyes focused, he took in the sight of Seren, sitting, head slumped forward on to her knees. Mordwyn's mocking voice sounded from the darkness somewhere behind him.

"Feel free to sit up. You are not bound." Calon dragged himself to a sitting position, his vision blurring in and out of focus; the agony in his head almost making him vomit. It took a while for him to be able to sit and open his eyes. He took in his location; a small chamber, barley lit by a *carreg-fwyn,* a light stone; a trick of Mordwyn's he remembered all too well. Something that brought a little relief, as he realised that, other than how he ended up in this cavern, his memory was intact.

"Perhaps I hit you too hard," Mordwyn laughed. "I thought I'd killed you at first, and your head does feel a little soft where the rock I used connected." Calon found it hard to concentrate and understand what the gwerin was telling him, but found that the agony in his head was focused above his right temple. He raised a hand gingerly to examine the source of the pain, but even gently touching the wound was almost too much to bear. He withdrew his hand, alarmed by how much blood stuck to his palm. Mordwyn's manic giggling echoed in the chamber as the gwerin moved across to Seren and crouched in front of her.

Calon tried to focus on what was happening but his vision blurred again and he closed his eyes against the pain. Somehow, he was able to retain enough cognitive function to realise that he could heal himself. He raised his hand to his injury again and focused on the injury. He felt the familiar heat as the magic began to work, the agony easing almost instantly. Disconcertingly he heard the bones of his skull as their edges grated against each other as they reformed. With the pressure inside his head receding as the swelling decreased, his eyes came back into focus to find the gwerin crouched right in front of him, a quizzical look on his features; those black, unwelcoming eyes expressionless and still unfathomable.

"Good. You've healed yourself, judging by the golden glow. You have learnt some skill from one of those *golems* I take it?" Calon didn't answer so Mordwyn told him, "We can move on then." The gwerin stood and walked back over to Seren, hauling her to her feet. She stood head bowed for a time, before slowly lifting her head. She looked at Calon and he saw that a band of some sort had been fastened around her mouth. Her eyes remained fixed on Calon and she gave a clear shake of her head before looking down again. Calon decided that she wanted him to wait before attempting to free her.

"You have seen my handiwork," Mordwyn said. "Or some of it." Reaching out, he lifted Seren's chin exposing her neck, revealing another band tightly fastened over her throat. "I would have bound you the same way boy, but as you can weave stone, I felt it was probably not worth it. This," he pointed at Seren's throat band, "is to control you, not her. Observe." He reached down to the floor then and picked up a palm-sized stone. Squeezing it between his flat hands, he smoothed it into a stone circle, humming his magic as he did so.

He showed Calon the results of his work—a perfectly round, glassy disk. He then pushed his index finger through the centre of the stone, creating a hole, which he stretched wider, weaving the stone with his magic until it had formed a round circlet. He broke the perfect circle by pinching it with his fingers, then held it up for Calon to see. "All the while that I keep my magic focused. This will keep its shape. But," he snapped the two ends together again to reform the circlet, "if I lose focus," he grabbed Seren's arm and looped the rock over it, clicking his fingers immediately afterwards. "This is what happens." The circlet of stone began instantly to close and within a matter of heartbeats was squeezing into Seren's arm with such force, her muffled scream startled Calon into rushing towards her.

Mordwyn's hand slammed into his chest at the same time as he clicked his fingers again and the rock on Seren's arm opened and fell away. "We both know that you could never have worked that stone off her arm before it cut straight through. Imagine that on her neck. So, you see," the gwerin continued. "If you do anything to attack me, I simply end the spell that keeps the rock-torc open and she dies." He giggled then. "So, I assume I have your full cooperation?" He waited for Calon to nod his ascent, which he only gave after another gesture from

Seren. Pushing Seren ahead of him he told Calon to follow them, lifting the rock-light to help them. "Good. Your help will be most valuable indeed," he added, cackling again as he pushed Seren forward and moved off.

They travelled for some time before stopping. Most of the journey was through narrow fissures that followed an underground stream, always climbing up hill. The way was hard going, nothing like the Cawrroc fashioned tunnels he had grown accustomed to during his time with Cadfan. He was pleased that Seren had the light to see where she was going or she'd have fallen continually. He determined not to ask any distracting questions of the gwerin, but kept all his attention on Seren. He stayed as close to her as Mordwyn would allow, terrified that if the gwerin slipped, his concentration would break.

He began to reason that he may have been tricked into believing Mordwyn's tale of how he needed to maintain focus on the spell, but he could think of no way he could call his bluff without risking Seren. He just hoped a chance to free her would present itself. Eventually, the trio stopped to drink and rest. They had no food, so went hungry. Mordwyn left Calon in the dark while he removed Seren's gag to allow her to drink.

After a short rest, they moved on. The going levelled out for a brief time and the easier travelling prompted Calon to suggest that travelling above ground would have been much quicker. Mordwyn laughed at that suggestion, claiming they could have left the caves at various points on their journey so far had he wished. When Calon muttered that his fear of the Marwolleth warriors was justified, Mordwyn stopped and faced him.

"Those Marwolleth are not the reason I fear to walk above ground. The Cŵn Annwn, 'the hounds' roam these mountains. No Celtyth would travel there other than the Marwolleth who have made peace with Arawn and his spectral hounds. Maybe, this far in, Arawn would not take kindly to even you two blundering through his realm. Maybe I should push you outside."

"Who is Arawn?" Calon asked him.

Mordwyn walked on for some time before answering. "He is a great weaver who has many titles; to my people he is the King Under the Mountain or King of the Underworld; but for the Hethwen he is just The Mountain King. Who knows what the Marwolleth call him, dog boy probably," he said chuckling at his own joke. "He is the reason Penrhyn was an empty land; anyone Celtyth who ventured here was slaughtered. Legend has it that Anghenfyl and the Cawrrocs brokered a deal with him, so it was here the Marwolleth were exiled. He is a fickle and bitter being, best left alone, best avoided."

Calon had a raft of questions but held them in. Chiefly, they were under the mountain and this Arawn was King Under the Mountain, so they must surely be in the most dangerous place. He also began speculating to himself what Mordwyn wanted here. It surely had something to do with gold, silver or precious stones, but he got no further than that thought as their path suddenly grew a lot steeper and harder. At the top of a particularly difficult climb, Mordwyn halted. Telling Calon to lie down, he wove stone over his feet and legs, placing a glowing rune enchantment on the stone.

"If you free yourself, I will know," were his only explanation, but it was explanation enough. Besides Calon was too exhausted and hungry to do anything rash. In addition, he was left in total darkness as the gwerin moved away. Calon therefore had no way of knowing exactly where the gwerin was. Remembering his time in captivity he realised he could be right above him as easily as anywhere else—his eyes able to see in the darkest cave. Whilst cloaking his eyes allowed him some night vision, he realised that still required some light. Underground there was none at all. Calon regretted that he had no idea how to activate his own enhanced vision, a 'gift' bestowed after Anghenfyl had licked his eyes. Sleep claimed him before he found the answer to that particular riddle.

Mordwyn woke him with a kick to his leg. Calon jerked awake, instantly aware he was no longer bound by the stone. His next thought was for Seren. He looked in the pale rock-light, but could only see her back as she slumped upright against the wall further along from where he now sat. After drinking from the small trickle of water than ran through the tunnel they were in, the three moved on. A strenuous climb followed and Calon could see that both he and Seren were nearing the end of their endurance. Without food for what felt like days, they were both weakening. Mordwyn by contrast was getting more excitable the further they went. He was now continually pushing Seren forward with a hand in her lower back, whilst also turning around and yelling impatiently at Calon to keep up; and keep up he did, the threat of injury to Seren his prime motivator.

After another interminable trudge up ever steeper inclines, a shout from the gwerin made Calon stop and lift his head. He could see that the steepness was at last levelling out, but also that a source of light had filled the cavern some hundred yards or so ahead. Mordwyn's rock-light blinked out, plunging Calon into near darkness, but he could see the silhouetted forms of Mordwyn and a stumbling Seren lurching towards what he hoped was the journey's end. Calon wearily followed, hopeful of food and rest but dreading what lay ahead. He still had no idea of how he could free Seren, especially as he was so weakened from lack of food. He found the last few yards the hardest of the whole trek, but at last stumbled into the light.

A huge, translucent column of ice stood in front of him, nearly eight yards wide, but with enough space to one side for him to walk through. As he could no longer see Seren and Mordwyn, he traipsed through the gap between ice and wall and found himself on a wide rock ledge on the steep side of a mountain, the cold air slapping his face. The long ledge, wide enough for a few men to walk abreast along it, was cut *into* the granite rockface of the mountain. It was thus sheltered by an overhang that would keep the worst of the weather off, but snow had blown in and drifted near the edge. The side closest to the cliff was lightly dusted and it was here that he saw the footprints of Mordwyn and Seren leading away from the cave mouth.

Looking out across the land below, he would never have guessed they'd climbed so high. The soaring sun was bright enough, but with its' light reflecting off the snow sided cliffs and peaks that surrounded them, Calon's eyes stung and watered. As his sight adjusted, he could see that they were ringed by snow-capped mountains, but none he suspected, as has high as the one on which he stood now. Calon looked back at the column of ice and saw now it was a tall waterfall, frozen still by winter, that extended down to a small lake, its ice stretching across half of the surface of the water before it melted away leaving impossibly blue water reflecting the cold mountain and the long icy vein on its glassy surface. All around, the soft snow blanketed the hard rock, flowing down to the hordes of trees that crowded the lower slopes.

A strident shriek shattered Calon's reverie, dragging his attention back to his predicament. He looked to his right and saw that the ledge extended precariously along the side of the cliff and he could see Mordwyn and Seren planted before a huge, sprawling nest on which an enormous eagle stood, wings spread, as it raged at the two intruders before it. Calon judged that it was at least three feet in height with a considerable wingspan, it's beak dark and hooked. This powerful eagle, with light golden-brown plumage on its head and neck, had stark white feathers down it's chest and on the underneath of its wings.

Calon watched awestruck as it launched itself into the air, plummeting over the side of the ledge, before catching an updraft and pounding its wings furiously to gain height. It ascended quickly, screeching as it rose, but was soon lost from sight. Calon switched his attention back to the nest where Mordwyn had now climbed, watching in horror as the gwerin launched two large eggs off the cliff, before kicking at the huge jumble of sticks and twigs that had formed the nest and sending them the same way. After grabbing Seren and pushing her onwards, he turned and gestured at Calon to follow. Still shocked by the gwerin's callous actions, Calon forged on, his anger at Mordwyn growing hot again after the long journey, giving him energy and resolve. He had nearly caught up with the pair in front of him when another shriek from above diverted his attention.

He looked up and saw the eagle, hovering above the cliff, its head perfectly still and focused on Seren and Mordwyn. He looked at the two a few yards ahead and watched as the gwerin bent down and grabbed a handful of scree and began chanting as he stood back up, looking at the great eagle above him. Calon's gaze switched back to the sky just in time to see the eagle drop, wings folded, in an incredible dive, spearing straight at Seren who lurched behind Mordwyn. Within a few yards of its target, the great eagle's wings shot out, breaking its dive and its huge taloned claws rocked forward, aiming straight for Mordwyn, when the gwerin launched the handful of gravel into the air and shouted a word of command that immediately solidified the mass of scree into a solid object that the eagle struck with devastating consequences.

It was as though the bird had hit the side of the mountain at full speed. Its body shattered by the impact, the eagle simply slid down the mountain side. Calon looked at Mordwyn, a twisted grin on the gwerin's face that lasted a heartbeat before another eagle descended unseen from the sky and hammered the hateful gwerin into the rock ledge, crippling itself in the process. It lay face down, claws still clenched around and inside the gwerin's carcass, as one wing flapped uselessly while the other barely stirred.

"Seren," he shouted, suddenly realising with dread what Mordwyn's fate meant. He leapt towards her, her hands clutching at the torc on her neck. His magic without thought at his fingertips, he grabbed the cold stone barely in time, the rock falling away from her as blood coursed down her throat and neck. He quickly clamped his hands on top of her wounds and surged what healing magic into her skin that he could, her hands clutching his wrists as golden light bathed them. He could sense the strength in that grip then the heat as her magic poured into him, adding to the healing.

Within moments, the bleeding stopped and she pulled away, still holding his wrists which she lifted to her mouth, still clamped shut by the rock gagging her. He could see her eyes, were wide with fear and her nostrils flare as she tried to suck in enough air to control her evident panic. In one swift movement, he cut his fingers through the stone and eased the gagging band away from her face. Seren immediately sank, retching and gasping to the rock ledge. Calon bent to see what else he could do for her, but Seren pushed him away,

"Eryr Mynydd," she mumbled, pointing at the eagle.

"Mountain eagle?" he repeated.

"Save it. Heal it," she told him. Calon turned and saw the great bird lay still now. Its head faced him and both eyes open, breath hushing in clouds from the nostrils on either side of its large, yellow beak. As Calon approached, the eyes tracked him. He noticed that the irises were the most brilliant golden yellow. The creature stirred and tried to flap its wings as he approached. Calon could see that one wing looked ok, but the other was clearly broken. He was about to turn to Seren when her hand clamped down heavily on his shoulder, bracing herself against him for support.

"Mountain eagles, our legends say, were bred by the Cawrrocs when they lived in these mountains. They were said to be tame and we believe they grew wild when the Cawrrocs moved underground. But Uncle has always said differently. He claims that they were trained to protect the Cawrrocs from the gwerin who would climb these mountains, killing and looking for gold. I think that explains its reaction to Mordwyn."

Her breathing still laboured but Seren continued with her thoughts. "Is there anything you learned from the Cawrrocs that might help us approach it safely? Any language or spell?" The bird now was fighting furiously to right itself. The one good wing flapping wildly, showering the pair with ice, snow and scree. Calon thought back to his training with Cadfan, remembering how he was taught to cloak himself in stone to hide, pass through rock or protect himself.

"If that's the case, there may be something I can try," he told her. "Stand back." She moved to the side and leant against the cliff face. He knelt, putting both hands flat on the rock ledge and let his magic cloak him; the stone 'skin' running up his hands and arms. He could feel the tell-tale prickly heat as it coated him. Standing, he turned to face Seren who gasped when she saw him.

"*Diafal roc!*" she uttered. "We have legends of rock devils—beings that can't be killed. Try the eagle." Calon turned back to the injured bird, still hopelessly fighting against its injuries and tentatively approached. He held his hands out, hoping to placate the beast, which still stared fixedly at him. As he got within touching distance, the eagle blinked then gently closed its eyes and settled down with a loud huff of breath that steamed the cold air. At first Calon thought it had died, but it saw that the creature's chest was still moving up and down, and its breath resumed its small gusting. He looked at Seren's astonished face, who nodded her approval, and Calon moved in.

Under Seren's instruction, who it transpired had some experience of healing animals, Calon started by smoothing his hands on the eagle's beak, letting her get his scent. Simultaneously, he muttered softly to her so she'd get accustomed to his voice when he began healing. As soon as the eagle was calm, Seren instructed him how to induce a sleep like state to keep her calm whilst he healed her wing. The healing of the bird's minor injuries he managed comfortable thanks to Seren's guidance, but the broken wing was beyond him however as he couldn't carry out her instructions. Seren tried to heal the eagle's wing but the touch of her hands just roused the great bird.

In the end, they discovered that if Calon held the back of her hands and he cloaked over her hands as well, she could use this magic touch to keep the eagle calm whilst she healed the wing which was 'broken in two places'. Having checked the bird over for other injuries, they stood back, letting it regain full consciousness. Its powerful wings created a snow storm that left them both rimed in white as it took off into the cold evening sky as though nothing had happened.

With the eagle gone, the crumpled body of Mordwyn was revealed. Great gaping wounds were testament to the devasting strike that had killed him. Calon felt nothing looking at the corpse of the being who had killed so many. Seren spat on the body, before walking away, back to the frozen waterfall to get out of the bitter wind. Calon followed. They sat just inside the cave, side by side, Calon's arm wrapped around Seren's shoulders and discussed their next steps. It was while they were deciding what to do with the gwerin's body that Seren suddenly stood and walked forward to look down over the ledge.

"Myllane!" she called, and was answered by a howl.

Calon looked at her. "How did you…" he began to ask, but then a nudging of his consciousness revealed the answer. Laughing, he too looked down and saw two shadow-foxes looking up from the valley way below, tails wagging furiously.

"Hela," he called down.

"I will teach you how, Calon. I have been aware of Myllane since we were pulled through the rock. That's why I was so quiet; I was holding Myllane with me so she could track us. Uncle is probably close behind with his fox, Gelert." They didn't have to wait long for Gelert to appear, but it wasn't Uncle who loped into view below them. "Gethyn!" Seren called to attract his attention. Gethyn looked up and waved. He was joined moments later by several other of the Marwolleth, with Uncle doggedly bringing up the rear. After an echoed conversation shouted back and forth, they had decided a few things.

Firstly, there was no way up the cliff; Seren and Calon had no way down to the valley and had no idea how to get back from where they were; and finally, with night drawing in the Marwolleth warriors below needed shelter. They could stay warm by using magic but that was draining over a long period and a shelter warmed by hearth-stones would provide what they needed. The warriors below had collected the nest rubbish Mordwyn had kicked from the cliff and woven the many sticks together, creating a framework that they leant against the cliff. They then began cutting good sized branches from the fir trees lower down and carrying them back up the slope. They wove these into the framework creating a stout wall that would provide a barrier against the wind and cold. Calon knew from his lessons with Cadfan that they would lay the small hearth-stones they carried inside, and these would be heated to warm the space they had created.

Having agreed with Uncle to see out the night as they were, Seren and Calon moved back into the shelter of the cave. They had water, and a small amount of sustenance that had been sent up the cliff attached to an arrow. More substantial food had been too heavy to make that journey. Having retrieved Mordwyn's rock-light, Calon walked further up the narrowing passageway, as much to stay active and keep warm without magic, as to really search. He was curious, however, as to why Mordwyn had marched them all of this way; he had seemed to have a purpose. This curiosity however was short lived as the passage way ended in an impassable rock fall.

So he made his way back to Seren, thinking as he clambered down about how to get down the cliff. Having come upon a possible answer, he talked it through with Seren who seemed a little uncertain about his plan, but agreed, and they huddled together for the cold night ahead. Seren had insisted she would use her magic to keep them warm through the night as Calon would need his to get them down the cliff in the morning.

As the dawn light perforated the darkness of the cave, Calon rose and wandered out to the ledge. Fresh snow had fallen, blanketing the rock and, thankfully, Mordwyn's twisted corpse. Thinking of the gwerin stirred Calon again to wonder what he had brought them here for. As all was quiet in the camp below, he headed further down the ledge to the site of the eagle's nest and beyond. The ledge hugged a curve in the cliff face that had obscured what lay beyond.

As Calon turned, he saw immediately that the ledge narrowed dramatically so it was barely wide enough to stand on. He could also see the gwerin's prize. The ledge terminated at a sheer cliff face; solid granite grey and unforgiving, that was scarred by a wide band of gold; probably three yards thick that stretched horizontally from a crevice to Calon's right across a sheer drop. As he stood and looked at the seam of gold, a familiar wrongness tugged at him. Looking more closely at the band of gold he could see black veins threading through it. *Void-stone*, he muttered to himself. He backed away, aware he could fight its influence, but not wanting Seren to come close.

The rockfall inside, he suddenly realised, was probably engineered to prevent anyone getting close. The ledge he was on, now he thought about it, was also not a natural phenomenon. It was too flat and hidden under an overhang that looked smooth. Where he had found the gold, the edge was narrow and not covered. "It wasn't' finished,' he said to himself. Mordwyn, he decided, must have created it. How long had he been travelling here? His thoughts were interrupted by Seren appearing behind him.

"Gold," she whispered. He turned to look at her, noting instantly how her eyes remained fixed on the great seam. He tried to gently usher her away, but she shoved back hard, almost knocking him from the ledge. As she forced her way passed him, he caught her around the waist with one arm and pressed his other hand to her face, finger and thumb stretched to touch both her temples. Before she could fight him off, he had whispered a word of power to send her to sleep.

Dazed as she was by the void-stone, she had no will to resist and he was able to drag her back from the gold seam and all the way back to the cave. Once inside, he fixed her feet into the rock, as Mordwyn had shackled him, and went back outside. The need to get off the ledge was now paramount. He had to find a way down and quickly.

Calon's plan was to create steps or holes in the cliff face for them to climb down. He had noticed when looking over the ledge the previous evening that there was a small outcrop approximately a third of the way down. If he could get Seren down to it, the distance would help her to shake off the effects of the void-stone. He experimented with how to create the steps on the granite next to the cave opening. By cloaking his hand and stabbing it straight into the rock face, he could scoop a handful of stone out, leaving a hole and also a small lip that offered a good foothold with toes able to jut into the hole, whilst the lip created made a good grip for hands to hold on to. His main problem was how to achieve this whilst leaning over and down.

It wasn't until he remembered how Mordwyn had clung to the rock and scampered upside down on cave ceilings, that he had a solution. He began by removing his moccasins and working bare foot. Cloaking both his hands and his feet he stood on the precipice. Kneeling down he forced his hands into the rock and eased himself over the edge so he was hanging. He then was able to force his feet into the cliff face to hold his weight whilst he made hand holds; one at head height and one at waist height. By moving down methodically, he repeated this process as he gradually lowered himself. Reaching the outcrop where he could rest took him a good deal of the morning.

The Marwolleth warriors below had come out to watch; Gethyn and Uncle had called up to encourage him, but he kept his focus on his task. A task that was more exacting than he had thought it would be. Still, he reached the outcrop, about the size of a large bed, before noon and took some time to rest. Climbing back up he discovered that he had created too many holds, and by spacing them out more he would still have been able to climb easily. This realisation meant it would be quicker going from the ledge to the ground.

Reaching Seren, he found her staring into space. She seemed more aware than she had been last night, but was still vacant and unresponsive. She didn't seem to understand anything he asked her, although once he had her on her feet, she seemed content to let him guide her. The journey down to the outcropping was a fraught experience. Several times Calon almost fell as he had to manhandle Seren's hands and feet down to each hold and impress upon her to keep them there.

Fortunately, the further they moved away from the ledge above, the more she understood what he wanted, but she was exhausted by the time they reached the outcropping. Warming her with a spell, he had her lie down and sleep, carefully extending a 'belt' of stone over her prone form to prevent her standing up or falling off. He then immediately set about creating a way down to ground level.

Below where he toiled, Uncle had obviously seen that something was wrong with Seren and shouted up to Calon. Calon had no time to explain but simply reassured Uncle that all would be well when he got her down as he toiled away. After most of the afternoon, he was less than halfway down the remining cliff, his body exhausted, when he heard Seren calling his name. He immediately stopped and wearily climbed back up to the outcropping, smiling to himself as he heard the indignation in her voice. He arrived to see her staring up into the sky. She smiled when she saw him.

"I'm stuck," she told him, seemingly unaware of how she came to be there. "What am I doing here?" Not wanting to waste energy and more importantly time, explaining what had happened, he busied himself with freeing her so she could sit up, then ordered her to climb down the rock face with him. It was easier to work with Seren now she was more conscious of her own actions and more aware of the danger they were in. She repeated more than a few times how high up they were.

When at last they reached the final hold he had made, she was a few holds above him, so her lowest foot was level with his highest hand, he told her to keep still. With daylight beginning to fade he decided to make smaller holds, meaning the hand grips would be as good but their toes would have to take their weight now rather than the whole foot. This helped him work a little more quickly, but made him worry more about Seren's ability to hold on.

By the time it was dark, he still had nearly thirty yards to negotiate before they were at ground level and he was exhausted to the point where he barely had the strength to hold himself on the rock face, let alone Seren. Stopping, he pressed his face against the rock and thought about how easy it would be to simply let go. It was then that Uncle solved his problem. He shouted up to Calon that they would try and get a rope to him. A rope he could embed in the rock and then shimmy down. He looked down and could just see Gethyn, dark against the snow, with rope in hand, twirling it in circles.

"We have weighted the end with a rock. We'll see how high we can get it. Judge then how much further you need to drop." Calon croaked out he understood, but tired as he was, he saw nothing. The consternation from below indicated the throw must have been close but it was simply too dark to watch the rope in flight. Calling out for then to wait, he took Mordwyn's rock light from his pouch, activated it then dropped it down to them with a shout of warning. Uncle immediately saw his thinking, and the rock-light replaced the other rock that had weighted the rope's end. When they were ready, Uncle told Calon to shout when he was ready.

"Now," he yelled down to them. This time he saw the rope arcing towards him but it struck the cliff a few yards below his feet. "Higher," he shouted. "It's close." In the end, too tired to go any lower, Calon managed to grab the rope on the thirteenth attempt. Again, Uncle had solved the problem by stacking snow to raise Gethyn a couple of yards. Calon used his magic to open a hole in the cliff face before jamming the end of the rope, bound tightly around the fist-sized rock-light, into the hole and sealing it, weaving more rock into the hole to hold it. In a matter of moments, the malleable stone he had worked with had hardened. They would get down now, he knew, he just didn't have the energy to move. He lay his cheek against the cold rock face and just stopped moving.

Perhaps sensing Calon was at the end of his strength, it wasn't long before Gethyn had shimmied up the rope and was talking to him. Calon couldn't find enough resolve to even listen so just mumbled 'Seren,' and waved an arm loosely in her direction. He was aware that getting her down the rope was going to be hard, but Gethyn simply slung her over his shoulder and eased down the cliff in a matter of moments. He came back for Calon and repeated the process. Calon saw that Gethyn's hands were cloaked, looking like tough bark, to avoid rope burns. Within moments he was lying in one of the snow shelters the Marwolleth had erected against the cliff face. He could hear Uncle fussing, heating the hearth-stones to warm the shelter. He was almost force-fed a thick liquid that tasted like pine resin, then felt hands at his temples, hot hands pulsing magic into his head and he slept.

Calon was woken by someone gently cupping his face with cold hands. He opened his eyes, taking a few moments to focus, to see a smiling Seren gazing down upon him. "It's time you got up Calon, we need you," she told him, releasing his face and getting to her feet. Calon groaned and sat up, accepting Seren's hand as she hauled him to a standing position. The shelter he was in had a curved straight wall of pine boughs. Above him a latticed network of twigs and sticks provided the frame for more in a wind and snow proof shelter that was wonderfully warm. Calon was surprised at how spacious it was.

"Come," Seren said, leaving the shelter. Calon followed noticing that a heavy cloak had been fastened back to leave the doorway open. The scene outside was not what he had expected to see. The warriors ringed the entrance to the shelter; all armed and all poised for action. Ahead of them, some ten yards distant the great mountain eagle Calon had saved stood menacingly, watching the warriors. As Calon stepped out into view, the eagle lifted its head to the sky and screeched. Leaping a few feet off the ground, the eagle thrashed its wings, sending flurries of snow swirling around them, before settling back to the ground.

"Calon," Uncle smiled. "As you can see, we have a stand-off. We won't harm the eagle unless it attacks, but it won't leave. We are trapped here. Seren says you healed it, which I think is why it's waiting for you. Like it or not, I suspect you are bonded with it somehow."

"What?" Calon asked.

"Bonded. Mountain eagles mate for life. This one's partner died, you healed it and in doing so you became its new partner. Similar I think to how we bond with shadow-foxes, who, by the way, are in the trees yonder," Uncle continued, pointing towards the forest ahead of them. "But they can't get any closer while the eagle is here." The bird was now shuffling about, bobbing its head, eyes fixed on Calon.

"What am I supposed to do?" Calon asked him.

"Damned if I know. Never heard of it before. Legends say the Cawrrocs used to tame them but how…" Uncle shrugged as he had no answer.

"When you healed it, you had cloaked your skin in rock. Perhaps it thought you were a Cawrroc," Seren suggested. "Whatever, it's not going anywhere. She's yours, like it or not."

"She?"

"Definitely the female," Seren told him. "She's bigger and more aggressive than the male and doesn't have a black crest. She'll be an interesting companion. She can hunt, protect you, maybe even carry you. You'll just need to find a way to communicate with her and train her."

"Thinking about it," Uncle added. "With the shadow-foxes, we take a bit of fur and create a *craith*, to strengthen the bond with your own particular animal. Perhaps we could try that. We'd just need a feather. You could get one and hand it back to us."

Calon could see the sense in that and stepped past the warriors to stand before the eagle. He cloaked himself in stone, eliciting a few gasps from the Marwolleth behind him. Remembering his da's advice on dealing with birds, he approached slowly, so as to not spook or stress out the eagle. As he was moving towards the bird he began to talk softly, reassuring the bird he was no threat, that she had no need to worry; again following his da's advice that 'it is good to vocalise that you are approaching, but avoid making a noise that might make the bird uncomfortable or any sudden movements.'

Once up close, the eagle, standing about three feet tall, took flight again, hovering around him, wings beating. It was hugely disconcerting as the great wings flapped around him, the feathers sometimes flicking his head and shoulders. He tried not to duck or move suddenly, then at a shouted suggestion from Seren he held his arm out horizontal to the ground. The eagle immediately landed on it, claws firmly gripping his arm. Calon could barely hold the weight of the bird, but a spear was thrust into his hand from someone behind him, the tip already in the ground, so he had something to brace against and support his arm.

The eagle then began rubbing its beak on his head, once catching his ear with the sharp tip, causing a trickle of blood to dribble from his lobe, which it then nibbled and licked at. With his arm beginning to wilt, Calon began to gently ruffle the bird's white, chest feathers, managing to loosen a few that fluttered to the ground. With this accomplished and his arm muscles burning, he jerked his arm up and the eagle took flight. They all watched as the great bird rose high into the sky, screeching and keening as it went.

The Marwolleth all crowded around him, slapping his back, congratulating him and marvelling at his control of a wild bird. None of them had seen or heard of anything like it. He was about to speak when Hela came crashing in, jumping up to lick his face and sending him tumbling into the snow. Myllane too joined in the scrummage, both foxes yipping their pleasure. Having given Hela a good fuss, he stood and approached Seren who had gathered the eagle's feathers.

"This one, I think," she said, showing him a small, soft downy feather, as white as the snow. "Let's do this in the shelter," she told him and headed back towards the cliff with Calon and two boisterous shadow-foxes in tow. Once inside, she made Calon remove his leather jerkin and the two undershirts he wore. Bare-chested, he stood facing the open doorway to provide Seren with as much light as possible. She began by rubbing snow on his right bicep to clean and numb the skin. She made an inch-long incision in the skin with her nail, sharpened by cloaking it, and weaving magic to lengthen it. Closing her fist around the feather, she began to chant under her breath, causing her fist to burn bright with a pale blue light.

Then, with no warning, she opened her fist, took the feather and eased the quill into the cut in his skin. With the aid of magic, she forced the whole feather, miraculously keeping its distinctive shape, between the layers of his skin. She then sealed the cut and pressed her hand hard onto the feather and began a new spell. If Calon felt the first part of the process was painful, it did little to prepare him for the burning that accompanied the second part. He felt his arm had been scolded with a red-hot poker from Kort's forge.

At exactly the point where he thought he could bear it no longer, Seren took her hand away and pushed snow onto his skin. His relief was instantaneous and joyful. Moving her hand away again, he looked at his arm and saw what looked like an intricate tattoo of a feather etched into his skin in incredible detail.

Seren smiled at him. "I'm not sure what this will accomplish; I used the same incantation we use for binding the foxes. Whether it works with your eagle remains to be seen."

"It's hardly my eagle," Calon muttered. "More likely that I'm her pet human. I'll never control that bird."

"That's not what we saw, Calon. We were hours waiting outside, worried what it was going to do. Yet two minutes with you and she flies off happy." She smiled at him again and they gazed at each other for a few moments, Seren breaking the silence. "Now come on, we're moving back down into the forest. The warriors are anxious to leave."

Chapter 16
The Parting

After journeying back down into the forest, where they camped for the night, the party journeyed on to the Hafan Hills, passing as they went the site of the battle. With spring only just beginning to show herself, Calon was surprised to see that colourful flowers grew with abandon over the killing fields. He remembered how he had buried his 'parents' and realised that the Marwolleth must have returned every one killed to the land. Recalling that he had left his sword and Seren's bow embedded in a rock face, he told Uncle he would need to fetch them and ran off, Hela close in attendance, to retrieve the weapons. He agreed with Uncle that they would meet them at the coast. Seren peeled away from the group too and loped after him, Myllane racing ahead with Hela.

A half hour off towards the forest on the eastern side of the hills brought them to the right place. The sword and bow were as he had left them. The blade-wood sword was as beautiful as he remembered. Reaching out with a cloaked hand, he withdrew the sword from the stone easily, the hilt comfortable in his hand.

"My bow?" Seren demanded. "If you've finished dreaming of being a sword warrior." Calon pulled her bow from the rock and handed it to her. The two were grinning like fools as they set off to catch up with the others.

The Hafan Hills reached down towards the great inland sea, Llyn-dwr-Halen, Seren explained. What had once been a river rushing down from the Eiran Mountains in to great lake had been flooded by the sea bursting through the coast to the far west of their island. The way into this sea was a treacherous route for any ship. A route that was fraught with riptides, crashing waves, whirlpools and the needles, a series of huge rocks jutting out of the water that were unnavigable for all but the smallest boats, that would be swamped anyway.

"Then how are we sailing away?" Calon asked.

"Because we will sail on a *Rhedwr Mor* ship—the 'sea-runners' can weave water the way you can weave stone. They will have no more trouble than you and I walking along here." She paused before adding, "I forget how much you don't know about our people."

"Sea-runners? Can they run on the sea then?"

"Almost. I hope you get to see them in action. Many prefer to be called wave-dancers; again, you will see why if you watch them in action."

As they travelled on, Seren was assaulted by many more questions which she answered patiently and in full where she could, but she was a little relieved when they crested the final rise of The Hafan Hills and looked down over a wide, curved sandy bay. They could see that the other Marwolleth were all gathered on the edge of the sand in a wide circle and seemed to be discussing something. Disappointingly for Calon there was no sign of a ship or boat or any sea-runners or wave dancers.

As they approached the group, they sensed there was some kind of discord. The talking stopped as they arrived, some of the warriors shuffling away to let Seren and Calon join the group.

"Something is wrong," Seren stated. "Is it the wave-dancers? Are they not coming?"

"They are coming as far as I know," Gethyn told her. "They said the day after the new moon, which is today. Judging by the wind, it will be hard going for them to sail here from The Cursed Isle. They will be here soon enough. That is not the issue."

"I'm not going," Uncle said.

"That is the issue," Gethyn added. There was an uncomfortable silence. Uncle seemed unconcerned by it and just waited for someone else to speak.

Eventually, Gethyn felt compelled to speak. "We would have all our people together, Uncle. Gorllewinol is a wondrous land and free of humans. We have known for so long that they would come here. Our people could never have prospered in Penrhyn, you know this. There is little we can grow here to feed so many. Yes, we can hunt. But we would always be wary of war. Especially now our defences have been breached. What if more human soldiers come? How long can we fight and not become like them?"

"All you have said is true," Uncle responded. "But I am one old warrior. I have lived all my long life in this land and I will not leave. I am the oldest living of our people and I will not leave this land I have nurtured and loved, nor those

I have left here. Nor would I abandon the Hethwen people to human rule. If I can save one child, I have fulfilled a purpose."

"The Hethwen," Gethyn spat, "who exiled us here. You would aid them?"

"We were not exiled. We agreed to come here to be free. And yes, I would aid them. They are Celtyth. We are different tribes, but one people."

Seren's voice broke the rising tension. "If Uncle stays, I stay."

"So be it. I will argue no more. You have time to change your mind yet. But you are free to choose, as are we all." He looked directly at Calon when he said this. "Your father will be delighted to meet you Calon, especially with the tales we can tell."

"And I will be delighted to meet him and share those stories," he told Gethyn. "Be sure to tell him that I look forward to his visiting us." He felt Seren's hand slip into his and give it a light squeeze. Gethyn, head slightly to one side, simply looked at him and then gave the briefest nod, but Calon still felt compelled to add, "Seren and Uncle are the only family I *know*. Having just found them I can't leave them."

Again, there was silence, broken by a sudden staccato of high-pitched whistles from above as the great mountain eagle swooped down over their heads, making all except Calon duck. Calon felt a warm acknowledgment as the bird passed and caught himself smiling at Seren. "It worked," he told her excitedly. "I felt her," he added, tapping his head.

But a screech of a different kind prevented any further talk. They all looked up and saw the eagle heading out over the water. "She's warning us, I can sense her wariness." Within a few heartbeats, they all knew why as a ship sailed around the headland. The great boat was awash with colour. Every plank of her long, slim hull was a different colour or different shade of a same colour. Adorning the hull were large round shields, all exotically painted with various eyes, fins, fish and seabird insignia. The single mast was canted forward and sported a sail of deep blue with a white wing emblem stretched across it. It gracefully slid through the water then stopped some distance from the shore.

From where they stood, Calon could see a buzz of activity on the deck as several of the shields were lifted off. Around him faces were grinning, a few of the warriors even cheered.

"Are they…" he began to ask.

"Wave-dancers," Seren confirmed as eight of the crew jumped overboard. Calon expected them all to disappear under the water's surface, but as they neared it, the wave-dancers all whipped their shields around and down to stand on them, landing on the sea with barely a splash before speeding towards them. He had never seen anything like it. In fact, it was the most exhilarating thing he could remember having witnessed.

Balanced on a shield, feet apart, each wave-dancer sped over the surface, skimming across the water like the flat stones he would throw as a child, spinning and jumping as they did so; turning sharp corners without losing speed and dousing their shipmates with water. Not a one approached them in a straight line, they all careered across the sea in twisting patterns, leaping from waves, spinning in the air, one even somersaulted holding her board to her feet. The whoops and screams of sheer joy and delight reached the shore and Calon could only marvel at not only their skill but their exuberance and how easily they lifted the mood of all who watched them.

When they reached the beach, their shields slid part way up the sand and they leapt clear. They greeted the Marwolleth warmly, clearly enjoying the admiration. All of the eight were females, who Seren told him, were far better water weavers than males as they were more in tune with the sea. Few males, she added, were even capable of working water with magic. All were dressed in silvery, glittering, tight fitting clothes that Seren explained was a 'leather' cured from the carcass of a great fish they loved to hunt. All eight warmly hailed Seren and Calon, who felt suddenly shy and oafish in the face of such happiness and warmth. A friendlier group he had never met, and suspected he never would.

Only one of the eight was armed, a sword hilt jutted over one shoulder. She was also the least colourfully attired of the wave-dancers. Her garb was a shimmering black material; her very difference made her stand out. The wave-dancer was dark skinned, as he was, but was bronzed by the sun as well. Her dark hair was bound tightly into a ponytail that hung down her back, and her eyes were a startling blue. It was only when Seren nudged him in the ribs that Calon realised he had been staring. The apparent leader of the group, she was hugging Uncle, then cupped his face in her hands before kissing him on the lips. She laughed aloud then spun away, grabbing a Marwolleth by the hand and dragging him running down to the sea.

On the way, she stamped on the edge of a shield and flipping it up, she caught it in one hand. On reaching the water, she dropped the shield onto the surface and in tandem with the warrior they leapt on to it, the wave-dancer's arm wrapped around the warrior. Calon knew he would never have been able to stay on his feet as the Marwolleth did, but envied him nonetheless. The wave dancers all ferried one of the warriors back to the ship in this fashion, although with much less flamboyance than the journey across. They repeated the journeys for the remaining warriors, who had all clasped hands with him, hugged Uncle and Seren before they were taken over to the ship. Gethyn was the last to leave, after embracing Uncle and Seren, he gripped Calon and thanked him again for his work in saving and healing them both. He nodded one last goodbye.

"We'll be back next year, Uncle; summer solstice," he called, before he jumped on to the shield that would carry him over to the ship.

Knifing through the water, the ship turned as it left, bringing it closer to the shore. The Marwolleth lined the side of the ship and waved their goodbyes, arms still moving as the ship moved out of sight, shadowed by the mountain eagle, which swooped down to the surface of the sea and sped behind the headland as well once the ship had gone. The three were about to turn when the screeching of the eagle drew their attention back to the headland around which the ship had just vanished. The huge raptor appeared, skimming the water, closely followed by a wave-dancer, who managed to catch a wave and leapt over the eagle, whooping with delight. The eagle tilted to one side, a wing tip flicking the water, and the two waltzed around each other this way as they approached the shore at great speed.

On reaching them, the eagle extended her wings to break her momentum, raising her up before them in all her magnificence, before settling on the sand. The wave dancer came in more slowly, gliding to a halt in front of them, before skipping off her shield. She stamped on the edge of it, flipping it up and catching it. She was beaming.

"That's some eagle," she smiled as she approached. Walking up to Uncle, she hugged him, hugged Seren then approached Calon, her face serious. She took his face in her hands, surprisingly warm but still wet from the sea. She planted a salty kiss on his lips.

"Why have you come back?" Uncle asked her.

"To stay," she replied, smiling at Calon, "with you."

As Calon blushed a deep shade of red, Seren's laughter peeled out. Seeing how taken aback he was, she added, "It is the *Rhedwr Mor* way," she told him. His confused gaze skipping from face to face must have been a picture as even Uncle was laughing.

"I've chosen you," the wave-dancer told him, taking his hand.

"But…" he began.

"And you have no say in the matter," the girl told him. "My name is Tarian. The eagle told me she'll share you with me." Calon, still dumbstruck, watched as his two companions laughed themselves stupid, the eagle keening along.

"The eagle talks to you?" an incredulous Calon blurted out.

"Yes. We *Rhedwr Mor* can link with birds the way you do with shadow-foxes, but we don't bond." Indicating the eagle in front of them, she added, "This one is lonely and grieving and thinks you deaf to her. Don't worry, I'll teach you." Calon absently rubbed at the *craith* on his right arm. The eagle's head bobbed up and down in response. "She wants to know what you want. You really can't hear her?"

Calon looked from the eagle to Tarian. "No. I was just scratching… We put her feather in my arm, a *craith*, to help me link with her and I sort of can but I don't really know how."

Uncle interrupted the conversation, "Enough, it's time to move. Talk on the way."

A short while later, as they finally left the beach, Calon looked around for the shadow-foxes, but they were nowhere to be seen. Uncle saw him looking. "I think we'll not see much of those foxes while that bird is so close," Uncle said, suddenly grabbing Calon and Seren into a hug, Tarian pushed her way in as well. "Thank you for staying," was all he said, before dropping his arms and heading back into the hills.

"Where are we going, Uncle?" Calon called as he loped after him.

Uncle stopped and turned. "Back into the Glendow Valley," he said ducking as the mountain eagle brushed over his head with a huge flap of her wings. "That's going to take some getting used to," he muttered. Turning back to Calon, he told him, "It's time we taught you what you need to know. It's time we made a Marwolleth out of you, Eagle-Heart."

Tarian, her shield slung onto her back, slipped her arm around his waist as he walked and Seren's laughter shadowed him as they followed Uncle up into the Hafan Hills.